Born in the UK, **Becky Wicks** has suffered interminable wanderlust from an early age. She's lived and worked all over the world, from London to Dubai, Sydney, Bali, NYC and Amsterdam. She's written for the likes of *GQ*, *Hello!*, *Fabulous* and *Time Out*, a host of YA romance, plus three travel memoirs—*Burqalicious*, *Balilicious* and *Latinalicious* (HarperCollins, Australia). Now she blends travel with romance for Mills & Boon and loves every minute! Tweet her @bex_wicks and subscribe at beckywicks.com.

Traci Douglass is a *USA TODAY* bestselling romance author with Harlequin/Mills & Boon, Entangled Publishing and Tule Publishing, and has an MFA in Writing Popular Fiction from Seton Hill University. She writes sometimes funny, usually awkward, always emotional stories about strong, quirky, wounded characters overcoming past adversity to find their for ever person. Heartfelt and Healing Happily-Ever-Afters. Connect with her through her website: tracidouglassbooks.com.

Also by Becky Wicks

From Doctor to Daddy
Enticed by Her Island Billionaire
Falling Again for the Animal Whisperer
Fling with the Children's Heart Doctor
White Christmas with Her Millionaire Doc

Also by Traci Douglass

Their Hot Hawaiian Fling
Neurosurgeon's Christmas to Remember
Costa Rican Fling with the Doc

First Response in Florida miniseries

The Vet's Unexpected Hero
Her One-Night Secret

Discover more at millsandboon.co.uk.

A PRINCESS
IN NAPLES

BECKY WICKS

ISLAND REUNION
WITH THE
SINGLE DAD

TRACI DOUGLASS

MILLS & BOON

First Published in Great Britain 2022
by Mills & Boon, an imprint of HarperCollins*Publishers* Ltd,
1 London Bridge Street, London, SE1 9GF

www.harpercollins.co.uk

HarperCollins*Publishers*
1st Floor, Watermarque Building,
Ringsend Road, Dublin 4, Ireland

A Princess in Naples © 2022 Becky Wicks

Island Reunion with the Single Dad © 2022 Traci Douglass

ISBN: 978-0-263-30124-3

04/22

A PRINCESS
IN NAPLES

BECKY WICKS

MILLS & BOON

Dedicated to my travel partner in crime
and fellow writer/sound therapist Farzana Ali.

We may have the English Channel between us, but
you're still one of my most royally excellent friends.

CHAPTER ONE

'THE NAME NAPLES comes from the Greek Neapolis, meaning new city. Its close proximity to an abundance of interesting sites, such as Pompeii and the Bay of Naples, makes it a great base for exploring the area...'

Adrienne Marx-Balthus zoned out of the audio guide in her ears. The woman in gold-rimmed sunglasses was still staring at her from the table by the window. Picking up her glass, Adrienne forced a smile in her direction. Of course she was going to be recognised here, too. Crown princesses like her didn't just leave their home country and turn invisible.

Still, this was rather awkward.

The woman pulled out a phone. Adrienne slid the earbuds from her ears as her heart started to pulse behind her blouse. It was one thing to be recognised, but to be photographed by a tourist on her first day as a junior resident doctor at the Cancro Istituto di Napoli wasn't ideal. Especially not when she'd already refused Papa's proposal of an official press photographer. Why would she want that? She'd come here to be...normal.

Signalling for the bill, she gathered her things. Outside, the birds chirped in the trees and the buzz of the latte she'd picked up and brought with her propelled her through the streets of downtown Naples. Thankfully, the woman hadn't followed her. Running in high heels was not advised.

Papa's voice was in her head now, warning her that she'd be spotted in Naples, no matter what kind of white coat she was covered up in. Alexander Marx-Balthus, Prince Consort of Lisri, wasn't particularly thrilled about his only daughter—his wife's heir apparent—veering away from her monarchical duties for anything. Not even to pursue her career in medicine.

Adrienne sipped her latte on the move, taking in the piazza to her left, the way it smelled, the way the locals smiled. Everything was so vibrant here, colourful, promising. She wouldn't be dragged down by her own restless mind.

Her mother the Queen's quiet words in Papa's ear had allowed her to pursue this role and she would be grateful to her for ever. Her father would have much preferred her to engage in finding a suitable husband than follow a career, but that was not exactly at the top of her list of ambitions right now. At twenty-one, when she'd fallen in love with the dashing Prince Xavier of Molizio, she'd been too young to know better, and too blind to see through his cunning charade, as it had turned out.

Sometimes she still couldn't believe Papa had encouraged her to go through with the engagement even after they'd all discovered what a lying, cheating... *No.* She frowned to herself. She would not dwell on that night at the Military Ball again; she'd done enough of that. But even after everything that had happened, and all the salacious rumours spread by the press over their sudden split, Papa had cited Xavier as an excellent match—in terms of his royal lineage, at least. He'd even told her that not everyone found love in a royal marriage, as though that was supposed to reassure her!

'I just won't have a royal marriage, then' had been her firm reply. 'I won't marry *anyone* unless it's for love.'

Papa only wanted the best for her, of course, she reminded herself...as long as 'the best' was someone with blue blood running through his veins, like Prince Xavier. Well, no chance of that here...

No chance of falling for anyone—not that I want to. It's going to be all about work, work, work.

At the other end of the piazza a line of scooters blocked the road, shoehorning into every inch of space around the cars. Gosh, it was hot here—hotter than at home in the summer, where Scandinavian breezes blew in over the mountains and cooled the rooms of the royal palace beautifully. But she pressed on.

If it were up to Papa she'd be letting her security guard, Ivan, take her straight to the hospital from her gated apartment, but she'd smiled and batted her eyelashes and convinced the man to let her walk this morning, saying she'd meet him there. It would be far nicer to walk and to get her bearings on day one, surely. Besides, her headscarf and giant sunglasses should hide her identity nicely.

Passing a dog straining on its lead to reach a fat pigeon, she let her thoughts run over her impending rotation again. She'd stood her ground at home, fought for the right to train as a doctor, and now she was finally away from Lisri and her royal engagements. At last some breathing space. There were no press photographers with her here, documenting her journey on yet another 'first day', which lifted her spirits again as the sea swept into view.

She must have walked uphill without realising. Inhaling the salty, damp air deep into her lungs, Adrienne flashed back to sailing trips on her yacht, *Amada*. One day, when she had some time to herself, which she knew would be rare, she'd take *Amada*, cast her sails again and conquer the sea herself. Ride the waves, the wild curves around the Amalfi Coast, out deep where the dolphins swam.

Dr Franco Perretta liked sailing too. She'd read it in one of his interviews in *Medical Heroes* magazine. For a second she thought of her new soon-to-be boss, sailing with her through caves, mooring at coves or in the shallows of secret bays. At thirty-one, she was still several years his junior—no thanks to spending time when she could have been focused on advancing her medical career attending silly social engagements instead, all while her family did their best to marry her off again.

It had only been a month or two after her relationship with Xavier had gone up in flames that her darling uncle Nicholas had received his terminal cancer diagnosis… But ultimately the tragedy had led her here, to this point. She hoped Franco Perretta would see and appreciate everything she'd had to overcome to get here, and not dwell too much on anything the press had written about her. They still loved to speculate endlessly about her and Xavier, and the fact that she'd been determinedly single since she'd broken up with him.

'Flowers, *signorina*?' someone called.

She bought the flowers. They'd look good in the hospital, all bright and cheery, signalling her new rotation and a new chapter in her life. As she walked, she felt a little nervous about meeting Franco Perretta in person for the first time. Had he heard about her reputation as Lisri's Ice Princess? Seen the stupid memes? Most people had.

She was ashamed that such things had to follow her, but not ashamed of how she'd got the name in the first place. Of course she hadn't given any of those suitors a second more of her time than she'd been forced to give them by her family—they could all think what they liked about that. She'd got her studies back on track over the last five years, and her career came first now. With Dr Franco Perretta as her mentor she'd soon be in line for success on her own account—not because of her family name or their wealth or influence.

Would he be as charming as he'd sounded on the phone? Since first reading about him, and then talking to him about this position, she'd been putting a jigsaw puzzle together in her mind and filling in the pieces herself.

A thirty-six-year-old Florence native, Franco Perretta was undeniably the talk of the institute. And the country. And most of Europe. Franco had done more for cancer research and developing biotechnology in the last half-decade than anyone. Who else could she learn more from faster?

And Dr Franco Perretta wasn't just the cancer institute's senior consultant. He was a philanthropist. He'd joined the Cancro Istituto di Napoli after his fiancée had died. She'd battled a rare kind of cancer that had taken her life quite quickly. The exact type hadn't been mentioned in the interview she'd read, just the fact that no one had known enough about it at the time to tackle it easily. The interview had been more photographs than words, come to think of it, but it had sounded as if his tragic loss had been the foundation for a whole lot of gain.

Franco Perretta and the institute, co-founded by his father, the billionaire insurance tycoon Marco Perretta, were behind the research and development of almost every cancer-related drug the European Medicine Advisory Board had approved in Italy in recent years. As an aspiring oncologist herself, completing this rotation with Franco meant she'd be right on the front line of cutting-edge techniques, technologies and therapies. Thanks to all his connections, she'd also be involved in real humanitarian acts, and that was experience any medical leader should have behind her.

Even though all the females in her family had so far lived very long, healthy lives, Adrienne would have to take the crown in Lisri someday, and she wasn't going to waste any more time doing anything she wasn't passionate about. It might be decades before she stepped into the reigning role—her mother was only in her early fifties.

There was a screech. Adrienne stopped in her tracks. A scooter had collided with a car up ahead and she saw its rider, like a human-sized bullet, shooting from the bike to the ground.

She reached the scene to hear a flurry of Italian curse words and to see men with raised fists. The guy from the scooter was staggering to his feet, tugging at his helmet.

'Are you hurt?' She took his shoulders gently, calmly. It was never good to raise your voice with people in shock.

He blinked as if he didn't even see her. Then a torrent of raging abuse flew from his mouth directly at the driver in the car. Stunned, she watched him limp purposefully towards his overturned moped, still yelling and gesticulating.

OK, so you're not that hurt.

'Princess? You're the Crown Princess, aren't you? From Lisri?' The red-faced football-shirt-wearing man in the car had stopped mouthing obscenities and was now striding towards her, one huge step at a time. He'd left his car door wide open, much to the annoyance of the other honking moped drivers. 'Your Highness, can I get a photo? My wife is a huge fan.'

Oh, God, what now?

'Get on.'

The unmistakable voice came from behind her.

She spun around. There he was. Straddling the seat of a matte green scooter—an MP3 Sport 500, no less—was

Franco Perretta. For a second she just stood there, stunned. He was all man, wearing a fitted white shirt and an open leather jacket. Taller than she'd thought, and utterly drop-dead gorgeous.

'How did you…?'

'I was driving past. I saw the headscarf and I thought you might be trying to hide your identity.'

'Am I that obvious?'

'Get on,' he repeated.

She tugged the helmet he gave her over her head. The machine was more motorcycle than scooter, sleek and well-cared-for… Expensive. Her skirt was too long and close-fitting for her to ride a bike of any kind, but she didn't really have a choice. Squashing the bouquet of flowers under her arm, she yanked up her skirt and climbed onto the back behind him.

'Go!' she cried, pulling the tight fabric higher and hugging his hips with her thighs.

Mr Football Shirt was only a hand's grab away. 'Just one photo, Princess?'

Franco flipped the footrests. Her arms looped around his waist and she felt the flowers tickling her cheek between them. Only the helmet stopped her face landing smack against his broad, leather-shielded back as he put his foot down and sped from the scene.

A rush of heat and man and power and freedom flooded her senses as they left the crowd in the dust. In three seconds flat they were bumping across a cobbled footpath and skidding down a narrow alleyway.

CHAPTER TWO

'YOU'RE ABSOLUTELY RIGHT, Your Highness, there should be more of these in use around Europe.'

Franco had been listening to Irina, one of their palliative care nurses, agreeing with everything Adrienne was saying for the last ten minutes. It was almost as if she didn't want to risk any opinion of her own being something the Crown Princess might not agree with.

'If you need me for anything at all, Princess, inside working hours or out, I can give you my phone number...'

'You don't need to call me Princess, or Your Highness. No one does when I'm working. Thank you though, Irina—for everything.'

Adrienne was smiling kindly, but there was a definite weariness there. He could tell she was a little exhausted by Irina's attention, and trying not to show it. But Irina wasn't good at getting hints sometimes, and she'd been extremely excited about what she'd called 'the royal arrival' for weeks.

He listened as they spoke, pulling up the patient files he'd need for the rounds himself, trying not to let his eyes linger on Adrienne's profile.

A member of Lisri's royal family...here in his institute. She was joining his team for her next rotation and this was her first time living away from Lisri. He'd hired her because she seemed a good fit, and also, if he was honest with himself, because in between their phone interviews he'd been thinking almost non-stop about her voice—her Italian was tinged with a sweet, lilting Lisri accent and was sexy as hell.

It had crossed his mind that she might have chosen to live outside of Lisri as a means of escape. Drama seemed to follow her—at least as far as the media was concerned. But even if that was the case she was certainly proving keen about her rotation, and he admired a woman with an enterprising spirit.

Count Nicholas, her uncle on the Queen's side, had passed away from cancer of some kind. Franco assumed his death had propelled her studies up to this point, the same way it had compelled her country to donate generously to the Perretta Foundation on a regular basis.

She hadn't said so, but it was clear she was the driving force behind those 'Marx-Balthus' donations. The woman deserved her chance here. She'd worked damn hard. But all the staff knew that having a member of royalty on staff was not going to come without its challenges. People liked to talk about Adrienne. They called her the Ice Princess of Lisri, he mused, still half listening to her conversation with Irina.

Allegedly, she'd given no man the time of day—not romantically, at least—since her break-up with Prince Xavier of Molizio a decade ago. Most people had assumed an engagement between them was on the cards, but it had never happened and the two had gone their separate ways. He hadn't paid much attention at the time, but he seemed to recall the press had written some pretty humiliating stuff about Adrienne that couldn't have been easy to deal with—especially at such a young age.

Irina was agreeing that Lisri was most beautiful in the

spring, and that it had wonderful mountains for skiing, while Franco was appreciating the way the sun was falling like some sort of golden worship on the Princess's cheekbones. Before he'd met her in person that morning he'd assumed all those flawless photos of her had been airbrushed.

Ansell Ackerman would hit on her—probably before the week was out, he mused. The playboy surgeon wouldn't be able to resist. She was incredibly beautiful. She'd also just caught him looking at her, which made him square his shoulders. He'd hate for her to think he was yet another one of her adoring fans. He'd leave that to Ansell.

Giovanni the caretaker poked his head around the door and did a double-take when he saw her. 'Sorry, Princess... er... I left something in here. I will come back later.'

Adrienne fiddled with the sleeves of her lab coat for a moment, then crossed her arms and looked between Franco and Irina. 'You know, I don't expect any special treatment while I'm here,' she said with a slight frown, her head held regally high. 'I've had quite enough of that in Lisri. It's nice to be somewhere I can be normal for a change.'

'So we're just "normal" to you, are we?' he shot back as she rearranged a lily from the crumpled bouquet of flowers, now in a vase. They'd got pretty squashed on the way here, crushed between their bodies on the bike. 'You know, we usually try to be more along the lines of exceptional.'

'Which you are,' she said, narrowing her eyes in response, though he detected a hint of playfulness that stirred something at his core. 'Everyone knows that. Your reputation certainly precedes you.'

He sat on the corner of the desk. 'And it was your qualifications, Dr Balthus, and your passion that brought you here—not your family name.'

She looked surprised for a second, as if she really hadn't

expected anything of the sort to come from his mouth. But he was damned if he'd allow her notoriety to preside over her work. The Lisri monarchy had ruled for a thousand years. It was amongst the oldest royal houses in the world. Her words and her presence could move mountains in any direction she chose, but right now she was here to work for him.

Why was he suddenly irritated?

Adrienne slid into a chair and her face was obscured for a second by the lilies. Maybe she'd anticipated how dull the residents' room would be. It was just an open-plan set-up, nothing special, several desks, a dull mud-coloured carpet that extended to the corridors outside. He'd wondered if she would want her own room, but her request was not to give her special treatment.

Not that it was stopping some people.

'It means a lot to me, being here with all of you,' she said now. 'This institute, this space. It's perfect—thank you. I can't tell you how nice it is for my first day here not to be filmed and documented for everyone to see.'

She sat back in the chair and closed her eyes, as if she was sitting on a throne for the first time…as was her destiny. Once her mother either stepped down or passed away she'd be right up there. Queen Adrienne. He couldn't look away from her serene face. She was going to be the most beautiful Queen there had ever been. Slim, but almost as tall as him, save an inch or so. Almond-shaped eyes the colour of a blue moon on the water, framed by pale expressive brows. Shapely, yoga-honed legs, soft as silk. He knew that; he'd felt them around his hips on the bike this morning, and he swore he could feel the imprint of them even now.

Irina had left.

'Should we go and do some rounds?' he suggested, suddenly feeling an urge to fix the lapels of his white coat. Then, 'I'll show you the assessment centre and the chemo suite—they're expecting us…'

Adrienne crossed her legs on the seat behind the desk and he caught the telltale red sole of a Louboutin and the flash of a milky pale calf.

There it was again…the stirring deep inside him, where nothing had moved for so long. Same as this morning, even before he'd had her wrapped around him on the bike. Instant attraction.

That's why you're so irritated. This is highly inconvenient. Why now? Why her?

'Dr Perretta, I really do have to thank you for this morning's rescue,' she said, swivelling the chair this way and that, slowly.

'It's Franco. And you're welcome.'

She stood up and crossed the room towards him, touched a hand lightly to his arm. The move made a swift knot in his stomach. 'I'm just Adrienne. And I really loved riding your bike this morning.'

He cleared his throat. 'You need a ride home?'

'No, I need you to help get me a bike of my own.'

He stood taller, thrown for a second.

'Or at least maybe you can recommend someone else who might help me get one?'

OK. This was interesting.

'I thought you didn't want any special treatment?'

'I haven't done anything that exciting in a while,' she said, dazzling him with a knockout smile.

For a second or two he swam in her oceanic eyes, waiting for his ability to form words to return.

He shouldn't be doing anything with this woman outside of work. His brother Benni would warn him about that. She was probably watched wherever she went, her every move scrutinised, which meant he would be watched too, by proxy. His worst nightmare. He'd always been an intensely private man. When he wanted attention for his work he knew how to get it, but his grief over losing Lucinda had only made it harder for people to get close to him, and he was fine with that.

There was something about Adrienne, though. He'd felt it during that very first phone call. Then her arrival had stirred him up for the first time in a long time…since losing Lucinda. And now that she was here, flashing that smile at him… Damn.

No, Franco, you will not be getting involved with her. Keep it professional… Keep your head on straight.

Somehow, though, for reasons he couldn't even comprehend, his mouth refused to co-operate with his brain. 'Let me see what I can do.'

CHAPTER THREE

IT HAD BEEN a long week for Adrienne. Her schedule at the cancer institute had been a whirl of patients and papers and research and administrative tasks.

Three mornings a week her day had begun with research working groups, rounds or academic conferences. On clinic days she'd typically seen her first patients at eight-thirty a.m., and she'd seen anywhere from ten to twenty patients a day.

And every time a door had opened and Franco had walked in she'd found herself holding her breath. Like now, as she waited for him in his office.

'*Buongiorno*, Dr Balthus. I mean Adrienne.'

He dropped a stack of files down on the desk in front of her and she wondered if he realised how gorgeous he actually looked with his touchable mass of midnight-black hair.

His broad shoulders looked like the perfect resting place for a weary head, and she'd noticed over the week that whenever he picked up a cup, or an instrument, or pointed, or gestured at a whiteboard or a screen, his muscles strained the sleeves of his white coat in the most delicious way.

'Our patient will be with us in a minute. I thought I should give you this first. Our next guy needs a smile.'

Franco produced a bright pink stethoscope from behind

his back. He placed it before her as softly and proudly as he might the crown jewels, and she caught a golden glimmer in his green eyes as they trailed the length of her body, from her practical new shoes to her small stud earrings. He'd been sneaking glances all week and trying to be unobtrusive, but of course she'd noticed.

'It's pink for breast cancer awareness, but it also complements every white coat.'

'Wow. OK!' She looped the dazzling piece of equipment around her neck, still feeling his eyes on her.

'Looks good. As predicted,' he told her.

He had a way of saying a lot without saying much at all. While some people had been fawning all over her, acting as if she was some kind of celebrity they had to woo or impress, like that slick-haired sleazy surgeon Ansell Ackerman, Franco had remained casually on the sidelines, as though he was observing her from the outside.

He hadn't asked her one single personal question. Usually men couldn't wait to ask her about her life. She'd known she was beautiful since childhood.And in her late teens men would fall quiet when she entered a room, all eyes on her. They would talk at her too much, trying to catch her alone when they thought no one was looking.

Someone was always looking. Even here in Naples. Mirabel, the housekeeper, seemed to be permanently installed in her apartment, and Ivan was waiting outside the institute's gates right now, just in case she needed him. Luckily she'd grown quite adept at escaping such constraints over the years, much to her family's annoyance.

The sun was blazing through the window straight onto Franco's face now, spotlighting three faint freckles like a constellation on his left cheek. She wondered what his neatly clipped beard would feel like against her face. Soft and slightly scratchy, a tingle to the lips…?

The thrill of having her thighs around his hips on that bike had not yet worn off—she wanted more thrills like that. It was quite surprising, actually, the way he'd awoken something inside her that she hadn't even realised had been sleeping quietly. Usually the only men she met were those politely introduced to her by her family, who invariably turned her off before they even opened their mouths, but here was Franco, rendering her fascinated.

'I love it.' She smiled, only half talking about the stethoscope. 'People will certainly see me coming.'

Franco perched on the corner of the desk, the way he did sometimes when he was reading patient files, and frowned at her. He looked like an ancient Roman statue in the sunlight. God, he was handsome. She'd promised herself not to think like this about any doctor, or indeed any man she couldn't possibly have, as what was the point in that? But all week, in every consultation, every talk, she'd been soaking up his words like a sponge and wondering if his heart was buried with his late fiancée.

'Are you having trouble out there?' he asked her now. 'Do people see you coming?'

'Of course. But at least I can run away faster now.' She gestured to her feet and the sensible trainers she was now wearing. Not her favourite style of footwear by far, but they were comfortable at least.

Franco laughed under his breath and drew a hand across his chin. 'That would be my worst nightmare…getting followed everywhere.'

'If I could keep things as private as you seem to, trust me, I would.'

She cursed herself under her breath. She'd pretty much just admitted she'd searched for him online and found nothing—which was the truth. Facts about Franco seemed to be as elusive as they came, but it only added to his appeal somehow.

'I liked the heels. Sorry it's taken me all week to get back to you about the bike—things have been busy.'

Her heart bucked. 'Same here. It's no problem.'

Her eyes fell on the movement of his fingers under the fabric of his white coat. She pictured the two of them as they'd been on Monday morning, one hand on the brakes, the other firm hand righting her ankle when her foot had slipped from the pedal...

She knew he'd been busy, so she'd asked around about a bike herself. But she hadn't obtained one in the hope that he'd still offer his assistance.

'I've made an arrangement for you,' he said now. 'A bike I think you'll like. You can come and see it later if you're free after your shift.'

'That's...that's very kind of you. Thank you.'

Adrienne clutched the stethoscope between her hands as her heart thrummed. A bike arranged for her by Franco Perretta was exciting. But also risky for him, if he valued his privacy as much he seemed to. The paparazzi would have a field day, snapping her out on a bike with a handsome colleague. He must know that. He must be doing it to help her, because he probably suspected she was here to experience freedom as much as to learn from him and the team.

A gentleman. A gentleman with a heart and courage. How many girlfriends had he had since his fiancée, Lucinda, had died? She'd bet he could have any woman he chose—if he was even in the market for being with anyone. His mysteries intrigued her suddenly. She was envious too, she realised. What would it be like to successfully keep a secret once in a while?

'Where should I go if I make it out of here at a decent hour?' she asked.

Before he could reply, footsteps pattered down the corridor. Their next patient and a nurse. Franco moved from the desk at exactly the same time as she stepped towards them to go and greet them, and she almost bumped straight into him. She tried to move away quickly before embarrassment could flush her cheeks, but he caught her elbow and somehow her fingers rushed on impulse to his hair.

'You should watch your step,' he said lightly. She caught the gleam of desire and danger in his eyes right before he looked away, seemingly flustered. 'Even in trainers you're dangerous.'

Suddenly her heart was a crashing cymbal in her chest, but she swept back her blonde hair, rearranged her lapels, stood tall in his commanding shadow. She was here to work hard— not to get distracted.

But, seriously, why on earth did he have to be so damn attractive?

She stepped past him to the door. When she turned he was still looking at her like...*that*. She would tell him not to worry about the bike. Maybe she shouldn't get involved with him at all outside work.

'I'll take you where we're going later,' he said before she could summon the words. 'Just give me an address and I'll pick you up.'

'I'll send it to you if you'll give me your number,' she dared, against her better judgement.

Damn it, I'm never usually like this with men. What is wrong with me?

He huffed a laugh that turned her heart into a circus. Then he took her phone and entered his private contact details. Had he planned for this to coincide with a Friday night? she wondered. Did he have any idea how she'd always had a thing for smart, altruistic types who gave nothing away about themselves when most men clamoured eagerly for her attention? The cool, calm, sexy, aloof ones were the only ones who had the power to hurt her, really.

Not that she was going to give him the chance to do that. This man was her boss and her mentor for a start. If her pride and professionalism were going to stay intact she was going to have to remind her libido that looking and not touching—not anything—was the best path to follow around Franco from now on.

Their patient was a forty-five-year-old male barrister, recently diagnosed with oropharyngeal cancer, whose name was Mr Geordano. She'd seen many patients like him already—wary, scared, sometimes in denial. She liked the way Franco was with them all: professional, kind, always letting them speak and shower him with questions before handing out calm, considered answers. No doctor knew the answer to every question, but he had answers up his sleeve for most things and she made an effort to remember all of them.

'This is an area of major research at the moment. There are several options available to you, Mr Geordano, and I'll let Dr Balthus walk you through her planned programme...'

Franco asked for her input a lot, she noticed, as if he was keeping her on her toes, and she was glad she'd paid full attention on the round earlier that week when the medical director of a centre for head and neck cancers had come to give a lecture. It mattered what Franco thought of her, even though she wished it didn't.

She was excited about tonight—to see him, to talk to him outside of work. To learn more about him...on a professional level, of course.

Maybe that would be enough.

Or maybe it would leave her wanting even more.

'What do you think, Pink Princess?'

Adrienne blinked. Their patient had addressed her directly, but both men were awaiting her opinion and she realised she'd zoned out momentarily. Franco was shaking his head, and Mr Geordano's grey eyes said volumes even before he spoke. 'Here just for the publicity, are you? Did you run out of red ribbons to cut?' He turned to Franco. 'I thought you had real doctors working here…?'

Adrienne pursed her lips. She should have been prepared for this. The guy had walked in agitated and he had every right to feel anxious, but his fear was the kind that bubbled up and came to boiling point as an imperious rage. She'd seen it before.

'We call her Dr Balthus,' Franco said firmly. 'And I can assure you we only have the very best doctors on our team.'

'I'm still in training,' she explained to the surly patient, shooting Franco a glance that said *I can handle this*. 'And you're absolutely right, Mr Geordano. I am a princess. But it's a royal's duty to be perpetually in service, is it not? I'm here only to offer my knowledge and skill to you, believe me.'

She paused a second, then took a gamble.

'I lost an uncle to cancer, Mr Geordano. I have no problem admitting that his diagnosis changed my life. He's the reason I studied oncology, and the reason I'm here, trying to help as many people as possible to beat this disease.'

She cleared her throat, feeling Franco's laser gaze on her cheek. She'd mentioned her uncle only briefly before now, but his cancer diagnosis and consequent death had shaken her even harder than Xavier's philandering and the press's own interpretations of what had really happened between them. She wouldn't waste her life on worrying about the past when she could help better someone's future.

'Any royal obligations aside,' she continued, 'I consider it my mission on this earth to fight the fight for others who are enduring what he did—as a *real* doctor. Here or in Lisri. Anywhere the fight takes me.'

Franco's eyes were still on her. Had she said too much? She thought she caught a flicker of approval in his green gaze before he took over.

'I lost my fiancée to cancer seven years ago.'

Adrienne's heart jolted. His statement seemed to pulsate in the still air while their patient fell quiet.

'She's the reason *I'm* here.'

Franco's fingers intertwined—perhaps a sign that he was nervous, maybe not used to saying such things aloud.

'I started my oncology fellowship to understand more about what took her from me. Like Dr Balthus, I felt that was the only way I could get on with my life—to stay on this road, find better treatments, even cures. You see, you're surrounded by people who know the reality of what this journey is like, in and outside of this facility. Everyone here, the Crown Princess included, just wants to help you through it.'

Adrienne realised she'd been holding her breath. She blinked away a tear, which she knew Franco saw, and she didn't know where to look. She didn't quite know what to do with all this personal information, but their patient was now gripping his seat on the other side of the desk from them, looking between them.

'Thank you, Doctors, for your honesty,' he said, and Adrienne felt an immense rush of relief—right before the knots in her stomach rendered her breathless.

The way Franco was looking at his shoes told her he

probably wished he hadn't said anything at all about Lucinda. It was quite clear he wasn't over her. Maybe he never would be.

Later in her apartment she looked less at the view of the glowing Mount Vesuvius, always on the verge of eruption, and more at her laptop, trying to find a photo. For some reason she wanted to see Lucinda. Franco was still grieving for her, even after all this time. Maybe he'd never got over losing her. When had he proposed to her? How long had they been together?

It had been her hope that seeing an image of Lucinda with Franco might help her to associate him with the source of his grief and his work here and cure her of this insane attraction she had before she saw him tonight. But she hadn't been able to find much at all. Franco was incredibly private, she reminded herself. Maybe he'd managed to delete any photos of them together, so they wouldn't mess with his broken heart even more.

She could relate to that, if that was the case. Even when she tried not to think about it she could still see him on the night of that hideous Military Ball, launching himself at the security team before they'd dragged him away.

Willing herself not to think about the past—not her own, at least—she went on with her search, knowing she should probably stop. This man was her boss, not some casual romantic interest, and definitely not someone to be sitting here wondering about.

But…

Did he miss Lucinda every day, or were some days better than others?

Experiencing pain like that had been bad enough over her uncle, she thought, feeling the little grey kitten who seemed to have adopted her on day one curl about her ankles. She'd named her Fiamma, the Italian word for flame, because of the little white patch of fur on her forehead that was shaped like a flame.

'But a partner, a *fiancée*…how would anyone ever get over losing that, Fiamma?'

Soon after, with the birds flocking to roost outside her windows, she pulled on jeans and a casual button-up shirt that she tucked in at the waist. Her heart pounded under her bra as she applied a deep maroon satiny lipstick, given to her by her cousin Emmaline, her uncle Nicholas's daughter.

'It puffs up your lips and turns you into a goddess,' she'd said.

Smacking her lips together, she wondered if she should be wearing it at all to go and meet her boss. Then she realised her jeans were perhaps a little too tight. In fact, her backside looked great in them.

Not good, Adrienne!

Maybe she should be wearing something less sexy— something that was more suitable for two colleagues meeting casually after work…

The doorbell rang.

Too late now, she thought, fixing a headscarf over her hair and sucking in a deep breath to calm her already frayed nerves.

CHAPTER FOUR

'IT'S A VESPA. Urban Club 125.' Franco patted the seat fondly, as he would a well-trained German Shepherd. To him a good bike was a man's best friend. 'About as safe and comfortable as you can get.'

'Not to mention stylish.'

Adrienne was obviously impressed. He watched her circle the bright red gleaming Vespa in the orange evening sunlight. Those tight blue jeans made her body impossible not to look at, but he'd have to try. He was her boss, her mentor. A fact he'd have to keep reminding himself of if they were to be spending time together.

He'd brought her to his sister Aimee's gated apartment and fetched the bike out of her garage, where she and Benni kept their collection. The Vomero neighbourhood was what you might call upscale, in a hilly part of Naples, with Vesuvius doing its thing in the background. His dad had a couple of apartments close by. His own penthouse was several streets away. It wasn't a surprise that Adrienne was staying in the exclusive neighbourhood too.

He'd heard her tell her security guard that she didn't need him tonight, as she wouldn't be going far from home, and he wondered, as he recalled the frustration in the man's eyes, how often she managed to dodge her staff in order to have a little fun.

Not that this was a night of fun, he reminded himself. This was about getting Adrienne a bike.

But he'd been thinking about her a lot—especially after what she'd said in the last consultation. She'd spoken so openly about her uncle, and that had flipped some kind of switch in him. He'd talked about Lucinda too—not a lot, but more than he had in a while to anyone, let alone a patient and a colleague.

Even now he wasn't sure what had made him do it, or specifically what it was about Adrienne that had made him do it, but he'd told himself it wasn't an entirely bad thing that he'd let his defences down. He'd even felt a little lighter afterwards.

'Are you sure Aimee doesn't mind me using it?' she asked him now. She looked raring to go, straddling the seat in her designer trainers, her fingers working the clutch. She looked pretty fabulous on the bike, and he almost told her so, but didn't. What good would come from flirting with danger?

'Aimee's in Costa Rica till October at the earliest,' he explained. 'She's joined a conservation team somewhere in the rainforest, so she won't be needing it. If she comes back early she has more bikes to choose from.'

He crossed to the front of the bike, putting his hands over hers on the grips. He heard her breath hitch, saw her blue eyes searching his.

Damn, if she didn't rile up his manhood, looking at him like that…

He considered whether maybe he was a little starstruck around her. Anything was possible, he supposed, but whatever it was that had her constantly hovering in the corners of his mind whenever he wasn't with her would have to be stamped out. This was the future ruler of Lisri; there was no future for the two of them even if he *was* interested in a relationship.

Was she really such an Ice Princess, though? He thought about her warmth at work and couldn't help but wonder more and more about her past. She hadn't always been portrayed particularly kindly by the world's media.

'Brake. Clutch. Stop. Start. That's about all you need. And the lights are here.'

She flipped them on, dazzling him for a moment. He hopped sideways and she scrambled off the bike, flapping her hands around his face without touching him, as if she was more afraid of touching him than blinding him.

'Sorry! Franco…?'

'I'm fine,' he told her as her face came back into view. She was laughing now, just like he was.

Back on the bike, Adrienne rode a few more laps of the driveway, looking as if she'd never done anything as exciting in her life. What kind of life had she led before this? She'd mentioned a press team, who always followed her to official events, and he'd seen for himself the suffocatingly vigilant security guard who looked as if he'd follow her into a toilet stall if he saw fit.

He'd arrived at the idea, over the past week, from her few carefully considered words, that she'd been forced to delay her studies a lot, thanks to her royal engagements, which was why she was starting her last rotation at thirty-one. Also that it had taken her leaving Lisri to stop a persistent stream of titled courtiers from sticking their noses into every aspect of her life.

He knew practically nothing about her personal life in Lisri, and there was hardly anything online about her aside from a few mentions of her ex, Prince Xavier of Molizio, who'd recently had a third child with the woman he'd gone on to marry. It didn't seem as though she dated much. So, sure, he was curious about what had happened to put her off men back when she'd been barely in her twenties and he'd been in the thick of things with Luci.

But every time that curiosity got the better of him he reminded himself that he was dealing with the future Queen of Lisri, and it was probably not wise to ask personal questions. In fact, they could be followed and papped at any moment.

No, thanks. He'd had far too many people interfering in his life after Luci had died. They might have meant well—unlike the media most of the time—but it had made him tense, and even more angry. He still felt a chill remembering the reporter who'd shown up at his door one day, wanting intimate details of their relationship for an obituary. Benni had gone nuts. All Franco had wanted was peace and space to grieve.

If he was smart he wouldn't take Adrienne anywhere else... He'd just have her sign the insurance papers for the bike and take her straight back home. But then, she wouldn't have asked him so specifically about the bike if she didn't think he could show her where to ride it. And he was a gentleman after all.

She slowed the bike as she came towards him, stopping next to him. 'Where are we going now?' She revved the clutch with purpose and eyed him through the slit in her helmet.

He should say *nowhere*. He could already feel the sparks of something dangerous here—and what good would it do to blur the lines of professionalism with someone like her when it would only blow up in their faces? Losing Luci to cancer seven years ago, five long years after her diagnosis, had been pure hell, and Adrienne would be leaving eventually, too, going back to a royal life in Lisri that would never have anything to do with him. It would be just as final.

'Is there anywhere more exciting we can go?' she asked, still looking at him expectantly.

He pulled his helmet on, took his time with the strap, and zipped up his jacket, considering his options. If he took her home this early on a Friday night she'd know he was giving her special treatment. Making decisions for her, overprotecting her—wasn't that what people had done to her all her life?

And if he took her home he wouldn't know she'd be safe out on the bike—not really. Surely it was his duty to take her farther, to at least show her the roads.

What the hell?

'We should probably do a test run before it gets dark. I don't trust you with those lights in public yet,' he told her.

In Spaccanapoli the alleys were small. In the daytime they were crowded with shoppers, and stalls selling wares for tourists, and fruit-sellers and fishmongers. It was a little quieter now—the perfect training ground.

He told her she was a natural when they stopped at a red light, and when it turned green she sped ahead of him, grinning. She was deft and considerate, weaving through all the traffic they came across, so she'd probably be OK out on the coastal roads…maybe after a few more test runs. Those roads were as twisty as snakes and the drops were steep. Maybe he should offer to go with her…just the first time…just to keep a friendly eye out.

'There's a route you can do through the Archaeological Park of Pompeii and the Vesuvius National Park,' he told her when they stopped at a water fountain modelled as a mermaid and took off their helmets. 'It'll take you a whole day from Naples on the bike, but it's the best way to see everything you were talking about.'

He watched her mouth as she drank thirstily, leaving

no lipstick on the bottle. He liked the shape of her mouth, the way it twitched when she thought about saying something but kept it inside instead.

'Unless you'd rather go by car…which might be safer for you, I guess,' he added, reminding himself not to look at her mouth, or even to think about it.

'What do you mean? You just said I'm a natural!'

Adrienne turned her back towards a passer-by who suddenly seemed to recognise her. Her headscarf had slipped, and she hurried to pull it back over her hair, resuming her disguise, such as it was.

'I mean, you're *you*,' he said, moving impulsively to shield her, catching a nose full of her enticing scent. It stuck in his throat, forming a new craving in the space of a heartbeat. 'It would take you a week if you stopped to talk to all your fans. We need you at the institute. Shouldn't you have security, anyway?'

She stepped away from his shielding as the passer-by hurried on, swigged from her bottle again, then wiped her lips with her hand. 'You heard me tell Ivan that you were my security tonight.'

He almost laughed. 'I'm not exactly used to watching out for paps, you know,' he pointed out.

He realised he should be irritated by her assumptions, but to his surprise he felt extra-protective as he saw her frowning eyes dart around, looking for protruding lenses. She was here under his guidance, so to speak. Of course he should look out for her—and not just at the institute.

'Not everyone's an adoring fan, you know,' she said a little wearily. 'And I don't deserve fans. I haven't done anything of merit yet. Not like you have.'

He dropped to the stone wall around the fountain, watched a pigeon peck the cobblestones by her feet. He wouldn't shower her with praise. Everyone else did that. No, he'd simply tell her the truth.

'I know you had something to do with your family's donations to the Perretta Institute after your uncle died,' he said.

She sat beside him, nodding, her eyes on the pigeon. He noticed a little engine oil on her expensive jeans, but she didn't seem to care. She'd been so enthralled with everything he'd shown her, all night.

'There are new drugs that went from phase two to phase three much faster because of your involvement...your interest behind the scenes. But you knew that, didn't you? You know you've done plenty of things with what you call "merit"—and not just because of some royal obligation. I saw how much this work means to you today...when you spoke about your uncle.'

He paused and watched her contemplate his words, still breathing in her perfume.

'There's a lot more I want to do,' she said after a moment. 'Thank you for your encouragement, though, Franco. It means a lot.'

'Do I sense that you feel there are some things you *can't* do because of your position?' He had to ask.

She pushed her honey hair from her face, tucking the loose strands back under her scarf. 'You mean apart from the fact that I'm followed everywhere and paraded around like some kind of poodle in a dog show whenever I touch ground in Lisri? If I hadn't fought for a real career before I take the crown I'd just be opening some hospital right now, instead of working in one.'

For just a second her eyes turned glossy and hurt, and they pierced his heart before she looked away. Some protective urge made him want to pull her in and hold her close to his body, just like the thought of her plunging off a cliff on Aimee's Vespa had done earlier. She was so far out of his reach, though, he kept his arm where it was.

'I shouldn't complain about my birthright or the family traditions I'm expected to continue, even after what happened with Xav... I mean...' She sighed. 'It doesn't matter.'

He cocked an eyebrow at her, waiting. He could tell it did matter to her. A lot. She'd been about to mention Xavier, too. Her ex.

Franco frowned, wishing he wasn't itching to ask more. It didn't sit right with him that she felt inadequate in any way. Surely she could do a lot with the power she'd been given? She wasn't just a pretty face. She was clearly someone who made things happen. But what could he say? He barely knew her. She came from a whole other world, and however wealthy his own family was, she was way out of his league.

'You know what you *can* change, right now?' he said, getting to his feet as it started to rain.

'What's that?'

He pulled her up impulsively. She froze a second under his touch, and the wariness in her eyes made him drop her hands quickly. Too quickly, maybe.

'The fact that you've never had a *real* margherita pizza before—not till I've taken you to Riviola's,' he said, pulling on his helmet.

The whole ride to the restaurant he battled with his own brain. What was he doing? He knew he shouldn't extend their night, or even their conversation. Her security guy might have second thoughts about allowing her to run around without him and catch up with them at any second, meaning his own authority or motives might come into question. If her thin disguise escaped her again they might even be photographed together, which would not look professional at all.

But the distance behind her eyes just now had filled him with a crazy urge to break down her carefully constructed walls. One quick dinner. Then home, he promised himself.

CHAPTER FIVE

'IT WAS GOOD of you to explain your decision to work with us to Mr Geordano this morning,' Franco said, folding his tanned forearms on the table opposite her.

A waiter squeezed past behind him with three pizzas the size of steering wheels, but Franco didn't flinch. Thank goodness for the low lighting in Riviola's pizzeria. She hadn't much wanted to ride home in the rain by herself, so here she was, continuing the night in his company.

You could have handled the rain. You're just enjoying flirting with danger.

'There were so many other ways you could have coped with that situation. He was rude to you.'

'I'm used to it.' She shrugged, finding the salt shaker with her fingers, feeling his eyes hot on her. 'It wasn't about me anyway, Franco. You know that.'

'You're right,' he said, 'the man is angry at the world, and you were there to take the hit. You turned it around, though, and he left spouting praise about you. I've noticed that about you, Adrienne. You don't enjoy the attention, but you know how to use it to your advantage when it's necessary.'

She folded her arms to match his stance. 'I'm learning,' she replied, breathing in the fragrant basil and tomato air, trying not to let self-deprecation consume her. Her position didn't always give her an advantage.

'Well, from what I've seen at the institute, and on that bike, you're brave,' he said, and her heart contracted in a fluttery spasm.

Any compliment from this man seemed to lift her somehow, him being who and what he was: successful, admired, the sexiest doctor ever to straddle a Vespa. But all she could see now was the way he'd looked that morning, when he'd told them how Lucinda had been…maybe still was…the reason for his work. He was the bravest one of the two of them.

'I can't imagine what you must have gone through, losing your fiancée so young,' she heard herself say.

Franco tore his eyes away, and she cursed herself.

'I wasn't sure how to bring it up, or even if I should, but I'm so sorry for your loss. I could tell she's the reason for everything you do even before you mentioned her to Mr Geordano.' She put a hand lightly to his forearm and felt him tense. All muscle.

'She was only twenty-two and I was twenty-four when we got the diagnosis,' he said, looking at her hand as if it was a foreign object he didn't know what to do with. 'I used to wish it was me the cancer had got, not her. What did she ever do to deserve that suffering?'

'No one deserves it,' she replied softly.

'She was funny,' he continued. 'Right to the end. I mean, she had her dark days in the course of that last year, but mostly she was all light.'

'You were engaged? Why didn't you get married before she…?'

The question left her lips before she could recall it, but Franco sighed deeply and frowned.

'She was adamant that she didn't want to make me a

widower. I'd only just proposed when we found out she was sick…and we weren't much more than kids ourselves, you know?'

He looked at her then, as if he was only just realising this fact.

'We were pretty young to get engaged, I suppose, but I was more impulsive then. She was smart. And brave. She accepted her fate maybe faster than I did.'

Adrienne sat back in her chair, listening intently as Franco went on to describe Lucinda in a way that caused the lump in her throat to disappear. Far from evoking more sadness, his stories about her made Adrienne laugh and shake her head, and try not to shed a tear, sometimes all at the same time. And the shape of his mouth in the candle-light made her long to taste his lips, as if she might absorb his passionate free spirit by osmosis.

She almost forgot where they were. He had a way of talking when he got going. His passion was enthralling and commanding. Fascinating.

Sexy as hell.

He wasn't only talking about Lucinda's illness either, as if he was determined not to let it define her. Instead he was sharing with her who she'd been before: a traveller, a fighter, an avid reader, a rememberer of everyone's birthday, an outspoken red wine drinker and a bad guitar player.

Hearing him talk just made Adrienne admire him more. Here was a man who was not afraid to love. He had more than enough to give. He *would* find love again. Because *he* was free to rain his passionate, all-consuming, unending love on whoever he wanted.

The rain was easing off on the windows outside, but somehow she could have sat there all night. Being normal. But just as she dared to think it she remembered she'd told

Ivan that she wouldn't be going far and she'd been out for hours. He might be out looking for her even as they spoke.

'So, what about you and Prince Xavier?'

Franco's sudden question took her by surprise. 'What about us?' She sat up straighter, wondering what exactly he'd heard. The press had speculated to the point of insanity and published flat-out lies about why they'd broken up, but no one knew the truth about Xavier's affair.

Of course there had been rumours about him, too, but being powerful and male he'd come out of it in a far better light than he'd deserved. In fact, the press had glorified his next relationship, while she'd been left as the eternal Ice Princess for turning every other man down since. Infuriating.

Franco was looking at her somewhat sympathetically, which irked her. She didn't need his pity! She told herself to breathe it out, but thankfully their pizza arrived and threw a cheesy barrier between them.

He made a masterpiece of eating an entire slice without oozing one bit of sauce anywhere, and then he said, 'So, are you enjoying it here, far away from Lisri and whatever happened there to make them call you the Ice Princess?'

She swallowed. So he had heard, then. It was only to be expected, though. Was there anyone left on the planet who hadn't?

'Not that you seem particularly icy to me,' he continued, and she felt her shoulders square. His brow furrowed. 'I'm sorry you had to suffer whatever it was you went through, Adrienne. I don't expect you to talk about it, but like I said before, it's your work here we're interested in—not your royal name or your past.'

She lowered her slice of pizza to her plate, grateful for his words even if she did feel a slight twinge of regret that he was definitely only interested in her professionally. It was just as well, she reminded herself. She didn't need another man coming between her and her studies—let alone the one who was supposed to be mentoring her. But the way he was looking at her...

Why on earth was she halfway tempted to talk about Xavier with this man? Because he'd just talked about his Luci so openly?

That was different. Lucinda hadn't destroyed him willingly, or lied, or harboured secrets.

She must not be swayed back onto the subject of Xavier. Then she'd have to get into that night of their engagement announcement, at the Military Ball, when she'd gone for a breath of fresh air in the grounds beforehand, only to find him whispering with Contessa Estelle. She'd stood there in the shadows of the hedgerow, feeling cold to the bone at the words she was overhearing. It had become clear they were sleeping together on a regular basis.

She'd even heard Xavier admit to his lover that he had no plans to stop seeing her once he was married to Adrienne.

'We'll just be a hot secret, you and me. We'll go away together every other month, I promise you. Even if she finds out she'll never admit it. A scandal will tear the royal family apart.'

Estelle had challenged him, begged him not to announce the engagement, but Xavier had told her he was caught between a rock and a hard place. He'd wanted Estelle in his bed, but he'd also wanted the prestige of being married to the future Queen of Lisri.

Adrienne had never felt so used in her life. She'd confronted them both, of course, right there, and told him she was calling off the engagement herself.

She could still relive every horrific detail of what had ensued in the throne room, when he'd chased after her and in the face of her fury denied everything she'd told her parents.

'He knew I would never divorce him once I'd married him, Papa! He knew I wouldn't drag our family name through the dirt!'

Thank goodness her mother had taken her side in the matter and the engagement had never been announced. But even after Security had led Xavier away, still shouting obscenities at her…and even after one magazine had published the fact that Xavier had found her 'frigid and terrible' in bed, her father had had the audacity to suggest a reconciliation.

'Maybe you can work this out if you'd just agree to talk to him again. His family is a great match with ours, Adrienne. He knows what it's like to be royal.'

She realised she was biting the insides of her cheeks again. And Franco was still watching her speculatively.

'I always had an interest in the biology of cancer, and I liked the way clinical oncology mixed pharmacology with the communication skills necessary to really connect with patients,' she said to fill the silence, picking at a fallen leaf of basil on her plate.

She sounded like a robot.

'I like to see how strong the patients are, Franco, how hard they fight and how their families come together when they're sick. You catch people in this time of distress and you can help to make them feel calm. You can make them feel cared for.'

'You're certainly good at doing that,' Franco said, but he was still looking at her as if he saw right through her, sea-green eyes penetrating every layer of her defences.

She shuffled in her seat, toyed with her napkin. She'd been babbling, avoiding getting back on topic, but he was astute…awake. Not easily fooled.

Franco served himself another slice of pizza and gestured for her to eat hers. He changed the subject adroitly, talking about his family instead. The Perrettas were an industrial, enigmatic bunch—from what she could garner from Franco, at least. They weren't aristocrats, but they were rich and well-regarded, successful, compassionate and driven. Franco's brother Benni ran Italy's second biggest automobile insurance company, and his eco-warrior sister Aimee was deeply into conservation efforts and community-strengthening initiatives. She was currently in the running for a position in Geneva as Environmental Affairs Officer with the UN.

Still, they weren't of aristocratic blood, she thought, picturing the stink it would cause in Lisri if she should start a relationship with Franco. She frowned fiercely. Why could she still not stop thinking about starting something with him?

Even as they made more small talk, about sailing, and Charles Dickens, the food in Sicily and the state of political affairs, their sexual chemistry sparked brighter than the candles between them.

'You're thinking. I can almost hear it', he said eventually, toying with a piece of garlic bread.

'I was just thinking about…the cat.'

'The cat?'

'Yes, Fiamma,' she lied, feeling guilty.

She just wasn't ready to admit how broken she'd been by Xavier's fetid, stinking lies, or how utterly embarrassed she still felt, knowing she'd been so infatuated with his handsome face and charming manner that she hadn't seen what was going on right under her nose.

It still stung that Xavier had only slept with her to persuade her that he loved her. So maybe she'd been pushing people away ever since not just to defy her parents' wish for a royal wedding, but because she simply wouldn't survive if her heart had to go through something like that again.

'This little grey thing seems to have adopted me. I didn't think I'd be out this late. I should probably get home quite soon…make sure she's got some food,' she managed, fixing her headscarf again.

Suddenly paranoid, she hoped no one was taking any surreptitious photos that might somehow get back to her family. She imagined they didn't look much like colleagues right now.

'Someone else will feed her…don't worry. Everyone has about fifteen cats that they feed here. I'll get you home safe.'

She knew he would, too, but she was torn between the desire to be with him for as long as possible and the need to pull away, get back into her safe space and protect herself. She was starting to feel as if this was a date. At least that was what it might look like to outsiders. This was her fault. She'd done this, planned this, let the excitement of being with him override all common sense. Even when she'd sworn to complete her studies before even *thinking* about another man in a romantic light—especially one like Franco, who she couldn't even have.

Franco must have noticed her discomfort, because he raised his hand for the waiter. When he'd paid she felt that stirring take hold again—the fury over her Ice Princess reputation. He might not have thought it true before, but she was surely acting like one now.

Even so, Franco didn't need to know any details about Xavier, she decided. It wasn't as if anything was ever going to happen between them anyway. She wouldn't dare allow it.

* * *

By the time they pulled their bikes to a stop at her place, close to midnight, the tension between them was thicker than the jasmine-scented air.

'Thank your sister again for the bike, please. I'll be sure to take good care of it,' she said, squinting through the drizzle. 'I'm better with the lights now, see?' She flicked them on and off again, just to prove her point, and the soft huff of his laughter ruffled her nerve-endings. He seemed to linger a moment, immediately sparking all sorts of fantasies. If he kissed her…what would she do?

No. Don't even give him the chance. You would only regret it.

'Goodnight, Franco. Thank you for the pizza—it really was life-changing.'

Holding her head high, Adrienne steered the bike up the street towards her apartment and forced herself not to look back.

That night she slept fitfully. Her restless thoughts woke her up at four a.m., when she took a cup of coffee to the balcony and stared at Mount Vesuvius across the water.

Despite her disguise, she was still paranoid she might have been photographed on the bike or with Franco. She'd been reckless, putting him in a situation that might come back to bite both of them.

He didn't need to be dragged through the world's press because of her when he was simply a man going about his business—saving lives, for the most part. What kind of impact would the media's attention have on his considerable workload and the welfare of his patients? It would likely make him stressed and distracted. The man had something good going on and he'd worked damn hard to

get it. And God knew he'd been through enough already…
with his Lucinda.

Only Adrienne couldn't deny that she had badly wanted
him to kiss her, to pull her in against his jacket, all leather
and cologne and sexy Italian intensity…

No, she told herself again. She couldn't kiss her boss—
no matter how tempting he was. It wasn't even worth con-
templating.

His family didn't need her complicating things for
them either. And there was Papa to consider too. He would
cause a riot if he knew anyone had taken her out on a
motorcycle—let alone someone who was supposed to be
a colleague and a peer. She'd come here to learn and to
work, not to elicit another royal scandal. Her father still
liked to think he could make his own rules for her, even
now she was over thirty.

She suddenly realised she was simmering more than
the volcano, just thinking about his autocratic decrees. It
made her want to break every single one of the rules she'd
agreed to live by. In that restaurant and out on that bike
with Franco she'd felt that secret part of herself that had
lain dormant for far too long getting restless again—like
a lioness ready to pounce. And it had felt good…as if she
was coming to life again.

It was not going to be easy, locking that part of herself
away around Franco. But she had to. For both their sakes.

CHAPTER SIX

FRANCO WAS PLEASED to see that Adrienne was interested in the work being carried out in the chemotherapy day unit, and thankfully Irina had stopped being so starstruck. The team were now happily delegating duties and patient dismissals to her on a regular basis, and Adrienne handled them all with grace and gratitude. Everyone loved her.

Perhaps he'd been a little too quick to judge her before meeting her, assuming she was coming to Lisri for a new adventure away from home as much as for her work. She was early to every lecture, and he'd seen her hunched over a desk long after her shift ended on several occasions, working on treatment plans for patients. Her confidence and passion shone through every time she addressed him or the nurses, the surgeons, the radiologists and the oncology consultants. She was going all out to be of use and gain merit, and he was seriously impressed.

He realised he wanted to talk to her again—get to know the Adrienne who was still hiding beneath her professional white coat.

Ever since he'd taken her out to the restaurant and lent her his sister's bike two weeks ago she'd been on his mind, slipping into his daydreams and his night ones too, if he was being honest. Maybe he shouldn't have opened up so much about Luci, but in a way he'd done it in the hope that she'd tell him something about herself in return. But she'd changed the subject—clammed up. He probably shouldn't have mentioned the 'Ice Princess' label they'd stuck on her. It was obvious there was more to the story of her and her ex than what had been reported, but it wasn't as if he could pretend he didn't know what people called her.

He made up his mind not to probe any more—he'd only be getting himself in too deep. Getting his heart involved was out of the question, especially under the circumstances, and he'd do well to remember that.

He found Adrienne in the residents' room fifteen minutes before her second consultation with thirty-seven-year-old data analyst Candice Trentino.

'So you're coming with me in case someone else calls me out for being a princess instead of a *real* doctor?' she teased as he approached her desk.

She was wearing her hair piled high in a bun today, and he thought again what a shame it was that she was forced to wear a headscarf whenever she went outside.

'Maybe,' he admitted. 'You already called me your security once.'

'Well, at least we weren't papped," she said before frowning. 'But just because you're paranoid, it doesn't mean nobody's following you. We should be more careful next…'

He bit his smile as she trailed off. So she'd been thinking about a next time too? He'd done his best not to imply there would be one. She was a closed book and the least available woman in Naples. He was here to assist her in becoming Lisri's best oncologist—that was all. Keeping her at arm's length was the only way forward…keeping her focused on her work, where her full attention belonged.

'I was impressed by this paper you wrote on the importance of evidence-based medicine in treatment decisions.' Adrienne tapped a printout on the desk as she swivelled fully in her seat to face him. 'Your passion shone through—which isn't usually the case in a medical or science-based paper. But then your passion seems to shine through most things, from what I've observed so far.'

'I'm surprised you've read that,' he said, pretending not to have noticed her compliment. 'I wrote that paper years ago.'

'I've read everything you've written,' she replied, as if he'd composed a book of award-winning poetry and not a collection of two-hundred-page documents full of charts and diagrams. 'Maybe I can pick your brain some more some time. I know you're busy, but I'd value your opinions, Franco. That twenty-four-year-old who came in this morning—Rosita Vettraino—the girl showing early signs of Ewing's sarcoma...' She paused delicately. 'I expected you to be present at the examination, but you weren't.'

'I know. I had to be somewhere else.'

He turned away from her as a rush of coldness ran through him like a wave. Even the mere mention of the rare cancer that had taken Lucinda from him could catch his heart off guard. He'd been bracing himself for this conversation.

'That's why I sent Dr Hernandez,' he said.

'He told me.'

He cleared his throat, turned towards the window. 'Did you get the MRI test results back yet?'

'Yes, and it's not looking good. Symptoms all checked out, so we've asked for a bone marrow biopsy. The family asked for you.'

Franco bowed his head at the palm fronds outside, as if sensing their judgement. He'd missed the appointment with Rosita that morning on purpose, accepting a last-minute emergency appointment in the radiation room instead. He wasn't proud of himself.

When it came to Ewing's, he was more than on top of current research and treatments, but meeting any woman who was even so much as *suspected* of suffering the rare form of cancer always felt a little too close to home. He'd seen Rosita's file. He would meet the young woman soon. But he was stalling and he knew it.

His researchers had successfully reduced tumour growth in young patients just like her with a new biotech drug, but the trial was still stuck in phase two, bound up in legal procedures. They needed phase three status so they could take on more patients—so they could start offering more hope to people like Rosita and her family. His lawyers kept saying it was only a matter of weeks until phase three was approved, and he wanted—needed—to deliver better news than he currently had.

Adrienne was looking at him curiously. He knew he hadn't mentioned to her the kind of cancer that had taken Luci when he'd talked about it before.

Ewing's sarcoma was a very rare type of tumour that grew in the bones—or, in Luci's case, the cartilage and nerves around the bones. He'd watched it snatch her away, all of her—her energy, her tireless drive... And the beautiful body he'd worshipped for several years of his young adult life had been reduced to a brittle shell. He'd watched her crumble on the inside too—watched the sparks fade from her eyes and listened to her crying late into the night towards the end. Not out of fear of dying, but out of sadness at leaving *him* behind. They'd only released her from the hospital in Rome so she could come home to die...

'In the case of Lucinda it spread to the lungs before it was even diagnosed,' he murmured, lost in thought.

Adrienne's neat eyebrows shot up. 'Lucinda had Ewing's? Franco, I didn't mean… You don't have to…'

'As you know, it usually affects people between the ages of ten and twenty. Luci was a rare case, contracting it in her early twenties like Rosita.' He paused to meet her eyes finally. He saw sympathy pulse in her pupils, but he didn't want it. 'There are new forms of treatment, Adrienne—more since I wrote the paper you read. The drugs currently in trial are the ones we need.'

'What trial?'

He paced the room, still lost in thought. 'One patient out of two hundred had an adverse reaction to the drug and the whole damn thing got put on hold. I offered to give them whatever they needed to launch phase three through the Perretta Institute, but it's not about the money—it's more bureaucratic red tape holding things up as usual, while people suffer.'

He paused.

'My first thought when I heard about Rosita was that we have to get the trial moving again. Just one cycle of this drug could reduce the cancer's spread to other parts of her body in weeks. This is a revolutionary advancement, Adrienne, and it will make a difference to so many others too. The authorities know it's big—that's why they're being extra-vigilant about it—but we're running out of time to help Rosita…'

'What do we have to do?'

He frowned. It wasn't easy to expedite things like this. 'I don't know,' he admitted. 'But I can't stand watching people suffer when they might not have to. I've already been on the phone personally to everyone I can think of—several times.'

He busied his fingers with the patient file on his clipboard, aware of the way she was still studying him thoughtfully. Shame rippled through him at the memory of avoiding the consultation that morning even now, as he talked about the promising drug, the kids and adults it had already helped, and what it could do in the future. He knew he was the most knowledgeable medic on Ewing's in the entire institute.

But this wasn't all about waiting for the trial. He couldn't talk about this specific rare cancer without bringing Luci up—and remembering everything they'd gone through in their battle to fight that soul-sucking disease. The work he'd launched himself into because of Luci kept him going, and kept others going too, even when he rarely spoke about her. But Adrienne hadn't even mentioned her before he'd cut in at Mr Geordano's consultation. What had he been thinking, making this all about himself and Luci when it wasn't about them at all? He was here to do a job. That had burned in his mind all day as he went about his duties.

He had no intention of letting his attraction to Adrienne affect his work in any way, but already he was finding it hard to concentrate on what he should be doing—and he'd spoken too much about Luci in front of Adrienne.

He hadn't looked at his photo album in weeks, either. Those memories of him and Luci were in a box under his bed and he hadn't pulled it out, trying to wish her back to life, since Adrienne had started working here. Unlike what he had done after several disappointing dates with other women.

He hadn't exactly been a paragon of virtue since Luci had died. She'd made him promise he wouldn't become a monk, and there had been a few women at first… OK, maybe more than a few women, when he'd needed to bury his grief and loneliness for even a handful of minutes. The brief relationships he'd managed after that had been little better. He'd felt numb, and he knew he'd given women the impression that he was aloof and emotionally unavailable. He hadn't cared if they stayed with him or not.

So why was his heart refocusing now—slowly, like a squeaky old camera lens—on the one woman he couldn't ever have? The Crown Princess of Lisri. What kind of card was the universe dealing him now?

His insides gnawed at each other like starving animals as they walked in silence to the chemo lab, and before his thoughts could spiral any further their patient arrived, dressed all in black, just like her mother. As they ran through copies of Candice Trentino's scans, X-rays, CT scans and pathology slides in the lab's all-white consultation room Franco tried to keep his eyes from Adrienne's as Candice's mother began to weep.

'It's a frightening situation when you're waiting for results like you have been,' Adrienne empathised.

He watched her pour a glass of water for both women. The white-painted room was made less stark by the platitudes printed and framed on the walls, but he knew nobody could focus on anything for long in this room. In this situation. Most people left loathing it—at least the first few times.

'We've examined the cells and tissues from your liquid biopsy earlier this week, and it seems that what we're dealing with is a pre-cancerous condition of the larynx,' Adrienne explained gently.

'You mean I might get throat cancer?' Candice croaked, squeezing her mother's hand. 'I don't even smoke!'

'But you do drink too much—I've always said that,' her mother cut in. 'That can't be good for her, can it, Doctors?'

'You try working where I work!' Candice exclaimed, pulling her hand back.

For a second she put her head between her knees, but it

was her mother who started gasping for breath. Candice reached for her hand again, gripping it tight like a steel vice.

Franco caught Adrienne's glance. Patients sometimes acted stronger than their family members at first, but he knew discussing a new diagnosis could affect people differently.

Bad news was unstoppable—like a rampant bull you wanted to run from but couldn't. It pinned you down, then stamped on you over and over again whenever you tried to get up. Luci had been shell-shocked at the time, almost deaf to her diagnosis. Later, in a heap on the bathroom floor of a hotel in Rome, the full extent of it had struck her. Her sobs had racked the entire corridor, and someone had even knocked on their door to check no one had died.

'Not yet!' Luci had replied.

Typical Luci. He'd tried so hard to be the strength she needed, but he'd never felt as strong as he'd looked.

He scanned the slides, wishing he could shake off his earlier conversation with Adrienne about Rosita and Ewing's sarcoma. It was his job to be everyone's strength now, and Adrienne must think him completely unprofessional for sending another doctor to that consultation earlier.

Adrienne was still talking. 'There are plenty of treatment options these days, of course, which we'll run through with you if you feel up to it...'

Candice was shaking her head. 'I can't do chemo,' she said adamantly. 'I can't lose my hair.'

'You might not have to.'

'I don't want to take any drugs.'

'It might not come to that either, Candice,' Franco said gently. 'There's now immunotherapy treatment, which we call biologic therapy,' he explained. 'The treatment uses your own immune system, your body's natural defences, to fight the tumour...'

They had both women listening attentively for the duration of the appointment. But the second they were alone Franco pulled Adrienne aside before she could leave. He knew his mind would keep spinning over their new Ewing's sarcoma patient unless he talked it over with Adrienne first.

'I need to talk to you tonight, if you're free,' he told her.

CHAPTER SEVEN

THERE WAS A letter waiting for her on the doormat. After showering the day off her, she opened it out on the balcony, feeling her heart pound in anticipation as she slid a nail under the scarlet wax crest. Her mother the Queen still insisted on sealing all her letters with it.

My darling,
I hope this finds you somewhere peaceful. I've been thinking of you fondly over the past few weeks...the royal palace feels empty with you gone.

I trust you are taking some time for yourself and enjoying the sights of Naples—it was always a secret dream of mine to travel for an extended period outside of Lisri.

I know I don't tell you this often enough but I'm proud of you...

Adrienne was startled as a silky swish of warmth curled around her ankles. She lifted Fiamma onto her lap and shook off her shoes, then read the last sentence again, picturing her mother's wise eyes and soft, kind face.

A pang of guilt struck her from nowhere. She herself was living a dream that her mother, Lisri's own Queen, had been forced to abandon when she'd married Papa when she was twenty-one.

Not that they hadn't been in love. Her parents had been smitten the moment they'd set eyes on each other, so the marriage arrangement had been welcome when it came some six months later. Even so, Adrienne was coming to learn with age that her mother harboured certain regrets about marrying so young and having to assume the crown without having done anything for herself first.

I've been inspired by your adventures, Adrienne, so I've been in the kitchen again. Chef Maxy was very surprised when I offered to help her bake—it's been so many years, you know. But it's something I dared to dream I might have done for a living, had I not been so fortunate as to be born a future monarch, and we made the most wonderful cake together. In fact I might even make another one when you come home for the polo match.

I also write to tell you, Adrienne, that Baron Vittorio La Rosa of Laughterhaven South will be in Naples next month, to visit the Military Academy. I happened to mention you were there and that you might be interested in showing him the sights of the city.

I wouldn't suggest this if he wasn't a handsome single man, my darling. I'm sure I don't need to mention that we'd be thrilled to unite the La Rosa and Marx-Balthus families...

There she goes again. Adrienne slapped the letter to the table and pressed her nose to Fiamma's fuzzy head to calm herself. Just as the Queen was confessing how she might actually find her daughter's ambition an inspiration, there she went, attempting to matchmake in the hopes that Adrienne might fall in love on the spot and drop everything to return to Lisri, get married and start making babies.

As if.

But, then again, if I could feel anything like I felt when I first saw Franco for someone who wouldn't cause the kingdom to collapse, maybe I wouldn't be entirely opposed to getting married soon...

Her phone pulled her out of her dream.

Franco was here.

She'd told Security to give her a missed call when he was downstairs, signing in.

Even knowing he was in the building sent her temperature rising.

The purring grey cat sprang from her lap onto the marble tiles as Adrienne hurried for her bag. Smoothing down her dress, she made for the elevator.

He had asked if she would meet him tonight but hadn't said why, or where they were going. Every attempt made by her head to say no had been pummelled into submission by her heart.

Franco's eyes trailed her up and down, burning like coals from Vesuvius, as she climbed off her bike and unfastened her helmet, shaking her hair free before tying on a headscarf.

Again, she felt empowered by his appraising glances but wished she didn't still feel as if she was walking a dangerous line towards some unmitigated disaster. Her wild heart kept bashing her ribs in a way it had never seemed to do for any of her parents' set-ups, and it would probably never beat the same way for the Baron her mother had promised she'd spend some time with.

Her mother's letter had really got under her skin, but she had to forget it and try to enjoy tonight. It wasn't as if this was a date anyway—just as the last time they'd gone out together hadn't been a date.

Or *was* this a date?

'This place is stunning,' she enthused, taking in the view.

He'd brought her to Castel dell'Ovo, the oldest castle in Naples, rising like a sandy fortress on a peninsula called Megaride. The waves were crashing in the distance and a sea breeze softened the heat. Every boat on the ocean ahead of them created a riot of colour, like the flowers around them on the hillside.

Franco extended a hand to lead her down a stony staircase. 'Welcome to the first inhabited centre of ancient Neapolis,' he said.

His shirtsleeves were snug around his biceps, and he wore navy-blue board shorts that came to just below his knees. He had really strong legs—from hiking, she'd heard him say once. She'd bet he'd like the scenery in Lisri, as her island nation, off the Danish coast, was at its best in summer, and the hikes out into the mountains and fjords were breathtaking.

Franco was smiling as she reached the bottom step. For a moment she was so entranced by the sight of him against the rolling ocean waves, and daydreaming of him hiking with her in Lisri, that she almost forgot to appreciate what he was actually showing her.

A three-hundred-and-sixty-degree panorama of the sunset across the gulf smiled before her, with the city sparkling in golden light.

'It's beautiful,' she breathed, just as her eyes landed on his. The deep green hue reminded her of home, of all the colours of new things born in the spring.

'It certainly is.'

He almost sighed, and he was still looking at her. Persistent butterflies assaulted her stomach as she became aware that he was looking at her long, slim legs in the short light blue sundress she wore. She'd opted to wear it so she could easily ride the bike…but she couldn't deny how it thrilled her to see him looking at her and clearly liking what he saw.

He led her along the seafront in front of the castle and set his backpack down on the sweeping stone wall. There were a couple of people lingering up ahead, pointing cameras at the views, but thankfully no one close enough to recognise who she was.

'Just us,' he said, as if reading her mind, and she sat beside him on the wall, daring to push back her headscarf a little and swinging her legs towards the sea about ten feet below. 'Well, just us and your security.'

Franco nodded towards where Ivan had positioned himself in the shade, several feet away, fanning his face with a pamphlet. Too far away to hear their conversation, thankfully.

'Ignore him,' she said.

Summer air blew warm about her cheeks, playing with her hair, blowing strands against his shoulder, which he may or may not have noticed. She wanted to feel 'normal' again, but she was starting to realise that maybe she'd never feel normal around this man.

He poured them each a glass of something sweet and cold, and told her a legend about a siren who'd landed here and given a name to the ancient city, the first settlement of the Greeks.

Franco was different from the Italian men in Naples, she thought. In her opinion guys from Florence were far more attractive, and he was the cream of the crop—the foam in the cappuccino. Exactly her type, she realised.

Funny… She'd never even thought she *had* a type till now.

It was clear he worked out from his impressive muscular physique. Not like most of the men who peacocked around her normally, who thought their money and their status could buy them every woman's desire and wouldn't know a barbell if it hit them on the head.

He could kiss her now, she realised. She'd be powerless to resist. She stifled a giggle. She really should start reading more than romance novels and medical journals, she decided.

Then he spoke.

'I have to tell you something.'

His eyes on the sea made her stomach lurch.

'That appointment today…the girl with Ewing's sarcoma…'

She nodded. Of course he would bring that up. 'I'm so sorry I mentioned you not being there,' she said. 'I didn't know it was Lucinda's diagnosis…'

'How could you have known?' He cut short her profuse apology with a wave of his hand. 'I didn't attend it on purpose, Adrienne, and not just because I'm waiting for the trial. It was selfish of me not to go. I know I painted a happy picture of her before, because that's the Luci I like to remember, but that doesn't mean I enjoy talking about what happened to her in front of everyone. However, I'd like you to understand.'

He met her eyes, and she knew he meant he wasn't comfortable talking about it with *her*.

'I do understand,' she said, even as her heart's own beat skipped away from her.

His knuckles turned white as he gripped the wall between them. 'Ewing's sarcoma...the type of cancer she had...it's so rare. The fevers and the pain in her bones were unbearable...' He trailed off a second, and she saw his Adam's apple quiver in his throat—just before she noticed Ivan, motioning for her to put her headscarf back on properly.

'There was only one treatment protocol for first-time patients when she got sick,' Franco went on. 'And because it's most commonly found in adolescence, and mostly considered a paediatric cancer, she was treated at a children's hospital in Rome. We spent *months* there—and I hate Rome. The food there is all tourist food...it was better in the hospital—which was the only good thing about it.'

Adrienne followed his gaze out to sea, wishing she knew what to say. This was an unprovoked outpouring she hadn't expected. It made her want to loop a comforting hand around his, but she busied her fingers with her headscarf.

To her surprise, once she'd finished, Franco took her hand. He gripped it like a vice, almost as though he were absorbing some kind of strength from her, and then he relaxed his hand in hers. It felt natural to touch him, she observed, looking at her slender fingers entwined with his. It also made her heart pound harder...

'Unfortunately, the type of chemo they used for Ewing's at the time meant Luci had to be an inpatient for longer than usual. She had an infusion every two to three weeks. Sometimes she was in there up to six days at a time. She wasn't too enthusiastic about being treated alongside children, as you can imagine. But the care she received and the atmosphere on the ward was better there than anywhere here. Not that it did much good in the end.'

'I can't imagine what you must have gone through,' Adrienne managed.

Then Franco told her all about the treatments they'd tried, and the researchers he'd gone to meet—even the week they'd spent in the Amazon, drinking a potent tribal brew called *ayahuasca*, just in case they could coax the demon out with magic. He'd done everything in his power to try and save his true love, and he hadn't given up or fled in the face of adversity. He really was the very best kind of man. The kind you could fall for hard and for ever, she thought to herself.

'The way you loved her... It's beautiful. Inspirational,' she said aloud.

He shrugged and dropped her fingers, turning his face to the sky. 'Not really. I just did what any man in love would do. When your heart is involved you have no choice but to fight for your person—right to the end.'

Your person. Adrienne repeated it to herself, wondering if she'd ever have someone she could call her person. She had trust issues now—and walls as high as the one they were sitting on.

She watched a seagull swoop for a fishing boat. 'Don't you think it's strange how some people think loving someone is just a bonus in a relationship...in a marriage?' she said quietly, remembering her mother's letter.

'What are you talking about?'

She closed her eyes, embarrassed. 'I don't know...'

Franco frowned at her. 'You're not being forced to marry someone, are you? Someone you don't want to marry?'

'Of course not. There's no one.'

Franco tossed a pebble over the edge and they watched it drop into the water.

'But my family *has* been quite adept at making strategic marriage connections over the years,' she continued thoughtfully. 'Maybe that's why I'm such a disappointment to everyone.'

She bit her lip, knowing she had a habit of revealing too much when she was nervous. But she suddenly felt a fresh urge to tell him *why* there was no one, to tell him that she was destined only for an aristocrat, even if her helpless heart should start yearning for someone else entirely. She should help Franco, she thought. Chase him away before her family did. Maybe then he'd stop looking at her like...*this*.

But she liked it when he looked at her like this.

'I won't claim to have any idea of what your life must be like in Lisri, but I *do* know that you're in my country now,' he said, nudging her gently as the breeze toyed with his hair, making her want to touch it. 'You're in my castle now—and in *my* castle you can never be a disappointment.'

She leaned into his shoulder, stealing a lungful of his scent.

'I'm sorry if I spoke too much about Luci,' he said. 'I just wanted to get everything out there, you know, in case any questions about her or her treatment come up with Rosita's family. A lot of people don't know me, or why I do the work I do. But some do...'

'I'm honoured to be one of those people,' she replied truthfully. 'For what it's worth, I know Ewing's sarcoma patients are rare. You're probably never going to be ready to see its impact on anyone else. But you will still be the best person in that room. People need a heart like yours, Franco. As well as your experience. And I'm here now. And I'm going to help you get that trial to phase three so Rosita can have the help she needs.'

An idea was forming in her head already... It would potentially ruffle some feathers in Lisri, but she was determined.

'We'll find a way to get it approved.'

Her breath caught as he brought her hand to his lips, letting them linger against the back of her fingers for a moment. The ground could have opened up and she wouldn't have noticed. She knew Italians kissed people's hands and cheeks all the time, but this gentle touch felt entirely different. He could kiss her lips right now... Was he thinking about it, just as she was?

'Has no one else proposed to you since Prince Xavier?' he asked her quietly, his green eyes slanted.

The question made jelly of her whole body. She shook her head, feeling her steady composure evaporating on the spot.

'I'm the Ice Princess, remember?' she told him, and she watched him visibly withdraw. She could have kicked herself. She'd completely ruined the moment.

Back at the end of her driveway later, Franco didn't get off his bike and he left the engine running even as her apartment keys burned in her pocket once again. Ivan pulled up on his bike just after them, and thankfully disappeared into the building.

'Thanks for letting me explain myself tonight,' Franco said, scanning her eyes through the gap in his helmet.

'I told you, it's OK.'

Her mind was a hurricane. He hadn't kissed her when he could have done. He'd asked her again if there was anyone, then left her hanging—as if waiting for her to elaborate, or kiss him first. Of course she hadn't. She'd let the moment linger and pass them both by, until he'd quietly suggested they ride home. Then again, knowing Ivan was several feet away, watching them, would have killed the moment even if she hadn't done it first.

'You're a good listener.'

'Well, you're even better at talking, so I guess we're a good match.'

She berated herself even as he muttered a laugh. *Why did you say that?*

Her brain was on overload. The night air felt thick with anticipation. Maybe he was waiting for her to make a move, she thought. She was royalty, after all, and he was nothing but respectful.

Rattled, she stalled her bike's engine by mistake. And in the end he took the pressure off in the simplest way.

'*Buona notte*, Adrienne.'

She watched him peel away into the night and felt as if something had ended before it had even started.

All night the fire in her veins burned hotter, as if she could feel the curse of her own royal blood working its evil magic.

He probably sensed she'd only bring trouble to his door, and he was right. She didn't give her past away easily, and neither did she put her emotions on display, where they could be scrutinised and judged. Franco, in spite of being a very private man, was trying to invite her in, gradually sharing parts of himself, while she kept shutting him out. Maybe *that* was why he wouldn't kiss her.

It didn't matter anyway. She'd avoided a potentially disastrous situation and so had he.

She should be concentrating on helping him professionally, she decided, by bringing more attention to the need for this trial. Who didn't want a role model like Franco? she thought. Someone strong, who fought for love and health and prosperity...and adventures. She was still overwhelmed that she'd been riding a Vespa with no accidents all this time.

Franco was an audacious explorer in many ways,

and she was already learning more from him than she'd thought she would. Now the idea that had struck her at the castle kept growing from a spark into a furious fire inside her, flooding her with a sense of purpose she hadn't felt in years.

CHAPTER EIGHT

FRANCO HAD BEEN on call since six a.m. with barely a break, and now he was looking at a screen displaying a portly thirty-nine-year-old man's insides. Beside him sat Adrienne, one of her long legs crossed elegantly over the other. But there was a rather large elephant lumbering around in the room with them. It had been hovering there ever since he'd left her on her bike earlier in the week, and not even the diagnosis they were about to give could make it fully disappear.

'Your MRI results have revealed a small spasm in your lower colon, but the colonoscopy, as you know, could not be completed. The surgeon had trouble getting the scope past an unusual lesion...'

'Yes, I felt that, thank you.'

Their patient, a Greek man named Diodoro, tapped his feet anxiously on the floor tiles. He wore too-white sneakers, and his plump arms shook with the movements, sending ripples through his belly.

The man's partner, a slightly slimmer Italian-Asian in a green V-neck sweater and fashionably mismatched socks, put a hand to his shoulder. 'You felt it? I thought you were sedated?'

'Obviously not sedated enough, Gabriel.'

Franco watched Adrienne wait patiently, and then continue unperturbed. She was always so poised, he thought—until she let her guard down. That night when she'd started to open up about her life—the real, personal side of it—he'd seen the Adrienne he wanted to see more of. But then she'd clammed up again.

Just for a moment she'd looked like a wilting flower, running out of water, but he was still none the wiser about her past. There was something that had pushed her to come here aside from wanting her oncology rotation. But she wasn't about to divulge any personal details beyond those he needed to know—that much was clear. He'd wondered if maybe there *was* a guy she was being urged to marry... and that was what had ended her other relationship.

No, he thought now, catching her eyes on him again. There was no one, as she'd said. Not with the way she'd started to look at *him*...

He could have kissed her the other night. He'd felt the build up, experienced a wave of lust he'd never felt before—and not just because she was so untouchable. Well, maybe not entirely untouchable, he thought. She hadn't dropped his hand when he'd taken it at the castle, and the thought of introducing her to a decidedly un-royal world of pleasure had made its way into his dreams on several hot, restless occasions this past week.

There was also the fact that women were usually intimidated by his wealth and his status in society. But Adrienne wasn't. She would always be the one people wanted to talk to, in any room. Part of him admired that—even if her status wasn't exactly her choice.

Knowing Ivan was always around, protecting her, made him burn even harder to get her alone, but there wasn't much point in letting this go any further anyway. She was the future Queen of Lisri, for God's sake. It was better this way...staying at a safe, professional distance. Better not to let that feeling in his heart rattle loose, nor allow himself this unsettling sense of dependence on seeing her and having her close.

Not if she ends up being someone else you might lose.

'So, we've looked at your CT pneumocolon…that's a virtual colonoscopy…and the results from your biopsy, and we can now tell you we've found something,' Adrienne was saying now.

She glanced his way and Franco bowed his head. This was always the worst part. Every doctor was trained to deliver bad news, but when it came to cancer it was still not the done thing to mention the C word outright. In saying they'd found *something*, Adrienne was leaving it up to the patient to come to his own conclusions and mention it first.

'It's cancer. Right, Doctors?' Diodoro wasn't beating around the bush.

'Yes, I'm afraid it is,' Adrienne confirmed.

'It's a death sentence, isn't it?' He wrung his hands in his lap, ran them over his dark denim jeans, then stood up, and Franco watched his shoulders fall with every step towards the window.

'Don't be ridiculous, Dio. You're always so dramatic.' Gabriel crossed one leg over the other, maybe trying to disguise his portly belly.

Diodoro turned, his face reddening. 'A lot of people just saw me hugging my knees with a tube up my butt, Gabriel. Am I not allowed to be a little dramatic?'

'Oh, honey, I've seen you do worse things,' his partner quipped, deadpan.

To Franco's surprise, Diodoro erupted into laughter, but when Gabriel got up and embraced him hard all laughter stopped, and both men fell silent in their trembling embrace.

'We'll get through this,' Gabriel whispered.

'It's not necessarily a death sentence. Fortunately, we've caught it early,' Adrienne went on.

Franco pushed the patient file closer to her, brushing the tips of her fingernails. 'When you're comfortable we can bring the surgeon in, and we'll discuss the details,' he said.

Diodoro nodded, sinking down into the couch again, apparently in shock. Franco felt for the man; it was impossible not to become personally invested in his patients—on some level, at least. Meeting the woman with Ewing's would be tough, but at least he'd be more prepared now... if his damn phone calls would ever get answered.

They needed just a few more weeks, the authorities kept saying.

Just a few more weeks to feed them the same old line about needing just a few more weeks, he thought.

Adrienne was walking their patient through the highlights of a new treatment—one that the Perretta Institute had helped bring out of trial and into general use. It was a revolutionary radiation technique that they would try prior to surgery—with the patient's consent. It had been a huge success so far, and just last week had sent two similar cases into remission in Rome.

When Franco took over, explaining what he knew, Adrienne took copious notes on her clipboard. She was so invested in the institute already. He knew she remembered almost everything she heard and read. He'd caught her poring over some of the documents she'd asked for a couple of days back, reading up on the patients on the Ewing's trial, the achievements and results they'd seen before it had all got held up. She was doing him proud and they were a good match in lots of ways.

But every now and then, watching her lips move, he wondered what might have happened that night if he *had* made the first move on the princess.

Diodoro's substantial mouth was compressed into a thin, grim line. 'Butt surgery. Who'd have thought it would come to this? By a princess, too.'

Franco bit his cheek, hiding a smile in his paperwork.

Adrienne drew a deep breath. 'I'm not a surgeon,' she said, 'but I can be present for any procedures if you want me to be.'

'I will indeed think about that. I'm grateful for your work here, Dr Princess,' Diodoro replied humbly.

'Dr Balthus is fine.'

Franco spotted Adrienne in the staff canteen later. She seemed to be engrossed in another research paper, alone at a table in the corner, until surgeon Ansell Ackerman made a move for her table.

Franco rolled his eyes and considered going over there himself, but she stood up abruptly and left to take a call, sweeping right past Ansell distractedly, without acknowledging him. Franco swore he heard her say something about the cat.

Ansell sloped dejectedly back to another table, which wasn't the way he usually exited a situation in this place.

But there was no time to waste on empty victories. Franco barely had time to grab a sandwich, as their Ewing's sarcoma patient, Rosita, would be here soon with her parents, and it was almost time for him to face some personal demons. It would be difficult, and painful, but Adrienne hadn't been afraid to tell him the truth. Ewing's sarcoma patients were rare, and he would never be fully ready to face one, but he was still always going to be the best person in the room.

He was frustrated beyond belief that phase three of the trial was still blocked at all angles. Still, Adrienne's determined words at the castle about her helping him get it through had stuck with him—as had the look in her eyes when they'd each silently dared the other to close the damn deal and kiss, regardless of any consequences.

'I just keep telling myself that this can't be right…she's only twenty-four years old.'

Mr Vettraino, Rosita's father, was in the denial stage. His well-cut navy double-breasted jacket, jeans and polished shoes reminded Franco of his brother.

'There must be something we can do.'

'That's why we're here,' Franco said kindly.

He'd prepared himself, reading late into the night, and before that chasing down more blocked avenues. He couldn't mention the trial now and get anyone's hopes up, and Adrienne knew it. But he would do the best he could.

The look on Rosita's face every time her father gave in to his emotions tore at his heart. Rosita was too thin already, with sad brown eyes and black hair in a slicked-back ponytail. She was turning her phone around in her hands, staring unseeingly at the leaflets and forms on the table.

'We know you have experience with patients who've developed this…this cancer,' her mother said. The prim-looking woman toyed with the top button of her pinstriped blouse and sat forward in her seat, making the pearls in her golden hoop earrings catch the sun. 'We're all so very grateful you're with us on this, Doctor. And you, Dr Balthus,' she added. 'Your work gives me hope. We'll do anything. Anything she needs.'

'The survival rate for localised Ewing's sarcoma is significantly higher than it was several years ago,' he explained, noticing that the woman's wedding ring—a thin gold band—was next to a not-so-modest-sized diamond. 'That's pretty high. But there are new treatments on the way, and we've caught it early. We do have options here.'

Adrienne pushed a box of tissues towards them and caught his eye. He knew they both wished they could talk about the success they'd seen in phase two of the new treatment. There was a young woman's future at stake—the future of a woman who should have the world at her feet, not a hospital floor.

'Now, Rosita, you're entitled to some help—and not just here at the hospital.' Adrienne's voice was warm, her manner well-honed. 'You'll have occupational therapy, palliative care and community nursing support. And we'll be here with you every step of the way.'

As Adrienne went on he watched the rise and fall of Rosita's emotions in her eyes and wondered what it would be like to have a daughter. He'd proposed to Luci with a ring not unlike the one on Mrs Vettraino's finger—big, lavish, with a diamond so sparkly it had sent rainbows across every white wall when the sun hit it. But Luci hadn't wanted children. Funny how he'd just accepted that, no question, without really thinking about if he wanted them himself. Maybe he would have considered it down the line. But he knew Luci would never have changed her mind. She'd been adamant.

For the first time he wondered if maybe…just maybe… they *wouldn't* have lasted for ever. They'd been so young, after all, and they'd both dived headfirst into a serious relationship. He didn't know many people who'd got together that young and still wanted the same things from each other years later.

He doted on his niece, Alina, only marginally less than her father, Benni, did—he had never missed a single one of her gymnastics competitions. Alina was eight years old now, with rosy cheeks, inquisitive round green eyes and a head of chestnut curls.

He and his family had become so much closer after

Luci died. He often thought her death had hammered home the importance of not sweating the small stuff, of talking things through and never going to bed angry with anyone or leaving anything important unsaid. He felt better for clearing things up with Adrienne over why he'd missed that first consult with Rosita, even if it had left things between them even more perplexing.

'How long before I die if no treatment works?' Rosita's voice was cool when she spoke, composed.

Her mother drew a sharp breath and snatched a tissue from the box. 'Don't ask things like that.'

'Why, Mamma? I want to know. It's my body, and I have a right to know how long it will be mine for. Will I lose the ability to walk eventually? Who will walk Bones?'

'You've called your dog Bones?' Franco asked her, and she nodded at her shoes.

'He's nine. If he dies before me, I guess at least he'll meet me up there.' She raised her eyes to the ceiling and jabbed at the air with her phone.

Her father took the seat beside her, exhaling deeply. 'She keeps talking like this, Doctors.' Then he turned to his daughter, revealing a hint of a gold chain under his white-collared shirt. 'I told you…this man can help you.'

'We will *all* do what we can,' Adrienne said.

'It's a rare but curable cancer if it's caught in time,' Franco told them, feeling Adrienne's eyes on him. She was clearly trying to take the pressure off him and it made him start for a second. Was she concerned that he might fall apart or something?

'Will she require chemo?' Rosita's mother grabbed for another tissue. 'Won't that just put her off her food? She's already lost so much weight—look at her.'

Rosita shot Franco a look that included an eye-roll. She was acting defiant, but she was probably back to being stomped on by that raging bull of bad news whenever she was alone. He knew it well.

Adrienne explained how a nine-week chemo course prior to surgery or radiation would help reduce the size of the tumour, and he focused on her calm, lilting voice, summoning strength by osmosis.

He knew the chemo drug they *weren't* talking about— the one on the trial—might possibly help Rosita faster. It would potentially cut the number of cycles in half…maybe even less. It would mean less pain for her, more time for doing regular things, like walking in parks, chatting to people online…maybe about her cancer? He wondered who she'd talk to about this. Luci had often complained that no one knew how she was feeling, and how could he have disagreed?

Back then, if he'd known about any treatment that might have saved Luci even an ounce of her pain, and someone had been keeping it under lock and key for no good reason…he didn't like to think what he might have done.

'I wish we could have told them about the trial. Any news on that? You didn't mention it, so I'm guessing not.'

Adrienne closed the door after the family, leaving them alone.

'Not yet,' he said, pacing to the window.

His brain was still whirring over all the questions they'd answered, and how he'd talked briefly about Luci when Rosita's father had brought up a child they'd read about who'd been treated in Rome. It hadn't been as bad as he'd expected. He had more hope for the future these days, and there was a new fire under his backside making him want to do even more.

'I offered to help, remember? And I have had a few ideas, actually.'

'I'm handling it—although I'm still waiting on the authorities,' he said distractedly. 'But I'll keep that in mind, thank you.'

He knew she could probably use her name to open a few doors, and he'd take her up on that if it came to it, but he owed it to his team to do everything he could personally regarding the issue before pulling a student into it—and that was what Adrienne was, after all, her royal status notwithstanding.

'Did I hear you say something about your cat?' he remembered suddenly as she pulled her phone out.

'She's gone missing.' She frowned into her screen, resting on the edge of the desk, revealing several more inches of smooth pale leg under her white coat. 'Mirabel the housekeeper hasn't seen her today, and she usually comes in for food.'

'Maybe everyone else is feeding her too?' he offered, but she shook her head.

'She never goes far from my apartment. I'm sure she's fine, but...'

'Go home,' he said, but she shook her head again.

'Don't be silly. I'm too busy.'

'Go,' he insisted. 'There's only an hour left of your shift. I'll tell one of the nurses to cover your last round.'

She offered him a thankful *namaste* hand sign and hurried out of the room. Then she stuck her head back in. 'Are you OK?' she asked. 'After...that?'

The question struck him deep. A missing cat on her mind and she was remembering to check in on *him*. And she'd already seen that he wasn't fine, mostly due to his frustration over all these vexing trial setbacks.

He told her yes, and motioned for her to hurry, then followed her, catching sight of her shrugging out of her white coat and swinging through the double doors.

Nothing would have happened to the cat. He was pretty sure of that. But he knew by now that Adrienne's cool exterior was all an act. She cared deeply about lots of things; she just didn't always talk about them with him. Who *did* she talk to?

She must really love that cat, he thought, hoping nothing *had* happened to it.

CHAPTER NINE

Mr Geordano, her oropharyngeal cancer patient, who had at first treated her royal presence with such disdain, had sent flowers again via the hospital. He was thanking her like this every few days now. She'd taken them home, and the scent of wild roses almost overpowered her the second she stepped inside.

'Puss?'

'She still hasn't been here,' said Mirabel, poking her head out from the kitchen holding a scouring pad and making her jump.

Adrienne tossed her bag to the couch, shook off her shoes and hurried the length of the apartment.

Panic was setting in now. Fiamma was the closest thing she had to a friend around here; she couldn't let her down.

In less than five minutes she'd sent Ivan off one way, despite his initial reluctance, and sped off the other way on her own.

As she headed south along the coast towards Solerno, the city soon fell into a backdrop. Looming mountains up ahead confirmed she was well out of her comfort zone. But she was not to be deterred. Upping her speed on the Vespa, all she could think about was Fiamma.

What if something was terribly wrong? What if she

never saw the kitten again? The cat was the only one who knew all her secrets.

'Puss!' she called out, and felt her scarf blow from around her neck, right into the branches of a tree. Damn. She couldn't stop and go back for it. What if Fiamma was out here somewhere, looking for her, lost?

But could she have wandered this far?

Pulling to a stop on a grassy patch, Adrienne left the engine on, checked her map again. The arrow was all over the place, telling her to ride into the ocean.

'Thanks a lot,' she grumbled at it, flipping the bike's stand down and cutting the engine. She shook her phone. As if in defiance the battery sign turned ominously red. Ten per cent left. *Great.*

Flustered and hot, and apparently in the middle of nowhere, between villages on a narrow coastal road, she turned the bike around carefully. It stuttered beneath her, hot and tired like she was, from a thirty-five-minute bakeathon in the sun.

'Don't you give up on me,' she ordered it, speeding back the way she'd come.

The road was beautiful. She tried to let the view relax her. It was all trees and wildflowers springing from mossy curves and corners. But she was still on edge after her work today, and the missing kitten was an added worry on top.

Franco was concerned that the trial would not be ready for Rosita in time. He wanted to try the new drug before she had too many cycles of regular chemo.

It sounded as if he didn't want her help in bypassing all the bureaucratic barriers—but that, unbeknown to him, was her speciality. She didn't just smile and shake hands with people in her royal life. Maybe he wanted to handle it on his own, like he'd handled things so far, without the help of a royal name—he was a proud Italian after all.

She hadn't told him about her idea yet. Instead, she'd confided in her mother the Queen about it in a letter, hoping that maybe she'd ignite a spark of excitement over something of such importance.

It had poured out of her so effortlessly—how a new website and app she had in mind would offer a network of support to cancer patients and survivors. How she already had an interview lined up with a young girl Bianca, now in her early twenties, who'd been in remission for over three years, thanks to having the new chemo drug when it was on trial. The drugs that were now being blocked from reaching more people. It wouldn't be so hard to find more interviews and get the word out...

I'm excited to have your support on this. I'm confident I can be someone who will in time help build a solid foundation for the health and prosperity of our country and beyond.

She'd also written about Franco, and the lives he was shaping and mostly saving, and how she felt useful now, but wanted to do even more.

Every time she'd written his name she'd felt her stomach bottom out, but she'd not mentioned her growing affections, just her work. *Their* work.

She had made no mention of Baron Vittorio La Rosa. Hopefully her mother would get the hint that she wasn't interested in him. But she *had* tried to be encouraging about her baking.

It's never too late to do something different, Mother, even something no one expects of a royal.

No reply to her letter had arrived yet. No phone call either. That was a little disconcerting…

Just then a motorcycle appeared from nowhere. It shot past her on the bend so fast she panicked, then shrieked and hit the brakes.

Everything happened in a blur. Skidding. Hot pain. The Vespa tumbling over the cliff edge. The next thing she registered was that she was flat on her back, grass bunched in her tight fists, and her right leg was burning like fire.

She staggered to the rocky precipice and peered down at the Vespa, clutching her arm. Her burnt ankle was sore, but she'd been lucky. *Very* lucky. The bike was now in pieces and smoking threateningly. Somewhere down there, she assumed, was her phone, gone to join it.

Lowering herself carefully beneath a tree, she studied her injuries. She would have a bloody and bruised ankle for a while, but she could walk. She turned her ankle, testing it, and winced, then tore the bottom off her shirt to make a bandage. It hurt like hell when she yanked it tight.

The road both ways was empty. But it was too hot to get back out into the sun. And what if someone else who felt like killing her came around the corner? The motorcyclist hadn't even stopped—what was wrong with some people?

Someone would find her, she told herself, and her shock was wearing off. But it wasn't safe, being out here alone like this. Hadn't someone said mountain lions lived out here? Or was that something else she'd imagined?

It felt as if hours had passed as she looked out for lions, waiting for someone—anyone—to come along. The sun gleamed its golden hues across the moss, like it did in Lisri an hour before their famous sunsets.

What would her mother say if she could see her now? She could never find out that this had happened, Adrienne decided. Papa would say her being alone again was not an option, like he always did. He'd probably remove Ivan, citing him as unsuitable, and send for a team of bodyguards to go with her everywhere.

She was just about to resign herself to limping down the road in search of assistance when another motorbike tore into view. She knew that bike.

'Franco?'

The strength she'd been summoning melted away as Franco almost skidded on his own bike in his rush to get to her. 'Adrienne!'

She tried to move away from the tree to meet him. It still felt too long until he reached her, and she held back a sob as he half fell to the ground beside her. Maybe she was in more shock than she'd thought.

'What happened? Stay still.' He crouched over her, deep concern etched around his eyes, his bare knees pressed into the scratchy grass. He started examining her leg and the gash across her arm, while she insisted she was fine.

'Where's the bike?' he asked. She motioned to the cliff-edge, wincing as she tried to move her foot again.

'Keep it still. You did a good job with the bandage… Can you walk?'

'Yes.'

His hand felt cool and soothing on her bruises. And his touch…dear God, his touch…

Her scarf was sticking out from under his bike seat. He must have seen it in the branches of that tree.

He shuffled to the cliff edge quickly. He seemed to take in the sight for less than a second before striding back to her, shoulders tensed, fists clenched, every muscle strained.

'I'm so sorry, Franco, but I had to swerve to miss another bike. Then this happened.'

His jaw ticked as his shadow consumed her. 'I don't care about the bike. It could have been you down there.'

He helped her up onto her one good foot, looping his arm around her waist and mostly carrying her as she attempted to hobble to his bike.

'I called your phone, but it's dead. I had a feeling you'd be out looking for the kitten and I was worried. You don't know these roads well enough.'

'I do now.'

'This is serious.'

His voice was gruff as he hoisted her up into his arms and paused with his face an inch away from hers. She told him she was sorry again as she searched his eyes. His pupils seemed to be dilated with repressed rage and something else... He cared about her more than he was letting on. The sudden recognition made her feel hot and weak all at once.

'Something really bad could have happened to you, Adrienne. You're probably in shock. I'm taking you to the hospital.'

'No,' she said, panic stabbing at her core.

He lowered her carefully onto the bike. The sun was sinking behind him now, and he gently placed her helmet back over her head, clasped it shut with purpose.

'No,' she said again as he mounted the seat in front of her. She clutched his shirt urgently and his muscles tensed, his back rigid as a wall. 'No hospital. Promise me.'

He turned on the engine and pulled onto the road slowly, carefully, so as not to hurt her any more. 'Why no hospital?'

'I can't have anyone knowing what happened and it would get out. Someone always talks. It would be awful, and ultimately unhelpful. And I'm completely fine, I promise.'

'You don't look fine to me. Where the hell is Ivan?'

'I sent him to look the other way. It's just a few bruises. Please, Franco, if you take me anywhere, take me home.'

She could hear her own voice trembling and felt his shoulders slacken.

'You're impossible,' he huffed, and she breathed a sigh of relief. She knew she could trust him.

But he didn't say another word the whole ride back.

CHAPTER TEN

A SHORT, ROUND woman in an apron stopped her vacuum cleaner abruptly when he stepped through the doorway.

'We need to get her lying down. I have to look at her.'

He helped Adrienne down the hall, using his right side as a crutch. The housekeeper fussed around them and cleared the path, then assembled a cushiony pillow at one end of a plush aubergine-coloured sofa. The sofa faced doors wide open to the sky, and the Gulf of Naples with all its stars. It was an impressive space.

'Mirabel, I'm fine…it's nothing,' Adrienne protested as he slid her shoes off and dropped them to the polished hardwood floor.

His heart was still high on adrenaline. He'd had a sudden feeling of dread that she'd gone out looking for the kitten instead of sending her staff, so he'd left an hour after her and taken three different routes before he'd seen her scarf.

She should be at the hospital now. He'd almost turned around several times to take her there for an X-ray. But… damn stubborn woman that she was…she'd trusted him not to do that.

'Where's your first aid bag?' he asked, and she directed him to the kitchen.

The apartment was too big for one person, with huge

appliances, a bigger fridge than his, and a dining table behind the sofa that would seat ten people. The views were truly fit for a princess.

She probably had a really good view of Vesuvius from the bedrooms upstairs, he thought idly as he located her first aid kit, but he wasn't taking her anywhere else with injuries like this—and definitely not with the housekeeper here.

Her ankle wasn't quite as bad as it had looked once he'd cleaned the grit out—and she could walk, thank God. She proved it when a soft meow from the balcony sent her leaping from the couch.

'Fiamma?'

He caught her, and Mirabel went for the kitten, scooping the small grey thing up in her arms.

'She came back! Oh, Mirabel, give her to me, please.'

Adrienne let him help her back to the couch, and he watched her press the kitten's furry grey head to her cheek. The kitten snuggled in for a moment, then sprang away to explore the rug around the gilded glass coffee table.

'That creature has no idea what you just went through,' he said crossly, and then bit his tongue. The sight of her on the road, and seeing that bike in pieces over the edge... It could have been *her* taking a cliff dive.

Mirabel was watching them, scrutinising him as he massaged Adrienne's leg from where he crouched on the floor in front of her.

Adrienne reached for her housekeeper's hand, drawing her in. 'Don't say anything about this to my parents, Mirabel.'

Mirabel looked uncomfortable. 'Does he have an appointment...? To be here...?'

'Of course he doesn't have an *appointment*, Mirabel. He just scraped me off the side of a road.' She paused, visibly regaining her composure. 'Don't say anything about any of this. I expect this to stay private—do you understand?'

Franco watched Adrienne jerk her gaze to him and back again, and took the hint and made his exit out to the balcony. The cat sprang after him and he watched it leap at shadows around the plant pots, trying not to listen to her and the housekeeper. She was trying to keep *him* a secret as much as her accident, and that grated on his nerves.

He'd noticed on the way in that someone had sent her flowers. The gift card was still sticking out of the bouquet. She probably had admirers everywhere. How many men had made it up here? Or was he really the first?

The door had closed after Mirabel and now Franco sat cross-legged on the soft rug. There was no way he was leaving her yet. His calls could wait. He didn't ask about her family—she'd panicked about them enough tonight—but he did ask if she needed anything, and she said that she needed stories to take her mind off everything that had happened.

'I like your stories,' she told him, settling back on the pillows on the sofa. 'You tell them with such passion, Franco. Anyone who's ever done anything great has been passionate about it, driven by it. Obsessed with it. Your passion was the first thing I noticed about you.'

'Is that right?'

Watching her lips singing his praises was intoxicating, as much as her penchant for secrecy was frustrating. He dared to reach a hand to her face, swept a strand of soft hair back behind her ear and let it linger as she scanned his eyes. He couldn't recall ever telling her a story with the passion she found so striking, but maybe she just liked the way he talked. Right now, he realised he was probably what Benni would call 'a sucker', but he knew he'd do anything the so-called Ice Princess asked.

So he told her of the legends surrounding the islands, of slayers and fighters and a fire-breathing dragon. He told her about the ghost he'd once seen in the catacombs, and how he'd befriended a pod of dolphins who had sailed with him to Capri in the wake of his yacht.

He'd thought she might get tired, but she kept her blue eyes on him, transfixed, till it took every atom of his self-restraint not to kiss her. What he really wanted to say was still repressed, like a dragon in a cave inside his chest. He hated leaving it to fester inside him...

Everything in his right mind told him to get up and leave her, but she was hurt, dammit. And stubborn.

CHAPTER ELEVEN

ADRIENNE HAD WANDERED out to the balcony, testing her ankle. It felt a lot better already, and Franco had had every excuse to leave her over the past couple of hours, but he hadn't. He'd kept her mind off reality, as she'd asked him to, but she felt his presence behind her in the doorway now, watching her like a falcon. It was strange and exciting, having him here, but if Mirabel told anyone...

'What the hell were you thinking—seriously?'

His voice made her stomach reassemble itself on the spot. She turned to him.

'I don't even think you understand the severity of what you just did—taking that bike out there on those roads, on your own. With or without a speeding bike coming at you, you don't know this place, how to handle those roads.You could be lying dead at the bottom of a cliff!'

She stared at him, shocked. She'd never heard him raise his voice, but she knew it meant he cared. She could see it—just as she had when she'd been collapsed at the side of the road—like a fire burning in his eyes, almost out of control.

'I've already told you I'm sorry.' Her mouth was dry.

'You have no idea, do you? What you're doing to me?'

His words struck her like a lightning bolt and his eyes tore through her weak apology to the very core of her.

They both knew what they were doing to each other—what they'd been denying for weeks. The realisation left her aching to reach for him, but he huffed and looked out at the expanse of sea on the horizon, as if composing himself.

She hugged her arms around herself. 'Listen, Franco. Whatever this is…'

She couldn't finish her sentence. As if magnetised by some invisible force, Franco strode to her from the doorway and a second later her arms had taken over, reaching for him so she could lose herself in his urgent, passionate kisses.

Her hands found themselves pulling at his shirt blindly and her lips fused to his as he walked them backwards, conscious all the time of her injured leg and her arm. Each kiss slowed into a sensuous new discovery, then sped up into another frenzied exploration until somehow they were back on the couch.

After weeks of waiting she felt sharp shocks of fire and lightning tear through her legs, her womb and her belly. She could barely breathe as he claimed her tongue in hot, delicious swirls, slowing down and speeding up like a song she instinctively knew how to dance to. They were chest to chest, hips to hips, in a cloud of cushions, and her whole world in that moment consisted of just his mouth, his lips and hands, and the places they took her to. She had never been kissed like this before.

'We should stop,' she heard herself saying suddenly. What the hell was she doing, giving in to this glorious, unrestrained, *frightening* passion?

Even as he uncoiled his limbs from hers, she bunched the fabric of his shirt in both her hands. She knew she had to let him go, but her body couldn't do it.

Franco slid from her grasp to the floor, ran his hands through his crop of messed-up hair and blinked at the room as if he'd been pulled out of a dream much too quickly. Her heart was on fire, her face still stinging with the friction from his stubbled jaw.

Reckless, reckless woman.

That heavenly place they'd just gone to together was exactly where she'd feared she'd end up if they got any closer. Her lips throbbed, wanting more of him. She sat up, grateful for the sea breeze blowing through the doors, and felt her breaths come hot and heavy as she forced herself up on shaky legs and walked past him to the kitchen.

'We didn't hurt your ankle, did we?' she heard him say eventually, his voice raspy like hers.

She wasn't even thinking about her injuries now. Dazed, she filled a glass with cold water and drank it thirstily, then pressed her hands to the counter, eyes closed, still tasting him, wanting more. So much more.

He stepped up behind her, dwarfing her in his shadow. 'I'm sorry,' he whispered gruffly, and she squeezed her eyes closed.

She wished he didn't have to be sorry. She wished he hadn't had to hear her telling Mirabel not to mention him being here. She wanted him here more than anything—surely he knew that. But just because she was being paranoid it didn't mean her family might not still try to stop her completing the fellowship, and warn Franco away from her if they found out her boss had been here in her apartment, tending to her wounds as a result of lending her a dangerous vehicle himself.

'That shouldn't have happened,' she forced herself to say. Because it wouldn't end well for him. It was stupid and selfish of her, at the end of the day.

He gently pressed his lips to the back of her neck, let his kisses rain along her skin, leaving a trail of tingles. She shivered involuntarily, surrendering momentarily to his worship, and he turned her around, took the glass from her. His eyes locked onto hers and his carnal desire churned up the air between them like a Catherine wheel.

He exhaled, saying her name again, and ran a thumb across the hollow beneath her left cheekbone. An electric thrill threatened to make her knees buckle. The gesture, and the desire in his eyes, resonated through every fibre of her being.

'I shouldn't have kissed you.' He drew her closer by the nape of her neck, and she closed her eyes despite herself. 'But, for the record, I do want to kiss you again, Princess Adrienne.'

'Don't call me that,' she groaned, pressing her forehead to his chest over his heart.

He broke away and turned away to the counter beside her. Instantly, she wanted his protective cocoon back.

His deep green gaze cut into her and he laughed without smiling. 'You are who you are, Adrienne. You're a member of a royal family. Why would you want to forget that? Don't you want to be a ruler for Lisri?'

She pulled out a chair at the dining table and dropped into it, needing to create some kind of distance between them as well as to have something stable beneath her unsteady feet. Her ankle was starting to throb again—all her fault…they'd got carried away.

'Of course I do. But it means this thing between us can't ever go anywhere.'

The words coming out of her mouth felt so wrong. The thought of going further, having his hand, his mouth, on her breasts and between her thighs, touching her and stretching out the night with endless incredible wanton sex, made her fold her arms weakly on the table and put her head down, as if blocking him from view might make the whole thing go away.

It was imperative now that she should warn him off, tell him why it wasn't wise for either of them to go down this road. Except they'd only had one kiss; he would think she was crazy, surely.

Her world was different from his. A kiss like that, and a heart like hers…it would be impossible for her not to keep on falling for him from this point forward. It might even turn into love on her side. But she'd be broken apart all over again when it ended. And so might he.

'It just can't happen again,' she affirmed. 'I mean it.'

He was too far away, even only at the other end of the table. Then he went and gathered up his bike helmet and jacket, sending a crashing agony right through her. She watched him shrug the muscled arms that had just been wrapped around her into the leather sleeves and knew she wouldn't rest unless she told him the truth.

'You're so different from him…you're everything he wasn't.'

'Prince Xavier?' Franco's eyes darkened.

'Xavier was cheating on me. That's the truth, Franco. I never told anyone, and no one else knows except my parents. So I couldn't marry him. But he's a royal, you see, like me. That's what they want most of all—a merger of two noble families.'

Franco processed her words in silence as she told him everything—what had happened the night the engagement was meant to be announced, how her father had still insisted Xavier was a good match because of his lineage, how the press had twisted everything, thanks to Xavier's lies. Holding his helmet under one arm, he studied her face and for once she couldn't read him.

'I'm sorry for what you went through,' he said after a moment. 'I have no desire to be "noble", if that's how your family defines it,' he added gruffly.

She swallowed. Of course he didn't want to be the next Prince Consort of Lisri. What she'd just told him would have scared him off for life, even if he wasn't still devoted to his dead fiancée. She fixed her aching head high, feeling the emotions inside her crashing harder than the real collision.

'They want me to marry some *baron* now,' she added for good measure. 'I haven't even met him myself. But if it's not him, it'll be someone else. They know, because I've told them often enough, that I'll only marry for love, but they will keep on lining them up...'

'Well, that's that, then, isn't it?' he said, studying her eyes again. 'We could sit here all night finding more reasons why that kiss shouldn't have happened, Adrienne. Or we could just leave it here.'

She couldn't tell if he was hurt, angry, or both.

Her insides were screaming. For a second she almost succumbed to her urge to pull him back to her, but he tugged the zip of his jacket up to his neck, and she pursed her still-stinging lips. God, she wanted to grab him again and not let go. He would probably never kiss her again now—ever—but it was for the best if he didn't. For both of them.

'Sleep on the couch,' he instructed from the doorway, back to being a doctor in a heartbeat. 'Don't try going upstairs. I'll come and check on you in the morning. Do I need an appointment?'

'No,' she managed.

'Do you need me to stay to make sure you're OK? I can carry you up to your room and I'll sleep on the couch.'

His question seemed to float around the chandelier, and she flashed her eyes back to the couch again, swallowing hard. She would never look at it the same way after tonight. 'I'll be perfectly fine, thank you.'

He lowered his head, as if biting back more words that would do neither of them any good. Then he left before she had the chance to change her mind.

CHAPTER TWELVE

FRANCO WAS FIVE minutes late. When he knocked on the door, Adrienne and Stefano, a radiation oncologist, were already present with Diodoro Merten.

Adrienne looked up as he walked in, and Franco swore he saw her cheeks redden slightly, though she was careful not to meet his eyes. Four days since their kiss, he thought, counting backwards in his head. And she'd been very careful to avoid being alone with him ever since.

Good. You don't need that drama in your life.

They were meeting briefly, prior to Mr Merten's first radiation treatment. Adrienne was explaining again how they'd seen some great success with it, and he took a seat behind the desk, explaining, when and where he could, the clear trend towards it in the colorectal cancer community worldwide, and this new treatment's ability to increase both pathological and clinical remission rates.

To anyone else in the room he was quite sure they seemed like nothing but professionals and colleagues, but their secret burned beneath every word they spoke to each other.

He'd kept himself busy away from her. He'd been through enough heartache for a lifetime with Luci—there was no way he was going there again, or putting his af-

fairs in the spotlight, to be raked through like garbage by
the media.

That bastard Xavier had come off almost saint-like and
unscathed after what he'd done to her, and here was Adrienne, still expected to marry the next aristocratic idiot her
family saw fit to pawn her off on. If that was what being a
royal was like—no thanks. He wanted no part of it. Though
he had also been thinking a lot about how strong she was—
probably more than she gave herself credit for—pulling
herself back together after all that nonsense and refocusing on her goals and career.

'Knock-knock!' Gabriel, Diodoro's partner, swept into
the room, carrying a large coffee. 'Sorry! I had to beat the
damn machine to get milk into this thing, and let me tell
you it wasn't worth it. Where do you get your milk from?
Pangolins? Otters?'

'Oats, actually,' Adrienne said as Gabriel took a seat.
'It can take some getting used to.'

'What happened to your ankle, Doctor?' Gabriel asked,
gesturing to her bandage.

Franco busied himself with the CT scans and treatment
plan in front of him as she said something vague about
coming off her bike. Had she told anyone the truth? he
wondered. Had that housekeeper said anything about him
being there without a damned appointment? Or asked her
why he, specifically, had come to find her?

'Sounds like you got lucky,' Diodoro told her, frowning.

'Can't say as much for the bike,' Franco cut in, looking
up from his paperwork.

Adrienne looked thoroughly embarrassed for a second.
He regretted the dig almost instantly. He couldn't care less
about the bike and neither could Aimee. It could be easily replaced. Adrienne couldn't. He was just on edge. Un-
settled by the fact that she'd been on his mind since she'd

called him the next morning, insisted her foot was fine and that he shouldn't come to the apartment to check on her.

He should be glad that his heart had been given a get-out clause. He wasn't a blueblood like her, for a start, and she wasn't free to love who she wanted to love—she'd said so herself. Some law would have her marrying the next suitable aristocrat, even if she *was* waiting for love. Why mess with a royal court pre-programmed to keep him away? Why get his heart all torn up? Again.

Forget her kiss…her addictive taste.

Forget those imploring eyes.

Forget it all.

Diodoro and Gabriel were laughing at something now, albeit nervously. Franco had zoned out, but Adrienne seemed to be doing a good job of warming them up prior to the first treatment session. He heard her tell them how impressed she was by their support for each other during this time. Ever the romantic, he thought, wishing he didn't have so much in common with the bits of her heart he'd been entrusted to see.

'I just love how he loves me, Dr Princess Balthus,' Diodoro said, laying his head on Gabriel's bony shoulder. 'He makes me laugh, and he listens to my soul. I think, when you find that with someone, you have the best thing this world has to offer.'

He exhaled deeply as Gabriel dropped a kiss on the top of his balding head. 'You big softie,' Gabriel said, and smiled.

Franco felt the same envy he saw in Adrienne's eyes.

'At least, I used to think that,' Diodoro continued despondently. 'Now I know good health is more important.'

When they'd left the room, the space was filled with the sound of Franco's buzzing phone.

'Hey, Dad.'

Marco Perretta asked after Adrienne, which made a ball of knots in his stomach. 'Yeah, she's here. But...'

Adrienne looked at him curiously, one hand on the door-knob. Trust his father to ask to see her now. He wouldn't wait for anyone—not even a princess.

Down in the busy entrance hall, his father stopped his low whisper of a phone conversation to address them both properly. Dressed in his trademark purple tie and his best suit, he looked ready to stand up in court—but then Marco Perretta always dressed ready for an occasion.

Adrienne smiled politely throughout his introduction to his father, and Franco wondered briefly what it would be like to meet *her* father, Alexander Marx-Balthus, Prince Consort of Lisri. It would probably be in some castle, or a private room draped in gold-plated accolades and trib-utes. Not that he would ever get to meet her family. His blood might be a rare AB negative, but it was still not pure enough for them, he thought bitterly.

'My daughter happened to mention there was some sort of misplacement issue with a bike you borrowed.'

Marco led them both outside into the bright morn-ing sunlight, which sent white streaks through his thick greying hair and made Franco wonder, as he always did, whether his hair would end up the same way.

'I've had Benni arrange a new bike. Same model. Where should I have it sent? Maybe to your place, son?'

'Oh, you didn't have to do that.' Adrienne seemed un-comfortable.

'Yes, Dad, you didn't have to do that,' he said, shooting him a warning look.

His father simply brushed them both off. 'It's a thank-you more than anything, Your Highness.'

Franco pulled his lab coat open and let the cool breeze free on the skin around his neck. The heat was insufferable.

He shouldn't have mentioned anything at all to his father—why had he done that? He'd brought his family into her affairs by telling them about the bike accident. She would probably refuse the new one, he thought to himself. Too afraid her family would find out.

'A thank-you for what?' she asked. 'It was a huge mistake, what happened to the first one, and I really am so sorry—very embarrassed, actually,' she said, pulling her sunglasses down over her eyes.

'It wasn't exactly all your fault,' Franco muttered in her defence, trying not to smile. She was kind of cute when she apologised—especially in that lyrical Lisri accent of hers.

'It's not like you haven't done enough for us, Princess,' his father said now.

'I wouldn't refer to her as "Princess"—she hates it,' Franco warned him.

His father looked confused. 'But she *is* a princess.'

'I know,' he agreed, maybe a little too enthusiastically.

Perplexed, Marco dragged a hand through his hair, and Franco knew he'd be getting questions later.

'Anyway, Your Highness… Dr Balthus…'

'Just Adrienne, please.'

'Adrienne. Franco tells me it was you who arranged for a hefty annual donation to the Perretta Institute's research and development programme on behalf of your family and the Kingdom of Lisri. I want to invite you both to an event at the weekend. Some potential investors will be joining us on the yacht—some guys from the biotechnology lab in Florence, the new executive from the pharma leadership team. I thought we'd cruise around the Bay Islands… have dinner, drinks, maybe some music—you know how it goes. Franco can give a presentation on the results from the trials currently underway. And I'm inviting Allegra from the European Medicine Advisory Board. She's been a little busy lately, but—'

'Allegra should be doing more with her time than sailing about on yachts,' Franco cut in, looking towards Adrienne now. He knew his father was trying to be helpful—Franco had told him about their newest Ewing's sarcoma patient and the chemo drug still on trial. The advisory board was harder to reach than Mars, and he'd never even heard of this Allegra. 'We've hit yet another roadblock.'

'Well, let's unblock it,' his father said, as if pushing a drug trial through endless bureaucratic entanglements was as simple as flushing detergent down a drain.

'Maybe this Allegra is the key,' Adrienne mused.

Franco said nothing. He didn't want to come off as negative, but decisions like moving a trial forward from phase two to three took more than one person. It was a convoluted process, and this one had already been stalled for almost three years.

His father was still talking.

'I thought an illustrious attendee and backer such as yourself, Adrienne, might be...'

'What? Something to talk about?'

Franco got to his feet, lowering his voice as people turned to look at them on the forecourt. He was all too aware of how she loathed being paraded around like...what was it she'd said? A poodle in a dog show? He wouldn't put her on show here, too.

'Dad, Adrienne is here to work with our patients. I'm sure she doesn't want to stand up and—'

'What? Speak for myself?' Adrienne interrupted him.

He caught the warning glint in her eyes as she tossed her hair over her shoulders, and in a flash he was back among the cushions on her couch, her fingers tugging at his shirt, her lips possessing his mouth. He could still taste all her words, some sweeter than others: *'They want me to marry some baron now.'*

'I know what I said before, Franco, but this is important,' she continued.

'I need you to focus on your work,' he protested.

His father was looking between them, his grey eyebrows raised in interest. 'Do I sense something going on here?'

'No, you don't,' Franco said acerbically.

'The new bike is a very generous gift. Thank you, Mr Perretta,' Adrienne said quickly. 'You can have it sent to my address. Franco knows where I live.'

Franco's pulse throbbed in his neck. Adrienne stood tall, defiant, as his father poked his buzzing phone again, and he wondered if she'd fixed her ankle by willpower alone—she certainly hadn't let the injury slow her down...not that he'd let himself get close enough to her to check on it.

'I'd be happy to attend your dinner, Mr Perretta,' she added curtly. 'Now, if you'll both excuse me? I have another appointment.'

'Where?' Franco knew they both had a break before Candice Trentino was due for her latest immunotherapy treatment, but Adrienne was already swishing back through the doors.

'She's quite a woman,' his father said, watching her, bemused. 'Bet she keeps you on your toes.'

Franco dug his hands in his pockets and felt the usual blast of annoyance that stemmed from his unfortunate attraction to a woman who was already proving worse for his heart than anyone he'd ever met.

'She's working for me, Dad,' he said tautly.

His father chuckled and slapped him on the back. 'Working *on* you, more like.'

'What's that supposed to mean?' he growled.

'I may be getting older, son, but I'm not blind.'

CHAPTER THIRTEEN

WAITING FOR HER call from Bianca Caron to come in on her brand-new phone, Adrienne read her mother's latest letter, swivelling in her chair in the residents' room.

She'd already read it three times, in fear that she might have missed something about her housekeeper mentioning a man in her apartment—a man who'd scraped her off the side of the road after a motorcycle accident, no less. But it seemed Mirabel had kept her word, and the Queen was even being rather encouraging about her new project.

It sounds like this means a lot to you, Adrienne. And from the way you write about Dr Perretta it does seem as though you made the right move, going to Naples.

She should be relieved, but instead she just felt worse about Franco. Of course her mother didn't know how she wanted him to be more than her role model and mentor. If she told her mother about that kiss, she'd feel it was her duty to tell her husband—she told him *everything*. And what if Papa flew here himself, or sent someone from court to confront him, warn him off? Franco didn't deserve that humiliation.

Rather than insult him by keeping their time alone a

secret, she'd done her best not to be alóne with him at all.
It went against every instinct, and every call from her
fired-up libido.

His father knew, though.

Marco Perretta had definitely picked up on the tension
between them, she thought, zoning out of reading the letter. The way Franco had acted outside just now, leaping
to her defence... She hadn't needed him to stand up for
her—she was doing fine on her own...most of the time.
But she knew why he wanted her to refuse to help with
progressing the trial: he felt the need to protect her from
the spotlight after everything she'd told him.

He'd been acting as if they'd never kissed, and now
this? Proof that he cared, whether he meant to show it or
not. Her heart fluttered wildly again, just from thinking
how she'd been putty in his big strong arms on her couch.

Her chiming phone pulled her from her reverie.

'Bianca, it's so good of you to agree to talk to me,' she
said, walking to the door and closing it softly. She was
alone. Just her and the palm trees whispering outside the
window.

'It's not every day I get to speak to the Crown Princess
of Lisri,' the twenty-one-year-old gushed.

Adrienne was quick to move on. 'I'm calling as a doctor and donor to the Perretta Foundation,' she explained
again, for the benefit of the cancer survivor's mother, who
was also on the call.

She told them how she intended to share Bianca's story,
along with the stories of others who'd seen encouraging results during phase two of the blocked trial, three years ago.

Her trusted cousin's media company was working on
the website and the app, under the strictest of confidentiality agreements. The new organisation—Survive&Thrive
would be a safe space for patients and survivors to share

their stories, which would be told from the heart, where Franco told *his* stories from. There would be links to helpful resources, real-life assistance on a live feed, updates on trials—the works.

It was coming together nicely. Soon she would have enough content to share—hopefully by the time they had to meet with that woman from the medical advisory board. She didn't know as much as Franco about the inner workings of it, but humans were humans, and hearts were hearts. Every story could move someone and make a difference.

'We need it moved on to phase three, so we can try to help more people,' she said now.

'Of course. I'm so excited to be a part of this.'

Maybe it wouldn't make a difference, she thought as Bianca waxed lyrical about the drug in the trial being the reason she was still alive and thriving. But maybe it would. Either way, it was better than sitting around on the phone, being put on hold, which was all Franco had been able to do so far.

Bianca seemed thrilled that people were about to read her story. 'I don't know why they blocked the same drug from being given to other people. It was only one person who experienced those side effects, and how those could be worse than cancer...that's just not possible!'

Candice had opted for immunotherapy treatment, and her new scans showed that her laryngeal cells seemed to be responding positively already, which only heightened Adrienne's buzz over her side project. She almost forgot the Franco-shaped elephant in the room, because she found herself so busy she barely had time to breathe.

Bianca had made firm friends with several of the other patients on the programme during her course of treatment and had promised to put Adrienne in touch with them. She knew she had a lot of work ahead of her, turning those accounts into moving, tangible evidence that the drug needed moving to phase three, but her mother's encouragement had lit a rocket under her, and she sped from the room after Candice had left, ready to get on the phone again.

Maybe she'd been softened by Adrienne's encouragement with her baking, but her mother hadn't mentioned the Baron's visit again. Perhaps she'd decided to forget she'd ever tried to set them up. Then again, maybe the Queen was biding her time before bringing it up again... with Papa's support, too.

Her mother's omission didn't sit right with Adrienne, now that she thought about it. She had mentioned Franco a lot in her last letter, and it didn't take a fool to fill in the gaps—as she was quite certain Marco Perretta had already.

No, Adrienne.

Her old anxieties were not permitted to follow her into this project. There was too much at stake.

Franco found her later, buried in a pile of notes and research papers in the residents' room. Her heart bolted as he closed the door behind him.

'What are you working on?'

'I'm writing discharge summaries. As well as about a thousand other things,' she replied truthfully as she felt the air grow thicker. He smelled like wood and citrus and sunshine. God, why did he have to be so gorgeous?

He perched on the edge of the desk opposite and eyed her thoughtfully. 'About my father's invitation,' he said. 'You don't have to come on the dinner excursion if you're too busy.'

She sat back in her seat. She should have expected this. He obviously didn't want her there, but she had to go. This wasn't about them. It was about patients like Rosita and getting the drug moved on in the trial, as well as the other contacts she'd meet.

'I'm coming.'

He nodded slowly, jaw clenched, then turned to the window.

'I thought perhaps this Allegra might help push our case with the board,' she added aloofly.

'I admire your enthusiasm, but let's not get excited. She's just one person, Adrienne.'

'We're all just one person, Franco,' she countered as he crossed to the window. 'Besides, I have an idea. I wasn't going to say anything yet, but—'

'I need you to focus on your work.'

Adrienne bristled. 'I am perfectly capable of multitasking.' She gestured to the pile of papers around her. 'And it sounds like you need me.'

Franco's mouth became a thin line.

'You don't have to protect me,' she said. 'I have Security for that.'

'I'm sure Ivan feels great, knowing he "protected you" from that motorcycle accident after you sent him off the other way.'

She stood tall, glaring at him as he rammed his hands through his hair.

'If you must know, I don't enjoy knowing the situation you're in, Adrienne. And this law that forbids you to marry anyone you damn well like is archaic.'

'There is no *law*, Franco,' she snapped in frustration. Then she lowered her voice as some people walked past outside the room. 'It's more of a tradition. Our family has always married other royals or high-ranking aristocrats.'

Franco looked confused.

'That's just the way it is,' she said. 'Other aristocrats

understand what's expected of them as consort to a monarch, you see,' she explained. 'They understand the restrictions and the responsibilities…'

'Well, that's good, Adrienne. Because any *normal* person would just think that was crazy.'

Ouch.

With a jolt, she realised how much he must have been thinking about this since that night. She fought the urge to close the gap between them as he started pacing the floor and his shoes made heavy, frustrated smacks on the tiles. What was she supposed to do? Her life *was* crazy—and what did he want from her anyway?

'How can you live like that? Bending to everyone else's wishes?' he growled—to his shoes instead of her.

She swallowed tightly. 'I'm not married yet, am I?'

Franco stopped his pacing suddenly and strode purposefully towards her. She barely had time to catch her breath before his lips found hers, and in seconds they were kissing furiously again, sprawled on the desk, papers flying everywhere. She gasped, and then moaned into his mouth as he hoisted up her skirt, pressing a possessive hand to the flesh of her thigh and making her arch up into him.

The sound of footsteps behind the door caught her ears. He sprang away from her, pulling her upright, one fraction of a second before it swung open.

Irina came in and made for a pile of papers on another desk. 'Don't let me interrupt you, Doctors,' she said jubilantly, stopping to pause at the window for a second.

Adrienne waited. Her heart was a hammer under her coat. She must have seen something.

'What a beautiful day outside! Look at that sky! Oh, while I'm here, Adrienne, can you sign this? It's a leaving card for Matteo, for when he goes on paternity leave.'

Irina thrust a card showing a picture of a baby in a sling

held in a stork's beak towards her and Adrienne took it with shaky hands, feeling her cheeks burn. So she hadn't seen them—thank goodness. That had been close. Too close. Franco had turned to the window, shoulders tense.

'I can only put my signature on official documents,' she said. 'Sorry.'

'Is that right?'

Adrienne caught Irina's look of disappointment, and yet again the fiery urge to dispel all the blue blood from her body consumed her. She had to remember who she was, but she was realising more and more by the second that who she *really* was had been pent up inside her for so long she barely recognised this whole new version of herself.

She snatched up a pen and wrote just her first name in block capitals.

'I hope he's looking forward to being a father,' she said of Matteo, their oncology social worker, handing the card back.

Franco had taken the opportunity to make his exit, leaving Adrienne hot and bothered even under the cool fan.

Irina tapped the door frame with the card on her way out. 'Is everything OK, Adrienne?' she asked. 'You look stressed. How is Candice?'

'Everything's fine,' she replied, resuming her cool, professional disposition. Although she was digging her nails so hard into her own palms they were leaving marks.

Irina closed the door after her and Adrienne could have kicked herself. She and Franco had almost been caught in an impassioned situation, here in their workplace, of all places. She really had to be more careful. There were eyes and ears everywhere...

But then, there always had been, and probably always would be. Wasn't that the problem? Franco wanted no part of that privacy invasion any more than he wanted to live by royal rules.

Her heart was on a dangerous path towards being a total wreck. She was still shaken by the kiss, and the smell of his cologne still lingered on her skin. That kiss had been as much her fault as his—they'd been winding each other up—but this had to end now. For both their sakes it must *not* happen again.

CHAPTER FOURTEEN

'We have to be on the yacht with Dad in two days.'

Franco had stopped his bike under a tree to take Benni's call. He could hear Alina in the background. His brother had called to thank him for sending her the new spangly leotard and matching socks she'd asked him for, knowing full well her doting uncle would spoil her. And then Benni had swiftly moved the subject on to Adrienne.

'Is she definitely going to go with you? After you told me you were trying to stay away from her?'

'It will be good for her to be there,' Franco replied truthfully. 'But keeping it professional the whole time probably won't be easy. She's trying just as hard as me to pretend nothing has happened.'

'Are you sure?' Benni teased. 'Maybe one kiss from a frog scared her off if what she needs is a prince.'

'Two kisses, actually, and thanks a lot for calling me a frog.'

'Two? You went back for more? Are you crazy?'

'Maybe I am.' Franco watched a boat streak across the ocean under the blue sky, wishing the sweet scent of blossoming bougainvillea would calm his mind like it usually did.

'The woman is destined for a throne, Franco. What are

you going to do? Move to Lisri with her and father her royal babies?'

Benni stifled a laugh at the thought, which hit a nerve. 'Of course not.'

He scowled at the ground, suddenly picturing another man by her side—someone she didn't even love. All for the sake of some outdated, ridiculous, hurtful tradition pushed upon her by the royal family.

Benni almost didn't even have to utter the words that came out next. 'Then walk away, bro. I'm warning you. This won't end well. You've already been through enough. Unless you can inject a few pints of blue blood into your veins, it's a lost cause.'

'Don't you think I know that? Besides, you should see what she has to go through, with her security and the paparazzi and…'

He trailed off, thinking how perhaps it wasn't all bad. She was strong and ambitious, and she had ideas on how to push the trial forward—not that she'd shared them yet. Which was probably his fault. He'd been all caught up trying to keep her out of the spotlight when actually she had every right to shine her light wherever she damn well wanted.

Benni was still talking. 'Don't walk, actually. Run. The last thing you want is the Lisri Prince Consort on your case, and I'll tell Dad to keep his nose out, too. He already seems to think you two have something going on.'

'Well, he's wrong.' Franco gritted his teeth as he looked at Vesuvius and the mountains looming before him like a judging jury. He was lying. To himself and to Benni. But the truth was tough to swallow. He was invested in Adrienne already—more than he wanted to be. And just this morning his father had insisted that they bring Adrienne's new bike aboard the yacht and go for a ride around Ischia.

'*It can't all be about business, son. You have to do our country proud...make her want to sing its praises to her people. You can take her to the thermal baths.*'

He could have put his foot down, told him not to meddle, but he hadn't. Maybe he *wanted* to take her there, just to see the look on her face. She'd love it. And damn if her smiles and excitement over all the new things he was showing her didn't give him new reasons to breathe.

For all the good it was doing him—or her.

'He just wants to see you happy again,' Benni told him. 'He doesn't care if she's the Crown Princess or if she stocks shelves all day in a supermarket. But I guess he doesn't know that her family only wants to marry her off into the aristocracy.' Benni paused. 'I don't want to encourage you when there's no hope whatsoever...but we all know plenty of people who consider you royalty anyway. And one of them is right here—isn't that right, Alina? Do you want to thank your uncle yourself for your new outfit before you cover it in grass stains?'

Thanks to his call with Benni and Alina, Franco was five minutes late for his shift, but Rosita and her family were also running late. Adrienne was exiting the residents' room when he passed, and she stopped in her tracks, as if she hadn't been expecting him to appear at all.

'Oh, you're here,' she said, flustered. 'I thought you were engaging with next-generation philanthropists at the university this morning.'

'I was,' he said, recalling the wide-eyed students he'd stood before in the lecture he'd been invited to lead. 'Then my brother called... What were you doing in there?'

He couldn't help his half-smile as she closed the door behind her as if she was shutting away a secret. She'd been hiding away in there a lot lately...on the phone, or huddled over her work. Probably keeping away from him, he thought wryly.

'Just another interview,' she explained, as if that explained anything.

'An interview? With who?'

'I'm working on something,' she replied evasively. 'It's not quite ready yet. I'll be more confident sharing when it is.'

'Try me,' he told her, intrigued.

Always a new mystery with you, Princess.

'How is it going, reaching the medical board about the trial?' she deflected, and he lowered his eyes, feeling the all too familiar bristling in his bones as he hit yet another brick wall.

'We should hear back in a few days.'

He walked with her towards the chemo lab. A kid walked past with his mother, stopping to stare at her from behind an IV pole, but Adrienne didn't even notice the attention.

'So, same as usual, then?'

'Pretty much. At least Rosita's tumour hasn't spread,' he said, examining the file she handed him as she opened the door for them. 'Regular chemo is better for Ewing's than it used to be. But as you know, if we can push phase three through and get her on board with the trial drug before the month is out, a mixture of the two might save her a few cycles.'

'Past results certainly seem to suggest that's the case,' she said thoughtfully.

Then she turned to him, fixing him with gleaming blue eyes that threw his mind off course for just a second.

'Your father called me here this morning,' she said. 'He wants me to bring the new bike on board the yacht at the weekend. He seems to think you might be willing to show me the sights if we have a couple of hours spare.'

Franco didn't know whether to be amused or annoyed. 'I'm sure he does…' He exhaled, raking a hand through his hair. 'He must have called you right after he called me.'

'Do you think it's a good idea?' she asked him, and he paused, handing her back the file.

'That's up to you. Are you confident enough on a bike after what happened with the last one?'

His cheeks felt like they might crack with the force of his fake smile. He'd take her anywhere she wanted, but he probably shouldn't. If he did he would just speak his mind in the end, and look what that had led to last time—a make-out session on a desk…one that had almost got them both caught. It wasn't his place to question any unwritten rules of the Marx-Balthus family, or the Crown Princess's personal response to them.

'I wasn't talking about the bike,' she said, her long fingers playing with the pink stethoscope around her neck.

Her actions defied her bold statement—she was nervous, afraid she had pushed him away too hard. A certain helplessness tinged her stare, but he forced indifference.

'I know things have been…difficult recently. I didn't mean to make things awkward between us.'

'Let's just put what happened behind us, OK?' he said quickly, before she could break his resolve. 'You were right—it's for the best, all things considered. I shouldn't have kissed you again. Shall we go and see if Rosita's here?'

He continued walking, trying to ignore the slick of perspiration building on his brow at the lie. The 'best' thing to do was to keep things platonic…only no one had riled him up like this since Luci.

The truth was shouting at him more loudly, the more

he tried not to hear it. As much as he'd loved her, Luci had never had him wanting her so desperately. Adrienne could break him harder than Luci ever had, with or without her family's help, and he simply didn't have the strength in him to lose someone else.

CHAPTER FIFTEEN

THE ISLANDS OF the Bay of Naples had been on her bucket list for a long time, but Adrienne was still not prepared for their beauty, even from a distance. A long weekend spent cruising around Procida, Ischia and Capri sounded ideal, but she wasn't just here for that, she reminded herself, stopping her Vespa by the dock and looking around her on the jetty for the others. The group of people she'd been expecting to meet prior to setting sail were nowhere in sight.

Her phone rang.

'Mother,' she answered, keeping her eyes on the crowds for stray cameras, as well as for Franco.

Ivan was lurking somewhere, watching for the same thing, but she was even more paranoid now. It had crossed her mind that maybe he'd seen Franco kiss her in the residents' room that time, even though she knew full well he'd been at the hospital gates outside. Her nerves were shot.

'How are you? I was expecting another letter. I know you hate the phone.'

'I just wanted to remind you that the Baron will be in Naples next week and he's looking forward to meeting you. You haven't mentioned when you'll be free.'

'I was hoping you'd forgotten about him,' she admitted, feeling hotter suddenly.

The Queen cleared her throat. 'Well, your papa has been asking me...'

'I'm sure he has, but he hasn't asked *me*.'

Adrienne frowned unseeingly into the crowds. She should have known her mother's silence on the topic was too good to be true. Now Papa was making her chase her down on the issue. He probably didn't want it to seem like *he* was pushing her. Typical. Their relationship had been tenuous at best, since his comment about a lying, cheating user like Xavier still being an excellent match because of his royal blood.

The Queen was quiet for a moment. Then she took Adrienne by surprise. 'How are things with that fine doctor? Dr Perretta? Have you told him your big idea yet? I happen to think it's marvellous, what you're doing. You could help a lot of people through this—'

'I'm up here!'

Franco's voice behind her took the air from her lungs.

'Mother, I'm sorry, I have to go.'

She hung up, heart fluttering, and turned to see him standing on the front lower deck of the yacht behind her, holding up a hand. His white shirt was open at the front, and he looked every inch the yachtsman who'd sailed to Capri with a pod of dolphins in his wake.

This was the yacht they'd be spending the weekend on? It had at least three decks, and a swimming pool she could see from the pier.

The breeze caught his hair and she forgot the conversation with her mother, noting with dismay how he looked sexier than ever against the turquoise water and the stark white exterior of the glamorous vessel.

'Princess Adrienne of Lisri? Is that you?'

Oh, no. Someone was calling to her from another boat, and within seconds a crowd of people had recognised her in spite of her headscarf. She looked up to the yacht again for Franco, but he was gone.

At first she panicked, as was her standard reaction, but then she reminded herself sternly that she was no longer accepting a life where her true self was squashed into the shadows.

'Of course you can have a photo,' she said to the lady who had stopped by her bike, wielding a camera.

Surprisingly, it felt nice to give a few people something they wanted instead of updates on their tumours. And even the Queen was excited by her involvement at the institute. Her mother had certainly sounded a little less enthusiastic than usual about meddling in her love life.

By the time Franco reached her she was busy signing tourist leaflets, with Ivan looming over the proceedings, and explaining to the people who had gathered how she was there as a doctor, working on cancer research amongst other things.

'Are you OK?' Franco seemed concerned as he moved to make a shield of himself between her and a young boy who'd run up to her on behalf of his bashful older brother. 'Allegra has had something important come up, so Dad wants us to meet later instead,' he said.

'That's no problem. And, yes, I'm absolutely fine, thank you,' she replied, moving him aside to sign the kid's map.

'You want me to leave you here?' he asked, one eyebrow cocked in amusement.

She considered saying yes, but as more people gathered she thought better of it—even with Ivan there. A little attention wasn't a bad thing, but she didn't want to look as if she was encouraging some kind of celebrity status.

The adrenaline rush hadn't subsided by the time Franco and a deckhand named Diego had steered her bike onboard to a special garage on the bottom level of the yacht. Franco's was parked there already.

'You didn't seem to mind the attention that time,' Franco observed, checking her brakes and tyres.

'I guess it's all part of the job. Or should that be jobs?' she said, removing her headscarf and shaking her hair loose. 'I have many roles—as do you, Franco, am I right? How's your niece doing?'

He seized the opportunity to talk about Alina and sent Diego off, saying he would handle her luggage. She studied Franco's biceps, filling out his shirtsleeves, thinking he was just as passionate about his role as Alina's uncle as anything else he threw his heart and soul into. For the first time she imagined he'd be a great dad someday, then admonished herself quickly for daring to fantasise that she herself might bear his children.

This is where it stops, she warned herself yet again. There was no point indulging in any fantasies about Franco. Things were too complicated as it was. In fact, she should distance herself as much as would be possible on a boat.

'I should get back to work,' she told him. 'I assume this vessel has a study?'

'Is this your secret project that you still haven't shared?' he replied, brushing off her mention of working in the study.

She nodded as her pulse spiked. 'It's almost ready.'

'I'm intrigued,' Franco muttered, shutting her bike seat down over the spare helmet and medical kit inside.

She didn't know quite how to take that, but then again she was distracted by his biceps as he screwed the oil cap tighter and then gestured her to follow him back outside.

'Wow!' she heard herself say suddenly.

Franco had led her up a flight of polished wooden stairs

to the second outer deck, where three more staff members were waiting behind a swim-up bar adorned with orchids and candles in jars. The rippling swimming pool was bluer than the sea beyond, and the cream-coloured oval lounge chairs, each with a single plush orange cushion on, quickly pushed all thoughts of work from her head.

'This is magical,' she gushed, allowing the romance of the setting to sink in in spite of herself.

Franco led her to the bar as a staff member dressed all in white slid two pre-made margaritas towards them. Marilyn Monroe smiled seductively from a pop art print behind him.

Something in the back of her head told her to insist she get back to work, but she couldn't quite make the words leave her mouth.

'Welcome to the *Lady Fatima*.' He clinked his glass against hers. 'It's the second yacht I co-bought with Dad and Benni. It's for entertainment, mostly.'

'Where's the first?' she asked, noting the extravagant indoor entertainment space beyond the giant double doors behind the bar. There was a piano, a dance floor, another bar, a table for at least fifteen people, and opulent chandeliers dangling over centrepiece arrangements of fruit and more flowers.

'The first was auctioned off. We put the proceeds into the Perretta Institute to fund the trial. Phase one and phase two.'

He slid out two white stools and she sat, noting the cool white leather and embroidered stitches—multi-millionaire touches she actually hadn't expected, now that she thought about it. Franco usually wore his wealth like an old sweater… like something that was comfy but nothing to show off about.

His knee brushed hers below the bar and she felt the

deep rumble of the yacht's engines before she noticed they were leaving the harbour already.

'Would you sell this too? If it meant phase three could go ahead?' she asked him, already knowing the answer.

'You know I would. But like I said, it's not about money. It's about breaking down bureaucratic barriers, and unfortunately we're dealing with hundred-foot steel walls here. I'm starting to think we won't get Rosita or any other patient on that trial anytime soon.'

'Don't think that,' she said, watching him trail a thumb idly around the salted rim of his glass.

His defeated tone made her want to tell him about her project now. But she'd share it soon enough. He put the glass to his lips and took a sip of his drink, and she saw new sunlit hues in the deep green depths of his eyes, and faint lines born of all those emotions he either expressed with passion or bottled up till they exploded. She'd infuriated him recently—she knew it, and she felt terrible.

Did anyone here see it? she wondered. This fizzing, bubbling champagne concoction of beautiful chemistry? Had her mother seen it in her letters? Was that why she'd changed the subject from the Baron to Franco in their phone call earlier?

Her heart sped up just at thinking of her mother telling her father. If she could, she would tell her mother everything. She'd shout her feelings from the royal rooftops. But she couldn't risk anyone coming down hard on Franco. He hadn't done anything wrong—and besides, it would jeopardise her project and the trial even more.

Just her presence in his life could be his downfall, she thought, her eyes shifting to Ivan, who'd taken up residence on a lounger at the other end of the deck.

Two staff members were standing over by the lifeboats, staring at her, speaking in lowered voices. She sipped her drink again, looking straight at them, till they scurried off, embarrassed.

'So, Franco…' she straightened up '…if you have some time later to discuss…?'

'We have all day now,' he said, a little wearily. 'But maybe we shouldn't think about work for a little while. Personally, I need a break.'

Crossing her legs in her tailor-made scarlet culottes, she found their knees touching again as they sipped their drinks in silence. Neither of them moved. Hot electricity zinged between them as she let her eyes run up the faint smattering of dark hair revealed by his unbuttoned shirt and he tried to pretend he didn't see her looking.

'If you insist,' she replied coolly, in spite of herself.

She would have thought he'd need a break from her too, but although he seemed unhappy about her being here, he hadn't put his authoritative foot down as he might have done. It struck her suddenly that Marco Perretta might have set this up on purpose. Maybe their fathers weren't so very different after all.

The thought of presenting Survive&Thrive to Franco filled her with hot anticipation as they made small talk about the yacht and the staff. She was proud of her work, and of the kids, teens and adults who'd so bravely told their stories. Of the medical professionals who'd consented to give their time and share their experience.

She would have told him sooner, but she'd only just completed the final interview that morning. The web designer was working on the finishing touches, and she was expecting to give the green light on it at any moment. It had to look perfect if it was going to be a success.

Franco was still watching her over his glass. He wasn't thinking about work. He was thinking about her. She could feel it. Drinking cocktails probably wasn't wise…

She put her drink down, mostly un-drunk, and as if reading her mind Franco did the same, and then told her he would show her around the yacht.

Adrienne followed him into a stateroom, feeling the tension snake around them as Franco placed her weekend bag on the king-size bed. It was adorned with golden and white cushions to match the window drapes. Brass and marble features stretched from the bedframe to the taps and tiles as he showed her the en suite bathroom with an impressive power shower.

'It's a little ostentatious, I know…sorry', he apologised, pointing out a display board of buttons next to the control that operated at least four different shower heads.

'It's more like a car wash,' she agreed, fighting a smile, and then went back to examining the embroidered towels as he pulled out his phone and frowned into it.

'I've been on fancier boats—if you can believe that,' she commented, wondering who it was that could be winding him up now. 'That must make me sound like a yacht snob, but…'

'I can only imagine what kind of royal vessels the monarchy keeps at its disposal in Lisri,' he said, sliding his phone back into the pocket of his low-slung denim shorts.

Suddenly they were face to face in the silence of the bathroom, and the walls, solid white marble, felt as if they were closing in.

'Did you have many men take you on dates out on the open water?' he questioned. 'Maybe a baron on a sailing boat? A duke on a speedboat?'

'No…' she replied after a pause.

She knew she had wounded his pride, explaining how her family had a strong preference for royalty and noblemen, but his words stung. It wasn't as if she *wanted* the loveless marriage she was probably destined for in the end.

She stuck out her chin, determined not to show how he was getting to her. 'I think I told you before we met,' she said, 'how I learned to sail when I was twelve.'

'No, you didn't,' he said, and she remembered that she actually hadn't. She'd just read about how *he* liked to sail and imagined the rest.

'I don't need a man to take me,' she told him stiffly.

Franco's mouth twitched. He corrected the alignment of a slightly wonky picture of a scene from a James Bond movie on the wall by the round porthole window. Outside the ocean sparkled and the sun beat down hard with the call of freedom.

'Good. We don't have sails, but I'll put you in charge of the lifeboats if we need them.'

'Gladly.'

She made for the door. Suddenly she needed the breeze on her face. Air. Space.

Hot on her heels he caught her elbow, just as she made to leave the suite.

'That was out of line. I'm sorry,' he said on an exhalation, turning her to face him. 'I'm just... That was a message from another contact at the advisory board. He promised to try and move things on, but he's having no luck. More delays.'

She bit her tongue.

Diego appeared at the end of the row of staterooms, holding a pile of towels, and pretended not to notice them.

She lowered her voice. 'It's not just the trial that's getting to you.'

He looked surprised for a second—maybe even more surprised than *she* was to have said it out loud. Then his face darkened again. 'I don't know what you want from me, Adrienne.'

'Nothing,' she said—too quickly.

'Sometimes I think you want nothing. But sometimes I think you want a whole lot more.'

'And what about you?' she countered.

Right away she regretted it. He fixed her a with a piercing look that sawed right through her. She could tell he wanted her, but he was just as wary of getting hurt as she was because of Lucinda. He'd been hurt as much as Adrienne—for different reasons, absolutely, but pain was pain.

He was probably also wondering what the hell his life might entail if he entangled himself in her world even more. A private man and a dedicated doctor like Franco Perretta wouldn't be able to suddenly leave it all behind and become a ribbon-cutting prince, especially after glimpsing how complicated everything was in the goldfish bowl she called her life.

'Maybe it wasn't such a good idea for me to come here,' she said quickly. 'That's what you're thinking, right?'

'It's not what I'm thinking.'

Franco stepped so close she could feel his breath on her skin. In a flash she was back to that night on the couch in her apartment, and then their passionate kiss in the residents room. It was as if magnets had taken over again, and pushed all sense and reasoning aside.

He cupped her chin, traced a tender thumb over her lower lip that caused a sharp moan to escape her mouth. Time seemed to freeze. Her resolve was wilting in the heat of his stare. But before she could surrender completely and press her mouth to his delicious lips he broke contact... killed the moment.

He swiped a key card in the door opposite hers and she ran her fingers over her lips, catching her breath, absorbing his touch. Torture. He'd been about to kiss her again, but of course had thought better of it. She watched him throw his shoes inside the stateroom and slip on a different pair before closing the door again, heavily.

Wait.

He was sleeping in the room right opposite hers?

Her heart was already in her throat. Fresh need and lust tingled through her.

She would lie there alone in that bed tonight, seeing herself wrapped around him, both of them tangled in clean silky sheets, with the sound of the ocean lapping the boat through the open windows, the cool night-time breeze caressing every inch of their naked skin.

She would lie there imagining herself locked against that solid muscled chest, knowing she'd have to resist all her urges to go to him for real, denying herself his touch once again...if he would even go near her now she'd built her defences up so high.

For his own good.

This was hell.

He led her around the yacht, making small talk in front of the staff they came across.

He pointed out the games room, stocked with a pool table and more books than she'd ever owned or read. Then took her through the cinema room and another lounge with a marble chess board, a study overlooking a tempting outdoor hot tub, and on through the engine room, where he explained engine power and the twelve-point-five-knot cruising speed.

All the while she couldn't stop imagining him sleeping in that room opposite hers tonight. Did he sleep naked? Did he make gentle noises while he dreamed? Did he ever dream of her, or did he wish they'd never met?

A wave of fatigue washed over her, just from thinking of the long evening and the weekend ahead.

CHAPTER SIXTEEN

'TWENTY-FIVE CENTURIES TO its name,' Franco said over his shoulder as Adrienne trailed him slowly on the Vespa along the path leading up to the mighty Aragonese Castle. 'If walls could only talk.'

'I'm sure they'd have a few secrets to tell,' she said, fixing her eyes on the islet ahead, which had formed some three hundred thousand years ago after an eruption, to create a giant hill that protruded from the ocean.

Adrienne had seemed quietly enamoured of what he'd shown her of Ischia so far, even though things between them were awkward, to say the least. He'd taken her through Ischia Ponte, the oldest village on the islands, where they'd explored quiet back lanes and classic Mediterranean architecture. Then they'd sipped cold drinks on a jasmine-scented terrace, and he'd attempted to lighten the mood with more myths and legends about this very castle.

But the almost-kiss was still on his mind. He'd stopped himself, though he had the impression she'd been about to initiate more this time.

'They say that if you kiss someone here you'll be with them for ever,' he'd said at one point. Then he'd wanted to kick himself. The Princess was the wrong audience for such a romantic fact—especially now.

She'd let him fill the silence with more stories, but she

hadn't asked him any questions like she usually did. She'd checked her watch every now and then, as if she was counting down the minutes till she could escape.

They'd only be stuck on the yacht, though, if they turned around. That would be even more awkward, with the staff loitering around, listening out for gossip on the Crown Princess, and Ivan, who was probably behind them now, trying to appear inconspicuous.

He would keep quiet from now on. He shouldn't have made that dig earlier about her going sailing with some baron or duke or whatever, but the thought of her enduring dates for the sake of some ancient family tradition still had him just as riled up as the stagnation they were experiencing around the trial. And all the tension between them whenever they were alone wasn't helping. Especially in that bedroom…

God, if only she knew how much he'd longed to press her down into that mattress and show her the kind of night he'd been fantasising about since he'd met her. Self-solace just wasn't enough any more.

Not helping, Franco, he chided himself. It was hot enough out here already.

They drove on towards the castle, past idling tourists in sunhats and couples posing for photos with the ocean-blue backdrop. Adrienne overtook him and he watched the back of her, memorising her shape, the golden strands of her hair, reminding himself he'd done the right thing at least by not kissing her earlier.

But just the thought of her settling for some bog-standard, insipid baron just to appease her family made him feel sick to the core. Life was short and precious. It should be a rollercoaster ride, not a slow, drawn-out process of suffocation.

They toured the castle rooms and Adrienne took photos with her phone of the views from various precipices. Each window offered amazing panoramas of Procida and Ischia Ponte, but a call from the institute took him outside alone for a moment. He'd asked for updates, and was grateful now for something to take his mind off Adrienne.

It was as if they were stuck between this huge castle rock and a hard place, he thought to himself as Irina chattered on in his ear. There was nothing much new for her to report, and he was instructed to enjoy his weekend off.

Frowning to himself, he turned on the path to find Adrienne watching the swimmers down below, her red culottes billowing in the breeze, her hair blowing in gentle wisps about her neck. Picture-perfect. Without thinking, he snapped a photo of her against the sky.

'What are you doing?'

'I'll delete it,' he said quickly, embarrassed that he'd done it without asking, like some awestruck fan out on the street. 'You just looked...hot.'

She sighed. 'I am hot...and maybe a little bothered too,' she said, missing the double entendre and wafting her cotton shirt around her breasts, using one hand as a fan. 'I don't like this tension between us. We should be doing something else. Maybe we should just go back to the yacht and I'll show you what I've been working on.'

'It sounds important.'

'It could be,' she said, chewing her lip.

A rush of guilt swept through him over being so caught up in the trial—and in trying to stay away from her—that he hadn't even given her a chance to explain herself regarding whatever it was she'd been pouring all her hours into lately.

The sky was darkening with the threat of rain. He knew it would shift the humidity. Maybe they should get back to the yacht, where they could stay dry and she could walk him through her project. But then again, what was one more hour? He should at least show her the best part of the island...

Adrienne removed her helmet and took in the sparkling rocks and pebbles in the pools of hot water just back from the beach, with their vents of steam billowing up from the sea floor.

'Some people say they're healing waters,' he explained as they parked their bikes on a grassy patch overlooking the bay below. 'All you need is a few minutes in them.'

'That's a prescription I wouldn't mind receiving.'

'Well, be my guest,' he said, pointing to a small changing facility, where she could get into her bathing suit. 'I'll be in the water, over there.'

Franco took off his shirt and stuffed it underneath his bike seat, grateful for the chance to get into the water—maybe it would help his brain this time, he thought, more than his bones.

When he turned, Adrienne was still watching him from behind her sunglasses. He caught her eyes roving his body in what looked a lot like silent appreciation for just a split second before she hurried off in the direction of the changing room. He bit back a pleased smile and headed across the pebbles for the pool with the least people in it.

Pools like this were scattered among the coastal rocks all over the island and bubbled at temperatures between thirty and thirty-seven degrees all year round. He'd brought Luci here once, just to try it, to see if it would ease some of her pain. It had worked its magic for an hour or two. Not long enough, unfortunately, he remembered.

Franco was just relaxing into a warm, rocky nook, with the water up to his shoulders, when Adrienne reappeared. All thoughts of Luci slipped straight from his brain.

'This was such a great idea,' she told him as his eyes travelled up her long, lean legs from bare feet to glistening thighs. She put her bag down on the rocks. He knew damn well she was giving him time to take in her body, slender and yoga-toned in a blue and green bathing suit. It was the cruellest act of torture.

'There are better places like this along the coast,' he told her, trying to sound indifferent to the fact that something most unfortunate was happening to his lower body beneath the steam. 'I know pools that only boats can reach.'

'Mmm...' she mumbled, and slid like a slick dolphin into the water.

A rumble of thunder warned them that the change in weather was getting closer, but Adrienne dipped her head underwater, the very picture of the calm before the storm. Her hair fanned around her head before she came up with her eyes closed. Droplets clung to her eyelashes as she blinked.

'This is just what I needed,' she breathed, just as he was wondering how on earth he'd ever be able to leave the pool with her looking like that next to him.

For a few long minutes they sat in silence. The rain was now falling and making tiny ripples in the water. They were both stealing glances at each other through the steam.

'I don't like all this tension around us either,' he said after a moment. 'But I hope you're at least glad you got to see this place.'

'Of course.'

Then she frowned, casting steely eyes at a few people who'd stepped closer in their direction. It was as if he saw the cogs turning. She'd insisted Ivan stay back by the road, to keep a watch for any big groups arriving.

'Don't worry,' he said. 'No one will recognise you like

that. Besides, you're out with a regular guy like me, so who'd pay us any attention?'

Another dig. He couldn't help it. Just seeing her like this was infuriating, knowing he could look but not touch.

'There's nothing regular about you, Franco, and you know it,' she said tartly. Then she stuck up her toes in the water between them, wriggling them with satisfaction. 'For what it's worth, I feel honoured every time you take me anywhere.'

'But would you tell anyone back home that?' he asked, then immediately wished he hadn't. Why was he digging this hole for himself even deeper?

She sighed, drawing his eyes to her cleavage as she swept a wet tendril of hair back behind her ear. 'I talk to my mother, actually,' she said. 'About some things. I've talked to her more than I ever have before, lately. Sometimes I feel like she regrets the life she's been forced into. I think she's happy for me that I'm here…away from all that, seeing all these things.'

Franco felt his eyes narrow. '*Forced* into?'

Adrienne shook her head, as if she already regretted her words. 'That came out wrong. I mean, she loves Papa dearly—always has. But she inherited the throne so young, you know? She's never been expected to work, or to cook—even though she's an excellent baker—or to travel alone, or even to think too much for herself…'

'Whereas you will become a doctor,' he finished. 'Will you be able to practise when you take the crown?'

He'd never asked her before. He'd assumed she'd be too involved in other things when her time on the throne came, but she was frowning at him now.

'I'll do whatever I like with my days—including practising medicine—as long as it's for the good of my country. I have a list of things I'm going to do for Lisri and, trust me, it grows longer every day.' She looked at him sideways. 'But the Queen isn't going anywhere for a long time yet. Decades. So I have plenty of time. And she's taking notes from me, even if she doesn't say it. Papa too. They like to think they're not old-fashioned but…you know.'

He bit back a smile, struck by this different side to her. She was a superstar, challenging the paradigm of what a crown princess should be and do. This was a woman on track for a bright future, and she'd have it with or without a man.

'You really can do anything you want to do with power like that,' he heard himself say.

She smiled, lifting the tension. 'It's not all bad, is it?'

'You're going to change so many lives.'

'Well, it's not like *you* don't do that already, Franco.'

'Oh, my God, Emma? Where's Emma? Have you seen her?'

The panicked cry made them both turn to the next pool in shock.

A young woman was scrambling from the water ten feet or so away. Almost instantly she was lost in the steam. 'My daughter—she was just here, have you seen her?'

Frantically, the woman in a red two-piece bathing suit searched around her, asking everyone in sight, almost sliding on the increasingly wet rocks around the pools in her hurry.

'Be careful!' Franco yelled at her, heaving himself from the pool with his forearms in one swift movement. He turned to help Adrienne, but she was already hot on his heels.

'She was just here—right here. Emma!'

'How old is she? What does she look like?'

Adrienne had crossed the slippery rocks with speed to reach the woman alongside him. A crash of thunder slashed through the scene and impulsively he put an arm out to steady Adrienne. This place could be dangerous. Unsupervised children could wander off and get into trouble pretty fast—especially in weather like this, which was getting worse.

The woman was barely able to speak. Her dark panic-stricken eyes were darting this way and that, trying to locate her daughter. 'She's three,' she managed.

'What is she wearing?'

'Yellow bathing suit. She's hard to miss but I don't see her… Oh, my God, where is she…? She can't swim.'

Franco cast his eyes out to the ocean, scanning the horizon. The rain was coming down more heavily now, beating the ground in angry smacks. The steam made visibility almost zero, and the wind was throwing salty spray into their eyes, not helping matters at all.

'When did you last see her?' he asked.

'I was getting her drink from my bag. When I turned around she was gone. Less than two minutes ago, I swear.'

'Over here!' Another voice came from the shoreline. 'I think I saw something. I think she's in the water!'

Beside him, Adrienne and the girl's mother both almost slipped in their haste to get to the oceanfront.

'Be careful!' Franco called out as he followed them, watching in case they fell.

The last thing they needed was broken and twisted limbs, on top of a missing child, but Adrienne was already scrambling towards the sand.

'She's in the water!' she gasped in horror, just as he spotted a flash of yellow disappear beneath a wave.

Time froze.

'Emma!'

The distraught woman did her best to run into the raging water, but she shrieked as she was pushed back—half by a threatening wave, and half by Adrienne.

'It's too dangerous!' he heard her cry. 'Franco, where's the lifeguard?'

There was no lifeguard. He knew that. People were supposed to watch themselves around here…and their kids.

Several families were hovering around on the periphery of the sea now, squinting through the rain, observing the scene in shock. In the distance he could see Ivan, already on his phone to someone.

Franco didn't wait for the young girl's bathing suit to reappear in the water. Without thinking, he leapt into the ferocious waves and started swimming.

CHAPTER SEVENTEEN

BEFORE A CRY could escape her lungs, Franco was being smothered by a wave three times his height. Adrienne watched in horror, forcing her mouth not to emit the shrieks and urgent cries she felt building up inside her.

He was a strong swimmer—he had told her that once, when he'd talked about jumping off the yacht to swim with those dolphins. But now the sky was a deep, unforgiving grey and the lashing rain formed a cloak, concealing him from her view.

'Emma...oh, Emma.'

Beside her, the little girl's mother had her hands over her mouth and was sinking slowly to the wet sand on her knees, letting the violent surf wash up and over her lap.

'My baby...my baby...' she repeated, rocking herself slowly even as Adrienne tried to urge her backwards, before she got swept away too.

She yelled out for someone to call emergency services, but they already had—probably Ivan, she thought, catching him holding a hand up to her. She could hear a siren somewhere in the distance and she motioned to him to stay back, not to draw attention to her in the middle of all this.

She prayed it wasn't too late for the little girl. The toddler would have been swept so far out by now that even if Franco could get to her, who knew how much water she might have sucked into her tiny lungs in a frantic effort to get back to her mother?

'Where are they? I don't see anything!'

'It's OK…he *will* find her,' Adrienne promised, praying that by saying it, by promising it, she'd persuade whatever God might be up there to take it as a firm instruction to, please, let him find the child.

It felt as if an eternity passed as she stood there, scanning every frothy white crest of a wave for a hand, or a foot, or a flash of yellow like before. A bigger crowd had gathered along the shoreline, and several other guys had attempted to go in, but the waves were too big, propelling them backwards as fast as they could swim out.

'I have to go in!'

The mother scrambled to her feet and almost fell straight on to her face as another wave rushed at her, like an angry wolf guarding its cubs from a stranger.

Adrienne held her back with brute strength. 'Don't. It's not safe. I've told you he'll find her.'

'Then where are they?'

Adrienne felt sick, still holding her back. It took every ounce of her strength not to follow him in herself. But she was not a strong swimmer; she had always been more interested in sailing a boat than jumping off its bow.

She prayed with more fervour, ordering, begging, silently scanning the horizon for signs of Emma and Franco. Relentless waves crashed and rushed at them, hitting the shore but bearing no sweet gifts of life, no Franco, no Emma.

Please, please, let them both be safe. I don't want to lose him. Please.

Suddenly…

'Franco!'

He appeared like some kind of merman, head first, then

full torso. He was ten feet away, bobbing in the water and catching his breath. The girl's yellow swimsuit was a beacon in his arms, and the woman's harrowing sobs of fear and relief combined made the crowd gasp, then cheer, as Franco started swimming towards them.

He was swallowed again in a second by another wave, and several other guys waded in to help him. Adrienne got waist-deep herself before she was lifted by a current she hadn't even known was there. Suddenly there were no co-ordinated movements—just her hands and feet clawing through seawater to regain some kind of stability.

Oh, God, what had she done?

She tried to yell out, but she was dragged under and her mouth filled with water.

Someone was grabbing her. A big, burly, broad-shouldered guy, with a face half obscured by a greying beard, scooped her up in his arms as he would cradle a newborn baby.

'P-Princess?' he stuttered in alarm—just before he ducked them both below an approaching wave to avoid being smashed by it.

Franco was almost at the shore when she came up, gasping for air. 'Put me down,' she spluttered at her saviour, and he did so immediately, shocked. 'Thank you,' she remembered to say, as her feet found sandy ground.

Sweeping wet hair from her eyes, she waded towards Emma's mother, scanning the beach for Franco. He was fast approaching, carrying the child in his arms, abdominals straining.

'She's not breathing,' he told her, as quietly as he could in the chaos. 'Stand back!' he yelled at the others. 'We need some room here. We're doctors.'

'Someone get that backpack!' she called out, pointing to the bag she'd left by the pool.

She was still panting heavily, and doubly drenched by the now torrential rain. The sirens wailed closer now and she caught her breath, coughing the whole time. Impatience made her brush away someone's hand when they came to help her. All she could think about was Emma.

The paramedics would have to scramble down the slope, across the wet rocks. It would all take time they didn't have to lose. The young girl's pretty face was too still. Her eyes were closed and unblinking.

Shaken, Adrienne helped Franco lay her down on the wet sand as someone else put down a towel for her.

The burly guy who'd recognised her held Emma's mother back, watching from the sidelines in a way that would have made Adrienne uncomfortable if Ivan hadn't been close, and if she hadn't been completely absorbed by the situation. He seemed to be the only one who'd recognised her, but she wasn't exactly the focal point here.

The poor woman was sobbing wretchedly. 'My baby, my baby...please, help her.'

'I'm going for CPR,' Franco said, and cleared her airway as best he could.

She watched in a daze as wet jet-black hair tumbled over his forehead. Her bag was delivered from by the pool, tossed to her across the rocks. She scrambled for it as his hands started pumping at the girl's tiny flat chest, praying for a spark, just a tiny movement that would tell them it wasn't too late.

'Emma, my Emma...please, you have to help her.'

Painful pressure built in her throat as she watched the scene unfold like a dream, fighting back tears. Franco's hands looked so big across the child's small, fragile frame.

One... Two... Three... Nothing was helping.

She watched Franco start CPR again. *Please. Please.*

It felt like an eternity in the lashing rain before Emma

coughed and contracted beneath him. Then she bolted upright, tears pooling in her fluttering eyes, coughing and
spluttering up salt water.

Franco fell on to his backside on the rocks in relief as
the crowd cheered in unison. Her mother rushed over and
swept the child into her arms, just as the paramedics arrived on the slippery scene with a spine board.

For the first time, Adrienne caught sight of the line of
people who'd gathered at the curve of the bay, back where
they'd parked the bikes.

Where had all those people *come* from?

The next fifteen minutes were a blur of statements and
forms and tears and thank-yous. By the time the ambulance had driven off with Emma, thankfully the rain was
subsiding—along with the crowds—but Adrienne had a
headache from coughing too much and squinting through
the rain.

When she turned, exhausted and emotional, the bearded
ox-like man who'd pulled her out from under wave was
staring at her, pointing a camera. Her heart leapt into her
throat.

'Let's get out of here.'

Franco was walking up behind her. He must have escaped the gushing praise of a young girl in a blue bikini
who'd managed to win his attention after the paramedics
had left. Tracking the camera still aimed at her, she almost
slid on the rocks again.

'Careful!'

Franco's strong hands gripped her shoulders, steadying her. His face reflected none of the emotion making
jelly of her limbs.

He slung the backpack onto his broad shoulders, then
grazed her cheek with one palm, turning her face, as if

to inspect it for damages. The gentle touch sent a tingling rush through her stomach. Impulsively, distracted, she pressed her own hand over his, trying to forget the way she'd seen her whole life flash before her eyes when she'd lost him, and then herself, beneath the waves.

'Are you all right to drive?'

Remembering the man with the camera, she pulled away too quickly. She watched Franco's damp, bronzed face darken like the passing storm when he saw the guy in red shorts. His lens was now directed at both of them, and she was still exposed in her swimsuit.

'Hey! You! Put that away!' Enraged, Franco started off towards him, but the guy was already scrambling across the rocks to escape. 'You'd better delete those pictures!' he called after him, but before they could reach him, he'd set off on his own motorcycle and was speeding back towards the castle.

CHAPTER EIGHTEEN

IN THE CORRIDOR on the second deck, a couple of hours later, Franco caught Adrienne leaning against the wall outside her stateroom, eyes closed, hugging herself. He'd come to find her after she'd taken two sips of her drink, then disappeared from the group around the bar, shooting him a look that implied she wanted him to follow her.

'I need to talk to you,' she said when she saw him. 'I didn't want to say anything in front of your father, or any of the others.'

'We can talk,' he said, turned on by just the scent of her shower gel, still lingering on her skin. Its fresh, nuanced blend of lilies and roses with a subtle, underlying note of white musk filled his nostrils. It somehow matched the white cotton dress she'd slipped on for the evening, and for a second it pressed a delete key on the events at the pools.

They were still all talking about it upstairs. No news reporters had been at the scene, but a couple of eyewitnesses had spoken about what they'd seen. So far none of them had recognised Adrienne, except the guy who'd taken her photo, and Franco hoped for her sake that he'd keep the photos for his private collection and leave the press out of it. The last thing she needed was pictures of herself in a swimsuit all over the Internet, and *he* didn't need to be seen standing like that next to her, either.

'That was pretty crazy, what just happened,' he said. She was looking at a framed print on the wall. 'We don't have to go back up there, you know. They're not expecting anything from you.' He studied the print alongside her, surprised to see a look of slight offence in her eyes when she glanced at him. 'I meant after what happened,' he added. 'They know you're tired, Adrienne, why don't you just rest?'

She ignored him and pulled her key card out from the tiny leather bag across her shoulder. 'I'll rest later.'

He watched her gather her laptop and some papers from the desk, while the width and squishy comfort of the inviting bed tortured him from where he remained in the doorway.

'Your father thinks the moon and stars of you,' she said, jamming her laptop into a leather bag with some cables. 'And everyone out there thinks you're a hero for going into those waves when the sea was…like that.'

He caught her eyes in the mirror on the wall, watching him…watching her. He felt a 'but' coming on.

'But you did a reckless thing. You had no lifebuoy, no nothing, Franco.'

'What did you want me to do? Let her drown?' He half laughed.

She raked a hand through her hair in frustration. 'Of course not! You can't know what went through my head this afternoon.'

'Maybe you're wrong about that,' he said as his jaw began to tick. 'You went off to find a kitten and left me thinking you'd plunged straight off a cliff.'

'It's not a competition,' she retorted, moving as if to press her hands to his chest and seeming to think better of it.

Just the almost-touch sent a lightning bolt of desire right

through him, and maybe her too, because to his complete
surprise she reached up with stormy eyes and pressed her
mouth to his, falling hard against him as he pulled her in.
He kissed her back hungrily, till she was breathing hot
and hard against his parted lips, arching into him with
her back to the wall.

'Adrienne...'

'Don't,' she said, her mouth to his cheek, and then his
forehead and nose, as if she couldn't force herself to move
away this time.

He felt her sigh gently against his skin and step away,
but before he could utter a word about having to stop, she
took his hand.

'Come with me.'

She led him to the study, where he stood by the window set into a wall of ancient maps of shipping routes.
People on the port bustled about with bags and trolleys
while Adrienne, still smelling like an intoxicating floral
bouquet he probably should be trying much harder not to
touch, set up a presentation. She seemed nervous. Was it
about her work? Or were the afternoon's events and that
last kiss making her angsty? Probably all of the above.

He could have kicked himself—what had he literally
just told Benni? This was getting out of control.

But he'd been just as worried about her out there. Adrienne had looked as if she'd had the soul sucked right out
of her, searching the beach for him and that little girl. He'd
seen the terror in her eyes—proof that she cared for him
if ever he'd needed it. But now here she was, back in her
fortress, fixated, agitated, insistent that whatever she'd
been hiding had to be shared with him *now*.

Why now? he kept wondering, but he wasn't about to
deny her a listening ear. This was why she was here, after
all. Doing all she could to become the best doctor she could

be—not just for him and their patients, but for the entire Kingdom of Lisri. Even if she'd become someone's bored, unsatisfied wife at the same time, he thought begrudgingly, wishing the taste of her wasn't so damn addictive.

They were due to sail to Capri at sunset. His father and his guests had been equally enthralled and horrified when they'd arrived on board and heard what had happened to Emma. Especially Allegra.

Allegra Aphelion, a specialist at the medical advisory board, was a tall, slender woman of French/Swiss descent, dressed as if to represent the best of middle-aged corporate conditioning. She had been beyond impressed to learn that Franco had brought a child back from the brink before the paramedics could reach them.

'You saved her life!'

'It's what we aim for every day in our line of work, Mrs Aphelion,' he'd replied.

The advisory board weren't his favourite bunch of bureaucrats, but perhaps Allegra had no idea of the situation they were in. There were hundreds of people behind the scenes of a new drug trial, drowning in paperwork and legalities. Maybe she had no real clue about the number of lives that depended on them all working together.

He knew if he had too many cocktails, he might spill his thoughts on it all, so he'd politely refused them all so far. As had Adrienne.

'OK, I'm ready,' Adrienne said behind him now. She had hooked up her laptop to the projector, and what he saw on the screen made him do a double-take.

'That's *you*,' he said pointlessly, thrown by what he was looking at—a photo of Adrienne in a white coat with her pink stethoscope, and a gold and red swirling logo above her reading *Survive&Thrive*. 'What is this?'

'I hope you don't mind that I haven't shown it to you

till now. You seemed to be so concerned about protecting my privacy, and I appreciate that, but this is too important. I didn't want you to stop me before I was ready. I want to do this.'

'Adrienne...'

'This is part of the new Marx-Balthus Foundation,' she explained, standing behind the desk.

Tendrils of her hair framed her blue eyes, and the fierce determination and pride in them struck him silent. The boat started juddering beneath them, but she didn't falter.

'I've had a team working on it for a while now. They're based in Lisri. We have a website and an app, so far. It tells a story of hope, based on your work with the cancer patients and survivors who took part in the trial. It offers them a place to connect.'

Franco sank to the leather seat by the window, his mouth agape over the spinning globe on the table.

What the hell...?

'I spoke to them all, Franco. All their stories are here— all the ways they were helped and how they're now thriving. I spoke to their families too. And there are links to new medical trials on the go—ones that are still in development—and incentives to push things forward, how and where to start collectively raising our voices...'

'How did you even come up with this?' His stomach was churning with all the emotions he had no clue how to put into words. 'You did all this by yourself?'

'I was merely being prudent,' she said. 'Trying something different to break the deadlock. I thought if we couldn't reach the medical advisory board by conventional means... There's always a back door, right? We can reach people like this instead. Look.'

She brought up images one by one. The website was

a medley of heartfelt stories told from the mouths of the patients for a change, instead of doctors and scientists.

There was Bianca. The girl was still cancer-free, after just half the predicted chemo cycles for her cancer. And Martijn from the Netherlands, just eight when he'd been on the trial, also cured. He'd gone on to become a swimming champion, and now held counselling groups at his hospital for other kids with cancer. There was Felicity, a striking blonde woman who'd been devastated by breast cancer in her late twenties. She was now cancer-free, thanks to her participation in the trial. She'd won a scholarship for a PhD in Natural Science and was the very definition of thriving.

The pictures kept coming. The stories were heart-wrenching—they'd tug at anyone's heart, he knew—but each one ended on a high. He and his team had done a lot of good with these people, and this was the proof. Adrienne had brought it all together—all of it.

At the end of each deeply personal story was a pre-designed social media post, and a plea to contact local representatives who might help push for more important research and medical trials—predominantly the one that was currently blocked.

'So that's why you wanted to be here this weekend so badly,' he said, remembering how she'd called Allegra the key.

It was still a long shot, but how could anyone fail to be moved by this? It was at least worth a try. It was creative, compassionate, empathetic, empowering, and leagues beyond anything all the medical teams he surrounded himself with had ever come up with.

'If we happen to show it to Allegra this weekend she might just take it on board,' he said. 'She'll talk about it with us, at least, and then hopefully talk to other people on the board.'

'That's what I was thinking.'

'You're amazing.' He sank back in his chair again, his mind spinning. His foul mood had been squeezed right out of him, to be replaced with sheer wonder. 'And you've put your name all over this. How did you keep it a secret?'

'Very strict confidentiality agreements,' she told him. 'But I can lift them any time I like. There's an embargo on the press release, but it can all be announced tomorrow morning if I say so. Your team will need to be briefed, of course, but we can easily align…'

'I wish you hadn't felt like this was something you had to do in secret.' He sprang from the chair, but stopped short of sweeping her off her feet. His breath caught as she stood there, frozen inches from him. Waiting. 'Maybe I've been a little overprotective of you.'

Like your family, he realised suddenly, ashamed of treating her the same way as them when she was clearly a force to be reckoned with.

This time he did reach for her, and swept a hand behind her head, urging her lips to his. He wanted to claim more than her mouth right now—more than he had this afternoon, when she'd turned her back on him and that woman on the beach who'd clamoured for his attention like a puppy dog. It had turned him on, knowing she'd been looking.

'You did the right thing, not involving me in this,' he said instead, reining himself in and crossing to the laptop, where he studied the Survive&Thrive logo up close. 'It needed your personal touch. Your heart and soul. It's all here. I would have ruined it—made it all scientific and medical—but you…'

'It's still those things. It's just personal too. And, actually, you were my inspiration,' she said.

Behind him he heard her exhale, like a rush of fire

leaving her body. She knew they had to stop surrendering to their impulses. Especially here. He was already too involved than was safe for his own heart. And now this.

'Do you think it will convince them?'

'Do you think what will convince who?'

Marco Perretta poked his grey head around the door and narrowed his eyes at them.

'What are you two doing, hiding out down here?'

'He should see it,' Franco told her. 'If you want the Perretta Institute to back this, that is?'

Adrienne glanced between them, as if weighing up whether or not to share it with someone else and his throat itched. She hadn't directly said she wanted his input. She'd done this all on her own, to her credit. She certainly didn't need them to back her. Not as far as the financials were involved.

To his relief, Adrienne beckoned his father closer and pulled up a seat for him in front of the projector. Then she stood in front of them both, ready for business.

'Let me run through my objectives for you, Mr Perretta.'

CHAPTER NINETEEN

ADRIENNE'S PRESS TEAM wanted to ask her a million things, and by eight a.m. she was starting to regret that she was on a yacht between islands on the Amalfi Coast. Still, timing had never been her speciality. And at least they had someone from the medical board here, in person, to watch it all play out.

She fetched a croissant from a fresh plate on the bar by the pool and accepted a coffee in a silver-crested cup. She was the first on deck, and today felt good already.

She and Franco had been up late, huddled in the study, going over the details of what would be announced by the press and how the Perretta Institute would correspond in alignment. They hadn't had a chance to be alone.

Finally Marco had called Franco to the entertainment hall for their customary midnight nightcap and she'd taken herself to bed, and fallen asleep the second her head hit the pillow. At least falling asleep exhausted was better than spending all night thinking about *him* sleeping in the stateroom opposite her, and wishing she could go to him.

This was about something else now, she reminded herself, adjusting her sunglasses and tying the robe around her swimsuit.

Her mother was the first to call, just as she'd settled on a lounger, and Adrienne allowed a small shiver of pride and anticipation to swirl through her with the caffeine as the Queen chattered on profusely about how proud she was. The embargo had been lifted on Survive&Thrive. And with her name attached to it, it was getting attention very fast.

'What does Papa think?' She had to ask.

Her mother paused, as if searching for the right words. 'He did say he'd like to meet this Dr Perretta one day. He's aware of the impression he seems to have made on you. Why don't you bring him to the polo?'

Adrienne's heart lodged in her throat. 'He's not the kind of man Papa would approve of.'

The Queen fell silent.

'But the kind of man he approves of has never been the kind of man for me. You know that, don't you, Mother?' Adrienne continued. She realised her heart was thrumming. 'I'll be a member of the royal family *and* a doctor, Mother. I'll do everything that's expected of me and more. But I've told you before: I won't marry any man I don't love.'

'Are you telling me you love this man?'

Adrienne balked. 'I… No, of course not. It's just that he and I have work to do. I don't want Papa to come between us, or put a spanner in the works for any reason.'

Still more silence.

Adrienne lost her appetite on the spot. Of course she wasn't telling her mother the whole truth, even though she'd probably read between the lines of her letters. But surprisingly, a huge leaden weight seemed to drift from her shoulders and she dared to exhale deeply. She might as well tell her everything now—God knew she'd been bottling it up.

She walked to the bow, cast her eyes over the sea and the boats with their sails jutting like shark fins in the distance. Then, in a hushed voice, she told her mother how she really felt about Franco. About how their lives were vastly different, how his future didn't align with hers and how it killed her. How Franco didn't want the never-ending circus that was her life, but how he'd shown her lately that sticking to her principles and staying single, instead of marrying someone for the sake of the throne, was simply what she had to do.

She would have sworn her mother took it on board, but then came her departing warning.

'My darling, just take care of yourself. I'm not going to tell you what to do at your age, but…why don't you just meet the Baron?'

And there she goes again.

Adrienne swiped at her face, pursing her lips. 'There is no law saying I have to marry a member of the aristocracy or another royal, Mother, only an archaic tradition,' she said tightly. 'And Papa would do well to remember that—both of you would—if I'm to continue our honoured legacy. I don't want to be a monarch who lies, Mother, not about my own worth, and not about my own heart's desires. What kind of role model would that make me?'

Adrienne was shaking; she had never said anything of the sort to either of her parents. But she'd summoned the strength Franco had given her out in that hot pool when he'd challenged her. It was high time she fought back and addressed some home truths.

'Buongiorno, sole.'

Franco's whisper in her ear made her jump, just as she was hanging up. Her conversation with her mother was unresolved, but she'd call again in a few days…talk to Papa if she really had to.

She spun round and swallowed back an anxious

flutter—first at the thought of telling Papa what she'd just told her mother, then at seeing Franco.

He looked even more handsome than yesterday, in another pair of low-slung shorts and a navy shirt, worn open. His taut abdominals gleamed in the morning sun and made her look twice, and then stifle a moan as he dropped to a deckchair and pulled out his phone.

'It's everywhere already,' he said as she stood over him.

He stopped scrolling through the web browser to eye her from head to toe in the swimsuit, then dragged another chair to his side for her, as if they were honeymooners or something, waking up to look at their wedding photos.

God, her imagination around this guy...

He still had a faint pillow crease on one forearm and across one cheek, and she imagined him some fifteen minutes earlier, sound asleep with no clothes on, just feet from her suite. The sooner they got off this boat, where she was already far too tempted by him, the better.

'"Princess Adrienne Marx-Balthus of Lisri garners support for new cancer drug trial",' he read aloud, as a deckhand brought him coffee. '"Revolutionary new connections for cancer patients..." "The Princess with a promise..." These headlines... Adrienne, everyone's talking about it.'

She flushed at the look of pure awe on his face. 'Lisri's *Evening News* called the press office,' she told him. 'They want some of the kids to do a TV piece. You and me too.'

'You and me, huh?'

His expression grew serious, and a smile played on his perfect lips. In spite of her apprehension about the whole thing, she felt a flock of excited butterflies take flight in her belly, followed quickly by a twinge of nerves. Everything hinged on their meeting with Allegra. Franco and his father had had no luck using conventional means so far—now it was up to her.

No one had put any pressure on her, but for once she was putting it on herself and enjoying it. She'd never been so fired up and flustered at the same time.

Hours later they were all sitting on a flower-lined terrace at the foot of Punta Carena Lighthouse. Essentially it was a terrace above the sea, overlooking a gorgeous cove. The seafood lunch was perfect, but every time Allegra looked her way Adrienne waited for her to bring up Survive&Thrive. She knew she couldn't be the first to mention it—the news would have spread on its own.

Before leaving the yacht, Franco and his principle investigator had given Allegra a presentation on the status of another current trial, to which Allegra had listened intently and quietly. No one had been looking at their phones. Which had given the news more time to circulate.

Thankfully it wasn't long before two men from the Perretta biotechnology lab in Florence started whispering, then looking at her. She put down her fork.

'What is this?' one of them asked, and her heart sped up as she took the man's phone.

Survive&Thrive was all over it. She could feel Allegra watching her, too, now.

'Survive&Thrive—It means going beyond your comfort zone. And also, using your courage to help the people around you.'

'That's Adrienne,' Franco said, and pride swirled in his eyes, hypnotising her for a second.

Allegra's phone rang.

Under the table, he knocked his knee against hers and she tried not to feel the zing of desire for him creep along her inner thighs.

'I'm getting hundreds of calls about this—and emails,' Allegra said, scrolling through her phone without answering it and looking between them in amusement. 'They know I'm here with you and they all want the scoop.' Her eyebrows furrowed as she read something else, then turned to her, shaking her head. 'This is quite an endeavour, Princess Adrienne, how did you find the time?'

'Well, to be quite honest, Allegra, I don't really know,' Adrienne answered truthfully, and a nervous laugh escaped her lips before she could stop it.

'I don't know what to say.' Allegra put her phone down on the table. 'I'm humbled, honestly, and I can only apologise for all the delays you and the institute have experienced so far, trying to push your trial through. All my CTAs are telling me to chase the board. They're getting calls already.'

'It's not your fault,' Adrienne said. 'But that was what we kind of hoped would happen.'

Allegra nodded, fighting a smile. 'I will do everything I can,' she said.

Franco and Marco let out a joint sigh of relief, and just hearing it made Adrienne reach for Allegra's hands. 'Thank you,' she said, 'from the bottom of my heart.' Allegra looked somewhat embarrassed for a second. 'We need more public awareness of the good these new treatments can do. We need all the support we can get.'

She couldn't help thinking of Rosita, waiting for another bout of chemo, and Candice, waiting for her hair to fall out when it didn't necessarily have to.

Cancer had a way of creeping into everyone's life at some point—if not directly, then by way of someone else. Furious determination flooded her veins. For her, cancer of every kind had merged into one huge iniquitous dragon she wanted nothing more but to slay, piece by piece, no matter how long it took.

Franco was quiet at her side, taking it all in, ignoring

his own vibrating phone. Her knee was still buzzing from where his had been pressed against it. He was with her on this. Even if it was as far as they ever went he was her partner in this mission, and for that, at least, she was satisfied.

Liar. You want him. More than just his kisses.

Allegra was wiping her eyes behind the sunglasses she'd chosen to hide behind for a moment. It was an emotional moment for everyone, it seemed. 'I give you my word I'll do what I can to get your trial moving. All your hard work won't be for nothing, Princess.'

CHAPTER TWENTY

FRANCO KNOCKED ON the door at ten p.m. and Adrienne answered with a radiant smile. She'd been locked away in the study fielding calls since they'd returned from lunch. Suddenly she was more in demand than ever, but she didn't look unhappy about it.

'Everything's coming together,' she said, stifling a yawn and rubbing her eyes.

She was clearly as exhausted as he was. He should say goodnight and retire, and he knew it. He'd been bursting with pride over her achievements all day—even more so after seeing Allegra's reaction—but as he'd scrolled through the news announcements he'd been hit with the fact that being linked to her on this project was bound to come with all kinds of unwanted attention—more than usual.

She rested her head on her hand against the door frame. 'When we get back to Naples tomorrow I have a couple of interviews to do, but then my team will take over. Don't worry, it won't affect my regular work, but I do have a lot of studying to catch up on.'

'I'm sure we can work out an extension for you,' he told her, letting his eyes run over her outfit—a lilac dress that emphasised her slim hips and full, round breasts. He was so tired it was all he could do to force his eyes away.

'An extension? Wouldn't that be special treatment?' She smiled.

He cleared his throat, forcing his hand not to adjust the strap of her dress as it drifted down over her shoulder.

'I guess it would, but you deserve it.'

He would not ruin her moment by asking if the royal family were dubious in any way about him being at her side in her latest venture. It was certainly bringing attention to her role at the institute already, as well as to him. News travelled incredibly fast—especially when a member of Lisri's royal family was involved. The Perretta Foundation had been flooded with calls all day.

'Big day,' he said, and she nodded, looking slightly awkward.

His words seemed to hang in the salty air, and for a second he considered saying goodnight, just as he'd planned.

'Get your swimsuit on,' he said instead, realising he'd only lie there imagining her in the next cabin.

'What?'

'I have something to show you. Meet me on deck.'

The grotto was just one of several sea caves around the island. Tonight, as he rowed the small boat from the yacht, the bioluminescence created a brilliant blue light that made the cave look alive.

Above them, the yellow half-moon lit Adrienne as she trailed a finger over the side of the small boat into the water, her hair loose around her shoulders. His thoughts were still crashing over him like waves, even though he'd tried to calm them down. The stakes would be higher than ever now. Her medical role would be under scrutiny along with his. Her family would be watching her even more closely, and more noble suitors would be rolled out. There was no doubt about it.

He was more than happy to be her partner in this new business venture, but one newspaper had already caused a stir online this afternoon, hinting that one day he might be trying to rule the nation alongside her, with no experience and no background, and no blue blood at all.

It was bothering him more than he cared to admit.

'Can we really swim in there?' she asked, pulling him from his thoughts.

The yawning mouth of the cave was an open invitation to a glistening blue-tinted wonderland. There was no one else around.

'We can in this one,' he said. 'When the tide is right.'

It was right tonight. He anchored the boat at the mouth of the cave and stood, kicked off his shirt and shoes. Adrienne's eyes trailed across his bare torso nervously, like a mouse that had been lured to some kind of trap and was considering whether or not to try and take the cheese.

'You don't have to swim,' he heard himself say. 'But I am.'

With that he dived into the cool, calm water, and in three seconds flat she was carving through the water behind him, swimming right into the cave.

He watched her tread water, spinning circles in the entrance. The bioluminescence glowed beneath her and swirled around her in a dream-like soup.

'It's like a movie set,' she breathed, floating onto her back.

Her silhouette against every shade of blue was worth filming without doubt, he thought, but it was just them here. No cameras. No one to see them at all. He could look, but he still shouldn't touch. It was glaringly apparent how different their lives were; they were on different trajectories.

His heart was not a toy for the media to play with.

She asked for a story about the cave, so he flipped onto his back beside her and told her about the Emperor's private swimming pool. This very place. It had once been elaborately decorated inside—a kind of temple in the ocean, in honour of the sea nymphs. Long ago, no one had known what made it glow. They'd thought it was magic.

'It *is* magic,' she breathed from where she was floating beside him.

Her shoulder knocked his as a wave swept in from a passing boat outside, and she reached for his hand.

'It's just a boat,' he told her, feeling her warm fingers tighten in his. 'I thought you were an expert sailor?'

'I am.'

She pulled her hand back quickly, and he tried not to notice how just one touch had, yet again, sent his heartbeat straight to his manhood.

'This is all just so different. Everything about this place. If my family could see me now...'

'What would they say?' He had to ask her now she'd brought it up. 'Have you heard from them?'

She kept her eyes on the roof of the cave. 'My mother is very proud of me. I haven't heard from my father yet, but I don't care what he thinks.'

'Yes, you do.'

She sighed. 'You're right. I do.'

'He wouldn't try and bring you home, would he? Now that you're involved in a different cause?'

'A cause that's not to do with marrying myself off to the nearest suitable man, you mean?'

He chewed on his cheek. He couldn't even find the notion funny. 'A cause that involves you being seen alongside someone who's not of blue blood.'

Adrienne turned to him. 'I know the media are already

speculating that we might be more to each other than colleagues. That's just what they do. I'm sorry.'

'It's not your fault,' he said truthfully.

'But I couldn't have done this without you. You give me reasons and avenues to push into and prove myself.'

She righted herself in the water, met his eyes an inch above the rippling blue hues. Her whole face glowed turquoise, her lips and eyelashes dripping.

'Is it wrong that I want you?' she whispered suddenly, and closed the gap between them. 'I know I shouldn't.'

'You're right...you shouldn't,' he heard himself say, as the bulge in his shorts screamed for attention.

He swallowed. This was the Crown Princess of Lisri, putty in his hands. Or maybe it was the other way round. He was the putty...

Ducking beneath the water, he swam away from her, trying to cool the heated blood throbbing through every inch of him. He came up three feet away to find her floating on her back again, sucking the air from the cave in huge, needy lungfuls, eyes closed.

'I'm not what you want?'

Her voice was small, and he hated what he was doing—to both of them.

'Adrienne, that's not it.'

Damn this. How was he supposed to forget what they'd already done? He could deny it all he liked, but he hadn't wanted anyone like this since Luci—and never as badly.

The Princess of Lisri...his for the taking. Certain responsibilities came with that...they both knew it. But he was so hard for her already. Blue blood, blue eyes imploring—how could he refuse her?

Excitement pounded and drummed in her veins as Franco's green eyes seemed to devour her. She let her gaze rake over his broad shoulders, bulging pectoral muscles and rippling abs.

'Make love to me,' she heard herself say, swimming up close to him again. 'I'm protected against pregnancy.'

Her words seemed to echo around the cave, and for a moment he caressed her face with a palm, eyes harrowed and tortured. It made her want him more, and without thinking another second she pressed her mouth to his, till they were kissing furiously, passionately, making for the line of rocks at the edge of the cave.

God, you're amazing, she wanted to say.

Every muscle was hard as he drew her closer with thick, heavy arms, and she thought he'd be able to wrestle a sea monster to the ocean floor if he wanted. Her hands slid like water over his shoulders, up and down his biceps, and all the while she kissed him, tracing the lines of his body, committing them to memory. She let her fingers tangle in his hair and trail downwards, to his shorts…

'Adrienne…'

His gaze locked to hers as his hands found their way to her hips. He was waiting to see what she would do, leaving it up to her. She wasn't going to wait now that she'd started. The water defined each line on his body as he swam with her, guiding her to a long, flat rock the right size for them to rest on. Or do whatever the hell they wanted on.

She slid a hand into his shorts, finding him so hard for her she moaned, and the need to explore more of him took over her entire thought process.

Franco's mouth fell open. His chest seemed to expand before her as he took in a huge lungful of the salty air. She hooked a finger into the waistband of his shorts, teased him towards her, hardly believing how daring she was, how desirous she was for him at her core.

He was still holding his breath as she drew his shorts

down, and she watched his biceps flex as he pulled them off and tossed them to the rocks, finally letting his breath out and crashing his mouth to hers again. In seconds her bikini was on top of them, making a wet pile next to their naked bodies.

He drew her against him by her hips, his back to the rock, and she found her hands caressing his tight backside, urging him closer. He was so hard for her—huge, in fact— and she heard herself gasp as he deftly pulled himself onto the rock, revealing the full extent of his manhood, every glistening inch of his rock-hard body. She wanted all of it.

He lifted her easily onto the rock beside him, and before she could touch him again he brought both his palms to her face and pressed his hungry lips to hers, kissed her till she was dizzy. As his palms slid expertly over the dripping curves of her skin she swooned audibly, till she found herself sitting astride him, naked before him.

Her knees quaked as he continued to kiss her and she slid her hand between them, along and up the straining length of him till he was making sounds she'd never heard...music to her ears. Pleasing him, it emerged, was her new favourite thing. She wouldn't allow herself to think about how she shouldn't be doing this...that she might regret it later. That *he* might.

Franco's own fingers were anything but idle. She took his lower lip in her teeth and grasped his thickness as they found her sweetest spot, revelling at the look on his face when she opened her eyes. Suddenly, neither of them could wait any more. He rolled her expertly onto her back, protecting her head from the rock with his hand, and slid inside her. With every thrust she felt herself falling deeper into him; it was futile trying to think of anything else.

This was the moment she'd been waiting for, and it was better than she ever could have imagined.

CHAPTER TWENTY-ONE

TWO WEEKS WENT past in a flash for Adrienne. The phone never seemed to stop, and she had her work cut out, making time for interviews about Survive&Thrive on top of her regular duties at the cancer institute.

'You look tired, Princess,' Rosita observed when she poked her head into her room one morning.

Rosita was hooked up to fluids and looked pale. Her cancer treatment plan was intense. Every time Adrienne saw her she yearned for something more positive to report regarding a place on the soon-to-be revived trial, but there was still no word from the medical advisory board. Although there was more pressure on them to get it moving than ever.

The people she'd interviewed had all been re-interviewed separately by various news outlets. The app had over half a million downloads already. All proceeds had gone straight to the Perretta Institute. It was now something of a buzzword on the medical scene...not that any of it had moved her father any closer to admitting he was proud of her.

He'd said very little, and she wondered if he was debating how to berate her for appearing so publicly with Franco Perretta in a cause that might lead her further from her royal duties than he preferred.

Not that she needed his approval, of course. But her pride and happiness over the project was overshadowed somewhat by the feeling that all was not well in the kingdom. Nor with Franco.

No, she would not be led back down that path, she reprimanded herself.

But how could she not?

They'd given in to their desires and it had been the most incredible sexual encounter of her life—but he'd been keeping away from her ever since, outside of the institute, and she had a feeling that this intense invasion of his privacy was getting to him. She felt awful, knowing that he was getting papped everywhere he went because of her.

'How's the latest round treating you?' she asked her patient now. She knew Rosita's chemo was already taking its toll, and this time she'd had to spend even longer as an in-patient.

'This is my third day...' Rosita sighed, pressing her raven-haired head to the pillows propped up at her back. The room was filled with vases of flowers. The TV on the wall flickered with no sound. 'At least I made it past Chapter Three this time.'

She held up the copy of *Great Expectations* that Franco had lent her. He'd insisted she should finish it. Adrienne smiled, even though the sight of it made her wonder where he was—still out entertaining a certain diet specialist named Nicolette de Luca, who was about to give a lecture in the hall with him?

'That's when it starts getting good,' she said, trying not to sound distracted.

'I've been on Survive&Thrive again,' Rosita said now. 'I contacted a girl in Austria, younger than me. She just got diagnosed with Ewing's sarcoma. She's written to the medical board every day about the trial, like my parents have. Do you think they're even reading the emails?'

Her eyes looked round and hopeful, and Adrienne felt a lump in her throat instantly. A downside to all the attention around the trial, through the website and the app, was that the people who weren't getting the help they needed were hearing about it. Not that ignorance had been blissful for them to begin with. Allegra had promised to help, but they couldn't really rely on one insider—they all knew that.

It felt as if some kind of clock was ticking.

What if her grand plan didn't actually work?

What if she'd dragged Franco into the limelight and encouraged all this relentless tongue-wagging about them both for nothing?

'There are other ways for you to get better,' she said, trying to sound cheerful in spite of herself. She squeezed the young girl's hand, wishing her thoughts weren't always such a tornado.

Franco himself stuck his head around the door. 'What are you two gossiping about?'

Her pulse soared. So he was back.

'Rosita has a massage soon.'

She was trying to sound impervious to his presence, but probably failing. She hadn't seen him now for three days. He'd been on Capri with a science research team. Then Nicolette de Luca had invited him to discuss the results of her study on the treatment of advanced cancer by diet therapy.

'Ah, you're getting into it.' Franco strode to her side and took the book from Rosita's hand. He ran a thumb over the embossed cover and threw a look her way. 'Charles Dickens…what a guy…' He put the book back down. 'Of course it's really a study on class and society.'

'I know,' Rosita said, and her eyes danced between them with interest.

Adrienne did her best to look busy, tucking in a blanket that didn't need to be tucked in at all. She wanted to apologise for bringing unwelcome speculation by strangers into his life, but every time she tried it was as if she was underlining another reason for him not to come any closer, and there was enough distance between them already. She'd read more than one piece of trash that accused him of trying to line himself up for his place as her husband. The thought of him seeing it made her cringe. He was such a private guy; this was probably a total nightmare for him.

'If you'll excuse me, ladies? Some people over on the radiation ward have "great expectations" for my afternoon. I'll see you shortly for the lecture, Dr Balthus?'

'I wouldn't miss it,' she answered before Franco strode from the room.

Rosita was grinning now, her clever eyes seeing deeper into Adrienne than she cared to show. 'Is something really going on with you and the hot doc? Like all the articles are saying?'

'Don't be silly,' Adrienne said lightly, willing her heart to slow down as the weight of it all came crashing back down onto her shoulders. 'I'll have Irina come back in…'

'Nicolette de Luca was kind enough to let me stay on the premises in Capri, where her patients are free to explore the most beautiful grounds. I've never seen such lush vegetable gardens… Even I might be going vegan after this.'

Adrienne sank a little lower in her seat in the study hall. Franco was doing his thing on stage, being as charismatic and charming as only he knew how. Even when the surgeon Ansell shuffled into the seat next to her, she couldn't keep her eyes off Franco.

The lecture was actually fascinating. The Perretta Institute was getting behind a grant for Nicolette de Luca's latest research programme, and its results on cancer-fighting foods, which they were being walked through now, were promising.

Nicolette's willowy figure was the picture of elegance in an open white coat, with her high, full breasts pert in a tight white shirt. She wore her bright red hair loose and spoke Italian with a refined accent.

And she was standing a little too close to Franco.

Jealousy was a wicked beast. Adrienne could picture the two of them these last three nights, drinking herbal tea, working late by candlelight… Franco would have been wooed by the dietician, eating her delicious fruits, maybe allowing himself to release some of the pent-up energy Adrienne had left him with after their one incredible, wet, hot night together that no one must know about—ever.

She'd given in to her burning, raging need to feel him inside her, and she'd have to live with the lack of that glorious experience for ever.

Wondering about it had almost been better. Now she knew exactly what she'd be missing when he moved on with someone more suitable for him than her. She should try to forget the rush of those salty kisses, the way his skin had glistened in that glowing cave, how powerful she'd felt, how *seen* and worshipped by him, and…

'That's absolutely right, Nicolette. Results show that polyphenols possess anti-cancer and tumour-fighting properties…'

Was he flirting with Nicolette to distract the press from the subject of the two of them, seeing as he loathed being in the public eye even more than Adrienne did? She wouldn't blame him. He hadn't asked to have his family history compared to that of every aristocrat now climbing out of the woodwork to try and set up a meeting with her. And it was up to her to do something about it.

'How are you doing, Adrienne?' Ansell nudged her slightly, so softly she barely felt it, and she remembered he'd slid in next to her.

'Yes, great…' she said, distracted.

There was no escaping this. She had to talk to her family—open up and be honest. She had to drive it home that she was her own person, paving her own future, with or without a man at her side.

'Dr Perretta, you should know an apple a day keeps the doctor away—but have you heard about what urolithins in walnuts can do? Our studies have found that these compounds, which bind to oestrogen receptors, may play a role in preventing breast cancer.'

Oh, Nicolette, you're good.

'So, I was wondering if you were busy on Friday…' Ansell's voice was in her ear now. He was asking her out again.

'Hmmm?' she managed, barely hearing him.

They were both just doing their job, Franco and Nicolette, and Franco was a free man. His kisses had not been promises, and their lovemaking, while it had been the best of her life, hadn't changed her situation, or his stance against being the centre of any kind of scandal.

It was up to her to turn things around—if not for herself, then for all future generations of women in Lisri.

'Your phone's vibrating.'

Ansell again.

'Oh, yes…thanks.'

She was about to turn it off when she saw it was a message for her from Reception.

Someone is here to see you.

Her heart jolted.

Something must be wrong. People didn't just show up unannounced—not for her, anyway. She had a schedule.

As quickly as she could, she squeezed through the rows towards the exit.

CHAPTER TWENTY-TWO

NICOLETTE DE LUCA WAS MAKING quite an impression on Rosita, telling her what she might try eating to help her feel less tired between chemo sessions. They were talking about horses now, comparing where they'd gone riding last summer, and the redhead kept shooting him looks, as if she was checking how impressed he was by her.

Franco rolled his eyes when her back was turned. Women who flirted so brazenly were almost always after one thing: one hot night with *Medical Heroes* magazine's Philanthropist of the Decade. These days he preferred those who wouldn't go near him at all— even if it left him hornier than a stag.

But it was better this way. The press were relentless, just as Adrienne had always said.

It wasn't that he minded his name being out there, attributed to *her* work—in fact, he was immensely proud of what she'd achieved—but being accused of being 'unsuitable' for her, simply because he wasn't an aristocrat...

He'd gone through enough torture, sympathy and gossip after losing Luci, thanks to keeping his grief and thoughts to himself. He didn't need his private life splashed in the world's press again. It made him cold to the bone, knowing that his every breath outside the institute was under scrutiny.

'Where is Dr Balthus?' Rosita asked him.

'I think she's in the Residents' Room,' he replied. 'She's busy.'

At least they'd both been busy…busy enough to justify keeping away from each other and keeping all temptation at bay.

With her website and the app a full success, Survive&Thrive was the talk of the institute—and most of Europe by now. It was all go. Over half a million downloads… New connections being made every minute… Hope delivered daily to people who needed it…

His phone rang.

Would it have taken off like this without her name behind it? Who cared? he thought. It didn't even matter. She'd been interviewed by everyone of any importance and, while he hadn't dared to say it aloud, he'd been expecting a phone call for days now.

'Excuse me,' he said to Nicolette, answering his phone at the same time. His heart was an ox, bashing his ribs under his lab coat. What if it *wasn't* what he'd been expecting…?

'It seems your Princess has caused a bit of a stir with this Survive&Thrive project,' said Nathan, chair of the medical advisory board. There was the sound chattering behind him, people talking excitedly. 'You'd better get your patient list together, Franco.'

Franco stopped short in the middle of the floor. 'Are you saying what I think you're saying?'

'Someone on the board has been fighting your case hard, and it seems we can finally approve the move from phase two to phase three within the month.'

Yes. Yes. Yes. Thank God.

Franco couldn't help it. He gave a loud whoop as he turned back to Nicolette, and Rosita laughed from the bed. 'The trial has got approval to move on,' he told them in jubilation.

'You're the first to know. We thought you'd want to tell Dr Balthus yourself,' Nathan said.

Franco told him, yes, of course, all the while raking his hand through his hair, picturing her face when he told her.

Nicolette spoke. 'Franco, do you want me to come with you?'

He realised he was headed for the door, his mind elsewhere. 'I have to go do and something—excuse me, ladies. I'll be right back,' he said, and left the room without her.

His indifference towards Nicolette was only making her try harder. She should have left an hour ago, but she'd said she wanted to meet Adrienne when she was free—and who didn't these days?

'Adrienne? I have some news.'

He hovered outside the door. She was being very quiet... maybe she had her headphones on. He considered for a second not telling her here at all. This warranted going somewhere special, with champagne... But, no, he wasn't doing things like that any more. Nothing that drew unwarranted attention to him as some potential wholly unsuitable suitor was not even an option. It was about the trial, not them.

'Adrienne?'

With a tentative hand he opened the door, expecting to find her there. All the chairs were empty, like the rest of the room. Frowning to himself, he remembered she'd left the lecture early. He assumed she'd come back here to push on with her studies.

He stood there for a minute, annoyed at how his brain was deconstructing her absence already. Not knowing where she was made him uneasy—which bothered him.

He pulled out his phone, annoyed again when his pulse

quickened in anticipation of talking to her. It rang out, and then high-heeled footsteps in the corridor told him Nicolette had followed him.

'Franco? I forgot to tell you…there's a restaurant launch in Rione Sanita tonight. I have two tickets. It's vegan—your new favourite.'

She wasn't going to quit.

He forced a smile, crossing to one of the desks. Adrienne's laptop was there, closed. It wasn't like her not to take it with her.

'I think we should celebrate,' Nicolette said from the doorway, folding her arms and wriggling her eyebrows suggestively.

The old him would have buried himself in her to get his mind off Adrienne.

He watched her eye the brown carpet of the residents' room with a hint of disapproval, tossing her long red hair over her shoulder. 'This is not exactly fit for a princess,' she said with a sniff.

He bit back a smile. The Crown Princess hadn't turned her nose up. Adrienne had given the institute nothing but compliments, and done nothing but good since she'd arrived. She'd also helped him address a few things about his own life. She was a leader, someone to look up to…audacious, driven, and so damn beautiful, inside and out…

He tried her phone again.

Come on, pick up… Where are you, woman?

Dropping to a seat, he stared unseeingly at Nicolette as Adrienne's phone rang out. For a second he considered that maybe she'd actually flown home without telling him. She'd mentioned something about an annual polo match this weekend in Lisri. She wasn't going to go, though—she'd told the team so herself, said shc was too busy. Had she changed her mind?

'Wow, what on earth…?' Nicolette trailed off as Irina entered the room, her face obscured by the hugest bunch of flowers he'd ever seen.

'I think we should keep these in here for the Princess. They're taking over the entire reception desk,' Irina said, wrinkling her nose. Then she sneezed. 'Gosh, have you ever seen anything like it? They're giving me hay fever.'

'Who are they from?' he asked, instincts primed.

'He just showed up with them before he left with her,' she replied, lowering the bouquet carefully to the desk in front of him, burying Adrienne's laptop under sunflowers, roses, and giant purple trumpet-like calla lilies. 'Charming man.'

'Who was charming?'

The back of his neck felt too hot under his collar. Nicolette was admiring the flowers now, fondling the satin ribbon around the base of the bouquet.

He bristled, stood up from the chair. 'Irina, who did Adrienne leave with?'

Irina shrugged, running her fingers along the head of a snow-white teddy bear, nestled in the blooms. Both women looked as awed as if an original Da Vinci had been deposited on the desk, and he didn't get a good feeling.

'I'm sure she said he was a baron. He had a very long, important name.'

'Lucky girl.' Nicolette looked impressed—and envious.

Franco felt a kick like a soccer ball to his guts.

CHAPTER TWENTY-THREE

ADRIENNE SCOOPED THE kitten into her arms and dismissed Mirabel the second she got home. She didn't feel much like talking. In fact, she desperately needed her own company after a day like today.

On the balcony, staring at Vesuvius, she felt her ears still ringing from listening to Baron Vittorio La Rosa going on about his tour of Mozambique, and wherever it was he'd been after that—she'd zoned out on a lot of it.

How infuriating that he'd tracked her down and just shown up like that. But it wasn't as if she could have just brushed him off, with Irina swooning behind her. And it wasn't *his* fault he'd been pushed on her.

He'd assumed she didn't want to meet when she hadn't contacted him, but his parents had insisted he try. He'd been pretty honest about that, once they'd started talking. It had been all their idea for him to come to the institute with a huge bouquet of flowers. His family didn't believe the rumours about her and Franco... *'Because obviously he's not husband material.'*

His words had boiled her blood, fired her up even more.

The Baron had talked a lot about a former boarding school friend called Carlos, who he'd just got back in touch with. After maybe the twentieth time of hearing his name she'd wondered if the Baron might actually be gay, and

not so secretly in love with Carlos. If that were the case...
wow. Imagine the pressure on him to be something he
wasn't—forced to knock on princesses' doors before being
shut back in the closet.

'My own situation could be worse, right, kitten?' she
said, stroking the creature's silky fur as she switched on
her phone again.

It pinged with the expected multitude of messages, and
she scrolled through for the important ones. Three missed
calls from Franco not long after she'd left the building.
Her heart soared.

She called him back.

No answer.

Jealousy consumed her like a dark cloud. Maybe he'd
gone out with Nicolette de Luca. He had every right to, of
course, but that didn't stop the furious butterflies flapping
when she called again and he still didn't answer.

The next morning she was surprised to see someone had
put the Baron's flowers in the residents' room, as well as
a huge card addressed to her. Bright red balloons and the
word *Congratulations* glittered on the front.

Dropping her bag to a chair, she flipped it open. The
whole team had signed it.

*Congratulations on your success with Survive&Thrive
and for helping to get the trial approved!*

What...?

'Well done, Princess... I mean, Adrienne.'

Irina's voice in the doorway made her spin around.

'When did you find out?' she asked, propping up the
card against the ridiculous bouquet and grabbing her white
coat from the back of a chair. This was monumental—

and she'd had no idea. Why had no one left her a message about this?

'Yesterday…late afternoon. Right after you left with the Baron. Franco was trying to get hold of you. I think he wanted to tell you himself…'

'He didn't call me back,' she said, missing a button on her coat.

Her head was spinning.

She found him after her rounds, before she was due to attend a radiation session. He didn't look too pleased to see her when she caught him exiting the consultation room.

'There you are,' she said, on edge immediately. 'Where have you been?'

'Busy,' he said curtly, making for the revolving door. 'Like you, I assume.'

She caught his arm in the corridor and couldn't help the grin taking over her face. 'Franco, the trial got approved!'

'I know,' he said bluntly. Then he straightened up. 'I called to tell you that yesterday.'

'I was out. I tried to call you back. This is so fantastic! We should talk… I want to stay involved.'

'We'll schedule a team meeting.'

His eyes narrowed at her, then moved to the floor. Her chest felt tight. He was angry with her. Maybe he'd seen the Baron's flowers. Who was she kidding? You could see them from the moon.

She cast her eyes around the corridor, then ushered him into an empty treatment room, closing the door behind them.

'Is this because of the flowers?' she said. 'Because I went for a coffee with the Baron?'

Franco made a thing of checking the clipboard he was holding. 'It's none of my business who you date, Adrienne.'

His coldness sent a chill through her veins. 'Franco, it wasn't a date. I just had to…'

'Regarding this trial… I assume you'd like to help reach out to potential patients?' He flipped through the papers on his clipboard, refusing to meet her eyes. 'Rosita and her parents have been informed. We can take two hundred people from all over Europe. And we'll start the first treatments at the institute next Friday.'

Oh, God. He's gone full doctor mentor on me. One hundred per cent colleague.

'I'd be happy to help, however you need me to,' she managed as her heart skidded and cracked. His eyes held none of the passion or sparkle he usually reserved for their encounters—not even now, after all his hard work had finally paid off.

'Franco, please don't be like this.'

'Adrienne. I have a life to get on with—as do you. Now, if you'll excuse me—?'

The ringing of his phone cut him off. Tutting, he whipped it from his pocket, and she watched his green eyes widen in surprise at the screen.

'What is it?' she asked, vice-like fear turning her voice tight.

Then her own phone went off.

All the breath left her lungs when she saw the screen. *Oh, no.*

There she was in her swimsuit, right next to Franco, wet, bedraggled, looking undeniably like more than colleagues. It was the photo that man had taken on the beach after they'd rescued little Emma—the one she had all but forgotten about.

He'd caught the exact moment Franco had walked up to her on the rocks and checked that she was OK. His big hands were frozen in motion, cradling her cheeks. Her eyes were gazing up at him in a way that spoke more than a thousand words about her feelings.

'I guess you got sent the same thing,' Franco said, letting out a harangued sigh. 'He must have waited for the right price…which they've given him now the drug trial has been approved because of you.'

Every breath felt tougher than the last. She felt as if the small white room was whirring around her.

This can't be happening.

Mortified, she sank into a chair by the wall. 'Someone from the royal court at Lisri sent it to me,' she said, trembling as reality hit her. 'Which means my parents have seen it.'

Franco's jaw was ticking. His face looked beyond enraged, the skin pinched around flared nostrils. She'd never seen him look like this. She'd humiliated him, just as she'd feared. Being at her side was causing him nothing but pain. To the world, this was confirmation of the rumours, and now he'd be badgered to death.

Her phone rang again. Someone at the royal court was calling her now.

Helplessly, she answered. Papa. The Prince Consort himself was on the end of the line. He wanted her home immediately.

She reminded him he couldn't summon her anywhere—that she wasn't attending the polo this weekend, nor the masquerade ball that followed it every year, that she had work to do at the cancer institute, and for Survive&Thrive.

But he wasn't having any of it. She was going to have to explain herself—issue a statement, which they'd have to construct together, in person, along with the Lisri media. Why had she gone out in a swimsuit, looking as if she was living some cheap Italian holiday romance?

'We'd just saved someone's life, Papa,' she reminded him.

'Do you know how this looks, Adrienne? I appreciate the work you and the doctor are doing is important, but so are we—so is your family name. You're embarrassing the royal family. We sent you there in good faith!'

He went on and on and on, and she wondered where the hell her mother was as she watched Franco by the window, shoulders held stiff, his face like thunder. She wanted to shout at the man who'd only ever half raised her, compared to his wife, her mother, the ever-loving Queen.

You don't care about me at all! You're just furious that none of your blue-blooded suitors will want anything to do with me if they see this!

But that wasn't a conversation she should start on the phone. She was going to have to stand her ground in person if she was going to make them listen to her once and for all.

'I have to go back to Lisri,' she told Franco when she'd hung up.

'I think you probably should,' he replied coolly, and strode from the room.

She sat there for a while, staring unseeingly at the walls, her thoughts a blur. Then she straightened up, gathering herself. Enough was enough. She would not let anyone control her any longer—not her family, not the media. She was the future Queen of Lisri. Even if she and Franco had no future, she had to protect *his* name now as much as her own family's.

CHAPTER TWENTY-FOUR

THE HAT WAS making the back of her head itch and she was hot. Far too hot. Stuffed into the royal box.

She'd left Mirabel in charge of Fiamma and the apartment and flown home just in time to ditch her bags at the house. Having changed into a dress she really didn't feel like wearing, here she was at the polo match, ten minutes before the start. Papa was playing, of course. She'd spotted him on the field already, in his hard hat, royal shirt and jodhpurs, making small talk with someone from the other team.

She raised her hand when he spotted her, and he waved dutifully as if nothing was amiss, putting on a show as usual. Ivan was on watch behind her, this time in a polo shirt. She had a sneaking suspicion that her guard was happy to be back. Things were never as crazy at the palace; no one would dare pap her with the Queen around.

She would talk to Papa later, over dinner. It was how they always did things. She was nervous about the impending conversation, but she had to stand her ground and, more importantly, she had to paint Franco in a new light. The light he deserved.

The players trotted in on their gleaming horses. The sun shone over the mountains in the distance. It should have warmed her heart like the roaring crowds—there was no place like home. But under all her fire and fresh determination the loss of him loomed heavy on her heart. He wanted nothing to do with her now—that much was clear. The photo had been the last straw…just the look on his face had said it all.

He'd loathe this royal life. There was no future for them…even if she did manage to convince her family that a few unwritten rules needed changing.

She'd tried to call him to say goodbye, and to apologise for the unwanted media attention surrounding the photo. It wasn't all bad—not like it had been after Xavier had turned her into the Ice Princess. People, it seemed, loved the hero philanthropist doctor. But that wasn't the real issue here. Franco didn't want all this—the baggage, the fuss. He'd survived a soul-crushing loss and was thriving on his own. He deserved more.

'Darling, you made it.'

Her mother swirled into the royal box in a sea-green dress, her greying hair glistening and styled. Whispers from the stands started up below, but the Queen batted her security away the second she was seated, and Adrienne couldn't help a faint smile.

'It was good of you to come, Adrienne,' her mother said, leaning in and touching her cheek to hers lightly. It was a public version of a mother-daughter kiss.

'I didn't have much of a choice,' Adrienne replied stiffly. 'But it's good to see you, Mother.'

'How are you?'

The Queen's silvery-blue eyes flashed with concern, and Adrienne struggled to hold back the tears.

She smoothed down the satin of her dress, adjusted her oversized hat. 'How do you think I am, Mother? Papa wants me to apologise…to make a statement. He wants me to pretend Franco means nothing to me so he can introduce me to...*them*.'

She gestured to the first row of seats below. A line of men in stuffy suits or too-bright shirts were toasting unknown achievements with champagne and slapping each other on the back. They'd approach her later, one by one, and probe her with questions she didn't want to answer.

'I won't do it, Mother. I won't lie.'

Her mother pursed her lips, stared at the field. The players were parading on the grass now, her father's team in the royal colours: green, orange and blue.

'You really love him, don't you? This doctor.'

Adrienne huffed a breath and leaned into her mother's soft, warm shoulder, summoning strength. 'It doesn't matter any more. He wants nothing to do with me. Can you blame him?'

Her mother stayed quiet, with her 'thinking face' on full display. They watched the match together in silence, but Adrienne barely followed the game. Papa wasn't a bad man, just overprotective, proud and stuck in his ways, and since the Xavier debacle she'd been too meek to confront him for fear of another scene that might embarrass the family.

But now the past was nipping at her heels, no matter how fast she tried to run from it. There was no choice in the matter now. No running away. Facing her family, banishing all subservient habits from her repertoire and paving a new way forward was something she had to do alone.

Franco was gone; he'd given up on her...realised he was better off without her.

Anger sizzled under her grief.

She realised now that she'd been testing Franco all this time. Every time she'd hinted at her real feelings—every time she'd let their flesh touch under a table, or met him in a kiss that spun her whole world upside down. It had all been a test to see how much fight he had. Because he'd need it if he was going to be with her.

Neither of them should have had to fight.

'Don't cry, my love,' her mother whispered.

The horses were a blur. People were looking, pointing, as they always did, and she hid her face, just as she'd done that night when Xavier had been dragged from the ballroom in front of her. Why did this feel even worse?

Xavier had fallen into her lap like a shining meteor, crashing from the sky. He taught her all about sex and red-hot sensual pleasures, showed her how to make love. Just nineteen years old when they'd met, she'd thought she'd known real love. Twelve years later it was clear she'd known nothing back then. She had never loved any man as much as she loved Franco. His happiness was everything to her. Just being in his light was the reason she threw back the covers every morning and faced each day.

Now that he didn't want her the pain was physical, gut-wrenching, as if there was a ball of steel in place of her stomach. Love was more than the act of sex. It felt as if she'd been walking through snow for years, just to reach his fire, only to have it snuffed out right in front of her.

How was she ever going to complete her oncology rotation after this, seeing him each day?

The family dinner was as she'd expected it to be. Her papa came in late, when she and her mother were already seated. Her dress felt too tight, and the cool mountain breeze gushing in through the double doors wasn't quite enough to stop the perspiration building at the back of her neck.

Ignore it. It's time.

The staff fussed around them, serving platters of food and jugs of juice, and she remained quiet at the ten-foot-long table, with her and her mother at one end, the Prince Consort at the other, and family members from the last ten centuries staring at them from the paintings on the walls.

Papa got in first—as soon as the butler was gone.

'You will give an official statement before the ball to-morrow, citing the fact that you were merely caught up in the moment…'

'I will do nothing of the sort.'

'Has our daughter not been through enough?' Her mother spoke now. She'd stood up, shoulders squared. 'We've talked about this, Alex.'

Wait. They'd talked about it already?

'Times have changed. It's a new world and Adrienne is making her place in it. We need to respect that together and honour her choices. That includes our daughter dating and even marrying any man *she* deems suitable for her hand.'

Adrienne fought the smile on her face. She hadn't been entirely sure her mother was on her side, but this was a pleasant surprise. Papa looked a little uncomfortable.

'I do not wish my girls to suffer…either of you,' he said, clearing his throat. 'I am merely trying to help you continue the line of—'

'No, Alex,' the Queen cut in resolutely from behind his chair. 'I love you with all my heart, but…no. There is no need for announcements. We don't need to humiliate this man any more than he's already been humiliated.'

Adrienne was stunned. Her mother had taken the words right out of her mouth.

'And your daughter, Alex—you've seen what she's capable of. She and this great doctor are doing excellent work. They're role models. That is what this country needs. Let them make their own way.'

Except he doesn't want me now, she felt like saying. *The damage is done. It's too late.*

Of course she wouldn't say it.

She put her napkin down, rested her head on her hands. 'I love you, Papa, but no one should have to hide who they really are or what they really want. Not for anything. And that's the message I want to convey as Crown Princess.'

To her surprise, her father sat back in his chair and studied her quietly for a moment. Then he shook his head, hiding a smile. 'How did I know this day would come?' He paused. 'I'm proud of you, Adrienne.'

Her mother swept towards the door, beckoning Adrienne to go with her.

'Of course you're proud of her—you tell me that all the time. It's about time you said it to her face instead. Now, come, my Princess. I'm expected in the kitchen. I've been baking the most wonderful cake for the ball tomorrow. If your Papa continues to behave, perhaps we'll save him a slice...'

CHAPTER TWENTY-FIVE

SURVIVE&THRIVE WAS THE talk of the masked ball. As the orchestra played and the guests danced and drank, everyone who came up to her had something to say about it. The app was up to over a million downloads now, and some of the patients due to take part in the trial had given more interviews—including Rosita, who was turning into somewhat of a Survive&Thrive mascot.

'What a great job.'

'You must have really impressed Dr Perretta.'

'Think about how many lives you might save!'

'What's going on with that guy, anyway?'

Of course people had been asking her about him, too. Every time someone said his name her heart sank.

Adrienne fixed her hair around her mask in the lavish bathroom, resting her hands for a moment on the cool tiles, wishing she could escape this silly thing. Then again, flying back to Naples, to Franco's inevitable disdain, was not a comforting prospect either. She still hadn't heard from him. She'd tried to call, but his phone had either rung out or he'd denied her calls. Frustration ate at her insides. And she hadn't slept properly since she'd left Naples.

At least Papa seemed amicable, she thought, once she was back in the opulent ballroom, with its candles flickering from every wall. Ten-foot-high paintings of royal ancestors peered over the evening's entertainment, and all the Dukes and Barons and Lords she was trying to avoid. She knew they'd try it on even without being encouraged by her father.

Not that she could tell who anyone was behind their masks. There were so many people here, their faces all obscured or partly hidden.

'Excuse me, Adrienne? Might I have a word?'

'So sorry—have to go.'

She gathered her floor-length gown and turned away from the oncoming Count, watching Papa work the room with his crowd of aristocratic cronies on the side-lines.

He'd conceded last night—in the kitchen, no less—that perhaps he'd pushed her a little too far. He'd even apologised for what had happened with Xavier all those years ago and promised to support her going forward. She'd resisted the urge to say *Too little, too late*—something about the look her mother had given her had stopped her in her tracks.

Whatever the Queen wanted was his wish too, he'd said. He'd also agreed that her mother's cake was the best he'd tasted in a long time.

'Princess Adrienne?'

The male voice behind her caused a lurch of nausea. When would they all just *stop*? The music was loud now, and she could barely hear what the man was saying. He was standing some three feet away, a picture of masculine elegance in the spotlights. His mask was all black feathers, with a crow's beak protruding in her direction, and it concealed his entire face. His suit looked like the stuff of a talented royal tailor. She had to admit he looked damn fine in it. He was looking her up and down in silent appreciation, and whereas usually she'd turn the other way something drew her closer.

'I have to warn you, if you're about to ask me to dance, or if you're about to try and woo me, it won't work. My heart is taken,' she heard herself say.

Better to warn him straight away—so he knew. It was going to take her a long time to get over Franco, even if they'd never even really got started.

Over his shoulder, she caught her mother watching with interest.

The crow stepped even closer. 'Who stole your heart?' he asked.

She realised the crowd around her had gone quiet. People were whispering, watching her, and the spotlights felt hot on the satin fabric of her dress. She held her head high, knowing Papa was probably watching too. And all the other men who wanted a piece of her.

'If you must know, his name is Franco Perretta,' she said, directly to the crow in front of her. 'You might have seen a photo of us, which was taken without our permission? He saved a girl's life that day.'

The crow cocked his head. All eyes were on them both now. She might as well keep going.

'He's a leader,' she proclaimed, squaring her shoulders. 'He's funny, and kind, and he always speaks the truth—right from here.'

She clamped a fist to her heart, and the crow's eyes narrowed inside the slits of the mask.

Sucking in a breath, she prayed for her voice not to tremble. 'He tells a story like no one else I know, and if he loves you, he loves you *fiercely*, with *everything* he has. He's the greatest doctor I know. The most passionate, inspiring human I know. Any woman would be lucky to have him. And we're going to save a lot more lives together… just as soon as I can get out of here.'

The crow was silent for a long time, watching her as

her heart pounded in a galloping beat. The music played on softly, but no one was speaking.

Maybe she'd said too much?

Swallowing her nerves, Adrienne almost turned to hurry from the room.

But the crow's hand caught her bare arm, just below the sleeve of her gown. The touch made her reel in swift recognition.

Gasping, she reached for his mask. 'Franco!' she cried as it dropped to the floor and feathers scattered across the tiles.

Her hands flew to her mouth. She blinked, not sure whether to laugh, cry or be furious.

'Franco,' she said again on an exhalation. It came out as more of a sob this time.

He pulled her in close, firm against his chest, cradling the back of her head and shielding her from the onlookers. Her hands found the lapels of his jacket, and her nostrils sucked in his familiar scent as if it was a life force.

'That was quite a speech,' he whispered in her ear, tangling one hand in her hair.

How was this real? Her legs felt as if they might fail beneath her.

'What are you doing here?'

'Your mother invited me.'

What?

He took her shoulders and she watched his green eyes dart around the room as people lifted their masks to get a better look at him—at *them*. Someone started clapping. Then someone else—the Count—followed suit.

'I couldn't refuse the Queen, could I?'

To Adrienne's utter shock, her mother raised her hand at Franco in greeting, and then the entire room erupted in an enormous cheer. He turned back to her, grazing her lips with his sea-green eyes. Then he swept her face to his in with one gentle, insistent palm and kissed her.

The room disappeared. The music grew louder, but Adrienne felt as if she was dreaming. She let him lead her towards her mother…watched him bow to her and smile, and laugh about something. Then, to her utter shock, she watched Papa give him the kind of handshake he usually reserved for royalty.

Surreal. She couldn't imagine what it must be like for Franco.

Later, out in the rose garden, he explained how her mother had summoned him, told him he was free to date Adrienne if he felt the same way *she* felt. She'd said she would come down hard on any publication that dared to pester them too much or darken either of their names.

'And the Baron…?'

'I wasn't ever concerned that you had feelings for him,' he said, cupping her face.

The Lisri moonlight accentuated every line and angle of his handsome face as he caressed her cheek, and she couldn't wait to get him alone, away from all these people, behind closed doors. Could she even dare to hope for a future for them now? So many questions were hanging on her lips, but he seemed to have all the answers.

'I was angry at myself more than you, for thinking that my privacy and the chip on my shoulder about my lack of blue blood were more important than the work we have to do together…the future we might build. You're my inspiration. You're standing up for the life you really want, and changing so many other people's lives while you're at it.'

'I don't care about your lineage, but I know your privacy is important to you, Franco. You hate the spotlight.

And being with me…that's a lot to take on. Even if I don't take the crown for another thirty or forty years!'

'Well, I guess that will give me plenty of time to get used to it,' he said, making her heart hammer under her dress. He was serious.

A lazy smile stretched his face. His kiss was all the answer she needed. He lingered, tilting her chin towards the moonlight, touching his lips to hers as if savouring the moment.

'I've had some pretty efficient defences up for a very long time,' he said. 'I didn't expect a royal superstar to blaze in and turn my life upside down.'

She smiled in his arms. 'I do apologise.'

'I forgive you,' he said as a firework lit up the sky from the palace rooftop. 'And I love you so much. I know it won't all be smooth sailing—far from it. Even if your mother does come down hard on the media in our defence.'

'Not as hard as I will if anyone dares attack my future Prince,' she told him, eyes narrowed.

She knew without a doubt that she'd have no problem speaking her mind about anything from now on. The press would always find something to talk about. The Ice Princess had melted, after all. They just had to ensure they were talking about the right things. Their work. Their values. Their goals.

Franco trailed a finger up her arm, along the seam of her dress to the flesh of her cleavage, then to her lips. 'I kind of like the sound of being your Prince,' he said, and breathlessly she sank into his kiss, letting herself fall a little further.

Whatever happened now, with Franco at her side, and her country cheering her on, she would be ready.

CHAPTER TWENTY-SIX

Six months later

'FRANCO! FRANCO, HOW do I look?'

Rosita hurried over to him in the garden, with Adrienne's cat, Fiamma, under one arm. Her loose, silky black hair swung around her shoulders, and she looked a picture of health in her rose-coloured satin dress.

'Do I look OK for the rehearsal photos?'

Franco stopped in his tracks with Benni, admiring his radiant Survive&Thrive ambassador and patient as she stood in the light of the flaming torches circling the icy lake. She'd become quite close to Adrienne, and she was gaining a following of her own.

'You and Alina are the most beautiful bridesmaids a man and a crown princess could wish for,' he said. 'What are you worried about?'

Rosita beamed at him and snuggled her face into the cat's fur. She'd taken full ownership of him lately, since Adrienne had been so busy, and he had an inkling the responsibility had given her a reason to get up each morning. She had a thousand reasons now.

He watched her take his niece's hand. Alina had been so excited ever since his brother and his family had flown in on the royal jet. Meeting the Queen and his bride-to-be the Crown Princess all in one day, then touring the royal palace with the Prince Consort was a story she'd be telling for months.

'I think Rosita's worried about her hair,' Benni said to him as they watched the girls hurry towards the others, past the twinkling fairy lights that had made a dream world of the royal palace's garden.

'But it's grown back beautifully,' Franco told him. 'And she didn't lose half the hair she might have done if we hadn't got her on that trial.'

They'd all been flown here to Lisri for the wedding—every one of them at Adrienne's insistence. Mr Geordano was here, Diodoro and his partner, and Candice. And the housekeeper Mirabel, who flushed every time she saw him, as if she was still embarrassed over asking him if he had an appointment that time after Adrienne's motorcycle accident.

It seemed everyone was thriving since the Crown Princess had arrived at the Institute. Even little Emma, the girl they'd rescued on the beach that day, was here with her mother. Adrienne had invited everyone who'd made an impression on her since she'd met him, which was so typically *her*.

It was going to be the royal wedding of the century. This was only the rehearsal, so tomorrow he'd probably be sick with nerves. But of course there was no way he'd show it. He'd been more nervous pulling the ring out when he'd proposed, in case she said no.

He'd taken her out on the yacht, just the two of them, two months ago. Someone had told him the dolphins had come back, and she'd cried when she saw them. She'd cried even more when he'd dropped to one knee and the whole pod had leapt from the water in their wake, as if they knew they had to impress her, too.

'Franco!'

Adrienne was sweeping down the steps now, with a backdrop of dramatic stormy clouds behind her, the Queen and Prince Consort Alex either side of her. 'Franco, we need a photo,' she said.

He was struck by her beauty all over again. The huge diamond on her finger looked as if it was on fire, reflecting the torches all around them.

Benni nudged him, bringing him back to earth.

'You got the girl of your dreams,' he reminded him, and it crossed Franco's mind, for just the fastest flicker of a second, that his brother had never said that about Luci.

But maybe he'd just been too young when he'd proposed to her. Too young to think too much about the future and what he really wanted from life. He knew now. He'd never thought about anything as hard as he'd had to think about becoming half of Lisri's new power couple. He'd thought about Luci the night before he'd proposed to Adrienne. In a way, his love for her had brought him here. He hoped somewhere, somehow, she was at peace with his decision.

Now, in her ankle length silver-grey dress, with a wreath of roses and a snug faux-fur-lined shawl, Adrienne looked every inch the Crown Princess. An outdoor winter wedding was something different, but it wasn't as if she'd ever have settled for something so pedestrian as Lisri's cathedral.

Something in her eyes made her look panicked for a second as she took his hands. Her father flashed his gaze towards him, then to the Queen, then cleared his throat.

'How about a photograph of Franco and the Queen and I first?' he asked. 'Benni, Aimee and Marco, too,' he added, beckoning them over. 'We all know you're like royalty in Naples.'

Prince Alex winked, to his surprise. He'd never seen

Adrienne's father wink at anyone before. It was nice to see how much he'd lightened up lately. Maybe he was happy to be unburdened of the weight of his own redundant rules, now they were being broken on a daily basis.

Adrienne dropped a kiss to her father's cheek. 'That's a great idea,' she said. Then she whispered, 'Thank you, Papa.'

Adrienne beamed and Franco smoothed his tailored jacket for the photo. It was emblazoned with the royal crest on the pocket. He was still getting used to how things were around the royal family of Lisri. It was a life he never could have imagined, even though they'd been living in Naples, continuing much as normal, albeit with a few obligations on certain weekends back here.

Further down the line, when Adrienne became Queen, they'd move here to the palace, to a home on the grounds they were designing together. He would be ready for it. Ready for the life they were already building.

'Our suite is all ready for tomorrow. I saw the chamber-maids going in with champagne and candles,' she whispered once their photos were done, sweeping him to one side while the photographers fussed and snapped more photos of the guests behind them.

He drew her in, pressed a kiss to her forehead, and she shuddered in his arms suddenly. 'I am nervous,' she said. 'More nervous about that than everyone watching us walk down the aisle, when we'll be televised around the world.'

'Why?' He almost laughed as he touched a hand to her flushed cheek, letting the faux fur shawl tickle his fingers. 'There won't be any cameras on our wedding night.' He smiled, leaning in. 'How will I survive tonight in our separate rooms?'

People were watching, but he was used to that now. She bit her lip, adjusting his tie, her mouth an inch from his. 'You'll just have to try. And tomorrow I will worship every part of you, for as long as I deem fit, as your wife,' she said, touching her lips to his in a way that made him want to pull her in by her hips in front of everyone. 'Over and over and over and—'

'Adrienne? We need you and the Survive&Thrive guests next. One for the website. Are you ready?'

Adrienne gave him a look that only he could see—one that spoke volumes about the lack of sleep they would both be experiencing on their wedding night. He rooted his feet to the floor as she floated back towards her guests, and he caught Rosita grinning at him knowingly.

Damn, he would have to get better at withholding the PDAs—but at least the press were only writing positive things about them now, portraying them as role models in love, career aspirations and everything else.

He made his way back to Benni, Aimee and his father. Benni slapped him on the back. 'Hey, Franco, we were just talking about the royal wedding dolls they've made of you both. Did you know Dad's ordered a hundred already, to give as gifts to the kids at the institute?'

Franco rolled his eyes. OK, so some things would take more getting used to than others, going forward. But they had support and allies all around them now. For ever with the Crown Princess of Lisri was going to be one hell of a ride...but he couldn't wait to get started.

* * * * *

ISLAND REUNION WITH THE SINGLE DAD

TRACI DOUGLASS

MILLS & BOON

To Princess Clara.
See you across the Rainbow Bridge.
Love and miss you, missy poo. <3

And to my Zoom Writing Cohort.
Thank you Aleks, Carol, and Lucy,
for all the words and support and wonderful chats.
Couldn't have gotten through this without you!

CHAPTER ONE

Dr. Morgan Salas stared at the large wooden sign near the pebbled beach, with its carved twin eagles and painted seascape, an image of the car ferry she'd just departed across the bottom. She took a deep breath of fresh Pacific Northwest air drifting through the window of the sedan, the late-September air crisp with the scents of fallen leaves and recent rainfall. For the first time in recent memory, she felt...happy. Lighter. More hopeful. Maybe she could find some measure of the peace and contentment she'd lost when Ben died. She had a month here. Perhaps it would be enough.

She'd enjoyed the trip from Mukilteo, Washington, on the mainland to the tiny, quaint coastal town of Clinton on the island. She'd had twenty minutes on the ferry to just enjoy the scenery and leave her cares behind. Hopefully. Maybe. Okay, probably not, but she was working on it.

From what she'd researched online, Whidbey Island was known for its "reserved individuality" and "effortless ease." She prayed some of that ease would rub off on her while she was here. First, though, now that she was on dry land again, she had to get to her appointment on the other side of the island near Freeland.

Morgan checked out the open window of her rented

sedan for oncoming traffic on the two-lane asphalt ahead, then managed to get around a few slower-moving cars until she was on the open roadway again. Cool wind in her hair, she passed several signs as she headed out of Clinton for the Scenic Isle Way, part of the Cascade Loop and the only section entirely contained within an island. She'd read about that, too, being something of a fact geek. The views here were gorgeous, no doubt. The knot between her shoulder blades and a bit more of her old anger and grief drifted away. And sure, maybe the roads here were bit narrow and…whoa! Those hairpin turns seemed to come out of nowhere, but it was all good. She'd take it slow and steady. That always won the race, right?

Well, usually. Unless someone cheated. Like Ben did.

Her pulse kicked a notch higher as she glanced at the clock in the dashboard. Twenty minutes.

She could still make it on time, barring any more hold-ups. She hated being late.

Except just ahead, traffic had slowed again. *Dammit.* Morgan slowed, then leaned out the window, craning her neck to see the problem. It was the middle of nowhere, farm fields bordered by forest on either side. But a slight incline ahead kept her from seeing beyond it. Huh. In the distance, animals grazed, and she spotted a few tourists gawking and taking pictures.

What could possibly be out here to cause such a ruckus?

Ugh. Morgan did not have time for this. Not today, anyway. So, after checking again for oncoming traffic, she nosed out of line into the opposite lane then hurried up the incline, thinking she'd bypass the crowd. Except when she got to the top of the hill, all she saw was sheep. Sheep everywhere. Including a big one square in her lane.

Alarmed, Morgan slammed on the brakes, only to have her back tires fishtail off the still-wet asphalt. *Crap.* Silence thudded loud in her ears as the sheep in front of her watched impassively, chewing its cud. Cursing, Morgan tapped her accelerator, hoping to nudge all four tires back onto the roadway. Except that, coupled with the slick and muddy berm, only made her slide farther into the ditch. Hands shaking, she closed her eyes as she careened backward, heart pounding, praying she wouldn't end up as a warning story on the news. *Woman illegally passes traffic, ends up trapped and dead beneath a ton of flipped steel. Kids, don't try this at home.*

In the end, though, the sedan's back end came to rest gently against the trunk of a huge pine tree while the front half of the car climbed crookedly up toward the road like a drunken college coed after a bender.

Lord, help her. She hadn't even been here an hour and things were already going downhill. Literally.

After a quick full-body shake to disperse some excess adrenaline and make sure she wasn't injured, Morgan set about figuring out how to get unstuck from her current situation. Her train of thought was quickly derailed, however, by the passenger door flying open. Stunned, she stared wide-eyed at the last person she'd ever expected to see again.

Ely.

No last name. They'd never exchanged them. The one-night stand she'd never forgotten.

Not even after ten years.

"Are you okay?" he asked, cutting through her befuddled thoughts.

"Uh…" Morgan frowned.

Am I okay? Maybe I hit my head after all, and this is all a hallucination.

She took a deep breath and gave a small prayer of

thanks that at least he didn't seem to recognize her. "Uh... yes. I think I'm—"

"Hang on a minute and let me check you over." Before she could finish, he'd reached over from the passenger side to run his hands over her arms and legs, checking for injury, but that only made her scalp tingle more.

"Stop. Please!" Out of sorts and far too aware of his hands on her body, she pulled away, heat prickling her cheeks. "I'm fine. Just a little shaken. Thank you."

Her voice trembled, to her eternal mortification. This was ridiculous. Ely was just a man. A man she'd had sex with, once upon a time. Also, a man who obviously didn't even remember her anyway. She was making a huge deal out of nothing. He shouldn't affect her like this. She obviously didn't affect him at all. Ely didn't seem to care in the least.

Well, other than the fact he was trying to get her out of her predicament. Okay. Fine. That part was helpful. She peered past his broad shoulder toward the crest of the ditch, where the same tourists who'd been photographing the sheep were now snapping pictures of her. Perfect. Exactly how she wanted to start her monthlong stint on the island. As a photo op. Morgan cleared her throat and fiddled with her horribly wrinkled shirt to avoid looking at him. "Did anyone else slide off the road?"

"Nope," Ely said, his tone a bit curt now, his expression clearly irritated. He leaned back, muscled arms braced on the door frame, filling the space like he had a right to, sucking up all her oxygen. He shrugged, then narrowed his gaze on her. "Probably because no one else was driving like a maniac. These roads get very slick after a rain. You could've killed yourself or someone else pulling a stunt like that."

Her hackles rose, her chest tight. "First of all, I'm not

a maniac. I have an important meeting to get to. And second, doesn't it rain all the time in the Pacific Northwest? That's kind of what you're known for it, isn't it?"

She forced herself to inhale. Arguing with him wouldn't get her out of this any sooner, and she couldn't risk missing her appointment. Time to end this here and now. And if that meant swallowing her pride, fine. "Sorry. You're right." She bit her tongue and forced a smile. "I wasn't thinking. Can you help me get out of here, please?"

"Of course." His voice and expression softened, and her heart did a weird little flip.

Damn. He looked so much like she remembered. Dark and handsome and windswept, his smile revealing dimples in his cheeks. Lord, she'd forgotten the devastating effect those dimples had on her common sense. Ely hiked his chin toward the door behind her and said, "Hop out and I'll see if I can't get you steered back onto the road."

Still dazed and shaky, Morgan undid her seat belt and opened the driver's side door. Stepped out on wobbly knees, only to find her new shoes stuck in mud almost up to her ankles. Before she could despair too much, Ely was beside her, his tawny gaze twinkling as he tried, and failed, to keep his smile from growing into a full-blown grin.

"Go on and help her out, Ely!" someone shouted from up top.

"Put those capable hands of yours to good use, Doc!" another guy yelled.

Blood whooshed in her ears, and Morgan wondered if it was possible to die from embarrassment. Because it certainly felt like she could, especially when Ely grabbed her around the waist and lifted her into his arms. A sucking sound echoed as her feet popped free of the muck, but all she could focus on was the feel of his hard chest against her, the heat of him through her clothes, his clean scent of soap and sandalwood. She'd forgotten how tall he was, a good foot above her own five-four. Strong, too. An unwanted shock of desire curled her toes inside her ruined pumps, and Morgan pushed hard against him. "Put me down, please."

He walked a few feet over to a grassy area and did as she asked. Their gazes locked and time slowed as the years drifted away. Suddenly they were back on a beach on this very island. Two young, stupid college kids living like there was no tomorrow.

Except life had taught her too well that there was always a day after.

"Sorry." She looked away, not sure why she was apologizing. Her stomach clenched, even though she'd done nothing wrong. Neither had he. Ely blinked down at her a beat or two, then took her hand to silently lead her up the side of the ditch to the berm. People clapped as they emerged at the summit, and she tried to look less discombobulated than she felt.

Morgan hated unwanted attention. The glare of the spotlight. The constant searing scald of gossip. She'd gotten more than enough of that after Ben's funeral. The whispers behind her back from the staff at the hospital. Conversations ending abruptly whenever she appeared.

Even though rationally she knew this was different, it felt all too similar. Moving stiffly, she sidled off to the side as Ely went back down into the ditch to gun the sedan's engine, sending a spray of mud flying as he zoomed the car back up onto the roadway. The crowd finally dispersed.

He left the engine running and walked back to Morgan, stopping a foot or so away from her.

"You've got…" he said, frowning.

"What?" Scowling, Morgan self-consciously wiped her cheek.

"No. The other side. Here." Ely tipped her chin up with a finger, then swiped his thumb across her jaw. Her lungs tightened and she thought she might pass out, completing her humiliation. Her skin still tingled even after he let her go. "There. Gone. Just a speck of mud."

"Oh..." she mumbled, touching the spot, nearly drowning in his eyes before pulling herself to safety. Flustered, she smoothed her hands down the front of her pantsuit to make sure nothing else was stained or missing. Yep. She must've hit her head and knocked something loose. Like her common sense.

Doing her best to regain her composure, Morgan stepped away and gave him her most polite smile, the one that appeased even her most irascible patients. "Thank you so much for your help. Now I need to go. Please excuse me."

Gah!

Unfortunately, Morgan had no idea how to greet an old one-night stand. Probably because she'd thought she'd never see him again. He'd never called afterward, even though she'd given him her number, so obviously he hadn't been interested.

Things had changed so much. *She* had changed so much.

"No problem," Ely called after her as she walked back to her sedan. "Take it easy on these roads. Next time you might not be so lucky, and I won't be there to help."

Feeling like a five-year-old who'd gotten caught eating paste, she climbed into the car and resisted thunking her forehead on the steering wheel. *Good Lord.* The last thing she needed right now was driving advice from the guy she'd banged on the beach a decade prior.

As calmly as possible, Morgan refastened her seat belt, checked her mirrors, then started down the road again with her hands at ten and two. She needed to focus on her meeting and not on the gorgeous man from her past, who was growing smaller by the second in her rearview mirror.

Dr. Elyas Malik stood there along the roadside, watching Morgan's car drive away, still a bit flummoxed. Who'd have thought helping a farmer herd his sheep off the roadway would lead to an unexpected reunion with the one girl he'd never quite forgotten?

Morgan.

After getting back into his old truck, Ely headed for home to change his clothes before he returned to the clinic. About a mile down the main road, he signaled, then turned off onto a winding lane that led through the countryside surrounding Wingate. The huge compound had belonged to his parents, his father's pride and joy. It was nothing like Ely would ever have bought for himself, though. But after the plane crash, he and his brother, Sam, had inherited his father's tech empire and everything that went with it. And while Ely had still pursued his dreams of becoming a doctor, his little brother, Sam, had chosen to take over the family business. Ely stayed at Wingate and Sam lived mainly in New York City, though he came back a few times a year to visit.

Most days, he didn't think about the money. It was just a part of him. He was privileged and he knew it, and he did his best to always give back to others, both in his work and his life. But today, Wingate, his vast, sustainable home, was at the top of his mind, probably because the anniversary of his parents' deaths was coming up next month. In fact, the internet was already awash with old photos of Ely's parents and the rise of the techno-titan his father had become.

He still missed them, even after all these years, and because of them and what had happened to them when he'd been just eighteen, family was the most important thing for him. He was happy here on Whidbey Island, living his little, private life, with his son, Dylan. And yes, his own ill-fated marriage hadn't worked out, but he'd gotten full custody after his divorce, mainly because his ex-wife, Raina, traveled so much for her job as a successful supermodel, and they both wanted Dylan to have some stability in his life. So, Ely's main goal in life was to be present for his son. Sunday dinners, the holidays and the warm, fuzzy nights playing board games by the fire. But unfortunately, he was also a busy doctor with a thriving practice.

He made another turn and pulled up to the keypad near the metal gates at the entrance. Punched in his code, then waited while the gates slid open before heading up the steep drive to the house. Modern architecture full of steel and glass sparkled in the hazy sunshine. Gardens and greenhouses and several experimental labs sprawled around the main residence, generating sustainable crops grown only with water and air. It all fit right in with the Whidbey Island vibe.

Every day, Ely was reminded of the great man his father had been, and how he'd failed to live up to his father's lofty ideals. Every day, Ely vowed to do better. For himself. For Dylan. There were many things money couldn't buy, and he knew that better than most.

He hurried inside to change his clothes then get back to work, where his colleague Dr. Gregory Anderson was waiting to introduce Ely to his new temporary partner for the month of October while Dr. Greg and his wife took a much-needed and well-deserved vacation to Australia.

"Ely," Mrs. MacIntosh, his housekeeper, called up to him when he was halfway up the stairs. "Is that you?"

"Yes. Why? In kind of a rush," Ely called as he continued to his rooms on the second floor. In his bedroom, he quickly stripped off his mud-splattered shirt and dress pants before hopping in the shower. After a quick scrub, he pulled on a fresh pair of pants, plus a shirt and tie. Smoothed a hand through his dark hair that always had a mind of its own, a flash of memory rushing through his mind, making his breath catch.

Morgan. Their night on the beach, bathed in starlight and nothing else. They'd both been so young then, so naive. The world had changed now. For him, at least.

He swallowed hard, pushing those memories away. No. Life marched onward. You either went with it, got out of the way or got run over by it. And Ely was determined never to be roadkill again.

CHAPTER TWO

MORGAN PULLED INTO the clinic parking lot at six fifteen and sighed. The place looked brand-new, due to a recent remodel Dr. Greg had mentioned. Squaring her shoulders, she changed her shoes, then took a deep breath and headed inside to where Dr. Greg waited for her in the reception area, looking the same as he always had—like an older Cary Grant. Same twinkling eyes, same square-jawed handsomeness, same tall, elegant frame.

"Morgan, my dear." He enveloped her in a big hug. "I was worried. The ferry company told me they'd arrived right on time. Was the traffic bad?"

"Sort of." No way was she telling him about the ditch incident with Ely. She returned his hug, then pulled back to smile up at him, leaving his question unanswered. "Well, I'm here now, and it's so good to see you."

"Same." He held her by the shoulders and looked her up and down. "Last time I saw you, you were still slogging away as a resident. You'd just gotten married." She did her best to hide the fact he'd basically sucker punched her in the feels, but obviously not well, because he hugged her once more. "I'm so sorry. Your father told me about Ben. What a horrible thing he did."

Horrible *doesn't begin to cover it.*

Inhaling deep, Morgan nodded, then stepped back

again, forcing a tremulous smile. "Yes. Thanks. It was pretty bad."

The loss. The cheating.

She cleared her too-tight throat, then tucked her hair behind her ear, desperate to change the subject. "But I'm here and ready to work. Where's your partner?"

"Dr. Malik called just before you arrived and said he's on his way."

"Great." Morgan glanced down and noticed a tiny spot of mud on her wrist. *Crap.* She brushed it away fast, remembering the feel of Ely's thumb on her skin, and damn if her traitorous skin didn't tingle again. Annoyed with herself, she shoved all those messy emotions aside. "Um, if you don't mind, I'll pop into the restroom and freshen up."

"Absolutely. Take your time."

Alone, Morgan stared at her reflection in the mirror. The new haircut, the new clothes, the same old wariness lurking in her eyes. *Get a grip, girl.* Once upon a time, she'd been a trusting fool. No more.

She washed her hands then headed out to the waiting room again.

"Perfect timing. Dr. Malik's here and waiting for us in the conference room," Dr. Greg said. "Since we're running a bit late already, maybe he can show you around the place in the morning. Don't want to be late for our dinner reservations in town. Afterward, Peggy and I will take you to the cottage where you'll be staying while you're here. Sound good?"

"Absolutely."

"Follow me, then." Dr. Greg led her down a hall lined with exam rooms that ended in a large, circular nurses' station from which other hallways spoked off, like a wheel. The conference room sat at the back of the facility, lined on one side with floor-to-ceiling tinted windows, giving them gorgeous views of the sunset and Puget Sound in the distance. You could still smell the fresh paint and drywall in the air. Morgan proceeded Dr. Greg in, then turned to greet the man sitting at the far end of the long table, overhead lights gleaming off his freshly showered damp hair, his brown skin glowing against his crisp white shirt.

Oh, no. No, no, no.

For a moment Morgan stood speechless. This could not be happening. Ely could not be the doctor she'd work with for the next month. Nope. Ten years with no contact at all, and now she'd seen him twice in one day. This was bad. So bad. Morgan did not handle surprises well anymore, and this was the second whopper in one day. Her pulse jackhammered against her temples and beat in her gums.

"Dr. Salas." Ely stood and walked down the length of the table, his tawny gaze unreadable. To the side, she felt Dr. Greg's gaze boring into her as well, the back of her neck prickling. She barely heard Ely's words over the thump on her own heart. "I hope your trip here was pleasant. Sorry I was late. I had to assist a stranded motorist. Got their vehicle stuck in a ditch."

He was acting like he didn't know her, like the accident in the ditch didn't happen.

Right. Okay. It took a moment for her brain to catch up to the reality racing around her and for her to realize that she needed to act, to respond, to do the job she'd come here for, because there was no alternative. She'd already given notice at her job in Boston and sublet her apartment there. Whidbey Island was her last resort—for the next month, at least. If this didn't work out, she'd have to find something else fast. She didn't have enough savings to survive long without a job. Six months in Africa had eaten through her nest egg.

Ely sat as well, across from her, still pretending he

didn't know her from Adam. Maybe he didn't—not any-more. "This shouldn't take too long, Dr. Salas. Dr. Greg assures me you're the right person to fill the temporary vacancy, and at this late stage, I must believe him. He couldn't say enough good things about you."

She blinked at him, nodded, still trying to gather her thoughts, feeling oddly numb now.

"We're lucky to get her, Ely," Dr. Greg said. "Morgan's very in demand."

She wasn't, but appreciated the boost of confidence.

"Well, then." Ely steepled his fingers, watching her over the top of them. "Tell me why you chose our little island."

Our little island...

His gaze had gone chillier now, and she got the distinct impression he knew. He remembered their night together as well as she did. But he was pretending he didn't. Which meant he was lying. Morgan didn't deal well with liars, either. Not after Ben. Voice tight, she said, "I recently re-turned from a mission in Africa, and I want to do good and be part of a community."

"I see." He glanced down at her hands, clenched atop the table, then met her eyes again. "Dr. Salas, I won't lie."

Really? Her mind spun. *Because you just did, about us.*

"I have my concerns. Mainly the fact you don't have much GP experience. It says on your CV you worked as an ER physician in Boston. Is that correct?"

She nodded, nausea building inside her.

"And you're recently back from a mission trip in Africa as well. This clinic might be a big change for you. Perhaps too big. All that adrenaline-fueled medicine is a big con-trast from Whidbey Island." He sighed, his gaze flicking to Dr. Greg as he flashed a rueful smile. "We do have our moments, though, right?"

Dr. Greg chuckled. "Right."

"This is what I want," Morgan said, struggling to salvage what was left of the situation. "Peace. Quiet. A chance to slow down and decide what to do next." She glanced out the windows, wishing she were out on the water. She always felt better on the water. "I like being by the sea."

The water had brought her here all those years ago, too.

"I've talked to her, Ely," Dr. Greg added. "She knows what to expect."

Do I?

Morgan was starting to doubt it now.

"I've still got my sailboat, too, Morgan," Dr. Greg chimed in, cutting through the roar of emotional clutter in her head. "Feel free to take *The Nightingale* while you're here. Please. I don't get out on her as much these days, with my hip replacement and all, but Ely takes good care of her for me. I'm sure he'd be delighted to take you out on the sound sometime."

Ely returned his colleague's smile, and Morgan's heart stuttered. His tawny eyes creased at the corners, and his dimples showed.

Stop! Abort! Abort!

She shook her head, straightening her spin.

Get it together. Now. Don't mess up this job. You need it.

The next hour passed swiftly. Her credentials were impeccable, as was her professional experience. She'd spent some time in family practice during her medical school rotations and had certainly seen her share of basic cases through the ER in Boston as well, so the adjustment shouldn't be as glaring as Ely thought. And Morgan expected this new practice would pose its own set of challenges, too.

"We're the best-equipped clinic on the southern half of the island and serve several communities, including Langley, Freeland, Clinton and Greenbank, as well as the small villages in between," Dr. Greg said once Ely's questions for her had run out. She answered them all as appropriately as possible, or at least she hoped she did, though she couldn't quite remember what she'd said.

Luckily, Dr. Greg kept talking, giving her something else to focus on besides Ely. "We can handle most things here. Ely's a double fellow in both general practice and pediatrics. He's also got extensive experience in ob-gyn. Our on-call schedule is pretty straightforward, too," Dr. Greg went on. "You'll have every second night and weekend on and the others off. Sound workable?"

She nodded. "Yep. I like to stay busy."

Busy had kept her sane the past two years.

"We're all sorted, then." Dr. Greg stood. "Morgan, let's go get some dinner, shall we? Ely, are you sure you won't join us? I can add another name to our reservation."

"No, thanks. Need to get home. But give my love to Peggy and have a wonderful trip. Don't worry about anything here. We'll be fine." Ely pushed to his feet. "I'll check in on you tomorrow, Dr. Salas. Make sure you have everything you need."

"Okay," she said, but he was already gone. She watched his retreating back down the hallway. "I don't think he's okay with me being here."

"Ely's a tough nut to crack," Dr. Greg admitted, then shrugged. "He'll open up more as he gets to know you. You'll see."

Morgan's heart sank. Maybe Ely had it right, keeping their distance and pretending there was nothing between them. Working together every day would be hard enough. Maybe she should just keep her head down and get through it. More drama in life was not on her list of things she needed, and this job was supposed to be a fresh start, not a new source of complications—especially ones like Ely.

Dr. Greg put an arm around her shoulders and added, "Don't worry, Morgan." He walked her back out to the lobby, then turned off the lights. "Ely's a good man. You can trust him."

But that was the trouble. She didn't trust anyone anymore. Not after Ben. She'd been there, done that, had her heart and future trampled on to prove it. And no matter what she and Ely might have shared in the past, Morgan wasn't sure she could ever trust him—or another man—again.

Ely drove home to Wingate, the twin beams of his headlights glowing on the quiet two-lane road. His thoughts were anything but quiet, though, looping around again and again to Morgan. Seeing her in that ditch had been jarring enough. Then learning they'd be working closely together for the next month…

Well, he wasn't quite sure how that would turn out, but his instincts told him it wasn't good.

He liked his small circle of family and friends and didn't let new people in often. The sudden loss of his parents had taught him that letting people too close only led to pain and heartache.

So having her reappear in his life out of the blue was unsettling, to say the least. Then there was the old awareness, the connection, flaring bright and vibrant as ever between them. She'd tried to play it off, tried to pretend it wasn't there, but it was undeniable. Always had been. Sizzling between them whenever they were close. He'd never had that with anyone else. Not even Raina.

But it spooked him, too. Ely got through life these days by staying in control. Protecting those he cared for and making wise, logical decisions. By not taking risks.

And Morgan all but had a neon sign above her head flashing Risky As Hell.

Dammit. It was his own fault, really. No one else to blame. He should've insisted on reviewing the details of the person Dr. Greg had insisted was the best choice for his temporary replacement. But he'd been so busy schedulewise lately, between the clinic and Dylan starting a new year at school, that he'd gone with whatever Dr. Greg wanted. The man had become something of a surrogate father to Ely, and if the new person was good enough for Dr. Greg, they were good enough for Ely.

He just wished it wasn't Morgan.

Not because he didn't want to remember their night together, but because he still couldn't forget it.

Distracted, Ely turned onto the long drive up to the estate and sighed. He supposed he might not have connected the dots anyway, even if he had reviewed her files. On that long-ago night, he and Morgan had known each other only by first names. It had been all about feelings, not details.

He frowned and typed in the security code at the gate.

After their night together, he'd always pictured Morgan as a warm, inviting, friendly person. But today she'd seemed cold, distant, withdrawn toward him. What could've happened to cause such changes in her? And why would she not have told him who she was earlier that day in the ditch? It all made him even more curious about her and the person she'd become after all these years...

No. Stop it.

He couldn't afford to get curious about Morgan. Becoming entangled in her life beyond the professional would take more than he had to give, no matter how intriguing he might find her.

Ely parked in front of the house again, then stood a moment, breathing in the scent of fresh, growing things. Part of the land here had been turned into something of a nature preserve, helping the native plants and wildlife of the island to flourish, and being in nature always calmed him. Tonight, though, he kept returning to the look on Morgan's face during that meeting. The lines of stress at the corners of her mouth. The vulnerability in her gaze. The tremble in her jaw. The tip of his thumb tingled in remembrance of the velvety warmth of her skin on his earlier…

Enough.

Determined to put her out of his mind, he headed inside. With Dr. Greg leaving tomorrow, there was nothing he could do. They'd have to find a way to work it out and keep the clinic running until his partner returned from Australia. He'd keep his errant emotions in check. Forget how his pulse kicked up a notch whenever she was around. This was business. Nothing more.

Nope.

Nothing at all.

CHAPTER THREE

MORGAN AWOKE THE next morning and blinked up at the sun-streaked ceiling, taking a few seconds to realize she was at the cottage. After Dr. Greg and Peggy had dropped her off the previous night, she'd been so exhausted she'd gone straight to bed without noticing much. Now, water lapped against distant shores, and seagull cries pierced the air. Not an unpleasant way to wake up at all.

After a yawn and a stretch, she got up and brushed her teeth, then turned on the shower to let the water heat. The amenities here at the cottage were nothing fancy, but what the place lacked in sophistication, it made up for in charm. Lots of exposed beams and cozy furniture. Wood floors and old pictures from the area on the walls.

But as she stepped under the steamy spray, thoughts of her temporary new home dissolved into memories of Ely. She'd been so sure he'd recognized her, especially at the interview, yet he'd said nothing.

Morgan sighed. Maybe she should leave well enough alone. After all, she'd built the Ely from all those years ago in her mind into a near-perfect fantasy, and there was no way reality could live up to that. Honestly, she barely knew him. What if he was horrible?

Except Ely didn't seem horrible. Not really. Distant? Yes. But not horrible. Not like Ben, who she'd only discovered had been cheating on her after the car accident that had killed him—and left his mistress untouched in the passenger seat.

A cold chill ran down her spine, and she stuck her head under the warm spray to chase it away, along with her lingering hurt and shame.

Why didn't I see it? The signs of his betrayal.

God. She felt like such an idiot.

She rinsed the conditioner from her hair, then turned off the shower before drying off. At least she had today to get situated and acclimate herself to her new home before starting at the clinic.

Once she'd gotten ready and dressed in jeans and a comfy sweatshirt, Morgan finished unpacking. The cottage consisted of one bedroom, one bathroom, a nice-size open kitchen area complete with a mini washer and dryer combo, and a small living room with a fireplace. Kindling had been set in the fireplace, which was a nice touch, but Morgan had no idea how to light it and didn't want to risk burning down the place, so maybe she'd leave that for a chilly night in the future.

A set of double doors off the living room led to a nice back patio area, surrounded by woods leading down to the water beyond. Sunlight filtered through the towering evergreens, and for the first time since the ditch yesterday, her sense of optimism returned. Perhaps she had made a wise decision in coming here after all, even with Ely complicating things.

She could handle him. She'd handled worse.

Morgan checked the pantry and found the shelves fully stocked. She started a pot of coffee, then made herself breakfast. After eating, she pulled her long, dark hair back into a ponytail, slicked on some lip balm, put on hiking boots and set out to explore. Whidbey Island was known for its trails, and she followed a well-worn footpath through the woods, not stopping until she reached the edge of the tree line and her breath caught. A green meadow stretched in front of her, bordered on one side by the bay and on the other by the road. More sheep grazed nearby. A few of them looked up at her, but they were otherwise more interested in the grass. She walked on a bit longer, then returned to the cabin, surprised to find a tall blond man waiting for her there.

"Hello," he said as Morgan approached, extending his hand with a friendly smile. "You must be Dr. Salas. My name's Jeremy Nelson. I'm the chef at Wingate."

Wingate. Why did that name sound familiar? Oh, right. She'd read there was some huge estate here on the island, owned by a wealthy tech family. She shook his hand. "Nice to meet you."

"Sorry to intrude on your day off, but Ely's tied up with another patient, and he asked me to call you. My daughter isn't feeling well, and since we're practically neighbors, I drove over to see if you're free to see her."

"Sure." Morgan headed for the front door. "Let me just get my medical bag. Please, come in."

Jeremy followed her inside the cottage.

"Wow. I haven't been to the cottage in years," he said from the living room as Morgan went into the bedroom to grab her things. "I'd forgotten how tiny it was. The landscaper for Wingate used to live here."

"Really?" Morgan changed out of her hiking boots into flats, grabbed her medical kit, then returned to his side. "Well, it's lovely. Perfect size for me. Shall we go?"

The drive only took a few minutes. As they went, Jeremy chatted about the places she should try to visit while she was there—Coupeville, Deception Pass, Ebey's Landing. Morgan nodded and smiled, but given her schedule, she'd have little free time. Maybe she'd come back for another visit. Or not, depending on how things went with Ely. Then they entered through a set of metal gates and drove up a long private drive to an estate that looked right out of the pages of *Architectural Digest*. All sparkling glass and cool steel reflecting the native flora and fauna. To the left of the large home was a large greenhouse area. To the right, a solar panel farm to harvest energy. Jeremy pulled to a stop under a side portico, and they got out. If the interior of the home was anywhere near as spectacular as the outside, Morgan was in for a treat.

Jeremy must've noticed her awed expression, because he chuckled. "The house is sixty-six thousand square feet total, with seven bedrooms, six kitchens and twelve bathrooms."

He opened the front door and led Morgan into a stunning foyer with gleaming parquet floors and wide-open space beneath soaring cathedral ceilings. A grand staircase curved gracefully up one side of the space to a balcony above, and an enormous abstract art–inspired chandelier sparkled in the sunlight streaming from skylights at least forty feet above them. The most striking features, though, were the floor-to-ceiling windows lining the entire opposite side of the house. They overlooked an immaculate deck and yard, a carpet of emerald-green grass stretching clear down to Mutiny Bay beyond. Her whole apartment back in Boston would've fit in that room.

"Wow. This place is spectacular," Morgan said, taking it all in. Over a massive stone fireplace hung a large portrait of a couple who seemed vaguely familiar. Something about the eyes…

"My daughter's upstairs," Jeremy said. "Gina's been complaining about her stomach hurting this morning. She vomited a few times, too. I gave her over-the-counter meds, but they haven't helped. I'm probably just overreacting, but…"

"No, it's fine. I'm happy to examine her. Better safe than sorry, I say." Morgan followed him up to the second floor. This space felt cozier, more lived in, though still light and airy. Jeremy took her to a pleasantly furnished bedroom in the corner. Elephants danced across a pink quilt atop a large poster bed. Beneath the covers was pale little girl who looked about seven. She had Jeremy's blond hair and wide brown eyes.

Morgan smiled and crouched beside the bed, pointing at a pink stuffed rabbit clutched in the little girl's hands. "Does your bunny have a name? I had a blue one named George when I was your age."

Gina eyed Morgan warily from between the rabbit's ears. "My tummy hurts. And I threw up. A lot."

"I'm sorry. Let's see what we can do about that, okay?" She straightened and pulled her stethoscope from her medical bag. "Can you lie flat so I can feel your tummy?"

The girl's gaze darted from Morgan to her father.

"Go on, honey," Jeremy said. "It's fine."

The child scooted down and put her arms by her sides, rabbit still held tight.

Upon palpation, Morgan didn't find any abdominal tenderness, which was good. Next, she checked Gina's throat for inflammation, but found nothing there, either. Pulse and temperature were good, too, as were her lungs.

"Well, I think you'll be just fine." Morgan finished her exam. "Nothing to worry about. But I am going to ask your dad to keep you in bed for the rest of the day and maybe tomorrow, too, just in case. Nothing to eat, but small sips of water when you get thirsty. I'll stop by tomorrow to see how you are."

She turned toward Jeremy and signaled for him to step out into the hall with her.

"I'm guessing it's just a stomach bug," she told him. "I'll give you my cell number, though, and please don't hesitate to call if there's any change in your daughter's condition. I suspect in a day or two, she'll be back to normal. Just keep her in bed today and let her sleep."

"Thank you." Jeremy gave a relieved sigh. "I know it's silly to worry, but she's all I've got. Do you have time for a coffee?"

Morgan checked her smart watch out of habit, but she had nowhere she had to be. "Okay."

"Good. Let me just tuck Gina in first."

Morgan waited for him, then followed Jeremy back downstairs.

"Are you sure? You don't need to go to any trouble for me," Morgan said. "I'm sure you're busy."

"No trouble at all. I've actually been up most of the night with Gina, so I could use the caffeine." He yawned, then smiled. "Honestly, you'd be doing me a favor. Talking to you will keep me from falling asleep."

She laughed as they walked into a large chef's kitchen at the back of the house, and Jeremy started a fresh pot of coffee. Morgan took a seat at a huge granite-topped island in the center of the room. Black-and-white tiles gleamed underfoot, and the appliances were all top-of-the-line stainless steel, including an Aga stove complete with double oven. Morgan looked out the wide windows over the farm-style sink while they waited for the brew to be done.

"Must be a dream to work in this kitchen," she said.

"It doesn't suck." Jeremy grinned and grabbed two white mugs from the tall cabinets surrounding the sink. Once the coffee maker beeped, he filled the mugs then carried them to the island, along with cream and sugar on a tray, before taking a seat on the stool beside Morgan's. "Seriously, though. Gina and I both love it here. Ely's parents built this house years ago, and it's one of a kind. Now that they're gone, it's fallen on Ely and his brother, Sam, to maintain it, though. Upkeep on a place like this isn't cheap or easy, but it's a labor of love for them, I think." He stirred sugar into his coffee. "Right now there's not much staff. Just me and the housekeeper most days. Have you met Mrs. MacIntosh yet? She looks after your cottage, too."

"Oh. No, I haven't." Her brain had glitched there a second, over the fact Ely owned this magnificent place. "What did Ely's parents do, exactly? This place must've cost a fortune to build."

"It did." Jeremy narrowed his gaze. "Ely's father started Malik Electronics. I'm sure you've heard of it."

Of course she had. Anyone living on the planet had heard of the tech giant, especially after it had recently merged with another company that produced half of the world's laptops. Her mouth dried, and she gulped more coffee to cover it. She should have connected the dots last night at the clinic, but then she'd been otherwise occupied trying not to have a breakdown after Ely's big reveal. *Wow.* Now the familiarity of the people in that portrait over the fireplace made sense. He had his father's eyes. And they were rich. Like *Forbes 100* wealthy. Which meant that Ely was officially a billionaire.

One more surprise to add to the list. She should probably be used to them by now. She wasn't.

While she was still trying to stop her foot from tapping against the rung of her stool, Jeremy fixed a plate of what looked like freshly baked cookies, then returned to the island. "Here," he said, winking as he held them out to her. "You look like you could use one of these."

Trembling, she took a cookie—chocolate chip, still

warm from the oven—and bit into it without looking. It was delicious, not that she noticed much. "Sorry. I just… I had no idea about Ely. About…" She gestured toward the kitchen as a whole, her half-eaten cookie still in hand. "All this."

Jeremy winced. "Please don't tell him I said anything. He's kind of sensitive about it, which is understandable. And really, he's just like everybody. You wouldn't know about his family or his fortune by talking to him. Or Sam."

"I'm sorry." She swallowed hard. "Who's Sam?"

"Ely's younger brother." His expression went a bit dreamy, and Morgan suspected there was something more there, but she didn't feel comfortable asking. "They're both very down-to-earth. In fact, last year they started opening Wingate for tours three days a week. The donations go toward helping local farmers during tough times. Plus, Ely also rents out some of the other buildings for receptions and stuff. And there's also the Halloween costume ball to raise funds for all the local shelters—animal and human. I stay pretty busy because of it all." Jeremy glanced toward the door. "Sounds like Ely coming."

Sure enough, the man they'd been discussing walked in, freezing as he saw Morgan. "Uh, hello. What are you doing here?"

"She came to check on Gina," Jeremy said. "I'll get you some tea, Ely. Just a splash of milk."

Ely nodded, then focused on Morgan again, his expression wary. "Everything all right?"

"Fine," Morgan said, hoping it sounded more confident than she felt. Not about her abilities. Morgan was an excellent physician, and she knew it. But her personal life was another matter. "Gina has a stomach bug. I ordered bed rest today, then she should be recovered tomorrow."

"She's napping now," Jeremy added, returning with

Ely's tea. "Mrs. MacIntosh is keeping an eye on her while I came down to tend to these cookies."

"Thanks." He took a sip, then asked Jeremy, "Where's Dylan?"

"Out back, with the gardener. As usual."

Dylan? Morgan was having trouble keeping up with all these new names.

Jeremy sighed. "Well, I should get back upstairs to my daughter. Unless there's anything else you need from me, Ely? Thank you again, Dr. Salas, for stopping by. I'll let you know if anything changes tonight with Gina's condition."

Ely waited until his chef left, then turned to Morgan. "Let me show you the backyard area."

It wasn't a question, so she couldn't really refuse. She tried anyway, needing time and space to process all that she'd learned. Not to mention the fact she wasn't ready to be alone with Ely again. Not with her pulse racing and adrenaline coursing through her system whenever he was near. She slid off her stool onto less-than-steady legs. "Um, maybe another time, actually." She started slowly inching toward the hallway behind her. "Your estate is lovely, by the way." Her nerves were firing on all cylinders now, for some reason, and if she wasn't careful, things would become awkward. Or more awkward than they already were, anyway.

"Morgan," he said, the look in his eyes leaving her no doubt that he remembered her now. "We need to talk."

Oh, God.

Well, if she'd learned anything from the last few months of her marriage to Ben it was that communication, even when painful, was necessary. Letting things go unsaid or fester was not good.

So, left with little choice, Morgan followed him out the

back door of the kitchen and onto a large flagstone patio. The sea-scented air surrounded them, and the sun finally broke through the clouds above, heating her already warm face. They followed a gravel path away from the house and down a gently sloping hill toward the water. Morgan kept pace with Ely's longer strides as a taut silence fell between them.

"I'm assuming you know about my family," Ely said once they'd stopped near the rocky shoreline. "And you probably have questions."

About so many things.

But she never got the chance to ask, because Ely rushed on.

"The money doesn't matter to me, in case you wondered. And as far as the locals are concerned, I'm just Dr. Malik, or Ely. All this other stuff—" he gestured toward the house and grounds "—I keep because it's a tribute to my parents. Their legacy. Not mine. Someday it will all be donated to the island. I just want to help people and do what I love, in a place that's important to me."

"Okay." Her paltry response was all she could manage. The fact he hadn't just come right out and told her triggered her worst fears, despite his intentions. Granted, he had a right to his privacy, too, but after their shared past, she wished he'd just been honest with her up front. But it seemed there were a lot of things she'd wished for with Ely that never came true. Just like Ben.

Ely turned to her again, his tawny gaze intense. "I've wondered about you over the years. If you'd gone on to accomplish all those dreams you'd had. You've become a doctor. Good for you. Not that I ever doubted it. You were always so determined. Nothing would've stood in your way, Morgan."

It wasn't true. Too many of her dreams had fallen by the wayside or been lost.

Too many hopes had been crushed.

Morgan stared out at the water, swallowing hard against the constriction in her throat, old hurts and grief squeezing her chest. "I guess we both got what we wanted."

He scowled, kicking a pebble with the toe of his boot. "Maybe."

Why didn't you ever contact me? Didn't I mean anything to you?

She wanted to yell, scream, something, but stuffed it all down instead. The reality was people's actions spoke way louder than their words. Another lesson she'd learned the hard way from Ben. If Ely had wanted to find her during the last ten years, he would have. The fact he hadn't was surely answer enough.

Ely knew he'd hurt her all those years ago, but life had not gone as planned for him, either. He'd been home a week when he'd gotten the call from Raina that she was pregnant. They'd dated off and on at college before finally breaking it off before Ely had ever met Morgan. They'd been careful when they'd slept together, but obviously not careful enough. When he'd found out, his world had shifted. Family was the most important thing to Ely, and he was determined to make sure his son never had a day when he didn't know how much Ely loved him. He'd made his choices then and there, and they didn't involve Morgan.

But now, things were different. For both of them. Life had changed him from the carefree boy he'd been back then. Changed her, too, apparently. In ways he was only just discovering. Seeing her again, being around her, had his emotions in turmoil. His heart pounded, and his blood sang in his veins. Mouth dry, he started to say something, then stopped himself. Maybe it was too soon. Or too late.

Tell her. Tell her the truth.

"I was going to call you," Ely blurted out, his voice rough as he watched the choppy water of the bay, feeling about as bleak and beaten as the craggy gray rocks along the shoreline. "But things happened, Morgan. Things I'd never expected." Then he paused, took a deep breath. "Are you happy?"

Morgan shivered, wrapping her arms tighter around her middle, like a shield. "I haven't been for a while, but I'm getting there." She sighed and stared down at her toes. "I've been through a lot the past two years."

"I'm sorry," he said, for lack of anything better. The ache in her tone tugged inside him.

She nodded. "Me, too."

They stood there a moment, neither saying anything, the air between them thick with possibilities and penitence.

Finally, she sighed and turned back toward the house. "I should go. Thank you for the tour."

He followed Morgan up the hill, not looking at the sway of her hips in the jeans she wore. Nope. Only to have her catch her foot on a rut and stumble back into him. Ely caught her elbow, the flowery smell of her shampoo surrounding him as her hair brushed his chin. The thump of blood in his gums grew stronger. He held on a second longer than necessary before stepping back and letting her go, fingertips tingling. Touching her felt good. Too good.

"Okay?" he asked, the word emerging rougher than he'd intended.

"Fine," Morgan mumbled, her cheeks pink and her gaze darting anywhere but at him. "Sorry."

Then, without warning, she started crying. Not sobs, just silent tears trickling down her cheeks. He froze, no idea what to do. Was this his fault? Perhaps he never should've brought up the past.

Then, to make matters worse, he reached up and cupped her cheek, swiping away a tear with his thumb without thinking. His breath stuttered, and his gut cramped.

Halt! Back away slowly!

Instead, he moved closer, lowering his voice to a near whisper. "What is it? What's wrong? Did you hurt yourself? Is this my fault?"

She waved him off and moved back, scowling as she searched her pockets. "I'm fine. I just… I don't know what's wrong with me."

Ely pulled out the packet of tissues he always kept close for his son in case of emergencies and handed them to her, chewing his lower lip. "Well, and if it helps at all, I swear I didn't know it was going to be you filling in for Dr. Greg. He'd given me your files and all ahead of time, but I didn't have a chance to read them. I trusted his judgment." He hesitated, then added, "I still do."

The weight in his chest lightened when he realized it was true. He and Morgan might have issues, but he did not doubt her medical abilities. Not at all.

"I'm not crying about that," she muttered, then turned away. "Or not only that. I don't know."

He hated seeing her upset like this and disliked even more thinking he might be the cause of it. "I'm sorry anyway."

"Stop saying you're sorry." She frowned. "It doesn't help anything. Show me instead."

Oh, boy. Oops.

Seemed he'd stepped in it again somehow. He swallowed another apology.

A beat passed, then two. Morgan finally met his gaze

again. "I was married. My husband cheated on me. Now he's dead."

Did you kill him?

The words hovered on the tip of his tongue before he squashed them. This was no time to be flippant. And he was sure there was way more to that story that he was not privy to. Maybe in time she'd tell him. Until then, he needed to mind his business. He rubbed the back of his neck as she yanked another tissue from the plastic packet in her hand, still scowling.

"And don't look at me like that. I don't want your pity."

The last thing he felt for Morgan was pity. If anything, he admired her strength, her fortitude for surviving whatever she'd endured with this deceased husband of hers. While she dabbed at her cheeks, he turned slightly to give her some privacy, staring down the shoreline to the place where they'd first met all those years ago.

She'd been working with a sailing crew going up the coast. Ely had been with his friends, having a cookout. By the time the introductions were made, the sky had become a riot of pinks and purples and golds. He could still picture Morgan, standing near the flames of their roaring bonfire, her bright smile rivaling the full moon above. Petite and curvy, with long brown hair and big blue eyes, her laugh had burned like a wildfire through his veins, and he'd been a goner. Couldn't help himself. Made excuses to his friends and led her away to where they'd had some privacy.

They'd talked a bit, between kisses. She'd been in her last year of premed, and he'd been ready to start his first residency. They'd agreed no last names, wanting to keep the magic of the moment alive. Then, as a lullaby of music and merriment drifted from the beach beyond, they'd made love. He'd been her first. She'd been the last woman he'd allowed himself to be so open with.

Afterward, they'd lain beneath the stars, the night breeze gentle on their skin, holding each other. She'd told him about her dreams, how hard she'd worked, holding two jobs to make ends meet and make up for what her scholarships didn't cover. He'd held her and listened, not saying much about himself. Not wanting her to see him differently because of who he was.

And the next morning, she'd left to sail back to San Diego.

"I wish you didn't have to go."

"Me, too. I gave you my cell number. You'll come visit me at Northwestern?"

"I will."

But he never had. Never called. Never visited. Had never seen her again.

Until now.

Heaviness weighed down his chest as he turned to face Morgan again now. His logical brain said to leave well enough alone, forget the past and just get through the next month. But the other part of him, the part sore with nostalgia and regret, forced him to say, "I'm here, if you want to talk."

"Talk?" She gave a derisive snort. "I'm tired of talking about the late Ben Morton. He cheated on me. And I didn't find out until the car accident that killed him because his mistress was with him that day. Sitting in the passenger seat. She walked away without a scratch." She blinked away more tears, her cheeks flushed, and his gut cramped.

"It was on the news, Ely. Everyone at the hospital. All our friends, family. They all knew. I tried to keep going as normal, but that's part of the reason I eventually went to Africa. Just to get away from it for a while. That's why I wanted to come here, too. Because no one would know me or my past. It could be a fresh start. And then you…you…"

Damn. He'd screwed it all up for her.

Now he felt bad. Really bad. He hadn't known and there wasn't much he could do about it now, but still.

"Come on," he said at last, continuing up the hill toward the house, feeling like a ton of bricks sat on his shoulders. "Best get inside. Those clouds on the horizon look like rain."

They returned to Wingate in silence, Ely sneaking glances at Morgan to make sure she was okay. They'd just reached the patio again when a high-pitched voice rang out from the side of the house, followed by a small dark-haired boy with a football barreling straight at him.

Suddenly, those bricks disappeared, and he felt a thousand pounds lighter again. Ely swooped his son into his arms and twirled him around, laughter filling the air.

"Daddy! Play football with me before lunch. Please?" Then Dylan's gaze locked on Morgan. "Who's that?"

CHAPTER FOUR

CONSIDERING WHAT SHE'D been through already on the island, Morgan's surprise threshold had long blown past its limit. She paused midsniffle and did a double take between Ely and the boy in his arms. Same dark hair, same features, but the eyes were different. Where Ely's eyes were a light golden-brown, the boy's gaze was sea foam green. So. Ely had a child. Huh.

"Uh." Ely set his son down, then cleared his throat, shuffling his feet. "Morgan, I'd like you to meet my son, Dylan. Dylan, this is Dr. Morgan Salas."

The little boy peered up at her, his football now tucked under one arm. "Nice to meet you."

"Nice to meet you, too." The kid was super-cute, and she found herself smiling despite her rapidly drying tears. Morgan loved kids. Which made the fact she couldn't have any of her own now even more tragic. She crouched in front of the boy, smiling. "How old are you, Dylan?"

"I'll be ten in December," he said, looking enormously proud of himself.

As she made the mental calculations in her head, her smile faltered. Dylan would've been born shortly after she and Ely had been together, so…

Guess that explained why he'd never called.

Bile burned hot in her throat. No. Just no. Not another cheater.

Ely inhaled deep and raised his chin, as if steeling himself for battle. "Dylan, go toss your ball around while Dr. Salas and I talk. I'll be there in a minute."

She waited until the boy was out of hearing range before asking, "Ten years old? Seriously, Ely?"

He shook his head and looked away. "It's not what you think."

Another red flag went up in her brain. Ben used to tell her that, too.

Bastard.

"Daddy, I'm hungry." Dylan suddenly ran up to them again. "Can I have a snack?"

"Go check with Jeremy," Ely said, ruffling his son's hair.

"What about Dr. Salas?" Dylan peered up at Morgan. "Can you stay for a snack, too? I'll show you my room. You can see my model boats. I love boats. Do you sail? Daddy does. Maybe we can all go out sometime?"

Morgan glanced between Ely and his son, her cheeks tight and her body tense. "And I'd love to see your room sometime, but I can't stay now. I need to get back to my cottage. Maybe later?"

The little boy nodded then rushed off once more.

Leaving Morgan and Ely alone again.

"Right, well…" He looked painfully awkward. Good. That made two of them.

"Right." She shoved her hands in her pockets, feeling far too vulnerable and raw for her liking. Despite her barriers, Ely had a way of cutting her down to the bone. Even more reason to keep clear of him outside work. "Goodbye, Ely."

Ely winced. "Wait, Morgan. I—"

"Save it. Really. We're work colleagues, Ely. Nothing

more. How you choose to conduct your life is your affair."
Inside, though, she was seething. Her skin felt too tight,
and heat clawed up her neck regardless of the cool breeze
off the water. She hated being the last to know things.
Being on the outside. Secrets. And while Ely hadn't outright lied to her, he hadn't been exactly forthright, either,
so same difference.

Their gazes snagged, but then an impenetrable, busi-
nesslike facade shuttered his face, and it was like a door
slamming between them.

"I'll see you tomorrow, then," he said, his tone icy.

He walked away, and Morgan followed the trail to her cottage, grumbling to herself all the way about stupid men and
their stupid choices. Lost in thought, she barely registered
the fact she'd reached the woods surrounding the cottage
until a strange female voice called out, jarring her. Morgan
stopped in her tracks and peered through the evergreens to
see an older woman waving from the cottage's porch.

"Hello, Dr. Salas," the woman said as Morgan neared.
"I'm Mrs. MacIntosh, the housekeeper at Wingate. Wanted
to check in on you and make sure you were settled."

"Hi." Morgan shook her hand. "I'm sorry if you've been
waiting long. I was just up at Wingate, checking on Jeremy's daughter. Do come inside. And please, call me Morgan."

They went into the cottage, and Morgan hung her jacket
on a hook by the door, offering to take Ms. MacIntosh's,
but the woman declined.

"Hope this place is working out for you okay," the older
woman said while Morgan went to the kitchen to start a
pot of coffee. "Heard you had quite a drive onto the island yesterday."

Yikes. Word traveled fast around here. Morgan winced.
"Does everyone on the island know?"

"Probably. This end of it, anyway." Mrs. MacIntosh laughed. "But don't worry. People in the area are just interested in the new doc and how our Ely swooped in and saved you."

"Well, I don't know about saving." Morgan bristled. She was hardly a damsel in distress. Helpless female wasn't her preferred look. "I would've figured a way out on my own eventually."

She started the coffee maker, then walked back out into the living room to find Mrs. MacIntosh lingering by the door. "Please, sit down."

"Oh, I can't stay. I have to get back to work. I'm already late." The older woman grasped the doorknob and smiled. "Just wanted to introduce myself and let you know I'll pop by in the morning to clean the place. After that, my schedule is three days a week. That's what Dr. Greg arranged, if that works for you."

Morgan had never had a housekeeper before, but she didn't want to be rude, so she nodded. "Okay."

She spent the rest of the afternoon tinkering around, staying busy so she wouldn't dwell on her discussion earlier with Ely. Why did she have to be so aware of him as a man? She didn't want to fall in love again. Didn't want another relationship. Didn't want romance. Especially with a man who hadn't been completely honest with her. She'd been there, done that. Had the scars to prove it. No. She was safer, happier, on her own. And yes, working together at the clinic would make keeping her distance from Ely more difficult, but it was necessary.

One month. Thirty-one days.

Then she could get on with her life and leave Ely Malik behind for good.

CHAPTER FIVE

MORGAN CRANKED THE heat in her rental car as she drove to the clinic the next morning. Wind howled and rain hurled against the windows of the sedan, and she clicked the wipers higher. Perhaps she should've worn a rain poncho instead of the well-cut beige suit she'd chosen for her first official day at work, but she'd wanted to look nice. She had an umbrella, so it should be fine.

According to the schedule the clinic had emailed her last night, they'd see patients in the morning, then she'd accompany Ely on home visits that afternoon. In between, Morgan planned to stop by Wingate to check on Gina as well, although she was pretty sure Jeremy would've called if there'd been any problems.

She navigated the twisty two-lane roads, doing her best to focus on the day ahead and not the past, but damn if that conversation hadn't stirred something up inside her again. She'd even dreamed about Ben last night, which hadn't happened in a long time. Anger sizzled inside her, and she gripped the steering wheel tighter with both hands. Ben didn't deserve that prime real estate in her brain after what he'd done. Morgan shifted in her seat, a familiar painful pinch of shock in her chest making her antsy. Each time she thought of that day, that phone call from the state police, it was like she was right back there again—phone slipping from her damp hand, legs threatening to buckle, throat choking her. Even after two years, the visceral explosion inside her was still strong, like a wound that refused to heal.

It was the reason she worked so hard, stayed busy. Because then she didn't have time to think, time to feel. An old coping pattern of hers, one that had probably kept her marriage to Ben going far longer than it should have. In their final six months together, they'd barely been a couple, barely talked to each other more than passing pleasantries, barely had sex at all. She'd been too emotionally drained from losing her baby, and he hadn't known how to deal with her trauma because of that or his own. So, they'd fallen into a kind of weird half-life.

Not that any of that excused his infidelity. She'd not done that to him, and the fact he'd done that to her made her feel like a fool when the truth had finally come out after the accident. A stupid, trusting idiot.

Since then, she'd vowed never to be that vulnerable again. Never to feel that raw. Gone were her days of blindly accepting whatever someone told her as fact. No one got past her walls now without a fight.

Including Ely Malik.

She pulled into the clinic parking lot and pulled into one of the Staff Only spots, then cut the engine, steadfast in her resolve to keep things professional. Morgan exited her vehicle with her umbrella over her head, then ran for the front entrance. Some other staff were already there, including Ely. He was talking with two women at the front desk, looking far better than should be allowed in a dark gray suit and burgundy-striped tie. She cleared her throat and wrangled her umbrella closed in the vestibule before entering the lobby.

"Good morning, Dr. Salas," Ely greeted her from behind the large, circular reception desk. His crooked smile gave her heart an unwanted tug.

Stop it.

"Once you've put your things away, I'll give you a tour before we start seeing patients."

"Thank you." Morgan dropped her purse off in Dr. Greg's office before returning to the desk. "Ready for duty."

He introduced her to the rest of staff. Sandy, an older LPN who handled scheduling surgeries and procedures as well as assisting patients in the office. Didi, the receptionist, who was in her midtwenties with a blue streak in her hair that matched her scrubs and a sparkly diamond nose stud. Joan, the radiology tech, and Mark, who ran the lab. Plus, there were several certified medical assistants who kept the back clinic running like clockwork.

They started down one of the halls, and Ely pointed out exam rooms, procedure rooms, ultrasound and X-ray facilities, the lab, and a small ambulatory surgery area. "We do our own minor surgeries here. More complicated cases need to be transferred to either Oak Harbor or Seattle General, depending on the severity. There's an air ambulance service, if needed. Even so, we're equipped to handle most emergencies in a pinch." He glanced over at her. "How are your surgery skills?"

"Good," Morgan said. "I handled a variety of things out in the field in Africa."

"Excellent." Ely looked impressed. "Well, if you ever have questions or need a second opinion, call me. You have support options."

"Noted."

The morning went by faster than Morgan had expected. Her full roster included mainly colds and flus, rechecks, and the occasional laceration that needed stitching. After they finished seeing everyone, Ely ordered in lunch and the staff ate together in the break room to get to know each other.

"I heard you went up to Wingate to treat Gina," Didi said, sliding into the chair next to Morgan's at the long table. "Jeremy and I are good friends."

"Yep, I did," Morgan said, amazed at how quickly news spread on the island. "Jeremy's great. I'll tell him you said hello when I stop by later to check on his daughter."

"Hey, Doc?" Sandy said from the other end of the table, and both Ely and Morgan looked her way. The older nurse cringed. "Sorry. Dr. Malik. I got a call from Karen Greene right before clinic ended this morning. She's having some anxiety. Doesn't think her baby's moving as much. Can you stop by and see her this afternoon?"

"How many weeks is she now?" Ely asked.

"Thirty-six, barely. She's booked into Oak Harbor for delivery two weeks from now."

"You're inducing her?" Morgan frowned. "Is she high-risk?"

"No. Karen's thirty-three, and this is her first baby." Ely wiped his mouth with a napkin. "But her husband's a long-haul trucker and wants to be there for the birth, so we agreed to induce her while he's here. Given her clean medical history, I don't see any harm." He turned back to Sandy. "My schedule's pretty full this afternoon. Could you stop by first, Sandy, then call me with an update?"

"Sure thing."

"Great." He checked his watch, then glanced at Morgan. "As soon as you're finished, we can go."

On the way to their first home visit, Morgan didn't say much, just stared out the window beside her at the passing scenery. Which was fine with him, since he was still churning through their conversation behind his house yesterday and the implications of it. He couldn't blame her for her anger and resentment toward her deceased husband after hearing what the man had done, but it was still hard for him to reconcile the woman Morgan Salas was now to the fantasy version he'd carried in his head for years. Then again, he tended do that, he knew. Romanticize things from his past, turn them into something bigger and grander than they really were. He'd done that with his parents after their deaths, too. That had never happened with his marriage to Raina, though, probably because she was still around, reminding him of why they were not a good match, even though they remained cordial to coparent Dylan.

They rounded a bend in the road, and he hazarded a glance at her again, finding Morgan watching him now, and the hairs on his forearms stood on end with wariness. He was a man who valued his privacy, sometimes to his own detriment. He didn't like talking about himself, a by-product of growing up in a family where his parents' every move had been splashed all over the tabloids. He didn't want to live like that. Didn't want to put Dylan through that, either. So, he kept a low profile, both professionally and personally.

"Your son is very cute," she said after a moment, her gaze slightly narrowed. "How long have you been married?"

He gave her a side glance, uncomfortable heat prickling up from beneath the collar of his white button-down shirt. *Relax. She's just being polite. You can open up a little, especially after what she told you.* Except it was difficult. So difficult. He rolled his stiff shoulders and stared straight ahead. "I'm divorced."

"Oh. I'm sorry."

He could've just left it there, but he kept talking for

some reason he didn't want to examine too closely. "Things with Raina, my ex-wife, didn't work for a lot of reasons. We were both too young, too driven in our own careers. Mainly, we were just too different. We tried to stay together for Dylan's sake, but it was better for everyone for us to part ways. We divorced two years ago."

Morgan nodded then stared out the window again, her expression unreadable. But he could imagine the wheels turning in her head as his old sense of failure burned hot and heavy in his gut. Ely wasn't a man who liked to fail. Even in a marriage that had been doomed from the start. Even with a woman he hadn't seen in ten years but had never forgotten. Their old connection still simmered just below his surface, and it terrified him. He didn't want to get involved with Morgan. Didn't want to get involved with anyone. Because that would mean risking his heart and his future, and he never wanted to do that again.

Luckily, before Morgan could ask him anything else, they arrived at their first patient's home, giving them work as a distraction. John Morris was an elderly man suffering from shortness of breath. He had a difficult time making it into the office, so house calls here were routine for Ely. Didn't stop the man's wife from apologizing continuously for putting them through a visit on such a rainy, miserable day.

"It's fine, Mrs. Morris," Ely reassured her. "We're happy to do it. This is Dr. Salas's first day, so it gives me a chance to show her where all the patients live. You're doing us a favor. No trouble at all."

"I've made you both a batch of brownies, just the same," Mrs. Morris said. "Let me get them while you two examine my John."

She went to the kitchen while Ely gave Morgan a rundown on the patient's condition.

"Mr. Morris is seventy-five and complains of shortness of breath for the last few days." Ely listened to the patient's lungs with his stethoscope, then stepped aside so Morgan could do the same.

"I'm fine." The patient harrumphed, flushed and drawn as he sat in his recliner in the living room. "Mildred's always worrying and fussing. I'm old, but I'm not dead yet."

Morgan caught Ely's eye and bit back a smile.

"Since we're here, why not let us check you over?" Ely asked. "Better safe than sorry, eh?"

He checked the patient's extremities for swelling, then took his temperature, which was elevated. "I'm guessing this is an upper respiratory infection," he said, straightening and hanging his stethoscope around his neck. "We'll treat you with antibiotics. Take it easy, John, and drink plenty of fluids. You should feel better again in no time."

"A little cold never killed anybody. And what about my animals?" The older man pointed out the window toward the animals grazing in the field. "Somebody's got to tend to the sheep."

"Mr. Morris, at your age a chest infection can become pneumonia if not treated properly," Morgan added. "Better a few days resting now than a week or more in the hospital later."

"Let me call your neighbor," Ely said, pulling out his phone. Small island practices offered services above and beyond the standard. "I'll see if Dave can keep an eye on your herd until you've recovered."

Mr. Morris scowled, looking like he wanted to argue, but he was outnumbered and knew it. Finally, he scoffed and gave a dismissive wave, crossing his arms. "Fine. But make sure he can do it first."

While Ely made the call, Mrs. Morris returned with a huge plate full of brownies. She set them on the coffee table, then took a seat on the arm of her husband's chair. Ely got through to the neighbor, who was happy to help, then he returned to his patient.

"Dave's got you covered," he said, reaching for a brownie. They were the best on the island, even better than Jeremy's. Not that he'd tell his chef. He swallowed a delicious chocolaty bite, then smiled. "Amazing as always, Mildred."

"Glad you like them, Dr. Malik. I've packed a box of them for each of you to take with you."

Ely finished his brownie, then went over prescriptions and instructions with Mr. Morris. By the time they left, he noticed Morgan had downed not one but two brownies, and she groaned uncomfortably once they were back in his truck.

"Too full?" he asked, grinning as he started the engine. "I should've warned you not to overindulge at lunch. Same thing happened to me when I first started. I didn't want to be rude, so I ate everything my patients put in front of me. Now you'll know for next time." He signaled, then pulled back onto the main road. "As a rule, I visit our elderly, sick patients first to prevent minor ailments from becoming serious illnesses."

"Makes sense." Morgan fastened her seat belt. "And that was nice of you, making sure his sheep were handled." She smiled over at Ely, a genuine one this time, and his chest warmed. Man, he remembered that smile. More than he should. Sunny and bright and unguarded. He'd missed it.

So much for keeping things strictly professional.

Ely scowled and focused straight ahead again.

Enough of that.

Morgan continued talking, which he hadn't expected. "In the ER in Boston, we rarely saw the same patient twice. That's another reason I wanted a change. I'd rather get to know people. Figure out what makes them tick, what worries them. I believe that can help us treat them better."

"Agreed." He believed much the same, that medicine was more than tests and procedures. That to truly heal a person, you had to take a holistic approach—body, mind and spirit. Ely drove on, tapping his thumb on the steering wheel. Huh. They agreed on something. Imagine that. After yesterday, he wasn't so sure he hadn't completely made up the synergy he'd felt with her that night on the beach. But nope. They did have things in common. Professionally, anyway. That was good for the clinic.

What about in the bedroom?

Uh…no. Where the hell had *that* come from?

He cleared his throat and shifted his weight, doing his best to eliminate the now-burgeoning swell of awareness inside him. Not going there. Not at all. His scalp tingled, and he resisted the urge to scratch it.

Concentrate on work. That's why you're here. The only reason you're here.

"On the downside, we get too attached to patients." He shrugged one shoulder to release some tension. "And when things go badly, it's harder because we know them so well." Over the years, Ely had lost several patients who'd been friends and mentors to him, and it never got easier. And wasn't that just the wet blanket he needed to calm down inside? Feeling more in control again, he straightened and leaned an elbow on the edge of the window beside him. "But this way of practicing medicine is worth it to me. It's what I like best about living here on the island. I've known most of these people my whole life."

Two more house calls followed—one to an elderly man with pulmonary edema and another to a child with chicken pox. Both cases were straightforward, and Morgan handled them well, her bedside manner easy and engaging.

She seemed to really listen to each patient and put them at ease. Even Ely relaxed around her after a while.

"Who's next?" she asked once they'd climbed back into his truck again.

"Roger Cayman. He lives near Langley, the farthest distance from the clinic. Then there are two more who live closer, and we'll see them on the way back."

They passed Karen Greene's house on the way, and Ely got a bad feeling as he saw Sandy's car still parked out front. The nurse should've been done with a simple OB check by now. He signaled, then turned into the circular drive in front of the house to park. Checked his phone, but there was no signal.

Dammit.

"What's going on?" Morgan asked, her tone concerned.

"This is Karen Greene's house. The OB patient we discussed earlier in the break room. Just want to pop in on Sandy and make sure everything's okay." He cut the engine and unbuckled his seat belt. "Be right back."

Sandy opened the front door before he got there, and he knew then there were issues. His LPN had been doing her job for years and had seen and done pretty much everything. It took a lot to rattle her, and based on Sandy's pale face and white-knuckled grip on the door frame, things were serious.

"I tried to call you," the nurse said. "But the service here is terrible."

"What's going on?" Ely asked, sidling around her to get into the house.

"Low fetal heart tones, around fifty. And Karen's water just broke. I can see the umbilical cord."

Damn. A probable cord prolapse.

Ely's pulse notched higher. If the umbilical cord became compressed too much during delivery, the baby would suffocate and die. Extremely bad news, especially on an isolated island, because if the baby did survive delivery, they'd need a NICU right away. Time was of the essence.

"What's happening?" Morgan rushed into the house beside him.

"Probable cord prolapse," he said, mind jumping ahead ten steps already. "We need to get Karen delivered ASAP. Have you done an emergency C-section?" Ely asked Morgan.

"Yes. Once in my OB rotation, and once in Africa." Her eyes widened. "Why?"

"The clinic is ten minutes away. Our surgery room is fully stocked. One of the GPs in Langley used to be an anesthesiologist. Sandy can call him now and he could meet us there."

From the back of the house, Karen screamed as another contraction wracked her body.

Decision made, Ely went into emergency mode, giving orders as he walked down the hall toward Karen's bedroom, medical bag in hand. "Sandy, get ahold of Dr. Lake. Tell him we need him at our clinic stat for anesthesia. Then, when you get a moment, reschedule the rest of our house calls this afternoon to another day. Morgan, call Seattle General and tell them to dispatch their air crew to our clinic. Then call Didi and tell her to have the CMAs prep the surgery room so it's ready to go when we get there. I'm going to insert a catheter to help relieve some of the pressure from her bladder off the umbilical cord and buy us some time to get her to the clinic."

It was a tense time, but the three of them managed to get the patient prepped and loaded into the back of Ely's truck, Sandy by Karen's side as they drove to the clinic. By the time they got there, thankfully Dr. Lake had arrived and the staff had everything in place. Ely and Morgan scrubbed up together while Sandy monitored the baby's heartbeat in the OR.

"Ely?" Morgan asked, rinsing off her hands and forearms.

"Yes?"

"How many C-sections have you done in the last two years?"

He took a deep breath and stepped off the pedal to shut off the water, keeping his hands and forearms elevated. "None. Why?"

"Let me take the lead on this, then," Morgan said firmly. "The baby will need your pediatric skills the moment it's delivered."

Ely backed into the surgery room ahead of Morgan and slid his arms into the sterile gown one of the medical assistants held for him. "But it was my decision to operate. If anything goes wrong, it should be my responsibility."

"For the record?" She slid into her own gown, then waited while an assistant put on her gloves and tied a mask on her face. "I agree with your decision. But if we want to save them both, the best chance that baby has is for you to stand by to resuscitate, if needed. Okay?"

Ely wasn't one to give up the fight, but it made sense. He gave a curt nod. "Let's do it."

The patient was on the table already with Dr. Lake ready to administer the anesthetic. Karen stared up at Ely, eyes wide and overly bright with fear. He squeezed her hand and spoke slowly, reassuringly. "We'll do everything we can, I promise. Once this is over, the air ambulance will take you and the baby to Seattle General. I'll fly with you to make sure you get settled properly, okay?"

"What about my husband?" Karen asked, tears welling. "He wants to be here."

He glanced at Sandy, who nodded. "He's on his way. Just relax. This will be over soon."

She nodded, gripping his hand even tighter. "Please save my baby."

"We're going to do our best," Morgan assured her.

Within seconds of Dr. Lake administering the anesthetic, Karen was out. Ely stood opposite Morgan as she began the procedure, making a deep, steady incision across the patient's abdomen, then another through the uterine wall and the placenta before reaching in and lifting out the baby and placing it in Ely's waiting hands. A few clamps, a quick snip and the cord was cut.

"It's a girl," he informed the room. "Good size, too, considering she's early."

He moved over to a separate table set up for the infant. The baby was blue and unresponsive, and he quickly cleared the tiny baby's mouth and nose of mucus clogging her airway, then checked her pulse. Still slow. Precious seconds ticked by. No change.

"We need to intubate." Ely inserted a small breathing tube into the infant's trachea, then attached a bag to force air into the baby's lungs. Sandy placed a hand lightly on the infant's chest, her solemn expression slowly replaced by a smile. "Heartbeat's improving, and baby's pinking up nicely." A collective sigh of relief echoed through the OR. "She's going to make it."

Ely removed the breathing tube, and moments later the welcome sound of a newborn's cries filled the air. Morgan nodded, her blue eyes shining with triumph and appreciation over her mask, and Ely's chest warmed with gratitude and grace and something far closer to affection than he was ready for. She turned then to finish closing on the patient's surgery while he continued cleaning up the baby and getting the infant ready for transport.

It was another half hour before Morgan had finished with Karen, and Ely rolled and stretched his stiff shoulders and neck. Finally, he could breathe again. He and Morgan walked back into the scrub area together, peeling off their gloves and soiled gowns, tossing them in the biohazard bin before scrubbing up once again, a sense of satisfaction palpable between them.

"The patient did well," Morgan said, her voice quieter now, faint lines of fatigue at the corners of her eyes. Ely wondered how much that surgery had taken out of her. Having experience was one thing. Being called to perform at the drop of a hat was another. "Karen's beginning to come around already. Hopefully the air transport will be here soon. How's the baby?"

"Good. The sooner we get them both to Seattle General, though, the better I'll feel. The baby will need round-the-clock care in the NICU for the next few days, but I think the biggest danger is past." He sighed and grabbed paper towels from the dispenser on the wall. "You did fantastic in there, Morgan. Thank you."

"You're welcome." Her cheeks pinkened slightly, and he felt an unaccountable urge to hug her tight. Instead, Ely finished drying his hands far more aggressively than necessary before tossing his used towels away and making a beeline for the door.

Coward.

Maybe, but at least his heart was safe. He could not allow himself to care about Morgan again. Not that way. She'd be gone at the end of the month. He had to remain logical about this. Had to remain in control. Even if his pounding pulse and buzzing knees already said he was too late.

Morgan joined him and the rest of the staff in the hall after she'd finished cleaning up, thankfully not mentioning his hasty retreat.

Ely swallowed hard against the lump of unwanted yearning in his throat and instead focused on the people around him. "Nice job, everyone. Especially you, Dr. Salas. We—"

The loud whirr of approaching helicopter blades overhead cut his speech short. Which was just as well, he supposed, given the turmoil inside him. He had to get a handle on all these feelings she evoked in him without even trying—need, nostalgia, regret, want—if he had any hope of keeping things professional between them.

Head down, Ely helped Morgan wheel Karen's gurney out of the surgery room and down the hall to the back entrance. The helipad for the clinic was still under construction, so the air ambulance landed in an open field adjacent to them.

"My baby?" a groggy Karen asked as they loaded her into the helicopter.

"Got her right here," Sandy said, handing the infant in to her mother once Karen was settled by the paramedics.

A loud horn sounded from the parking lot, and a huge semi screeched to a stop. A burly man with a beard and baseball hat climbed out and hurried toward them. "Sweetheart, I got here as fast as I could." Karen's husband promptly started crying the moment he saw his daughter for the first time. "She's the most beautiful thing ever."

There was enough room for one more person, and Ely and Morgan exchanged a look.

"Go on, then," Morgan said after a moment. "You promised her in the OR you'd be there."

He grinned—couldn't help it. "I did." He shouted to be heard over the roar of the rotors. "I'll be back in a few hours to give you an update."

"Take your time," she called back, waving. "I'll hold the fort down here while you're gone."

CHAPTER SIX

MORGAN WROTE UP her notes on the surgery and stuck around to handle phone calls and anything else that might pop up until closing, then she left. It was well after five now, but she still wanted to stop by Wingate on her way back to the cottage to check on Gina.

Jeremy had followed her advice and kept the little girl in bed for the day, and now Gina was bouncing off the walls with energy. With the patient feeling better, the recheck was fast, and Morgan ended up in the kitchen again with Jeremy afterward, glad to have made a new friend. She told him about the emergency C-section while he made them tea.

"Sounds like you had an eventful first day," he said. "I saw a snippet about it on the local news. The air ambulance getting called in always makes for a big headline."

Morgan smiled. "I keep forgetting how quiet things are usually on this island. I hope emergencies aren't a regular occurrence around here. I had enough of that in Africa."

"They're not." Jeremy slid onto the stool beside hers and rested his elbow on the black granite countertop and his chin in his palm. "You look exhausted."

"I feel exhausted." She grinned. But more than fatigue, it was the growing ache inside her that bothered Morgan. The one that had been growing since she'd walked into

Karen Greene's house earlier today. Which was silly, honestly. As a physician, she saw lots of pregnant patients. They'd never bothered her before, not even after her own disastrous outcome. But something about today… She sighed and rubbed her tired eyes. Seeing Karen come so close to losing her precious baby today had brought back the grief and guilt and shame about her own ectopic pregnancy. The knot of sadness in her chest tightened. That, as much as the surgery, zapped her energy reserves. But it was too early to share that with Jeremy. They'd just met. So, she fell back on her standard excuse. "I just need a good night's sleep."

Liar.

What she needed was a hug and a cuddle. From Ely.

Stop it.

"Do you know how Gina and I came to live here at Wingate?" he asked over the rim of his mug. The always cheerful Jeremy looked far more serious now than she'd ever seen him. "We moved in after my partner, Scott, died of a brain aneurysm. One second he was fine, the next he was gone." The edge of sorrow in his tone broke her heart. "We'd been out shopping, and he collapsed in one of the stores. I called the EMTs, but by the time they got him to the hospital, he was gone. Gina wasn't even a year old then. We'd adopted her at six months, thinking we'd have a lifetime of memories to make together. Then, just like that, I was a single father, trying to raise a baby on my own while also processing my grief. It wasn't a good time for any of us."

"Oh, gosh. I'm so very sorry for your loss," Morgan said, putting her hand over his. "That must've been terrible."

"It was. I tried to keep my restaurant in Seattle open, but my heart wasn't in it after Scott died. I'd grown up on

Whidbey Island, and my mother was the chef for Ely's family for years. And I needed to work. Scott had been our breadwinner. He was in finance and made great money at it. But his medical bills ate through our savings after he was gone, and I couldn't be homeless, not with a child to support."

He gave a sad little shrug. "Then Ely stepped in. He'd heard about Scott through people on the island and tracked me down. Offered to pay for everything, too, all the medical bills. Everything. But I couldn't let him do that. I wanted to work. Needed to after losing pretty much everything I loved. I needed to show myself and Gina that I could stand on my own. Have some pride again. So, Ely offered me the head chef job here at Wingate. Room and board, too. He saved my life. He's a good man."

"Wow." She'd wanted to believe that Ely was the man she'd met on the beach all those years ago, but after her arrival here and discovering so much he hadn't told her, her doubts had grown. Hearing Jeremy's story made her think that perhaps he was a decent person after all. And working with him today with their patients had confirmed that, too. The past had been a girlish dream. This was reality. Still, she'd been through too much to defeat her apprehension quite so easily. She tucked her hair behind her ear and sipped more minty, sweet tea, grateful for the warmth on her constricted throat. "That sounds pretty incredible of him."

"It was." Jeremy smiled at her. "He gave me a future, Morgan. Not the one I'd expected to have, but a good one just the same. And if I'd never moved in here, I'd never have met Sam, so…"

He pulled out his phone and showed her a picture of the mysterious younger Malik brother. Tall, muscled, dark haired, handsome, just like Ely. Same dimples, too. God, those dimples. An image of Ely grinning at her from the helicopter earlier flashed into her head, and her stomach fluttered.

Whoops. No. Stop thinking about Ely and his dimples.

Or any other part of him, for that matter. They'd done well together today. She needed to keep that going, not mess it all up by getting personal with him. Personal never worked out well for Morgan. She took a deep breath and passed the phone back to Jeremy, hoping he didn't notice the slight tremble in her fingers. "I look forward to meeting Sam. Will he be coming to the island while I'm here?"

"He's returning for the Halloween ball at the end of the month. It'll be the first time we've seen each other in months. His schedule's so crazy in New York right now, with the merger and everything. He still calls me every night, though. So sweet." Jeremy gave a rapturous sigh. "You'll love him, I'm sure. Oh, and you'll get to meet Raina then, too."

That took Morgan aback. She frowned. "Really?"

From her own experiences with marriages ending, she'd expected Ely's relationship with his ex-wife to be acrimonious, too, but apparently it wasn't, not if the woman returned to Wingate for visits. "Is she here a lot?"

"Once a month or so." Jeremy shrugged. "She and Ely keep things cordial between them. Why?"

"No reason." Morgan frowned into her tea, doing her best to hide her inner turmoil. "Sounds very…modern."

Jeremy snorted. "Why, Morgan Salas. If I didn't know better, I'd think you were jealous."

"What? No." She protested too much, because the uncomfortable niggle inside said he might be right. Which was complete nonsense. She had no right to be jealous about Ely's relationships. They were work colleagues. That's all. His private life was none of her business.

Jeremy laughed. "Seriously, though. If you're curious, his relationship with Raina is friendly, but that's all. And it works for them. They live in completely separate worlds otherwise. Ely's happy here on the island. As a supermodel, Raina's always flying off to some exotic locale for a photo shoot. If it wasn't for Dylan, I honestly don't think they'd ever have ended up together. They wanted very different things in life. But Ely's devoted to keeping the family support there for Dylan's sake, so they make it work."

Interesting. She'd have to ask Ely more about that sometime. Or not. Since it was none of her business, even if it felt like it was.

"Anyway," Jeremy said, patting her arm, "we should go out to dinner one night in Langley, just the two of us. I can show you around the area, introduce you to some people."

"I'd like that."

They set a date, then Morgan headed home. By the time she arrived at the cottage, it was a bit after eight. She got a fire going in the fireplace with the help of detailed instructions left by Mrs. MacIntosh, and had just settled in with a good book and a cup of cocoa, warm and snuggly in her pj's and blanket, when someone knocked on the door. Scowling, she got up to answer, hoping it wasn't something that would mean she'd have to change and go out into the night again. Rain pattered on the roof, and a cold wind blustered against the walls. She shivered and opened the door a crack to find Ely on her porch.

"Hey," Morgan said, surprised. "What are you doing here?"

"Just stopped by to give you an update. Karen and the baby are okay."

"That's great!" She pulled her fleece pj top tighter around her as the wind gusted once more.

"Yeah. They named her Serenity," he chuckled. "Ironic, since her delivery was anything but."

"Right?"

They stood there a beat or two, her fingers twisting in the hem of her pj top to keep busy. An odd mix of anticipation and apprehension fizzed inside her like soda pop. She should ask him in—that would be the polite thing. But it was late and very dark, and it felt weirdly intimate to let him into her cottage just then. She didn't want to give him the wrong idea.

Is it wrong, though?

Of course it was wrong, she chided herself. She didn't want Ely that way anymore, no matter what the shiver up her spine might say. She was just cold, that's all. To prove her point, she stepped back and opened the door wider. "Please, come in. Get warm by the fire."

"Oh, uh…" He hesitated, perhaps as conflicted as her, before the stiff breeze pushed him closer to the threshold. "Well, maybe just for a second. To get warm, like you said. I won't stay long."

She closed the door behind him, catching a whiff of pine and spicy aftershave as he passed her. With him there, his broad frame seemed to take up all the oxygen in the space. For lack of anything better to say, she pointed toward the coffee table. "I was just going to settle in with a book. Can I get you some cocoa?"

"Oh, no. Thanks. The sugar will keep me up."

"Yeah. I get that." She stared down at her stockinged toes, wondering what the hell to talk about now. Morgan watched as he bent slightly to warm his hands near the flames, the fabric of his jacket stretching across his back, revealing the strong muscles beneath, and…oh, boy. Molten warmth pooled low in her belly, and she looked anywhere but at him then. Not helping. Not at all. "So, busy day, huh?"

"Very busy," he said, staring into the flames, the shadows catching the dips and hollows of his high cheekbones before he stood and faced her once more, his expression serious. "Thank you again for performing the surgery so well."

"Happy to do it," Morgan said, her voice quivering slightly as she took a seat and pulled her blanket around her like a shield from all the things she didn't want to feel with him. "And thanks for showing me around with the home visits."

"No problem." He shoved his hands in his pockets, rocking back slightly on his heels. "Can I ask you something?"

Butterflies swarmed inside her then, and her heart lodged somewhere in her throat. "Uh, okay. Sure."

"Great." Ely took a seat on the sofa, catty-corner from her, and rubbed his palms on the legs of his pants like he was nervous, which only ratcheted the bubbling energy pinballing inside her higher. His Adam's apple bobbed as he swallowed, then said, "What's Boston like? I've never been there and always wanted to go."

"What's Boston like"? Seriously? Such a lame question.

He should have left after telling her about the case. That was what he'd intended to do. But no. Now he was sitting on her sofa asking her stupid questions instead of the things he really wanted to know about her, and…

Gah! This was all a mistake. A horrible miscalculation.

Except, the more time Ely spent around Morgan, the more he wanted. Seeing her in action today with the C-section had reminded him of her passion—in work, and in life in general. And while his life was neat and ordered and perfectly wonderful, it lacked passion. He wanted that passion back dearly.

Morgan watched him a moment, apparently as stunned by his silly question as he felt. But he couldn't think of anything intelligent to ask her now that he was here. He, a physician, well respected in his field, had absolutely no game at all where this woman was concerned. Of course it didn't help, either, when his gaze slid downward against his will to her breasts, their outline more pronounced since she'd crossed her arms beneath them, pushing them up and out into that soft fleece top she was wearing. His palms suddenly itched to touch them, cup them, see if they were as plump and full and just the right size like he remembered. He licked his dry lips and glanced away.

No. Stop looking there. Stop it.

And now his lower body was responding as well, dammit, as the tension inside him grew stronger. Heat climbed his neck from beneath the collar of his white button-down. Maybe she wasn't going to answer. Maybe she sensed the things he was feeling. Maybe she'd kick him out on his butt as he deserved.

Instead, she just gave him an odd look and snuggled down farther in her chair. "Uh, Boston is a nice city. Brutal winters. Not that I saw much of them. I worked in the ER, and it was very busy, so I didn't have much free time."

"Right." His pulse thumped harder against his temples. Now that he couldn't look at her boobs, it seemed that was all he wanted to do. But he couldn't. Nope. He wasn't that type of man, ruled by his desire. Flustered, he asked the next question that popped into his head, which turned out to be the complete wrong one. "Is that where you met your husband?"

Hell.

Morgan's gaze narrowed, and Ely rushed to cover his blunder.

"Sorry. No idea why I asked that."

Stop talking, idiot.

He couldn't. "I mean, I'd like to get to know you better, but…" He swiped a hand through his hair and looked away. "I didn't mean anything by it."

Morgan untucked her legs from beneath her, placing her pink sock–covered feet on the floor. And now he was looking at her toes, wondering what she'd do if he massaged them, kissed them…

What the hell is wrong with me? Leave. Now.

But he couldn't stand up without knocking into her, because she was close now, too close. Close enough for him to catch the scent of her perfume, something floral and sweet and entirely too intoxicating for his liking. He clenched his jaw, a small muscle ticking in his cheek.

"I'm sorry," he said again, because that seemed to be all he could say tonight. Why couldn't he just let it drop? That would be the easy thing to do, but then, nothing was easy with Morgan, and damn if he didn't like it that way. His blood pounded, and his chest burned. He felt more alive than he had in years. Everything seemed sharper, clearer, including that pinch of regret that had never quite gone away where she was concerned, even after a decade apart from her. The one that got away.

And now, sitting in her cozy cottage on a chilly early-October night, the fire wasn't the only thing crackling. The air around them seemed charged with anticipation, expectation, longing.

Or maybe that was just him.

Morgan watched Ely, waited. For a long moment, neither said a word.

Then they both said in unison, "Look…"

He gestured toward her, feeling flushed and frustrated. "Go ahead."

"No, no," she insisted, her knee bumping his. "Sorry. You go."

Ely sighed. "I was going to say it wasn't my intention to hurt you. Now or last time." He hadn't meant to get into all this with her tonight, but it seemed as good a time as any. Full disclosure. "A few days after I got home from our night on the beach, Raina called me. We'd dated awhile in college, nothing too serious, but we'd had sex. And apparently we hadn't been as careful as we'd thought, because she'd gotten pregnant."

"Oh." The ice in Morgan's tone now nearly gave him frostbite. "And were you two together when you slept with me?"

"What? No!" Ely gave her a startled look. Given what she'd been through, he couldn't blame her for jumping to conclusions, but still. It stung. "I'm not a cheater, Morgan. I would never do that. Never. We'd broken up weeks before I ever met you." Stomach hard, he continued, "I made a mess of it all. With you, with her. Everything. But I'd like to start over fresh, if you're willing, to get through the next few weeks as smoothly as possible. What do you say?"

A silent beat passed before Morgan shook her head, her shoulders slumping. "I'm sorry, too, Ely. I promised myself after Ben died, I'd stop punishing myself. Stop being so suspicious of everyone and everything. And yet, here I am, taking it all out on you, just like I said I wouldn't." She snorted. "So, yes. Let's try this again. A fresh start. I'll try to make these next few weeks less stressful between us, too. I'm not saying—"

Before she could finish that sentence, something loud

thwacked against the side of the cottage. They both jumped in their seats.

"What the hell was that?" She frowned at the wall across from them.

"No idea." Ely stood. "Stay here while I check."

He walked to the door, only to find Morgan right on his heels, and glanced back at her over his shoulder. "Which part of 'stay here' did you not understand?"

"The part where you give me orders and I obey them."

Her tart answer made him smile. Safety wasn't a big concern out here on the island, but he'd better check just in case.

"Look, I've got my coat on already, and it's cold. You wait here where it's warm. Be right back." Ely opened the door only to have a blast of frigid wind knock him back a step into Morgan. She squeaked, and he turned around fast. "Are you okay? The storm's gotten worse since I got here, and..."

His voice trailed off as he realized Morgan was mere inches away, blinking up at him, looking as mesmerized as he felt. Neither of them moved. Time slowed as they both leaned closer, closer, so close their lips brushed once, twice, then latched on, kissing. Ely's brain short-circuited as Morgan melted against him, wrapping her arms around his neck. Every cell in his body remembered her—her soft curves, the scent of lilacs from her hair, the taste of sugar on her tongue. The catch of her breath and her mewls of pleasure when he touched her.

Some tiny part of his mind clanged with alarm. He shouldn't be doing this. Not after what they'd just agreed to. But the need roaring in his blood quickly drowned that out. Drowned out all of it except the fact that this was Morgan, the woman he'd thought about, dreamed about, believed he'd never see again. Now she was here in his arms again, and he couldn't get enough.

His hands drifted down her sides, barely skimming the sides of those breasts he couldn't stop staring at before, his resistance faltering as his fingers reached the hem of her fleece top, grazing her smooth, silky skin beneath...

Morgan shivered and moaned, and Ely's pants felt altogether too tight.

Buzz, buzz, buzz.

The vibrating of her phone jarred them apart, panting. Her blue eyes looked almost black with arousal, and his first urge was to haul her back to him before his logical side kicked in at last. Morgan was on call tonight.

Hell. He had to stop. They weren't kids anymore. They both had other things to consider. He turned away as she answered her phone.

While she talked to whoever was on the other end of the line, he went outside to check the cottage. Nothing there, no damage, thank goodness. Whatever had struck the place was gone now, but he stood in the cold anyway, letting it work its magic on his overheated body. *Deep breaths. Concentrate on boring stuff, like periodic tables and medical insurance codes.* Anything besides Morgan and how wonderful she'd felt against him. Over and over, he breathed until his pulse slowed and his body calmed.

By the time he stepped back inside, Morgan was ending her call by telling the person to schedule an appointment at the clinic the next day.

"Who was that?" he asked, using work to put some much-needed distance between them.

"Mr. Mowrey? Hurt his foot while hiking. I'm going to see him tomorrow."

"George Mowrey? From Langley?" Ely frowned. "He was on the schedule for the clinic today but no-showed.

He has a history of untreated type 2 diabetes. I've been on him for a while now to keep regular appointments so we can watch his blood sugar levels, but he isn't compliant. Hates doctors and clinics." He shook his head. "If he's calling now, I'm guessing the problem's worse than he's letting on. Let me know if he doesn't show up."

"Will do."

Awkwardness formed a kiss-size elephant between them. Ely checked his watch. "I should probably get going. I'll see you tomorrow, then."

Morgan stayed where she was, her lips slightly swollen and her cheeks pink. His traitorous fingertips buzzed with the need to touch her again. He clenched his hands in his pockets instead.

"Good night, then." Ely stepped out onto the tiny porch, looking anywhere but at her.

"Night," Morgan called as he shut the door behind him.

Ely walked into the darkness, wondering how on earth he was going to get through the next month without losing his mind—or his heart.

CHAPTER SEVEN

MORGAN STAYED BUSY the next few days, so she had little time to think about that kiss, which was good. If she'd ever worried that being a GP on a small island would be boring, she'd been mistaken. Her schedule was packed, and there were lots of genuine cases to keep her constantly challenged. She didn't see much of Ely, except in passing. He was polite but distant toward her after the other night, and honestly, that was fine. She was attracted to Ely, yes. But she wasn't looking for anything more.

Am I?

That question still churned in her mind as she took a quick break between patients to grab a cup of coffee in the break room. She'd just added cream and sugar when Sandy popped her head in.

"Hey, Dr. Salas. Do you have a minute?" the LPN asked, her expression worried.

"Sure. What's going on?"

"Can you to take a quick look at a patient for me? I'm doing the postpartum wellness checks today for Ely, and one of the mothers isn't doing so good."

"Anything specific?" Morgan followed Sandy out of the break room, coffee in hand.

"More shortness of breath than I'd expect, and she just doesn't look right. My gut says something's wrong. The patient claims it's the flu, but Dr. Greg gave her Tamiflu before he left, and there's been no improvement." They rounded the corner and headed toward the exam rooms. "I'm worried if I let the patient go now, she won't return."

"Of course." Morgan left her coffee at the nurses' station, then walked over to exam room three and pulled the file from the holder on the door and perused the patient's history. She and Sandy went in together, finding an exhausted-looking young woman with a baby in her arms. According to the chart, the patient had three children, including her tiny five-month-old infant.

"Hello, Mrs. Murphy." Morgan smiled. "I'm Dr. Salas. I hear you're not feeling well today."

"I'm fine." But the dark circles under the patient's eyes and the grayish pallor to her complexion told a different story. Her cheeks looked sunken as well, and her clothes practically hung off her body, signaling sudden weight loss, though Morgan wasn't sure if that was from sickness or the normal stress of parenthood. She glanced at the chart again and noted the woman's recent drop in weight.

"Since you're here," Morgan said, unwinding her stethoscope from around her neck, "why don't you let me check you over?"

"I… I really don't…want to be…a bother…" The woman stopped, out of breath, and Morgan and Sandy exchanged a look. "And please…call me…Rita."

"Okay, Rita." Morgan waited for the patient to transfer the infant in her arms to Sandy, then checked Rita's pulse and blood pressure, both of which were normal. "Where's the rest of your family today?"

"A neighbor's looking after my toddler while I came here. The older two are in school. My husband's working, as usual," Rita said, her breathing still too rapid. "I need to get home soon. They can be a handful. It's no wonder I'm so tired."

"Hmm." Morgan listened to the patient's chest. Lots of rattles and congestion. Her concerns spiked. "Do you have a history of asthma or TB, Rita?"

"No." The patient frowned. "Dr. Greg thought I might have a chest infection. He gave me meds."

"Did they help?"

"Not really." Rita shrugged.

"Did you finish the full course of antibiotics?" Morgan checked the file again. From Dr. Greg's notes, it looked like he hadn't been completely sure what he'd been dealing with. He'd wanted to see Rita back in a week, but there was no record that she'd kept that follow-up appointment.

"I did," Rita said. "But like I said, they didn't really do much."

"Why didn't you keep your follow-up appointment?"

The patient looked guilty. "I meant to, but with the kids and my husband's crazy work schedule, I didn't have time."

"Okay." Morgan moved to the patient's side again. "Lie down and let me do an abdominal check."

She palpated the area through the patient's baggy overalls, discovering swelling and distention around the stomach area, even though the patient was rail thin. Not good.

"Have you had any unusual vaginal bleeding or discharge recently?" Morgan asked.

"No. I mean after the baby, it takes a while for all that to get back to normal, so no. Nothing weird."

Morgan finished going over the patient's full medical history again, then looked over at Sandy. "Could you check if Dr. Malik is back, please? If so, ask him to come in a moment. Thanks."

The nurse handed the baby back to Rita, then left.

"Why do I need to see Dr. Malik?" Rita asked. "I'm

fine, really. I just need a good night's sleep. That's all. I seriously don't want to bother anyone."

Unfortunately, Sandy returned moments later sans Ely. "He's still at the hospital in Seattle, but I've got him on hold for you."

"Thanks. Excuse me a second, Rita. I'll be right back." Morgan stepped out into the hall, the sour taste of dread in her mouth. Unfortunately, she was pretty sure she knew what was going on with the patient, but she wanted another opinion. Because if she was right, she needed to arrange further tests, including MRIs and a lumbar puncture.

"Hey, Morgan," Ely said when she took him off hold. "What's going on?"

She quickly gave him a rundown of the patient's history and current symptoms. "My biggest concern is a tumor. She's only twenty-six, with three young kids, but…"

Ely waited a beat, then said, "I'd get a chest X-ray first, see what's happening inside, then wait for those result before going further. I should be back by the time that's done and I can have a look at her, too, for confirmation, okay?"

"Okay." Morgan nodded. "Thanks, Ely."

"No problem. See you soon."

Morgan ordered the X-ray, then returned to the exam room to tell the patient.

"Are you sure I need this today?" Rita coughed, protesting. "Is my insurance going to cover this?"

"Yes, you need it. And yes, your insurance should cover it, since it's medically necessary. I spoke with Dr. Malik, and we'd both like to get this done now so we can see why the antibiotics didn't help. We'll know more after that. If you're ready, I'll walk you over to radiology. It's just down the hall. Or, if you're too tired, I can have Sandy get you a wheelchair." Morgan smiled. "And you've got free baby-sitting for a little while. Might as well take advantage of it while you can."

"I guess you're right. Fine." Rita slid off the exam table and followed Morgan into the hall. "I can walk. How long do you think it'll take?"

"Not long. Maybe fifteen minutes for the X-ray, then we just have to wait for the results. And you're next in line."

"Okay."

Morgan left the woman in the capable hands of Joan, their radiology tech, then stopped at the front desk just as Ely walked in, looking at his phone, his dark hair tousled. She watched him for a second, weirdly comforted to know he had her back.

He looked up and saw her. "What's happening with your patient?"

"She's in X-ray now." They went to the nurses' station in the back together. "Then we can figure out what's going on with her."

"Yep." He hung his jacket in his office, replacing it with a lab coat with his name embroidered on the chest pocket. "Where's the chart?"

Morgan handed it to him. "I took another full history."

"Good. Let's wait and see what the films show, then."

Half an hour later, they had Rita's films up on the computer, and Morgan's heart sank. Both lungs were dotted with white circles, indicative of cancer. It was even worse than she'd suspected. Poor Rita.

"We need more tests to be sure. A lumbar puncture." Ely scowled at the screen. "Based on the metastases, it's already stage three, possibly stage four. We'll need to get her referred on to an oncologist in Oak Harbor, stat."

"Yep." Morgan's chest felt hollow and caved in. This was bad. So bad. So unfair. Rita was young. A mother. In the prime of her life. "She's got three children. One's a five-month-old. How do I tell her she's got a terminal illness?"

Ely shook his head, his tawny eyes sad as he placed a hand over hers on the counter. "How about we tell her together? I've known Rita for years. Delivered her last two babies. Plus, I'd like to examine her myself. It's a long shot, but…"

She picked up on that thread of hope in his voice. "Why? What are you thinking?"

He took a deep breath. "She's had some vaginal bleeding but dismissed it as normal after pregnancy, right? But it's been five months since she delivered. Her periods should be regular now."

"But she's also breastfeeding." Morgan considered possibilities. "Are you thinking she had the tumor during her last pregnancy and the hormones accelerated its growth?"

"No. But look at these." He pointed at the images on screen again. "They're called cannonball tumors."

"Okay." Morgan still had no idea where he was going with this. Diagnostically, those types of tumors could signal anything from endometrial cancer to ectopic pregnancy. She should know. She'd been screened for them herself, after…

Her throat constricted, and she swallowed hard, shaking it off. "Where are you going with this?"

"Let me examine her again first. I want to order a urine HCG test."

"Choriocarcinoma?" As far as long shots went, that was the longest. The condition was super rare and, with Rita's medical history, unlikely. Given the spread to her lungs, chemo and radiation might not give Rita much more time, but every second she had with her children now would be precious. Morgan did her best to stay objective, but if Karen's case had been hard, this was heartbreaking.

Some of her anguish must've shown on her face, because Ely pulled her aside as the patient returned to the exam room with Sandy. "Hey." He clasped her upper arms gently. "Let's not get ahead of ourselves. We're still not sure exactly what we're dealing with, okay? If you need to step out, I can handle this myself."

"No," Morgan said, pulling herself together, but still feeling awful inside. "I'm okay. Rita's who we need to focus on here. She's so young. Her life is just starting. This will change everything for her and husband."

As I know only too well.

He rubbed her arms through the sleeves of her lab coat, warming her despite the chill in her blood. "But at least we caught it now and she has a chance to prepare." He waited a beat or two. "Ready?"

"Ready."

They went into the exam room, and Ely ordered the pregnancy test. After Rita gave her sample and Sandy took it to the lab, the patient sat atop the exam table, feeding her baby. The infant sucked contentedly, falling asleep as they watched.

"Well?" Rita reached over to gently put her now-sleeping infant in their carrier. "Can I go?"

"Not yet, I'm afraid." Ely kept his tone gentle. "We need to wait for the urine test results first."

"What? Why?" Rita frowned, looking between Ely and Morgan. Her voice rose, edged with panic. "I'm not sure why you're running that test anyway. I had my tubes tied, Ely. You did it yourself." She scowled, rehooking the strap on her overalls. "Did you find something? We've known each other forever, Ely. Just tell me."

"Your X-ray showed something concerning." He hesitated. "But I'd like to examine you first before I say anything further, okay?"

Rita sighed. "Okay."

"Any unusual lumps or bumps anywhere?" Ely asked as he palpated her abdomen, same as Morgan had done. "Any unusual findings in your monthly breast self-exams?"

"No. Nothing I've noticed."

"Any other symptoms apart from the breathlessness?"

"Nope. Well, except for the tiredness. But I figured that was pretty normal with two kids and a baby." She gave a short laugh, then coughed. "Seriously, though, Ely. I can't be pregnant again. I love my husband, but we're barely making it as it is, and..."

"I don't think you're pregnant," Ely said reassuringly. "But there's a chance it could be something related to that. I won't know for certain until we get the urine test results. In the meantime, relax. Dr. Salas and I will be back shortly to talk again."

Morgan followed him back out into the hallway, just as Sandy returned from the lab.

"The HCG test is strongly positive," the nurse said.

Ely met Morgan's gaze, and a flush of adrenaline zoomed through her system.

"Choriocarcinoma," they said in unison. The rare condition originating in the placental tissue after a pregnancy or miscarriage suddenly became a real possibility for their patient.

The heaviness in Morgan's chest lifted slightly, and she could breathe again. It was still a cancer diagnosis, but for Rita the news was excellent. Those types of tumors responded extremely well to chemotherapy, and she should hopefully make a full recovery. "The hormones in her bloodstream are being produced by the tumor tissue, then, since her tubal ligation was successful."

"Yep." Ely's shoulders sagged with relief. "We'll still need to do additional testing and a biopsy to confirm the diagnosis. Lumbar puncture, too, to confirm it hasn't spread anywhere else. But based on the patient's history, the urine test and the X-rays, I'm confident that's what we're seeing."

Morgan couldn't stop smiling. "Excellent. Thanks for consulting."

"Thanks for asking." Tiny dots of crimson stained his high cheekbones, and Morgan realized he was blushing. The sweetness of it caused an ache in her chest. "Teamwork. Well done."

His gaze flicked to her lips. Morgan's heart did a little flip. *Oh, boy.*

"Come on," he said over the thud of her heartbeat in her ears. "Let's go tell her."

Saturday morning, Ely drove his old truck toward Morgan's cottage. They weren't expected, but he promised he'd take his son out on the boat today and thought maybe Morgan might like to tag along. As he parked to the side of the cottage, behind her sedan, Ely spotted her on the porch, coffee in hand, staring out at the pewter-colored sea.

"Are we going to surprise her, Daddy?" Dylan said in a loud whisper.

"We are." Ely got out and waved to Morgan, who stood now at the edge of the porch, looking far too good for his peace of mind. Even in faded jeans and a dark sweater, she was the sexiest thing he'd ever seen. He helped Dylan and Gina, who was along with them, out, then grabbed a picnic basket Jeremy had packed for them from behind the seats and locked the truck.

It had been a long, hard week at the clinic. They both deserved a break. He'd even gone so far as to call in a favor from a friend at a neighboring clinic to be on call for them so they wouldn't be disturbed. He glanced over at a some-what subdued Gina and smiled. "Ready to go sailing?"

The little girl looked up at him, clutching her pink bunny tight. She nodded and grinned back at him, two of her front teeth missing.

"Good." He ruffled her wheat-blond hair, then reined Dylan in beside him. The boy had enough energy for ten men and could be quite a handful sometimes. Ely had been the same at his son's age.

The minute they reached the corner of the cottage, Dylan took off running again, this time up onto the porch, where Morgan stood waiting.

"Dr. Salas. Daddy's taking us out in the boat today and he said I could ask you to come, too. If you want." By the time Ely rounded the corner with Gina, his son was bouncing around from foot to foot, arms waving. "Will you come with us, Dr. Salas? Please? We brought fresh orange juice and homemade muffins from Jeremy, too, for breakfast," Dylan said in an excited rush.

"Surprise," Ely said, his tone droll. "Sorry to just show up like this, but he's been on me to take him out and I know you love the water, so… But I completely understand if you have other plans."

"Oh." She glanced at the water in the distance, her expression wistful. He understood. Nothing better than being out on the sea, wind in your hair and the sun on your face. The weather was perfect, too, crisp and bright with a hint of breeze. Morgan looked back at him, hesitating, and for a second Ely feared she'd say no. His level of disappointment shocked him. Scary, that.

He cleared his throat and placed a hand atop Gina's head. The little girl was stuck to his leg like glue. "We should've called first, and…"

"Please, Dr. Salas!" Dylan pleaded, hopping up and

down. "Daddy says we need two adults on the boat if Gina comes, too. You have to come. Please. Please, say yes!"

Morgan bit her lip, clearly stifling a laugh. "Well, with an invite like that, how could I refuse?" She glanced at Ely. "What about patient calls? Is cell service good out on the water?"

"Already covered." He explained about his friend in Langley and how he'd made a deal to cover after-hours and weekend patients for them later in the year when one of their colleagues got married in exchange for his buddy covering this weekend. "So we're good to go."

"Great." Morgan headed for her door. "Let me grab a few things and lock up. Be right with you guys." She took her coffee cup back inside, reemerging a few minutes later with a small tote. She held it up and said, "Waterproof poncho, thermos of coffee, wool beanie and a blanket. Anything else I should bring?"

"Just yourself." He took the tote from her in one hand and held the picnic basket in the other.

She locked up the cottage, then followed them down a stone pathway to the bay, where Dr. Greg kept his boat rigged. *The Nightingale* was a pretty thing. Forty feet of cruising pleasure. Tons of deck volume and interior space and fast as a whip, too.

"We'll go out under the engine, then put the sails up once we're clear of the bay," Ely said, offering a hand to Morgan as she boarded, then lifting each of the kids into the boat off the dock. Dylan was already unable to stand still from pure excitement. They got each kid into a life vest, then had them sit on the padded benches. "It's pretty rocky close to shore, and I need more maneuverability than the sails allow. I'll be helmsman if you'll crew?"

"Absolutely," she said, even giving him a jaunty little salute. "Aye, aye, Captain."

And damn if Ely didn't feel a little shudder of pleasure from that.

They put on their own life vests, then Morgan cast off and they were on their way. Ely loved handling *The Nightingale*, steering them smoothly out of the dock and the bay, then into the larger Puget Sound. Being at the tiller always relaxed him, taking away the stresses of the week. He was in his element and grateful for his mirrored aviator sunglasses to hide his gaze, so he could watch Morgan as much as he liked without her knowing. Time slipped away as she sat with the kids, wind ruffling her hair, her smile wide and easy.

Once they were out at sea, they unfurled the sails, working together almost like they'd been a team for ages. Soon they were speeding along. His blood sang, as it always did, with the thrill of being back on the water again. From Morgan's blissful expression, she felt the same. He wondered how long it had been since she'd been out sailing. He doubted she'd had much time with everything else going on.

"Where are we heading?" she yelled across to him after a little while, interrupting his thoughts.

"Marrowstone Island. Thought we'd hike some trails at Fort Flagler, if you're up for it." He pointed toward the land in the distance. "It's an easy walk, even for the kids. We could have a picnic there, too, enjoy the great views. Sound okay?"

"Sounds great." She looked so happy he wanted to hug her. "How fast can this thing go?"

"Fast." Ely chuckled. "But this is the highest speed I'm comfortable going with kids on board. Maybe another time we'll go out by ourselves and see what she can really do."

"Challenge accepted!" Morgan laughed, and the sound washed over him like fine wine, rich and deep and oh, so intoxicating. His pulse skyrocketed, and his mouth dried. If he wasn't careful, he'd fall for her all over again. He looked away fast, concentrating on the water ahead and not the roar of blood in his veins or the sudden tightness in his body that had nothing to do with stress and everything to do with the woman sitting across the deck from him.

Before long, they sailed into a sheltered cove and lowered the sails. Ely took them to shore under the engine. Without the wind, sunlight prickled hot on his skin, and he tugged off his sweater, leaving him in his T-shirt. Morgan did the same, and his mouth dried to cotton as he took in her tank top, how the thin fabric clung to her body, leaving little to the imagination while covering everything at the same time. More flashes of their night on the beach cranked his internal temperature to boiling—the way she'd arched and moaned as he teased her taut pink nipples…

Not helping, dude. Not at all.

Flustered and frustrated, Ely turned the tiller over to Morgan, then he leaped off the boat onto nearby rocks to anchor them securely. "The tide will be on its way out by the time we get back," he said, not daring to look at Morgan again. "We'll be able to wade out then. In the meantime, start passing the kids across to me, please."

"I can jump!" Dylan yelled, defiant. "I'm not a baby anymore."

"These rocks are slippery, son," Ely said in the same tone his dad used to use with him. The one that brooked no argument. "On the boat, you always do exactly what the captain says. No argument."

Morgan bit back another grin and handed Gina over, then turned to pick up Dylan. The kid sighed but allowed it. Ely shook his head. His son sure knew how to be dramatic when needed. He'd gotten that from his mother. Yep.

"Wait for us just up the hill there, kids." Ely held out

his hand out to Morgan. She grabbed her tote bag from him, the touch of their fingers sending zings of pure desire up his arm as she leaped onto the rocks beside him. For a brief second, they were chest to chest, heartbeat to heartbeat. He'd swear hers was racing as fast as his. Their eyes locked, held. It was too much and not enough all at once. He squeezed her hand tighter, tugging her closer, closer...

A seagull squawked loud, diving into the water nearby and splashing them both. Reality snapped back. He cleared his throat and let Morgan go, moving aside to let her pass, his entire body vibrating like a tuning fork because of her.

Walking helped. They followed the trails at an easy pace, letting the kids run on ahead. Partway up to the summit, they stopped for a break. Even with the breeze, it was hot, and perspiration slicked his forehead. Ely used the hem of his T-shirt to wipe his face, not missing how Morgan stared at his bare abs. His skin tingled, like she'd touched him, and now all he could think about was her stroking him there, moving upward over his pecs, tickling through his chest hair. And now heat of a different kind flooded his system.

Enough resting for now.

To keep the kids in sight as they climbed uphill, Ely lengthened his stride, and Morgan fell back a bit. They didn't talk much, which was fine, since he wasn't sure he had enough oxygen for that anyway. Usually, these trails were easy for him. But today, he was having a hard time. Probably because his body was too busy lusting after the woman beside him.

When they finally reached a clearing at the top, Morgan stopped in her tracks, gasping. "That view is spectacular."

The summit wasn't particularly high, but you could look out over Puget Sound and Whidbey Island in the distance—all lush green grass and blue skies and wild-flowers.

"You should check out Camano Island while you're here," he said from beside her. "The San Juan Islands, too, up north. They're all beautiful and have their unique sights to see."

"I'll try. Thanks." Morgan shaded her eyes with her hand as she looked up at him. "Maybe we could take the boat up there some weekend, unless you think Dr. Greg would mind."

"Maybe," Ely managed to say past his tight vocal cords. Spending more time alone with Morgan on the boat would be a fantasy come true. A very erotic fantasy. He swallowed hard. "October can be a tricky month, weatherwise. It can be beautiful one minute and awful the next. The coast guard are always having to rescue hapless tourists this time of year. I'd hate for anything to happen. We need you at the clinic. I need..." He stopped, realizing how close they were standing now. How did they get so close? He stared into her eyes, and his gums thudded in time with his pulse. "I...uh..."

Get it out...

Nope. He turned toward the horizon again. "I need you at the practice, is what I was trying to say. With Dr. Greg gone."

Lame, dude. So lame.

Needing to get away before he made an even bigger fool of himself, he grabbed the first excuse that popped into his head. "I should check on the kids."

Morgan's stare prickled the back of his neck as he headed off in the direction of his son and Gina. God. Why did he become a blathering idiot around her? It wasn't like they were virgins. Hell, it wasn't even the first time they'd slept together. Maybe he was just out of practice. Or maybe it was because he liked things calm, cool, collected. Predictable. And being around Morgan, things were anything but predictable.

Dylan ran around with Gina in the meadow in front of him, playing tag and laughing.

Then it hit him, like a cartoon anvil right on the head.

Right there. That was why he had to be careful.

His son was the most important thing in the world to him. He needed to stay focused on Dylan and forget the rest. He shouldn't need love or passion or romance. The coparenting situation with his ex-wife wasn't ideal, and yes, he got lonely sometimes, but it worked for them. It was a known variable. Morgan was not. Her stint here was done at the end of the month, and she could fly off to Africa again or even Antarctica, for all he knew. And yes, she'd said she wanted a quieter, peaceful life going forward, but that didn't necessarily include him or his son. No. He couldn't take that risk.

"Yay! Muffin time. I'm starving!" Dylan ran past him to where Morgan had started laying out the blanket and the food. "Daddy, can we eat now?"

"Yep." Ely retuned to the blanket and plopped down on one side, opening one of the containers Jeremy had packed for them. "What kind of muffin do you want, son? Blueberry or cranberry?"

"Blueberry!" Dylan sat beside Morgan, and Ely put a muffin on a plate, then handed it to Dylan, along with a napkin. "Thanks, Daddy!"

"Sure." Ely looked to Gina. "What about you? Ready for a muffin?"

"Yes, please," the little girl said. "Cranberry. My daddy makes the best muffins."

"He sure does." Ely got a plate ready for Gina. "What

about drinks? Looks like we've got a couple juice boxes in here or bottled waters."

"Juice box!" Gina and Dylan yelled in unison.

"Guess that leaves us with the waters, huh?" Morgan snorted, jamming a straw into the top of each juice box for the kids, then taking the water Ely handed her. He was careful not to let their fingers touch this time. If she noticed, Morgan didn't say anything.

Once they were all eating, Dylan carried the conversation, chattering away about his schoolwork and the kids in class and his favorite subjects, history and science, just like his dad.

After they'd all finished and the kids went back to playing, Ely stood and scanned the sky. "Clouds are rolling in from the north. Might be bad weather coming. We should go. Wouldn't want to get stuck here during a storm, and the tide will be going out anyway."

Morgan gave him a skeptical look. "Really? It seems so nice out."

"I grew up here. Trust me." Then, realizing what he'd said, he glanced her way as he started packing up their stuff. "Or don't. Trust me, I mean."

She chuckled and gave him a reluctant smile. "I do. Trust you. At least about the weather."

Her words made him feel ten feet tall. By the time they made it back down to the shore, the tide was on the way out, as he'd predicted, dragging *The Nightingale* with it. Now there was an expanse of shallow water and sand to cross where there'd been several feet of sea before. He and Morgan rolled up their jeans and waded out. He tried not to notice her shapely, tanned calves or her cute bare feet with their pink toenails. Yep. Just as he'd thought, those toes were very kissable indeed.

"Kids, stay on shore and wait for me. I'll be back to get you. Understand?"

Both kids nodded, already working on a sandcastle.

About halfway to the boat, the water got deeper fast. Soon it was up to Ely's waist and Morgan's chest. He stopped and looked at Morgan, careful not to let his gaze dip to her now see-through tank top. "Let me carry you the rest of the way."

"No." Morgan backed away slightly. "I'm fine. In fact, you go back and get Dylan and Gina. I can make it the rest of the way to the boat on my own."

"Don't be silly." He scowled and scooped her up in his arms, despite her protests. "Crew all gets treated the same. Captain's orders." He hoisted her higher against his chest and continued toward the boat, digging his toes into the sandy sea bottom to keep stable. Waves battered against him, splashing up his chest and into his face, but all Ely could seem to concentrate on was how soft Morgan's curves felt pressed to his chest, the warmth of her breath over his skin drowning out the salt and the sea and all his fears and doubts. His swim trunks grew uncomfortably tight despite the icy water.

Oh, God.

Distracted, he stubbed his toe on a rock beneath the water, and everything went topsy-turvy. One second, they were standing upright. The next, Ely tipped forward. He tried to hang on to Morgan, but it was too late. They went under. Water gurgled in his ears as he surfaced, choking and gasping, to find Morgan across from him, doing the same, her hair slicked back and her eyes glinting with humor.

Well, that was one way to distract himself, he supposed.

They swam against the current the last several feet to the boat, and he helped her up onto the ladder so she could climb aboard. Morgan flopped down onto the deck like a landed fish, then clambered to her knees, a piece of seaweed stuck to the front of her wet tank top, right between her taut nipples. Her cheeks were flushed, and her blue eyes sparkled with something more than humor now. Something darker and a whole lot more exciting.

Ely swallowed so hard it clicked in his ears, then returned to shore fast for Dylan and Gina, praying the cold water would work its magic on his overheated libido.

By the time he got the kids into the boat, one tucked under each arm, Morgan seemed to have regained some of her composure, too. He cast them off from the rocks, then climbed the ladder himself.

"Are there any towels?" Morgan asked, pulling another bit of seaweed from her hair and tossing it over the side.

"Check below." Ely pulled off his sodden shirt. "Take the kids with you. It's probably warmer down there anyway."

"What about you?" she asked.

"I'm fine." He turned away to start the engine.

"Okay," Morgan said, heading down the stairs below decks. "Be right back. Come on, kids."

"There's a small gas stove down there, too," he called from behind them. "Maybe there's cocoa."

Cocoa was the last thing on Ely's mind, though. He was concerned about control and the fact that he was losing the battle to maintain it when it came to Morgan. Even more concerning was the fact he liked it. Liked feeling reckless and wild and free with her. And that scared him most of all.

CHAPTER EIGHT

By the time they arrived back at the bay in front of Morgan's cottage, the wind had picked up considerably. Dark clouds scudded across the sky as the first drops of rain fell. Ely had been right to cut their trip short after all. Morgan tidied the boat, then stood on deck, ready to jump out with the ropes to fasten *The Nightingale* to shore. As she did, she noticed a figure waiting atop the hill for them. Not Jeremy. This person looked to be female. Huh. A patient, maybe?

The mysterious arrival's identity was soon confirmed, however, when Dylan got ashore and quickly ran up the hill. "Mommy! Wait till you hear what happened. Daddy tried to carry Dr. Salas to the boat and they both fell in the water. And she had seaweed in her hair and we had muffins and juice. I wish you came with us."

Great. Not exactly an ideal way to meet the ex, with Morgan looking like a drowned rat and wearing someone else's sweater because her own clothes were soaked. Didn't matter. She wasn't trying to impress anyone, right? Still, she couldn't stop herself from tugging at the hem of the sweater, now hanging unevenly to her knees, as she stared at Ely's supermodel ex in front of her.

And honestly, the fabled Raina looked pretty much exactly like Morgan had expected her to—tall, thin, with long blond hair and sea foam–green eyes, the same as Dylan's. She was dressed immaculately, too, like she'd walked right out of a Ralph Lauren ad, only serving to make Morgan feel more like a soggy slug. The woman's smile was nothing but friendly, though, as she stepped forward to shake Morgan's hand, and now Morgan felt bad for being ungracious.

"I hope Dylan wasn't too much trouble today. Jeremy sent me down to invite you all for dinner at Wingate." She fiddled with Gina's braids, then looked over at Ely, who'd finally joined them. "I have to go back to Paris tomorrow for fashion week. But I'll be back in time for the ball at the end of the month."

Dylan's lower lip trembled as he clung to his mother's leg. "Do you have to go, Mommy? Can't you stay for a while this time?" He turned to Ely. "Daddy, tell her to stay."

Ely sighed and shook his head. "Your mom has to work, son."

"I hate work. Stupid Paris." Dejected, Dylan stalked off toward the truck alone, head bowed and little shoulders bent. Morgan's heart ached for him.

Ely looked from his son to Raina, frowning. "You did tell him you were staying awhile this time."

"I know. I'm sorry. But one of the top designers had a last-minute cancellation with another model, and my agent got me booked into the spot. It's a lot of money." She sighed, crossing her arms. "We've had this conversation, Ely. You know I love Dylan, and I'm sorry to disappoint our son this time, but he'll get over it. I'll bring him back something nice, too, as a present."

"Gifts don't make up for quality time," Ely grumbled.

The air chilled, and not because of the approaching

storm. Morgan did her best to inch toward the cottage. This wasn't her business, no matter how curious she might be.

Finally, Raina said, "I'll stay longer at the end of the month. Besides, Dylan's in school now. He won't miss me as much."

"Yes, he will. He always does when you're gone." Ely started to his truck with Gina as thunder rolled in the distance.

Raina turned her attention back to Morgan. "I'm sorry. But enough about that. Can I let Jeremy know you'll be joining us, Morgan?" she asked, pleasant as could be, like she and Ely hadn't just been having a polite disagreement.

"Oh, um." She pulled the baggy sweater tighter around herself. "No, actually. I think I'm just going to take a nice hot bath then watch a movie. Maybe another time." She waved to Ely and the kids, who were waiting by the truck. "It was nice to meet you."

"Same." Raina smiled, then turned toward the Mercedes parked near Ely's truck.

"Does that mean we can do it again?" Dylan yelled back at Morgan from the truck window, his expression brightening once more.

"Anytime," Morgan called back. "Ask your dad, and if I'm free, we'll take a picnic and go."

Once they'd all left, Morgan went inside and quickly showered and changed before making herself dinner then climbing under a blanket on the sofa. By then, the storms had arrived full force. The windows rattled against the onslaught of rain and wind.

Morgan tried to read a book, but the creak of the roof kept distracting her. She shuddered. At least she wasn't on call tonight. The lights flickered once or twice but thankfully stayed on. Morgan tucked her feet under her and snuggled deeper under her warm blanket, only to jump at a knock on the door.

Who in the world would be out in this?

Ely, apparently. He stood on her threshold, hair plastered to his forehead and completely soaked. "Sorry to ask on a night like this, but I need your help. One of the local fishing boats didn't return this evening. Coast guard search and rescue are sending a helicopter since it's too rough for a lifeboat. I'm going up with the flight crew. We'll need all staff at the clinic if we find them. Langley's sending people over, too, just in case. There were four men on that boat." His voice cracked with anguish. "I know them all."

"Oh, no." Her pulse tripped, and her chest constricted. "Let me get dressed. You should've just phoned and saved the trip. I would've gone straight to the clinic."

"Service is down again. It's usually the first thing to go during storms this bad." He took a deep breath and stared longingly at the fireplace. "And I didn't want you driving to the clinic on your own. High tide's coming in, and some of the bridges are already washed over. It's easy to get lost. You can follow me. I need to be ready to go the minute the chopper gets to the clinic."

"Okay. Just give me a minute."

Once she was ready, they made their slow way toward the clinic. Morgan gripped the steering wheel tight, nails digging into her palms. Even with the wipers on high, she could barely see the road in front of her, following Ely's taillights instead to stay oriented. They crossed a small bridge, and water splashed against the side of her sedan. For one horrifying second, Morgan feared she'd be swept out to sea, and her stomach plummeted. Finally, after what seemed a small eternity, they reached the clinic.

"Any sign of the coast guard chopper yet?" Ely asked the rest of the staff once they were inside.

"They haven't been able to take off yet," Sandy said from her post at a two-way radio. "Waiting for another crew member and for the wind to die down."

Ely cursed under his breath. "The longer those men are out there, the less chance they have."

"Coast guard crew on the radio," Sandy said, handing him the receiver.

Everyone listened in silence as he spoke with them. Morgan couldn't hear what was said, but based on Ely's grim expression, it wasn't good. At last, he replaced the receiver and turned to the anxious group.

"More trouble, I'm afraid. A tourist's car went over the side of one of the bridges. It isn't submerged yet, but the driver is trapped, and the tide is rising. The fire department is on scene. They're requesting medical assistance. EMTs are all busy on other calls. They may have to cut the driver out of the vehicle. I'm going to go. Didi, can you get my medical kit?"

"Let me do it, Ely," Morgan offered. "You wait here for the helicopter."

He shook his head. "Based on what the coast guard said, it'll be at least an hour before they arrive."

"Then at least let me come with you." She might not be as familiar with the area, but she wasn't going to just sit by and do nothing while people's lives were in danger. "I'll need a medical kit, too, Didi."

Ely hesitated then exhaled slow. "Are you sure? It could get dangerous."

"All the more reason for me to go, then."

He seemed to come to a decision and gave a curt nod. "Fine. We'll take my truck. It's got four-wheel drive."

They braved the lashing rain once more on the way to Ely's vehicle. The air temperatures weren't particularly cold, but the chilly waters of Puget Sound could bring on hypothermia and death within minutes this time of year. Travel was slow again, but they found the bridge where the tourist accident had occurred, mainly by letting the flashing red and blue lights guide them.

"Any luck, Drew?" Ely called to one of the firemen as they got out and approached the partially submerged vehicle.

"Not yet," the burly guy said. "Four people in the car—husband, wife, two kids. So far, we've got everyone out except the husband. His foot's stuck on something in there, and the tide is rising. Water's up to his shoulders now, and he's panicking."

"Any chance to pull the car out, occupant and all?" Ely asked, squinting down at the scene.

"Already tried, but it didn't work," the firefighter said. "If we had more time, maybe. But I'm guessing all we have is ten, maybe fifteen minutes before the car's submerged completely."

"Best take a look, then." Ely slid down the embankment and into the churning water surrounding the car. The eerie glow of the vehicle's submerged headlights rippled around his hips as he peered inside the vehicle, trying to find what was trapping the driver's foot in the car. Morgan knew that if they couldn't get him unstuck, they might be forced to amputate just to save his life. She'd seen it happen before, in Africa. Her pulse stumbled. But they couldn't let the man drown, either.

Determined to help as much as she could, she skidded down the slope, too, on the opposite side of the car from Ely, holding her medical kit above her head to keep it dry. Drew, the burly firefighter, followed close behind her. She reached the passenger side door and stuck her head in through the shattered window to speak to the terrified driver.

"Sir, I'm Dr. Salas. What's your name?"

"B-Bob," the man said between chattering teeth. "B-Bob Taylor."

"Well, Mr. Taylor, we're here to get you out. Please try to stay calm and this will all be over soon." Through the windshield, Morgan saw Ely toss his med pack atop the hood, then dive below the water. Her breath froze until he resurfaced a few moments later.

"It's murky down there," Ely called, water sluicing down his face. "Too hard to see. Sir, can you feel where your foot is stuck?"

"I—I'm n-not s-sure. I th-think m-maybe under the gas pedal," the man said.

"Could we pull him out if all three of us tried at once?" Morgan offered, looking from Ely to the firefighter beside her side.

"No. Too risky," Ely said. "We could injure him more that way. Let me look again on this side."

He dived below the freezing water once more. Morgan had been standing there only a few minutes, and her feet were already going numb. She couldn't imagine how miserable poor Mr. Taylor must be. To make matters worse, the car was teetering precariously on the rocks. Any slight bump or disruption could send it sliding deeper into the water, taking Mr. Taylor—and possibly Ely—with it.

The weight on her chest intensified, making her breaths shallower.

The clock ticked.

The victim looked paler now, and his lips were turning blue, sure signs of impending shock. Morgan propped her medical kit on the edge of the window and pulled out an oxygen mask. She handed the cylinder to the fireman beside her to hold, then carefully reached past the shards of broken glass to slip the mask over the man's face, using her calmest voice. "This will help you breathe until we can give you something for the pain, okay?"

An unholy screech of metal on rock sounded, and the car jerked downward. Her stomach lurched as the fireman stepped back, pulling Morgan with him. *Ely.* Where was Ely? For an awful second, she thought the vehicle might disappear completely into the choppy waves, but thankfully it stopped after a few inches. Morgan inched closer again, and through the open window, she held Mr. Taylor's hand as she searched the frothing waters around them for Ely. Hot bile scalded her throat. No sign of him.

Please let him be okay. I can't lose him. There's so much left to say, so much left undone...

He surfaced then, a few feet away, and relief so profound her knees nearly buckled washed over Morgan. She wanted to run and throw her arms around him, but she needed to stay with their patient.

"Whew. That was close." Ely spit out a mouthful of water. Instead of terror on his face, though, he looked energized. Like he enjoyed the danger. "I got a better look inside the driver's side foot well, and I think we can get him out if one of you pulls while I maneuver his ankle out from beneath the gas pedal." Then he said to Mr. Taylor, "Sir, your ankle is broken. We'll get you out, but it'll be painful."

Mr. Taylor let go of Morgan's hand to lower his oxygen mask. "I don't care. Just help me."

Gusts screeched like banshees through the night, and Morgan reached back into the medical kit. "Let me give him a shot of morphine. That should take the edge off while we get him unstuck." She pulled out a prefilled syringe and uncapped it with her teeth. With any luck, the guy would pass out completely and save himself the suffering.

Meds given, they got to work. Ely went back underwater to lift the gas pedal while Morgan held the car door and the burly firefighter pulled Mr. Taylor to safety. They got him out just in time, too, as the water began to overtake the engine block and the headlights winked out. Morgan felt like she was in an action-adventure movie. Except the chill in her bones told her this was all too real. She wasn't sure she'd ever be warm again.

Ely was shaking uncontrollably, too, when he joined her a few minutes later. They both huddled under thermal blankets while they waited beside Mr. Taylor's gurney for the ambulance to arrive.

"M-my f-family?" Mr. Taylor asked. "Are they all right, too?"

"Yes. One of the firefighters has driven them to the clinic to be checked over," Morgan said once her teeth stopped chattering, doing her best to soothe the man as the EMTs finally pulled up. "Don't worry. It's only a precaution. They're fine. We promised you'd be right behind them."

"Thank you," Mr. Taylor said, his words a bit slurred from the morphine before he drifted off again.

"You ride with him," Ely said to Morgan as they loaded the patient into the back of the rig. "I'll drive back myself."

He took off for his truck before Morgan could answer, looking entirely in his element. She climbed in beside Mr. Taylor for the ride to the clinic. When they got there, the place was a hive of activity. The man's family huddled in the waiting room, looking bedraggled and shocked but otherwise fine, according to Sandy. Still in his wet clothes, Ely got back on the radio again.

"The helicopter still can't take off," he said a few minutes later when Morgan joined him. "Another trawler spotted our disabled boat, though. It's still afloat, but limping. They couldn't get too close because of the choppy water, but there's still hope the crew is all right. For now, all we can do is wait."

"Go get changed, both of you." Sandy shooed them away from behind the counter. "You're dripping all over my nice clean floor." Despite her cross tone, the nurse's concern was obvious. "Mr. Taylor's in X-ray now, and depending on the severity of the fracture, we'll either set it for him or send him on to Oak Harbor after the storm is over. For now, they stay put. No one should go back out in this."

Morgan changed into a clean pair of scrubs and socks she'd found in the changing room. When she returned to the desk, Sandy thrust a steaming cup of coffee into her hands. She'd never felt such bone-deep weariness in her life, and the night wasn't even over yet. She slumped into a chair at the nurses' station and closed her eyes, letting the warmth from the mug in her hands seep into her bones.

She must've dozed a bit, though, because the next time she opened her eyes, Morgan noticed the wind had quieted, and the rain had slowed to a patter. Ely sat beside her, having changed into scrubs, too.

"What's happening?" she asked him around a yawn.

"Coast guard's taking off now." He raked a hand through his tousled hair. "They'll be here in about twenty minutes. They've reestablished contact with the fishing boat, and according to reports, one of the crew has a suspected head injury. I'll go down to the boat to make an assessment."

Faint lines around his eyes and mouth stood out in sharper contrast, and dark circles shadowed his eyes. Dark stubble covered his jaw, and there was a tiny cut on one of his cheeks.

"Maybe I should go instead of you," she offered. "At least I've had a nap."

"I'll be okay." Ely flashed a lopsided grin, showing off

those dimples of his again. She wanted to hug him and tell him everything would be all right, even if it wouldn't. "I volunteer with the local rescue team, so I've been trained for this."

"Hey," she said, frowning. "I thought we were a team here. There's plenty of people here at the clinic. I want to go with you, in case you need backup."

He seemed to consider that a moment, looked like he wanted to argue, but then exhaled slow. "I just don't want anything to happen to you, Morgan. I'd never forgive myself if…"

She took his hand and squeezed, her gaze earnest. "And you don't think I feel the same?"

They looked into each other's eyes a long moment, and a silent understanding passed between them.

"Okay," Ely said, kissing the back of her hand quick. "Let's go."

They pulled on dry coats and went outside to the open field to wait for the chopper to land. Ely introduced her to the crew while they put on their flight suits and harnesses. "This is Dr. Salas. She'll be my medical backup."

The crewman nodded, making final adjustments to Morgan's harness. "Been in a helicopter before?"

"No," she said. "But I love flying."

The crewman handed her a set of headphones, shouting over the roar of the rotors. "Gets pretty loud up there. You'll need these. I have to warn you, it's going to be a bumpy ride."

Morgan glanced over at Ely. He looked perfectly at home, like he'd been doing this all his life. Maybe he had. He gave her a thumbs-up, his obvious excitement infectious. Then he made a slight adjustment to her helmet, his fingers brushing her skin and making her tingle from more than anticipation.

"Last chance to change your mind," Ely said into his mic. The words reverberated in her headphones.

"No way." She climbed into the helicopter ahead of him. "We've got patients to save."

And yep. It was turbulent as hell in the air, just as the crewman had warned. The chopper lurched and dropped, and despite her bravado, Morgan held tight to Ely's leg, squeezing her eyes closed. When she dared open them again, she found him watching her, his expression amused.

"Okay?" he asked through the mic, laughing.

Embarrassed, she nodded, uncurling her fingers from his thigh, but the feel of his rock-hard muscles lingered in her mind, despite more pressing issues ahead. "Fine."

"When we get to the boat, they'll lower me down," Ely explained as they neared the site of the stricken boat. "I'll make the assessment on the head injury. Meanwhile, they'll send down a basket to lift the rest of the stranded crew to safety. Once the other men are onboard, you'll need to triage them for treatment."

"Got it." Morgan gave him a thumbs-up. "Or should I say 'Roger'? Like they do in the movies?"

Ely grinned, and there were those darned dimples again. Thankfully, the pilot interrupted before she could get too distracted, announcing they'd reached their destination. Morgan peered out the side of the chopper at the rain-streaked gray water below, but didn't see the disabled vessel. Then Ely directed her attention to a point forward from where she was looking, and she made out the vague shape of a listing boat, just large enough for the four-man crew and their catch. Three fishermen in bright yellow slickers stood on deck, waving their arms frantically. The absent fourth fisherman was the one to worry about.

As the helicopter hovered over the scene, Ely made his final preparations to be winched down.

She watched, chest constricted, as the cable lowering him swayed in the wind. The fishing boat was also moving with the waves, making the landing tricky. If not for the skill of their pilot, they could crash, or Ely could be crushed. Luckily, he made it onboard, giving them an A-OK salute before unhooking from the cable. Then the next part of the process began.

A few heart-stopping minutes later, the first fisherman arrived in the chopper. Morgan and a crewman pulled him on board, where the man lay gasping and shivering on the floor. She had enough time to do a brief check on him—cold and shocked but otherwise unharmed—before the next fisherman arrived.

The second man pulled on her sleeve to get her attention. "It's Jack who's hurt," he rasped. "The rest of us are all right. But Jack got hit on the back of the head by the winch. He's in a bad way."

"Don't worry," Morgan said, returning her attention to examining him. "Ely will look after him."

"I don't think Jack can move," the first man said. "Hasn't moved since the accident."

Satisfied the second fisherman was unhurt as well, Morgan moved on to the third man, who'd just arrived. Her mind raced with the new information. If the fourth fisherman had sustained an injury to his brain or spinal cord, things would become much more complicated.

Sure enough, Ely confirmed the worst by radio a few minutes later.

"Probable spinal fracture. I can't risk moving him. You'll have to leave me here for now."

"Roger that," the pilot replied. "Can you stay afloat until we can get you towed in?"

"I think so." Ely sounded less sure now, and Morgan's chest squeezed tight. "I need to go silent for a few minutes so I can listen to Jack's chest. Be back online when I'm done."

The third fisherman shouted something Morgan couldn't make out, but she could tell from the man's expression he was worried. She knew how he felt.

"What is it?" she asked.

"Ely hit his head going below to check on Jack," the fisherman said. "Nasty cut on his forehead."

Head injuries were nothing to mess with. If Ely passed out, the boat could get lost in the current or sink. Morgan grabbed the cable and hooked it to her harness. "I need to go down and help Ely."

"Sorry, ma'am." The coast guard crewman stopped her. "It's too dangerous for untrained civilians."

Jaw set, Morgan gave him the same look she'd used on belligerent patients in her ER back in Boston, the one that usually put the fear of God into them. "I'm not an untrained civilian. I'm an experienced sailor as well as a doctor. And it's my duty to help those in need."

Her fierce tone gave the guy pause, and he glanced at the pilot. "What do you think?"

"I don't like it, but if we're going to drop her down, we need to do it now. Fuel's low."

"Are you sure?" the crewman asked, and Morgan nodded. "Okay. Let's get you on that ship."

She kept her eyes closed tight as she was lowered, truly scared for the first time. The rope swayed with the combined turbulence of the helicopter's blades and the wind, and her stomach lurched. Ely would be furious, but she didn't care. Better him angry now and alive than dead in Puget Sound.

Sure enough, when she touched down on the deck, Ely ran up to her, unhooking her cable, seemingly oblivious to the blood streaming down his face from the gash on his forehead. The chopper flew away, leaving them alone on the stranded, disabled vessel.

"What the hell are you thinking, Morgan? Now you're trapped here."

"I'm not trapped. You need help, Ely. You can't care for your patient properly if you're hurt yourself," she said, gesturing toward his forehead as she set her medical kit down at her feet. "Teamwork, remember?"

The boat rocked precariously. With each wave, they took on more water, making it list even more. From experience, Morgan knew they needed to turn into the wind to avoid capsizing, then keep the boat on that course until they reached shore. A calm descended over her. Water had never frightened her. Treat it with respect and keep calm and you'd be fine. Besides, someone had to steer this thing until help arrived, and Ely needed to stay with his patient belowdecks. She told him as much. "Go back below. I'll stay here at the helm. If you need help, let me know. You should let me look at that cut, too."

Two hours crept by. Every now and then Ely would check on her, and she noticed he'd at least put a bandage on his forehead. Good. Eventually the rain and wind eased, and visibility improved. A lifeboat came toward them. She yelled to let Ely know, and as soon they were secured to the stable vessel, she went below. Ely sat beside Jack, looking bedraggled and in pain. She crouched beside him to carefully examine his forehead without undoing the bandage and risking the wound bleeding again.

"You want some analgesics?" she asked him.

"Nah." Ely gave her a tired smile. "Need to stay alert for Jack. I'll take something later."

Another hour passed before they were back on dry land. The air ambulance stood ready to transfer Jack to a neurosurgeon at Seattle General, although he'd begun to rouse and use his limbs again, which was a positive sign. Hopefully, there'd be no lasting damage.

Once they were back at the clinic, Ely reluctantly agreed to let Morgan suture his wound.

"Are you sure you're not too tired?" He looked at her, gaze narrowed.

"I'm more alert than you are." That seemed to shut him up, and he let her close the wound, flinching slightly when she injected the lidocaine. "And you're welcome for saving your butt today."

Ely held his breath, and for a moment, she thought maybe she'd gone too far. They were both exhausted and she'd let her emotions get the best of her there, but dammit. She'd been so scared for him. If he'd gotten badly hurt or worse... Her head spun just thinking about it. She concentrated on her stitches, neat and even and tight. He wouldn't even have a scar.

"I'm sorry. You're right. You were fantastic out there, Morgan," he said. "And I couldn't have done it without you. I just wish you hadn't put yourself at risk to help."

She tied off the last stitch then sat back, frowning. "We're partners, remember?"

"But I don't... I can't..." He leaned forward, rubbing a hand over his face, careful to avoid the area she'd just worked on. "Since my parents were killed in a plane crash, I've been terrified of losing control. Of losing the people I care for. I never want to go through that again. But I can't control you, Morgan. You scare the hell out of me, because I care. Way more than I should, and if anything happened to you today, I can't... I wouldn't..."

His voice trailed off as he hung his head, and Morgan blinked, taking that in. He cared. She cared, too. Way more than she'd intended, and whoa. That was scary. Way scarier than any water rescue could ever be.

In the end, she cleared her throat around the odd sudden lump of longing lodged there, her eyes getting misty as she grabbed clean gauze pads and bandages to finish patching him up. Morgan was glad she was facing away from him as she said huskily, "I'm sorry that happened to you, Ely. I wouldn't want to cause you any additional pain."

I care about you, too.

It had been so long since she'd allowed herself to be open and vulnerable like that, and it left her feeling raw and achy inside.

When she turned back around, Ely caught her hand, bringing it to his lips, and her heart stuttered. "Thank you, Morgan. For everything. It means the world to me."

And just like that, all her good intentions about keeping her distance, keeping things professional, went right out the window. It was a good thing she was sitting down, because otherwise she probably would've melted into a puddle of goo at his feet. That was possibly the sweetest thing anyone had ever said to her.

And while she was terrified, she also now felt...hopeful.

By the time they left the clinic, the sun was rising. The wind had died down to a gentle breeze, and it promised to be a fine day ahead. Morgan was so tired, though, she probably wouldn't see most of it and she certainly didn't feel awake enough to drive. So, she arranged with another staff member to dive her vehicle back to her cottage later, then accepted Ely's offer of a ride home. She planned a warm bath, a hot meal, then bed. Not necessarily in that order. In fact, they'd barely left the parking lot before she fell asleep in the passenger seat of Ely's truck.

She woke to the sensation of being lifted, her head cradled against a solid, warm chest as she was carried inside her cottage and lowered onto her bed. She wanted to reach out, say something, but she didn't have the energy. Just before she gave in to sleep once more, Ely kissed her temple, his lips light as a feather. "Sleep tight, *janaan*."

The sound of him leaving barely registered as she fell into a deep sleep.

CHAPTER NINE

DESPITE THE BUSY NIGHT, Morgan woke at her usual early time. After dressing, she checked her phone, relieved to find she had service again. Sandy had texted that all the patients from the clinic last night were doing well and not to worry about coming in, since Ely had already rechecked all of them earlier.

Reassured she wasn't needed, Morgan decided to take a walk up to Wingate to see Jeremy. The exercise would do her aching legs good. Plus, it would give her time to think about everything that had happened with Ely and how her feelings toward him were changing. Well, not exactly changing. She'd always cared for him. But now those feelings had deepened into more. Her step had a bit of extra bounce now.

Trust me, he'd said that day they'd picnicked on the summit with the kids.

The thrilling, terrifying thing she realized now was that she did.

She trusted Ely Malik, against all odds.

The rest of her trek to Wingate passed in a blur. She couldn't say exactly when she'd gone from doubt to certainty where he was concerned. Maybe it was the way Ely showed such kindness for those around him. Of how he always put others first. Or his devotion and loyalty to his family and friends. Ben had had a lot of good qualities, too, at first, she could admit now. But his main focus had always been his career and his status as a surgeon. When they'd married, she'd known that, but she had thought eventually that would change. She'd been wrong. So wrong.

She didn't worry about that with Ely, though. He would remain as he was.

Even to his own detriment.

Morgan stepped up on the granite steps under the portico at Wingate and knocked.

"Come in!" Jeremy opened the door for her with a delighted smile. "Perfect timing. I just finished a fresh batch of croissants for breakfast. We can sit and you can tell me all about your sea rescue last night."

Morgan wasn't even surprised he knew all about it now. She chuckled and followed him to the kitchen, inhaling the delectable scents of pastry dough and butter, then sat on a stool at the island to relay the previous evening's events, interrupted here and there by Jeremy's gasps.

Once she'd finished, he said, "The Malik men are something else, aren't they?"

Seeing as how she'd only met the one, Morgan shrugged. "Well, Ely was pretty amazing last night, that's for sure."

"Were you scared? I'd have been terrified."

Strangely enough, Morgan hadn't been. Not really. There'd been moments when she'd worried about the patients and more than once when she'd been terrified for Ely, but she'd never been truly scared for herself. She shook her head. "This sounds weird, but I honestly loved every minute of it. It reminded me of my time in Africa. And working in the busy ER in Boston. I guess I've grown accustomed to the adrenaline rushes. Last night was oddly exhilarating, actually." She smiled. "And to think I came to the island for the peace and quiet."

Jeremy laughed. "Yeah. How's that working out for you?"

"How's what working out?" Ely stood in the doorway to the kitchen, and Morgan's pulse tumbled.

"Oh, hey, Ely." Jeremy stood, winking at Morgan. "Come join us. We were discussing your heroics last night."

"Heroics?" He scowled and walked over to the island, touching the bandage on his forehead. "Getting beaned by a low ceiling going downstairs wasn't exactly a superhero moment for me." He stopped next to Morgan, the heat of him brushing her side and making her shiver with delight. He nudged her slightly, smiling down at her. "Luckily, I had the best surgeon on the island stitch me up."

Morgan stared down at the granite-topped island, unexpected euphoria swelling inside her at his compliment. She'd done millions of sutures in her career, could probably do them blindfolded. But Ely's sutures were the most important ones by far to her.

Her voice sounded thick to her own ears as she choked out a thank-you past her constricted vocal cords. Good Lord. She felt like a giddy teenager with her first crush. Morgan glanced up and found the same answering emotions in Ely's tawny gaze. The simmering heat inside her notched higher toward full boil, and despite her realizations about trusting him, this was all feeling too overwhelming. Morgan scrambled off her stool, desperate to get out of there before she tackled Ely to the floor and had her wicked way with him right there in the kitchen. She smoothed a hand down her jeans, palms damp. "I, uh, should get back to the cottage. Thanks for the coffee, Jeremy."

"No problem." He gave her a knowing little smile. "I've had an idea—I thought we could go up to Oak Harbor with Dylan and Gina this morning, since it's Sunday and they're out of school. We'll do some shopping, have lunch. And we still need to get you a costume for the charity ball, too. We can be ready to leave in an hour. What do you think?"

"Uh, that sounds great. Yep." Morgan edged toward the back door, discombobulated. "I'll just go and get ready. See you soon."

Except Ely foiled her escape, following behind her. "I'll come with you. I need to talk to the landscaper about decorations for the ball. Usually Raina handles that, but with her in Paris, it falls to me. Don't want to forget with work and all. We only have three weeks left, right?"

Three weeks.

When Morgan had first arrived here, a month had sounded like forever. Now, it was slipping by so fast. "Yeah," she said quietly, her former happiness dampened. "That's not much time."

"No, it's not." Ely gave her a pointed look as they walked across the patio together, then he turned to face her, stepping closer. "I don't like to waste time, Morgan. Come sailing with me later this afternoon, after you and Jeremy get back from Oak Harbor. I'll meet you at *The Nightingale* at two."

It wasn't a question. Not that Morgan would've declined. In fact, based on how her pulse was falling all over itself in anticipation, she couldn't wait. Whatever Ely had planned, she'd have the sea, the sun and the man she wanted more than her next breath all to herself. What more could she need?

CHAPTER TEN

An hour later, Jeremy, Morgan and the kids clambered into her sedan and started the forty-minute drive up to Oak Harbor at the northern end of the island. Dylan and Gina were excited but trying to be on their best behavior, because ice cream was the reward. And once they were there, true to his word, Jeremy took her to the premier party shop on Whidbey Island to try on costumes. Pirate wench, sexy nurse, courtesan. None looked quite right. Too short, too tight, too revealing.

While she stayed in the dressing room, Jeremy continued to sort through a rack of outfits and every so often pulled one out to pass through the curtains to her. She was beginning to think they'd never find one. Then Jeremy handed in a mermaid costume made of shimmering, silky green material with sequins and an iridescent faux shell–encrusted bodice.

"Oh! I think this one might be it!" he said, glee in his voice. "The color will bring out your blue eyes. Try it on, then let me see!"

Morgan gave the costume a skeptical look. Up close, she could see what had first appeared to be a lot of revealing areas were covered in flesh-toned mesh, so there was that. But the neckline still plunged far lower than she would've liked. She changed into the costume, then checked her reflection in the mirror, turning this way and that to see all angles. Huh. Looked better than she'd imagined. The slinky fabric clung to her body in all the right places without being too tight, and the color did make her eyes pop. Jeremy was right, this was the one. She made a few final adjustments, then pulled aside the dressing room curtain for her friend to see.

Jeremy wolf whistled. "You look ah-mazing! Everyone at the ball will be enchanted." He glanced over at the kids, who were playing in the corner, then leaned in to whisper, "Including Ely."

"Stop it," she said, unable to wipe the grin from her face. They weren't there yet, but maybe this afternoon would change things. She did a little twirl, holding her sparkly green mermaid tail out to the side, enjoying the sensuous feel of the fabric against her skin. Yep. Maybe this afternoon would change a whole lot of things.

"I know where we can get you some shoes," Jeremy said. "And a matching mask."

The kids giggled when Morgan looked over at them, then checked her watch. Almost noon now. Wow. They'd been in there for ages. "Maybe after we get a quick lunch?"

"Good idea."

Morgan went back in the dressing room to change while Jeremy returned to keeping Dylan and Gina occupied. Once she'd paid for her costume rental, they walked to a diner down the block. Halfway there, however, Dylan stopped her by hugging her legs.

"I like you being here, Dr. Salas," the little boy said, beaming up at her. "I hope you never leave."

Morgan's eyes stung, and her answering smile wobbled. "Aw. I like being here with you, too."

She had to clear her throat, her voice rough with affection as she moved them out of the line of traffic on the busy sidewalk.

Jeremy came to her rescue then, sending her a "that's so precious" look. "Come on, kids. Race you to the diner!"

The morning went by far too slowly for Ely. He ended up going back into the clinic to distract himself, then on a few house calls. Then, finally, it was time to head to the dock.

Honestly, he hadn't looked forward to something this much since Dylan was born. The weather today was what they called heavy—bright and sunny and surprisingly warm, but blustery as hell, making the waves choppy and strong. Challenging conditions for any sailor. Also exhilarating if you knew what you were doing. Steering the fishermen's boat to safety the way she had, Morgan had already proved she could more than handle it.

He checked his smart watch again. Nearly two now. His skin tingled all over as he continued prepping the boat, fingers a bit clumsy as he tied knots and tested ropes. Then she was there, the woman foremost in his thoughts for days—for years, really. Morgan waved as she walked out onto the dock, wearing a pink shirt and denim shorts that showed off her tanned curves to perfection. She waved again and called to him, "Hey."

"Hey," Ely said, straightening, hands on hips, heart in throat. "Ready to go?"

"More than ready." She grinned, then took his hand to steady her as she climbed aboard. "But I should warn you. You're going to get wet today. Very, very wet, if I have my way."

Her confidence made his body tighten even more. Never one to back down, he gave the cheekiness right back to her. "And you should know us islanders are never worried about getting wet. Besides, if I remember right, didn't we both go under on our last trip?"

She gave him a look, and Ely laughed. She didn't argue. How could she? It was true. But that twinkle in her eye was pure delight. Ely knew better than most how a boat could soar across the sound when it was set to the wind. How shortening the sails with roller reefing genoas and using a smaller jib could increase your speed and your control. How harnessing the power of the wind and battling the waves could be a mind-blowing experience. Almost as good as sex.

Almost.

And speaking of sex, it wasn't his top priority today, believe it or not. Not that he didn't want Morgan. He did. So much it hurt. And his hand was a poor substitute for the real thing. But he also didn't want to rush her. He knew she had scars from her past. He did, too. Today was about spending time together, away from work, talking through those old wounds from the past. Then afterward, if they both wanted it…

Ely swallowed hard and glanced at Morgan again. She looked happy today. Relaxed. Free. Freer than he'd ever seen her since she arrived on the island earlier this month. He took that as a good sign.

CHAPTER ELEVEN

MORGAN, TOO, CHECKED over *The Nightingale* because it kept her from checking out Ely. His outfit was similar to hers—shorts, T-shirt, sneakers. She had a bikini on under her clothes, and he had on board shorts again. He looked good, but then he always did. Ely had a way of making anything he wore flatter his body, all lithe male sinew and strength. Inside, she fizzed with expectation and molten need. Then she glanced up, and their gazes locked.

Oh, boy. Morgan looked away fast, taking far too much interest in the life vest in front of her. Nerve endings alight, she straightened and set the thing aside, concentrating on the trip ahead and not the dryness of her mouth. "I'll take her out this time. I think I remember the channel you followed."

Ely nodded and cast off. As soon as they were in clear water, Morgan set the sails, her confidence growing alongside the thump of blood in her ears. This was it. "I'm helmsman and you're crew. Ready?"

"Ready."

Within seconds they were traveling at speed. The brisk wind caught the sails, and Morgan hooked her feet under the toe strap, easing herself over the side and the rough waves, counterbalancing the cant of the boat with her weight, reveling in the speed. God, she'd missed this.

The freedom, the catharsis, the rightness of it all. Morgan pulled the sails in tighter, and the boat went faster still. She shouted to Ely over the roar of the wind, "Dr. Greg said I should take her out and put her through her paces whenever I wanted, so that's what I'm doing."

He joined her at the sail, copying her position then giving a whoop of pure excitement. "Amazing!"

They tacked upwind for the next forty minutes, working as if they'd sailed together for years. Eventually, however, Morgan's muscles protested, and she allowed the boat to bear away from the wind, slowing them to a more sedate pace.

"That was fantastic. Seriously. I've never experienced anything like it," Ely said. "Who taught you how to do that?"

"My dad. He started taking me out when I was four." She smiled. "I've always loved it." She looked over at him, feeling slightly flushed from the adrenaline pounding through her veins. "I even had the chance to join the pre-Olympic training squad but turned it down to study for my MCATs instead."

"Wow." Ely looked impressed. "I've never known anyone else like you, Morgan."

"Same, Ely. Same." She stared at the sparkling waters of Puget Sound, chest squeezing. Ely was such a good man. Not the idealized version she'd kept in her head for years. But genuinely good and true. Whip-smart intelligent, loyal to a fault, sexy as hell, dedicated to those he cared for. If she'd been a person who believed in fate, she might have wondered if it hadn't been love that had drawn her back here again after all these years.

The realization brought her up short.

Love? She didn't love Ely.

Do I?

She definitely liked him. A lot. More than a lot. It had nothing to do with his money or his name or even his looks. It had to do with how kind he was, how he knew the right thing to say at the right time to make people feel better. The way her heart raced and her knees went tingly whenever he was around. About how she felt comfortable with him, even when they talked about uncomfortable things. About how she missed him when he wasn't there.

Oh, God. I love Ely Malik.

But she was still afraid, too. Afraid of putting herself in that same vulnerable position again that she had with Ben. Afraid of being open and raw, then having that used against her. Anxiety pressed hard on her temples, and Morgan turned back to fiddle with the rigging, wondering when the temperature had risen so much. The last of the clouds had disappeared from the sky, and there were blue skies for miles. They were floating in a secluded little cove off one of the smaller, uninhabited islands. The sun beat down, prickling hot on her skin. She tugged off her T-shirt, revealing her pink bikini top as her shoulders baked.

Ely watched her, silent and still. Then he removed his shirt, too, giving her an eyeful of tanned torso. Her throat tightened as she gazed at all that bronzed skin begging for her touch. His aviator shades again hid his tawny gaze from her, reflecting back her own wanton expression. Her heart tripped as she imagined those brawny arms around her, pressing her against him, hot skin to hot skin, the fullness of his body inside hers, thrusting again and again and...

"How about a swim?" Ely said, his voice tauter than normal as he pointed. "To the beach there. It's not too far."

Morgan nodded, not trusting her words, as Ely dropped anchor. She slipped off her shorts and toed off her sneakers, then stood on the wooden deck at the back of the boat, poised to dive, hoping the exercise would restore her equilibrium.

Then she plunged into the depths, gasping as cold water enveloped her, icy and invigorating as she struck out for shore, not needing to look back to know Ely followed her. It was almost animalistic now, their connection, predator and prey. Though it was anyone's guess which was which. Morgan had nearly reached the shore when a hand tugged on her ankle. She stopped and treaded water as Ely surfaced not far away.

"You didn't wait for me," he said.

"I knew you'd catch up."

You always catch up.

Then he set off again with long, sure strokes, leaving her in his wake and beating her to shore.

"Hey, you cheated," she yelled once she reached the shallows near the remote pebbled beach. "Competitive much?"

He grinned wide from the beach where he let the waterproof tote on his back fall to the ground at his feet, then opened it to spread out the blanket inside. "Always. You know that, Morgan."

Yep. She did. Another area where they were well matched. To prove it, she splashed water at him. She wouldn't surrender without a fight. Battle lines drawn, Ely slowly faced her, water dripping from his handsome face, then he charged back into the water, sending a small wall of water in her direction. Soon they were play-tussling in the waist-high shallows. He was bigger and taller than her, but she could move more quickly, making it even. At least until he grabbed her by the waist and hoisted her in the air.

"Hey! No fair. What the—?" Morgan yelled, scowling down at him.

Ely held her aloft a moment, and their gazes locked.

His eyes darkened, and slowly, so slowly, she slid down his front until they were face-to-face. Her feet still didn't touch bottom, so she wrapped her legs around his waist against the current, and she kissed him. Like she'd been dying to do ever since that night at her cottage. Her heart slammed against her rib cage, desperate for release. His body responded in kind despite the chilly water, his length hardening against her, pulsing with undeniable need.

He carried her back to shore, and they somehow ended up on the blanket without breaking their kiss. She couldn't get enough of him—the way he tasted, the way he smelled, the way he shuddered against her when she stroked the sensitive spot between his shoulder blades. His hands seemed to be everywhere at once—her back, her butt, her breasts, between her legs. Shocks of pleasure zinged through her bloodstream, making her moan low and deep. Ely nuzzled her neck, then made quick work of her bikini top before taking a chilled nipple into his warm, wet mouth. The contrast made Morgan gasp and arch beneath him, crying out softly. It had been so long since she'd felt this alive. Too long.

He continued lavishing attention on her breasts with his lips and tongue as his hands drifted southward, his thumbs tracing under the top of her bikini bottoms, teasing her, making her shiver with need.

More, more, more.

She panted, writhed. "Please, Ely…"

"Please what, *janaan*?" he asked, lifting his head to meet her gaze.

She'd called her that before, at the cottage. Bewildered and bewitched, she focused enough to ask, "What does that mean?"

He blinked at her, eyes glassy with desire, color dotting his high cheekbones and his hard length pulsing against her thigh. Ely frowned, the muscles in his throat working as he swallowed hard. "It's Urdu. My father's family was from Pakistan."

Not an answer, really, but she didn't care anymore because Ely was kissing the skin above her bikini bottoms now, removing them to make love to her where she needed him most. Using his lips and tongue and fingers in the most extraordinary ways to make her feel the most extraordinary things until she cried out in ecstasy so many times that she lost count. By then, Morgan felt light as a feather and heavy as stone all at once. She wanted more, though. So much more. She wanted him, inside her.

She reached for him, only to have Ely stop her, kissing her palm.

"I don't have protection," he whispered against her skin.

"It's all right." She pulled him up for another kiss, tasting herself on his lips. "I can't get pregnant."

He stilled a moment, watching her closer. "Morgan, I…"

But she didn't want to talk about that now. There'd be time later for old hurts and pain. Right now, she just wanted to feel good, to feel free, with Ely. To help him along, she took advantage of his stunned silence to reach down again and stroke him through the soft fabric of his board shorts. Soon, he groaned low and closed his eyes.

"Please, Ely. I need you," she said again, nibbling his jaw.

Cursing under his breath in a language she didn't understand, Ely pulled away to remove his shorts, revealing the full extent of his desire. Then he was beside her again, and Morgan felt aflame from the inside out. She rocked against him, urging him on, scoring her nails lightly down his back as he rose above her, holding his weight on his elbows. Gazes locked, she parted her thighs to allow him easy entry, and he thrust deep inside her, then held still, their bodies joined. When he finally moved, she moved with him, setting a rhythm that had them both teetering on the brink all too soon. It was too much. It would never be enough. Ely reached between them to stroke her slick folds, and Morgan spiraled over the edge to another orgasm, reaching, straining, soaring.

Ely continued to thrust, riding out her pleasure, once, twice, then joining her in orgasm. Waves crashed over them in time to those on the shore, mirroring their sensations until, at last, they floated back to earth. Arms around each other, breaths ragged. Slowly, reality returned. Sunshine. Seagulls cawing in the distance. Pebbles *cushing* beneath their blanket as Ely rolled off her, then pulled her into his side, her head resting over his heart. Sated and happy, Morgan didn't want to break the spell.

At last, Ely said softly, quietly, his fingers tracing lazily up and down her spine, "Why can't you get pregnant?"

Morgan reminded herself to breathe. Even after all this time, it was so hard to talk about it. But it was time. He needed to know, deserved to know. She shifted slightly in his arms, cleared her throat, ignored the swell of grief inside her, then exhaled slow. "About a year and half before Ben died, I got pregnant. Turned out to be ectopic. They operated to remove the embryo lodged in my Fallopian tube and discovered the other one was badly damaged, too, most likely due to endometriosis. The doctors told me kids weren't an option for me. Not biological ones, anyway."

Chest aching and eyes sticky, she stayed where she was, awaiting his reaction, hoping for the best, fearing the worst. Family was so important to Ely. He had Dylan, but if he married again, Ely would want more children, she was sure. He should have more children. He deserved more children, but she couldn't give him that. The realization broke her heart. She continued when he didn't respond, turning her face more into his chest so he couldn't see her tears. "Ben and I…didn't deal with it well. It's one of the things that ultimately drove us apart. I withdrew, and he looked elsewhere for what he needed. For a long time, I felt like it was my fault. Sometimes, I still do…" Then there was no more holding back her grief. She cried, long, wracking sobs that tore at her soul, releasing the pent-up pain and guilt she'd carried for years. Ely held her closer, his face buried in her hair, whispering soothing nothings, letting her get it out of her system.

When she finally settled against him once more, drained to dregs, he whispered, "Jesus, Morgan. I'm so sorry."

She sniffled and held him tighter. "Thank you."

Long moments passed as more memories washed over her. She'd opened the floodgates and now there was no shutting them, apparently. "I was devastated. Ben and I both were. He'd always wanted a big family. At the time, he said it didn't matter, but I knew it did. We pulled away from each other. I threw myself into my work so I didn't have to think about it, so I didn't have to feel. We drifted apart…" Her breath caught on a hiccup. "During the last year of our marriage, we barely spent any time together at all. We ended up like strangers. That's when he started having his affair. Looking back, I guess I can't blame him now. Stuck in a loveless marriage."

Her body tensed as old emotions flared. Regret. Anger. Resentment. Denial. Coming home to an empty house, leaving before Ben was up in the morning. They'd tried at first to fix the broken parts, but after a while it seemed pointless. Too wrapped up in their own pain and loss to notice anything else.

"Then, I got the call one day from the state police." She went numb, frozen, same as when they'd told her Ben was gone. "He'd swerved to miss a car coming the wrong way down the road. Died instantly. I already told you that his mistress was with him. A colleague, going to the same conference." The next words cut like a knife. "She came to see me after the funeral, told me she and Ben had been in love and he hadn't known how to tell me." Morgan shook her head. "I would've given him a divorce. We weren't in love anymore, and I wanted him to be happy."

She sniffled, those last words hanging in the air a long moment before she mumbled, "Sorry."

Ely finally propped up on an elbow to frown down at her. "You have nothing to be sorry about, Morgan. None of that was your fault. Ever." He sat up and pulled her close into a bear hug. "Please stop thinking that way. People do what they do. We're all responsible for our own choices."

They sat there like that for a while then, him holding her, rocking back and forth slowly.

Morgan took a deep breath, somehow lighter, freer, emptier for having released all that. "Thank you for listening, Ely. For being there for me. I came to this island for a chance to start over, and it feels like maybe I have."

"Hmm." He kissed her temple, wrapping the blanket around them, then staring out at the horizon with her back pressed to his front, his legs caging hers in, both still naked. "As I mentioned earlier, my father was from Pakistan," he said, tone low, intimate. Morgan stilled, not wanting to interrupt him, knowing this was important. "My mother was Scottish. They were a great pair. Their talents complemented each other. I loved them very much. My father built his tech company from the ground up. A true American success story. The only time I think he was ever disappointed in me was when I told him I wanted to be a doctor instead of following in his footsteps. Thank God Sam was interested in carrying on the family legacy.

My father never held it against me, though. I always knew how proud he was of me. Of both of us. My mother, too."

He smiled against her cheek. "I never really paid much attention to the fact that they were famous growing up. It was just a thing about our lives, like the money my father made. I mean, I knew we were different than a lot of people, but living here on the island, no one gave us special treatment. I had a great childhood, running through the farm fields, getting dirty and muddy, sailing on Puget Sound." His fond smile faltered then. "Then the plane crashed happened when I was eighteen. Everything changed in an instant. I had to grow up fast—as the older brother, I had to become caretaker of the estate, the family. Sam was only ten at the time. He couldn't do it. I had to protect him from all the tabloids and the photographers that descended like vultures. The investigation into their deaths came back as accidental. They'd been flying over the Rockies, and the weather turned bad. Nothing the pilot could do, but that didn't stop people from speculating, from nosing into our private business, from spreading rumors and conspiracy theories."

"Oh, Ely." She placed her hands over his forearms around her middle and squeezed tight. "I'm so sorry."

He nodded, his stubble tickling the side of her neck as he rested his chin on her shoulder. "Me, too. But that's why I'm so protective of those I care for, why I stayed here on the island to raise Dylan, far away from all that." He tightened his hold around her. "It's not a life for everyone, though. It wasn't enough for Raina. I understand if it's not enough for you, either."

Morgan opened her mouth to answer, then stopped herself. They were still lost in the afterglow, still dizzy on sex hormones and requited lust. She knew how she felt, but not Ely. When she made a choice about her future, she wanted to do it with a clear head and a wide-open heart. No regrets, not anymore. So, instead of answering his unspoken question, she pulled away to kiss him fast then pull on her bikini top. They'd talk again once they got back to the cottage. They had time. No need to rush.

"Today was wonderful, Ely. Thank you." She smiled, tugging on her bikini bottoms, too. "Should we get back to the boat?"

"I guess we should," he said at last, standing to tug on his board shorts, averting his gaze. They swam back to the boat, raised anchor and set sail for home. The wind had picked up enough again to use the sails, and the late-afternoon sunshine was still warm. Morgan kept trying to touch him or catch his eye to make him smile, but he seemed to be putting some distance between them.

"Everything okay?" she asked at one point, concerned.

"Fine." He smiled, but his eyes were hidden behind his sunglasses again, so she couldn't tell what he was really thinking.

As they approached the bay, Morgan saw a figure standing outside the cottage, eyes shielded, looking out over the water. Jeremy. From the way he was pacing back and forth, he was agitated. She tensed. Something must be wrong. Was it Gina again?

Ely must've noticed at the same time she did, because he hurried to pull on his T-shirt and shoved his feet into his shoes before starting to take down the sails. "Something's up."

They reached the dock, and Ely hopped over the side to tie up the boat, then headed to the cottage without waiting for Morgan. As she finished sorting everything out on the boat, she kept an eye on Jeremy and Ely in the distance. Next thing she knew, Ely climbed into his truck and took off. Her anxiety notched higher. So much for talking about the future. It would have to wait until later.

By the time she hurried up the hill to the cottage where Jeremy still waited, her gut was in knots. "What's going on?"

"It's Dylan. I wasn't too worried at first, because I figured he'd probably caught the same bug Gina had earlier. Then the pain in his stomach got worse and... Oh, God." His words rushed out in a torrent of nervous frustration. "I tried to get ahold of Ely, but his phone was out of range, then I tried the clinic in Langley but couldn't get them, either. Then I rushed over here, and luckily you guys were coming in."

"Okay. It's okay, Jeremy." Morgan patted his shoulder, switching into full-on doctor mode now. "You did the right thing. Let me change, then we'll go back to Wingate together, all right?"

She darted inside, tugging off her bikini and T-shirt, exchanging them for jeans and a clean Harvard sweatshirt, then she scooped up her medical kit and hurried back outside to where Jeremy stood near her sedan. "Try not to worry, okay? Kids are tougher than they look."

Ten minutes later, they hurried through the grand foyer of Wingate and up to Dylan's room.

Ely was there already, examining his son, worry etched on his face. He glanced up at Morgan, frowning. "I'm almost certain it's appendicitis." He pressed gently on the boy's lower right abdomen, then released. Dylan moaned and squirmed in pain. "Positive for guarding as well."

"I want Mommy," Dylan cried, and Morgan's heart clenched. "Where's Mommy?"

"She's working, remember?" Ely crouched beside the bed to smooth damp hair from Dylan's forehead. "I'll call her. Promise. Right now, though, I need you to let Daddy finish examining you, okay?"

He looked up Morgan, eyes filled with anguish, and she placed a supportive hand on Ely's shoulder. A burst appendix was nothing to mess around with. Left untreated, it could lead to sepsis or worse.

"How about if I take a look instead?" she asked quietly. There was a reason you didn't treat your family members—loss of objectivity could often lead to bad decisions.

A beat or two passed before Ely gave a curt nod and moved aside. Morgan stepped in to perform the same exam and reached the same conclusion. "It's definitely appendicitis. What do you want to do?"

"Remove it." Ely raked a hand through his tousled hair. There was still sand on his feet. On her feet, too. Her chest felt heavy and tight. The surgery was relatively common nowadays, but that didn't make his decision any easier. Morgan wished she could comfort him, but now wasn't the time or place.

"Should we airlift him to Seattle General?" she asked.

"No," Ely said. "I'm afraid there isn't time."

"We'll do it at the clinic, then. I'll scrub in." Morgan had done her fair share of appendectomies, too. "Can Dr. Lake do the anesthesia again?"

Ely looked at her, pulling on his ear. "Are you sure you can handle this?"

It wasn't personal, his doubt. She knew that. It was the normal concern of a parent for a child, intensified because of what Ely had been through growing up. Her rational mind knew that. But it didn't stop the pinch of hurt inside her. Morgan tamped it down as best she could and gave him a firm nod. Time to put the personal aside in favor of the professional. Something she'd become all too adept at lately. "I am. I did many of these during my mission trip in Africa. But if you'd feel more comfortable calling in another surgeon from Langley, then that's what we'll do."

He blew out his cheeks, pinching the bridge of his nose, eyes closed. "I just want the best for him."

"I know." She squared her shoulders, determined to put Ely's fears at ease as she would with any other patient's father. "I'm confident I can handle Dylan's surgery." The boy cried out again, then writhed on the bed, flushed and in agony. "But whatever you decide, you need to hurry. The longer we wait, the higher the risk of rupture."

Ely cursed and stared down at his son, then looked back up at her. "Let's call the air ambulance first. Get a rough estimate of their ETA. We can also prep the surgery room at the clinic. That way if things go south before they arrive, then you can step in."

"Good." She crouched by the bedside again, reaching over to stroke the boy's fevered brow. "Dylan, you need an operation on your tummy. You won't feel anything because you'll be asleep, okay? We're going to move you now to get you to the hospital. Understand?"

"Will Daddy do it?" he asked, his tone plaintive.

"No, buddy," Ely said, taking his son's hand and moving in beside Morgan. "But I'll be right beside you the whole time, and I'll be there when you wake up, too. Promise."

"What about Mommy?" Tears filled Dylan's eyes.

"I promise you I'll call her and let her know what's going on." Ely's Adam's apple bobbed. "She'll be there as soon as she can. She loves you very much. You know that, right?"

Dylan nodded, and Ely gently hugged his son, whispering something to him, and Dylan finally relaxed in his father's embrace. Morgan realized then that it wasn't just Ely she loved. It was Dylan, too. She'd do everything in her power to make sure the little boy made a full recovery.

"Morgan, get ahold of Sandy and have her call Seattle General, please," Ely said as he carried his son to the door. "I'll drive him to the clinic in my truck. He can lie down on the seat in the back. And tell Sandy to call Dr. Lake, too, before she goes in to get the surgery room set up."

"Done," Morgan said, following him downstairs. "It's going to be all right."

Ely gave her a side glance, looking unconvinced.

"Jeremy," he called to his chef in the foyer. "Call Raina. Let her know I'll update her when I can. And call Sam, too. You have his number."

By the time they reached the clinic, Dylan's condition had worsened. Ely hurried inside with his son in his arms. Morgan met him at the door and filled him in on Sandy's conversations with the hospital on the mainland.

"Seattle General will send the air ambulance, but there was an accident on the I-5 and they're tied up triaging that. They'll work us in, but it could be up to an hour before they get here. We also need to factor in the travel time back to the hospital." Dylan moaned loudly, and Morgan leveled Ely with a pointed stare. "My professional opinion is we shouldn't wait."

He held his son a little bit tighter, the most precious thing in his world, as if that could keep him safe. As if that could make him well. *Dammit.* He shouldn't have gone out sailing with Morgan. If he'd been home at Wingate, maybe he could have caught this sooner, given them more time, more options for Dylan's treatment. Less risk. More control. That was what happened when he took his eye off the ball.

He should have known better.

Morgan took a deep breath, her tone calm and patient. "As you know, Ely, the longer we wait, the more likely

Dylan is to have complications. It should be a straightforward procedure. If it's done now."

"Dr. Lake's on the way," Sandy called down the hall where they stood. "Be here in twenty."

Ely stared at Morgan. An hour ago, they'd been cuddling on the beach, happy and carefree. Not this.

It wasn't enough for Raina. I understand if it's not enough for you, either...

He wanted Morgan to stay. Wanted to make a life with her, but not if she didn't want that, too.

He'd been there, done that, trying to make someone stay, trying to make it work when it wouldn't. He couldn't go back to that again. He couldn't let this interfere with his son's treatment. Morgan had switched back to professional mode here, and he needed to do the same. His feelings didn't matter.

What mattered was Dylan and making him better.

"Fine. We'll do it here." Ely's mouth pressed into a grim line. "But I'm scrubbing in, too."

For a moment, Morgan looked like she wanted to argue, but she didn't. "Okay. But only to observe."

CHAPTER TWELVE

ELY DID OBSERVE. Morgan felt his gaze on her the entire time—not intimidating, per se, but stressful. With Dr. Lake manning the anesthesia and Sandy acting as her surgical nurse, Morgan made her first small incision, then another, working precisely and methodically until Dylan's inflamed appendix was exposed.

"Irrigation, please." She waited as Sandy cleared the area with sterile saline.

From there it was as textbook perfect a surgery as she could have hoped for. A few snips, a pair of clamps to tie off the blood vessels and then she was placing the removed tissue into a specimen tray to send to the lab. Normally this procedure was done laparoscopically, but the clinic didn't have that equipment, so she'd done it the old-fashioned way.

Immediate danger over now, Morgan exhaled behind her mask, then began closing. Based on the size and inflammation of that appendix, they'd made the right choice to do the surgery now. It would've ruptured before the air ambulance arrived.

Dylan should make a full and swift recovery. With a small scar as a memento.

Ely remained by his son's side as Morgan stepped back

from the operating table, relief and gratitude shining in his eyes over the top of his mask.

After Dr. Lake finished with the anesthesia, they wheeled Dylan into a small recovery area set up next door. The kid was coming around already, but it would still be several hours before he was fully conscious again. He'd probably need a couple of days in the hospital in Seattle, too, to recuperate.

Sandy caught Ely as he followed Morgan into the scrub room. "Dylan's mother is on hold. I brought her up to speed, but she still wants to talk to you."

"I'll be right there." Once the door closed behind Sandy, Ely turned to Morgan, his voice gruff. "Thank you. You did an excellent job."

"You're welcome." She blinked back sudden tears, wanting to hug him, but not daring to in front of all the staff. "I'm glad it all worked out."

They stood there watching each other until Ely backed toward the door. "I need to take that call."

Morgan finished cleaning up, then went next door to the recovery area to check on her patient. Ely was there already at Dylan's bedside, cell phone to his ear. She started to back out quietly to give them some privacy, but not before hearing a bit of their conversation.

"Daddy?" Dylan said, his voice rough from the anesthetic. "Am I fixed?"

"You are. A few days of rest and you'll be all better." Ely bent and kissed his son's forehead, then stroked his hair. The sweetness of it all made her heart ache in the best way. He was such a good father—caring, attentive, engaged. She knew how much being there meant to Ely. She might not be able to have children of her own, but she'd love and care for Dylan like he was her very own. If

Ely wanted that, too. She didn't want to get too far ahead of herself, though. They still needed to talk.

Ely spoke into the phone, then turned back to his son. "Mommy says she's flying back from Paris early to be with you. She'll be here before you know it."

She must've made a noise, because Ely and Dylan both looked over at her. Morgan winced slightly. "Sorry. Didn't mean to interrupt."

"Come in," Ely said, waving her over. "Dylan was asking about you."

"You were?" she asked, stepping up to the boy's bedside.

"Will you stay with me until Mommy gets here?" Dylan looked far too small in the big bed. "Please?"

Morgan glanced from him to Ely, who was watching her closely, then propped her hip on the opposite side of the bed from Ely. In the back of her mind, a warning bell sounded. She was getting too far ahead of herself, getting too attached, too soon, but she couldn't just walk away. Not now. Not yet. She took Dylan's hand and smiled, eyes stinging again. "I'll stay as long as you two need me," she promised, meaning every word. "Now, try and get some sleep."

The next few days Ely didn't see much of Morgan, unfortunately. When he wasn't working at the clinic, he spent his spare time at Seattle General with Dylan. Raina had kept her word and taken a red-eye flight back from Paris and was there, too, rearranging her schedule during her son's recovery.

In the quiet moments alone, though, Ely's mind returned to the beach with Morgan. Honestly, being with her, holding her afterward, had been some of the best moments in his life—at least until she'd not answered him. He was a cautious man by nature, and he'd known from the start she was leaving at the end of the month, so part of him knew he shouldn't be bothered now. He'd gone into this knowing it was temporary. Knowing you couldn't force someone to do something they didn't want. That never worked out well in the end. And while the sex between them had been amazing, it was more than just the physical attraction for him. Always had been. Even if Morgan would never feel the same.

Looking back, he could see he'd fallen for her so hard, so deep, so fast it felt like a whirlwind. Which only served to trigger his already buzzing control issues. Ely was trying to do better with this stuff, but it was difficult. And the last thing he wanted to do was make Morgan think she had to stay here out of some sense of loyalty to him or their past. He certainly didn't want to put his son through another messy breakup. Couldn't put himself through that, either, if he was honest. Being vulnerable only to lose her in the end.

Then again, he feared it was already too late for him with Morgan.

The last car ferry of the day docked at Clinton, and Ely drove onto dry land, deciding to stop at the cottage and see if she was home. This was silly, speculating and guessing when they should just sit down and talk it out. It was after eleven now, a bit late, but hopefully she'd still be up.

The lights were on in the cottage when he pulled to a stop in her drive, and now he was second-guessing himself. Maybe he should go home and get a good night's sleep. Come back in the morning when he was clearheaded. But no. He couldn't do that. They both had to work the next day. There never seemed to be enough time to talk about things. Why wasn't there enough time?

His gut tensed. It wasn't nerves, really. Just uncertainty.

Ely liked to know what he was walking into, and he had no clue with Morgan. It brought up unpleasant memories of the time after his parents had died, when everything had been so chaotic and scary and sad. He'd had to step up and be the man of the house then, even though he'd felt very much not ready. Sam had needed him. Same as Dylan needed him now. He was used to putting others' needs ahead of his own for the sake of the greater good. But now it was just him and Morgan, and he needed to know.

So, he took a deep breath, then got out of the truck and walked up to knock on the door.

Morgan opened it, looking far too adorable in her pink flannel pj's and socks. His heart rate kicked up another notch. "Uh, hi."

"Hi," she said, giving him a curious look. "I wasn't expecting you tonight. Come in."

She moved aside to let him enter, and as he passed by, Ely caught the scent of her flowery shampoo, taking him right back to the beach, to making love on that blanket, her warm, welcoming body tight and wet around him, and...

Stop that.

His throat constricted, and his heart thumped harder. He was here to talk, that was all. Given how tired he was, he wasn't up for anything else, anyway. He followed her over to the sofa and sat down, lifting his arm over her shoulders when she cuddled against him, warm and soft.

This was nice. Cozy. He could get used to this. That was the problem.

They shared a brief kiss, then she tucked her head under his chin. It felt good. Too good. He was never going to get through this if he let his emotions get the better of him. Distance. He needed to keep some distance. Distance and control. "How was your afternoon?"

"Fine," she said, her body relaxed against his. "Yours? How's Dylan doing?"

"Much better. I was just on my way home, actually, and thought I'd stop by."

"I'm glad you did."

A fire crackled cheerfully in the fireplace, and a mug of cocoa and an open book, spine up, sat on the coffee table. But the air smelled of wood smoke and desperation. Morgan had her arms around his waist, and her head rested on his chest over his heart. Which was aching and pounding, all at the same time.

Just ask her. Out with it...

As if hearing his thoughts, Morgan leaned up to look at him. "Something particular on your mind?"

"Uh..." An odd mix of arousal and apprehension zipped through his bloodstream. Why couldn't he just say what he wanted? Yes, it was scary, but he'd been scared before and pushed on. Maybe he was getting sidetracked by his body's response to her, which only intensified his anxiety at his lack of control. He scooted away from her, dropping his arm to his side, frowning. "How do you feel about things? Between us, I mean."

Smooth. Not.

Morgan tilted her head a little, her expression thoughtful. "Good, I think. Why?"

"Oh, well. I just wondered..."

Why didn't you say anything that day on the beach? Do you not want to be with me?

He scowled down at his hands in his lap, then fiddled with the buttons on his shirt. Being direct wasn't so easy when your heart was involved, so he asked a more roundabout question. "Have you thought about staying on at the clinic after Dr. Greg gets back?"

Morgan's brows drew together. "Um. I didn't know that was even an option."

Hell. What a stupid thing to ask, especially since she was right. He and Dr. Greg had never discussed taking on a permanent third partner. God, he was making a mess of all this. "Forget it. Not sure why I asked that. I'm sure you're more than ready to go when your time is up here, right? Probably already have some big job lined up back on the mainland and everything."

She blinked slowly, a bit of the old wariness slipping back into her expression. She bit her lip and went still, looking away. "Actually, I have been thinking a lot about my future lately."

"Oh?" He glanced up at her again.

Morgan nodded, scooting back to the far corner of the sofa. She was obviously skittish. He couldn't blame her.

Ely stood to walk over the fireplace, needing to move, needing to expel some of his nervous energy before it ate him alive. He'd made a mess of this whole thing. Of course, it didn't help knowing more about Morgan's past and trying to walk through that minefield, but still. He should've waited. Even as the clock ticked down on what little time they had together.

"Sorry," he said, scrubbing a hand over his face then staring down at the flames, the searing heat doing nothing to chase away the chill inside him. "Seeing Dylan on that operating table, then later in recovery crying for his mother and her not being there…"

He swore under his breath. "My main goal over the years has been stability. I've done my absolute best to create a stable life for myself and my son here on the island. Then you came along and blew that all to pieces. And while I've loved every minute of it, and while I—" He almost let the words slip out, but stopped himself. Ely hung his head and squeezed his eyes shut. "I shouldn't have said what I did on the beach. Pressuring you about seeing yourself living here on the island. That was a mistake. I never should've asked that. I'm sorry."

"I see," she replied, but from her tight tone, Ely doubted she did.

"Do you?"

She grabbed a throw pillow and hugged it tight against her like a shield. "We all say things we don't mean sometimes. Believe me, no one knows that better than me."

Ouch.

Okay, yes. This was definitely going off the rails.

Abort! Abort!

Stupid Ely. Always trying to do too many things at once. Always trying to control everything. God, he was so bad at this. He rubbed the back of his neck, wishing for a complete reset of this conversation, yet knowing it was already too late for that. "I, uh, I should get home. Early day tomorrow."

"Hmm." Her voice cracked slightly, letting him know she wasn't as okay as she pretended. Every fiber of his being wanted to go to her, to kneel and beg her to stay, but he didn't, because that would only make this whole situation even more pathetic.

So, he headed for the door instead. Stopped on the threshold, staring down at his shaking hand on the knob, looked back at her one last time. "Three weeks left."

Morgan didn't get up, just watched him from the sofa, her smile bleak. "Yes. Three weeks left."

Those three little words—not the three little words he'd wanted to say—sucker punched him in the gut. They continued to pummel him all the way back to his truck. This was exactly why he usually kept to himself. Why he didn't open his heart to anyone. Why he didn't take risks. Because in the end, they always came back to hurt you.

CHAPTER THIRTEEN

THE REST OF the month passed by in a blur for Morgan. Between work and home and back again, she lost track of the days. She and Ely barely spoke now, other than passing pleasantries at the clinic, and it reminded her far too much of the final days of her marriage to Ben. A half-life of grays and beiges with no bright colors at all. Funny how things changed so fast. Things had been so good between them that day on the beach, until they weren't anymore.

She'd allowed him in, past her barriers. She'd trusted him. And look where it had gotten her.

Right back where she'd started.

Well, no more. She was done trusting people.

By the time the day of the costume ball arrived, Morgan didn't want to go anymore, but Dr. Greg and Peggy were arriving back from Australia, and they'd expect her to be there. So, she forced herself to get up and face Halloween, refusing to give in to the hurt inside her. She'd survived worse. She'd get through this, too. Eventually.

It would help once she was off the island, away from Ely. Seeing him every day, working with him, knowing they wouldn't be together, had been almost unbearable. But she'd worked hard to put on a happy facade, pretending everything was okay, keeping things light and normal in front of everyone else, as if her heart hadn't been ripped out and stomped on. She'd only been here a month, only been reunited with Ely for a few weeks, and yet she'd loved him. And she'd lost him, and deep inside she feared this might be it—the thing that broke her once and for all.

She absently tapped her spoon against the shell of the soft-boiled egg she'd made for breakfast to crack it, but as soon as the sunny yellow yolk ran out, a sudden wave of nausea washed over her, and she barely made it to the bathroom in time. Afterward, she sat on the tile floor, hot face pressed to the cool porcelain of the toilet, waiting for her heaving stomach to settle. Maybe she was coming down with something? On the bright side, that could be a genuine reason not to go to the ball tonight.

"Knock, knock. Is there a doctor in the house?" Jeremy let himself in, then walked into the bedroom, halting at the sight of Morgan on the bathroom floor. "Good Lord, what happened to you?"

He helped her up and placed a cool washcloth on back of her neck, then stood nearby as she sat on the edge of the bed, apparently concerned she might faint or something.

Morgan took a few deep breaths, then looked up at him. "I think I'm coming down with something."

"Oh, no! Don't say that. You can't miss the ball tonight. Everyone will be there." Jeremy smiled. "Including Sam."

The last thing in the world she wanted to do at that moment was meet more Maliks. She sat up, glad some of her dizziness was subsiding, and forced a smile for her friend. "I feel like I know him already, since you've said such nice things about him. How are things with you two now that he's back at Wingate?"

"Good." Jeremy blushed and took a seat beside her. He had it bad, that much was obvious. "Always nice to reconnect whenever he's here to visit." His besotted grin beamed brighter than the sun, casting her own heartache in deeper shadows. "Sam's so charming and nice and wonderful." Then his smile faded, and his shoulders slumped. "But I'm not sure he's as enamored with me. I mean, I'm just the chef. And I've got Gina." Jeremy shook his head. "It could all be a one-sided crush on my part, but I can't help myself."

She put her arm around his shoulders. "You are not just the chef, Jeremy. You're a funny, smart, talented man raising a child all on his own. And you're an excellent cook. Sam would be lucky to have you. Any man would be lucky to have you."

Jeremy laughed, then hugged her, and Morgan felt slightly better. If nothing else came from her stay on Whidbey Island, she'd made a good friend in him. But she was leaving Sunday night, the day after the ball, and that made her sad. There was no way she could stay, though, not without a job and with constant reminders of Ely around every corner. She'd thought she'd hidden her misery pretty well, but apparently not, because Jeremy gave her a speculative stare.

"What's wrong?"

Morgan shook her head. "Nothing. Just thinking about everything I have to do once I leave."

"Liar." He nudged her with his shoulder. "Dr. Greg might offer you a permanent spot at the clinic."

"No, he won't." Morgan sighed. Ely had said as much during their last ill-fated conversation. "Besides, I promised my parents I'd visit them next month." Not the whole truth, but not a total lie, either. She really did have those things to do, even if the real reason she couldn't stay was Ely.

"But I thought you loved it here. And you seemed so happy. Is it too boring? It is, isn't it?"

"Uh, no." Morgan chuckled. "My time here has been anything but boring."

"I'll miss you. I hope you'll stay in touch."

"Or course I will."

Morgan stared at her hands in her lap for fear Jeremy would see the tears in her eyes. God, she'd been so emotional lately, too, above and beyond the regular breakup-heartache stuff. What was even happening to her?

"Dylan will miss you, too. And Gina. And Ely." He reached over and covered her hands with his. "You know, Ely has this weird way of thinking that putting his family first means putting himself last, but that's not true. The best thing he can do for Dylan is to show him what a healthy, loving relationship looks like. I love Ely like a brother and want to see him happy. He needs someone to share his life with, someone who shares his passions and interests, someone who cares for him as much as he deserves. Someone like you, Morgan."

It took a second for her brain to register his words. She looked up at him, startled. "What?"

"You heard me." Jeremy gave her a look. "I can see you love him. It's been written all over your face since a week after you got here. Remind me to play poker with you. You're a horrible bluff."

Oh, God.

She felt sick again, for totally different reasons now. She couldn't live through all the pitying looks again, not after what she went through with Ben. "Please don't tell anyone, Jeremy. I'll get over it. I have to, since he doesn't love me back."

Jeremy snorted. "If that's true, then Ely's a bigger idiot than I thought in this situation. You two are perfect for each other. And he cares for you. I know he does, because he gets that sappy look on his face whenever he sees you. If he said otherwise, it's probably just to protect himself."

Morgan took that in. Ely hadn't really ever said one way or another whether he loved her. She'd just assumed based on his actions the past few weeks that he didn't. But maybe that wasn't fair. He'd had a lot on his plate to deal with, so...

"Look. He sees it as his duty to look out for everyone. So, he works hard to stay in control. My guess is, you're a risk to all that."

"But I'd never do anything to hurt him or Dylan."

"Yes, but if Ely feels things are out of his hands— the way emotions usually are—then he withdraws. It's all about protection with him, remember?"

Jeremy stood then and sighed. "Well, I better get back to Wingate. I've got a ton to get done before the ball tonight. Keeping an eye on the caterers, and God forbid everything's not perfect when Mrs. MacIntosh takes over for me later." He stopped at the door and looked back at her over his shoulder. "Pick you up at six thirty?"

Morgan nodded, still distracted by what he'd told her. Was it possible she'd been wrong these past few weeks? After he left, she cleaned up her now-cold breakfast, her thoughts tumbling like wet socks in a dryer. It wasn't even noon yet. She should do something. Take a walk. Get outside. Then she caught a glimpse of herself in the mirror, and *ugh*. She looked like hell—face pale, dark circles under her eyes. She hadn't been sleeping well, either, come to think of it. Though that wasn't surprising under the circumstances. Partway through changing her clothes, another wave of nausea hit, and she ran to the bathroom again.

Man, she hadn't been sick to her stomach like this since...

She sat back on her heels, bile burning her throat and breath ragged.

No. No, no, no.

Her butt hit the bathroom floor, and she held on to the toilet for dear life. It wasn't possible. It couldn't be possible. Her period was late, sure, but that could be from stress. And the doctors had told her the chances of her conceiving again were slim to none.

They could be wrong...

Morgan clambered to her feet, pulse pounding in her ears. She splashed cold water on her face, then brushed her teeth again before returning to the living room and slumping down on the couch, running through dates in her mind. It had been three weeks since she'd been with Ely on the beach. Early still, but an at-home test could be accurate.

What if I am pregnant?

A tiny frisson of excitement sparkled through her before a second frisson of fear followed.

Even if she had somehow conceived, having a viable pregnancy was a long shot at best. With a history of ectopic pregnancy, she was at greater risk for another.

She took a deep breath, then exhaled, struggling to slow her racing pulse. More likely it *was* stress throwing off her cycle. That wasn't uncommon, and Lord knew she'd been under enough of it here on the island. No need to worry. She'd leave here tomorrow night, and her period would probably start right up again.

Then a sudden image of her holding a baby with Ely's dark hair and her blue eyes flashed into Morgan's mind, and she couldn't breathe. Couldn't do anything except cry. She wanted a family of her own more than anything, and the thought of that family including Ely and Dylan and a new baby seemed too perfect to be real. But she couldn't get her hopes up. Not yet. If by some miracle she was pregnant, it was still too early yet. She could still lose it. Or it could turn out to be ectopic again. And if that happened...

No.

Think logically. Take things slow.

First, confirm if she was even pregnant. That meant a drive into the pharmacy at Langley for an over-the-counter test. Morgan slipped her feet into her sneakers before grabbing the keys to the sedan and her purse. Do the test. Then at least she'd know, one way or another.

That evening, Ely fiddled with the tricorn hat of his pirate ensemble. Dylan stood watching him, eyes round with wonder. He was dressed as a battle droid from the latest sci-fi flick and looked more adorable than intimidating, but Ely wasn't going to be the one to tell him.

"Are you excited to go to the ball tonight?" Ely asked his son.

"Yes! Mommy said I can have all the candy I want," Dylan said from the doorway.

Ely didn't buy that for a second, but he let it pass. There'd be plenty of people at the party to keep an eye on Dylan's sugar bingeing, including Morgan.

Morgan.

With a sigh, Ely stared at his reflection. He looked ridiculous with his fake sword and a stuffed parrot on his shoulder. He felt even worse, but that had nothing to do with his costume and everything to do with that last awful conversation with Morgan. They'd avoided each other after that night, and with his busy schedule he hadn't had the time or the mental wherewithal to confront her again. And while it wasn't entirely true, that was the excuse he was going with anyway.

Honestly, he didn't know what to say, really. Didn't know how to just put himself out there and risk it all to be with her. No matter how much he might love her and want to be with her. Knowing he was doing the right thing didn't stop his stubborn mind from remembering her laugh, her smile, the way her lovely eyes lit up when they'd been out sailing, the way she smelled like sunshine and flowers and hope. So much hope. Hope for a different future, a different life, one filled with family and love and laughter.

All the things he wanted. All the things slipping through his fingers after tonight.

"Ely? Are you in here?" Raina called, walking into the room. She stopped short at the sight of his getup. "Wow. Maybe I should've said, 'Argh, matey.'"

"Ha-ha," Ely said. "Not."

She was dressed in a gown that would've made Marie Antoinette jealous, her long blond hair twisted into a sophisticated-looking arrangement atop her head and a pair of diamond earrings he'd given her as a wedding gift twinkling in her ears. In her hand was the matching necklace. She held it out to him now. "Can you help me clasp this, please?"

Raina turned her back to him, and he quickly fastened it around her neck.

"Dylan, sweetie," she said to their son, "can you go check on Uncle Sam, please? See if he needs anything?"

The boy ran from the room, eager to help, as Raina faced Ely once more. "Want to tell me what's bothering you?"

"Nothing." Ely scowled down at his shiny black boots. "I'm fine. Why?"

She shook her head. "Because you're walking around like someone kicked your puppy."

"I most certainly am not." He looked past her into the mirror again, adjusting his parrot. Okay. Fine. Maybe he did look a little mopey. He had a black hole where his heart used to be. He was entitled to some wallowing.

Raina watched him, arms crossed and a brow raised. "You love her, don't you?"

Ely tried to play it off with a dismissive wave. "I don't know what you're talking about."

"Don't lie to me, Ely. I always know. It's a mom thing." She sat down on the edge of his bed with the regal air of the queen she was dressed like. "It's obvious, you know. The way you look at her. Like she's your favorite Christmas gift, the present you've always wanted."

He snorted. "Morgan and I are friends. Work colleagues. That's all."

Raina snorted. "Right. Sure."

Ely met her gaze in the mirror and frowned. "It doesn't matter what I feel, anyway. She's leaving tomorrow night, and that's the end of it."

"Did you tell her?"

"No." He tugged at his coat again, even though it was fine. "Why would I do that?"

"Because she has a right to know, Ely." Raina stared at him in the mirror, speaking slowly like he needed the extra time to absorb her words. Maybe he did. "I wish you'd learn that love isn't something any of us can control. Not you. Not anyone. It's wild and free, and that's the beauty of it. Love is a gift, Ely. And rather than accept it and cherish it, you think it's something to be feared and locked away."

She picked at the pale duvet beneath her fingers. "Losing someone you love is better than never having them in your life at all. Don't miss your opportunity to change, Ely. Talk to Morgan. Dylan loves her. You obviously do, too. Ask her what she wants, how she feels. Ask her to stay. Maybe she'll surprise you. Think about it. Just because things didn't work between us doesn't mean Morgan's not your perfect match. Take a risk. That's the only way you'll know." Raina stood and walked to the door. "The guests will be here soon. Meet you downstairs in five minutes."

CHAPTER FOURTEEN

BY SIX THAT NIGHT, Morgan had that deer-in-the-headlights look, shocked and scared and stunned out of her wits. The test sat there on the bathroom counter, two pink lines glowing cheerfully up at her, even though she still couldn't quite believe it.

Pregnant. I'm pregnant.

On autopilot, she dried her hair, then got dressed, shimmying into her mermaid costume without really paying much attention. She still wasn't keen on attending the ball, and the thought of seeing Ely right now made her feel sick all over again. Morgan absently placed a hand on her lower abdomen, wondering how he'd react, knowing she was carrying his baby.

Not that she'd mention it tonight. Not after what had happened last time. And the last thing she wanted was for him to be with her out of some misguided sense of responsibility. She'd had more than enough of that with Ben, thanks so much.

Of course, she'd never really thought about being a single mother, either. She'd never expected to be a mother at all, honestly. But life had a way of surprising you. And even though she'd just found out, even though the embryo couldn't have been more than the size of a poppy seed, she already loved her baby fiercely.

Morgan took a deep breath and straightened her dress. Her boobs were kind of sore, too, and from the online research she'd done earlier, that wasn't uncommon, even this early in gestation. Her smile grew until she was grinning like an idiot. Couldn't stop. For the first time in a long time, she finally felt like she had a future to look forward to.

So, fine. Enough feeling sorry for herself. She'd go to the ball, if only to make an appearance. Show Ely she was more than capable of thriving on her own. And when the time came, when she knew for certain the pregnancy would go to term, she'd tell him about their baby. Let him decide how he wanted to proceed at that point. If he wanted to stay in their lives, great. If not, they'd be okay, too.

She left her hair long and draped over one shoulder, then applied shimmering green eye makeup and a final slick of gloss. There. Done. Ready to face whatever the evening threw at her.

Jeremy knocked on the door, right on time.

"Your carriage awaits," he joked when Morgan opened the door, her tail draped over one arm.

"Wow. You look amazing, Jeremy." He did, too. His hair was slicked back, and his Jedi robes looked like they'd come right off the movie set. He even had a trusty lightsaber at his side. "Is that your weapon or are you happy to see me?"

"Both?" Jeremy chuckled and walked into the cottage, shutting the door behind him. "And don't you look stunning, Princess of the Sea?"

"Thanks." According to the clock on the wall in the kitchen they still had a few minutes before they needed to leave, so they took a seat in the living room. "Can I get you something to drink?" Morgan asked. "Maybe some wine to take the edge off before the party?"

"Wine is always welcome." Jeremy relaxed back into

the sofa cushions. "This is the first quiet moment to myself I think I've had all day. Don't think I've sat down, either, since I was here earlier."

"What's Gina going to be tonight?" Morgan poured him a glass of white wine, then got a sparkling water for herself before carrying both drinks back into the living room. "Was it a witch?"

"Fairy princess," he said, then raised a brow at her glass. "You're not having wine, too?"

"Uh, no," Morgan said. "I'm not much of a drinker."

They sipped in companionable silence for a few minutes.

"I almost wish we didn't have to go," Jeremy said at last. "Would be nice to just have a night in."

"Don't tempt me. You know how I felt earlier."

"Better now?" She nodded. Jeremy set his empty wineglass aside. "Good. Mind if I use your bathroom before we go?"

"Not at all."

A few minutes later, Jeremy returned, his expression curious as he held up the pregnancy test. *Crap.* She hadn't even thought about hiding it. Add brain fog to her list of symptoms.

"Is there something you want to tell me?" He looked at the stick again. "I wasn't snooping, I swear. It was just sitting there on the counter, so... It's positive, right?"

For a moment, Morgan considered lying, but Jeremy was her friend, and she could really use a confidant right now. "Yes, it's positive. But you can't say a word to anyone."

"I swear." He sat beside her on the sofa again. "You don't look like this is good news."

She gave him a quick history of her previous pregnancy. "I honestly didn't think it was possible. All the doctors told me the chances of it happening again were basically nil after last time, but I guess they were wrong."

"Wow." Jeremy took her hand, his expression concerned. "Is this good news, then?"

Morgan stood and took the stick from him, frowning. "I don't know. Yes, I mean, I'm happy about the baby. But I'm also scared. I don't want to get too excited yet, because it's still early and there's a chance it could be another ectopic pregnancy, which would not be good, so…"

"When will you know?" He lowered his voice. "More importantly, who's the father?"

Morgan's cheeks prickled with heat, and Jeremy gaped. "Oh, my God! It's Ely's? Have you told him yet?"

"No. And that's why you can't say anything to anyone, understand? Not Ely, not Sam, not Raina. Not even Gina or Dylan. No one." She walked the pregnancy test back to the bathroom, then returned. "I'm going to tell Ely, eventually. Once I know for certain the pregnancy is viable, then—and only then—will I say a word to him about it."

Jeremy's smile fell. "Oh, Morgan. I really think you should tell him now. He should know. And if there are complications, he can be there for you, by your side. You shouldn't have to go through this alone."

"No." Morgan bit her lip. "I don't want him to feel like he needs to be with me just because of the baby. I want a man by my side who's there because he loves me, not out of some sense of obligation." Her voice shook despite her wishes. "And what if this pregnancy isn't viable?" She shook her head, blinking back tears. "No. I can't do that to him. I'm sorry, Jeremy, but you need to let me do this my way, okay?"

"Okay." He exhaled slow. "I won't say anything. Promise."

"Good." Morgan started toward the door. "Now, let's get going to this ball."

By the time they arrived at Wingate, the gala was in full swing. Morgan thought she recognized several faces behind the masks and makeup—a few patients and most of the staff as well. A wide variety of costumes filled the house, everything from superheroes to animals and even a few inanimate objects like dice and power tools. Spooky music filled the air, and the estate was decorated to the hilt with a corn maze set up outside for the kids, lots of black lights and spiderwebs and jack-o'-lanterns. Skeletons occupied many a corner, and ghoulish green garlands of strung-together bones surrounded the banisters in the foyer.

A small local band was set up in one room, along with a dance floor, and were cranking out "Monster Mash" at earsplitting levels. Everything was all so festive and fun, and soon Morgan found her cares and worries disappearing, her toes tapping to the lively beat. Through the throng of guests, she spotted Ely across the room, dressed as a pirate with Raina beside him, looking resplendent in a courtesan costume. They certainly made a striking pair, tall and gorgeous.

Ely's head was bent toward another guest as he listened to what they were saying. It wasn't until the crowd parted slightly that Morgan saw it was Dr. Greg and Peggy he was speaking to. Excited to hear all about their trip, Morgan headed over, too, despite her plans to avoid Ely as much as possible. As she approached, her gaze locked with Ely's, and for a moment the rest of the world fell away.

Morgan looked anywhere but at him as she greeted Dr. Greg and Peggy.

"Welcome, Dr. Salas." Raina hugged her. "You look amazing. I always wanted to be a mermaid."

"Sounds like things have been pretty exciting at the clinic since I left, Morgan," Dr. Greg said, picking up the thread of conversation and running with it. "Sea rescues, emergency surgeries. Ely says you handled it all like a pro, though."

"I did my best." She smiled. "It's wonderful to have you back. How was Australia?"

"Beautiful." Peggy beamed. "We'll have you over for dinner tomorrow before you leave to tell you all about it. Ely, too. That way you can both catch my husband up to speed on his patients at the same time."

"Daddy!" Dylan ran up to them, colliding with his father's legs.

"Hey, buddy." Ely laughed, hugging his son around the shoulders. "Slow down."

"Sorry." The little boy looked up at Morgan. "Where've you been, Dr. Salas? When can we go sailing again?"

"Oh. Well, I think we'll have to take a rain check on that, since I'm leaving tomorrow night." The words hurt more than she expected, and she swallowed hard around the lump in her throat.

"No!" Dylan said, transferring his embrace from Ely's legs to hers. "Don't go, Dr. Salas. I don't want you to leave. Please stay with me. You can live with Daddy and me and we'll all be happy ever after, just like the movies."

Her heart pinched, and Morgan's breath caught. Her gaze flew to Ely's, and he looked as uncomfortable as she felt.

"You know," Raina said, coming to her rescue and pulling Dylan to her side, "I never got a chance to thank you, Morgan, for all you did for my son. If anything had happened to Dylan…" Her voice cracked a bit, and Morgan's chest ached even more. Without thinking, she placed her hand atop her abdomen again.

She looked down at the crying little boy, then crouched in front of him. "Even if I'm gone, you can still call me, you know. I'll give you my number. Anytime, day or night, I'll be here for you, whenever you need me."

Dylan sighed, his cheeks damp and red. "I love you, Dr. Salas. You made me all better." He hugged her tight, burying his face in her neck, and Morgan closed her eyes, soaking it all in, saving it to comfort her later. "You look really pretty, Dr. Salas," Dylan said at last, leaning back slightly to look at her. "Don't you think she looks pretty, Daddy? You should tell her she looks pretty, too, Daddy, so she isn't so sad."

Oh, boy.

The last thing Morgan wanted was to cry in front of everyone. She straightened then, smoothing her hand down the front of her shimmering green dress. She could feel the eyes of the group on her, and her stomach lurched. She shouldn't have come tonight after all, especially with her hormones out of whack. It was too much. It was all too much. "Uh, please excuse me. I need some air. Dr. Greg, Peggy, so glad to have you back. Can't wait to hear about your trip tomorrow."

Morgan walked away as dignified as she could with her mermaid tail draped over her arm, aware of people glancing her way. She didn't stop until she found Jeremy standing near the buffet tables, eyeing the caterers' setup critically. Every conceivable kind of hors d'oeuvre and finger food seemed to be there—bowls of shrimp and platters of meat and cheese and crudités, even tiny cakes decorated with swirls of chocolate and cream. If her stomach hadn't been in knots, she might have tried some.

"I'm not sure there's enough," Jeremy said, his tone anxious. "Do you think there's enough?"

"You're kidding, right?" Morgan gave him an incredulous look. "There's enough stuff to feed the entire island twice over."

"Well, I guess that's good, because it looks like most of the island is here," Jeremy said. "I haven't seen a party at Wingate so heavily attended since New Year's Eve. Lots of people come to the island just for that event each year." He looked at Morgan. "Maybe you'll even be here for it, eh?"

No. She wouldn't. Morgan stared at her toes. It was best if she left. Went to see her parents, took some time to figure out where her life would go from here. Start over fresh somewhere new. It would be hard leaving Whidbey Island, though, especially since she was just starting to feel like she belonged there, but it wasn't the end of the world. She couldn't let it be.

"Hey." Jeremy put his hand on Morgan's shoulder. "Everything will work out. You'll see."

Before she could respond, a tall, dark-haired man joined them. He was slimmer and a bit shorter than Ely, but there was no mistaking the resemblance.

"There you are, Jeremy," the man said, slipping an arm around Jeremy's waist and pulling him close. "I've been looking for you everywhere. Don't tell me you're worrying about the food. This is your night off."

"Sam, let me introduce you to Dr. Salas," Jeremy said, ignoring his other statements. "Morgan, this is Ely's younger brother, Samuel Malik."

"So nice to finally meet you, Dr. Salas." He smiled, then bent to kiss her hand, a charmer for sure. Something else the Malik brothers shared, apparently. In the background, the band was halfway through a rousing rendition of "Don't Fear the Reaper." Sam grinned, looking between her and Jeremy. "What do you say we all hit the dance floor and get our groove on?"

"Uh…" Out of the corner of her eye, she saw Dr. Greg and Peggy talking to Raina, but Ely wasn't with them anymore. His location soon became apparent, though, when someone tapped on her shoulder and she turned to find Ely blocking her path.

"May I have the next dance?" he asked, holding out a hand to her.

The band started a lovely, slow rendition of "Zombie" by the Cranberries, and Morgan didn't want to make a scene, dammit, so she accepted. They walked to the dance floor, and Morgan did her best to relax in his arms as they swayed to the music, her tail draped over her arm and his fake parrot bobbing on his shoulder, but it was difficult.

"Okay?" he asked as more couples joined them.

"Fine." But between the warm, gentle pressure of his hand on her lower back and the brush of his body against hers, she felt like a complete mess inside. To make matters worse, the thought that this could be their one and only dance together made her eyes sting once more with unshed tears.

No. No, no, no. Stop it.

She would not cry here. She wouldn't.

"Penny for your thoughts?" he whispered near her ear, making her shiver.

Morgan sighed, then looked up at him. "I'm thinking about leaving."

She felt his intake of breath.

He glanced around before maneuvering her toward an open door that led out to the empty patio. A breeze blew, cooling her overheated skin and making her shiver. Ely slipped off his pirate coat and wrapped it around her shoulders, leaving him in his frilly white shirt and black pants, like some historical romance novel cover model. His arm brushed hers as he leaned on the railing, and her heart hurt even worse. For all they'd had and all they'd lost.

"I thought you should know." His quiet voice filled the darkness. Her breath caught, held. "Dr. Greg's going to ask you to stay. For the record, I told him I think you'll make an excellent addition to the practice." Ely gave a tentative smile. "We'd be lucky to have you."

Well, damn. Not what she'd hoped to hear from him. A job offer wasn't bad, but she couldn't take it. Working with Ely every day, knowing he wasn't hers, would never be hers, would be too hard. And what about the baby? Hard to hide that once she started showing. Her throat dried, and she swallowed hard. "I, uh… I don't know. Won't that be awkward? Us working together, after what happened?"

The breeze blew again, harder this time. Through the soft, dim light filtering out through the open doors behind them, Ely looked…broken, somehow. Vulnerable. She'd never seen that in him before.

"What I said that night, Morgan… Not just about staying. About everything. Or what I didn't say." He shook his head then sighed, his broad shoulders slumping. "I wish you didn't have to go." The words were so soft, she would've missed them if she hadn't been paying attention. Then he turned slightly and touched her hair, pain lurking in his tawny eyes. "I wish…"

"What?" she whispered, the rush of blood in her ears drowning out everything but him. "What do you wish?"

His fingers traced down her cheek to her jaw. "I wish I'd called you all those years ago."

They both gave a short laugh, then stilled. Time slowed as Ely kissed her again. Morgan froze at first, then melted against him. His pirate coat fell from her shoulders and hit the ground as the kiss turned hungry, desperate, until finally Ely pulled back, their ragged breaths the only sound in the otherwise quiet night. "God, Morgan. I want you so much."

"I know," she said, summoning every ounce of will-power she had to push him away. "But that's not enough."

The sound of a clearing throat had them both looking at the door again. "Sorry to interrupt," Raina said. "But Jeremy's looking for you, Ely. A problem with the caterers or something."

Morgan stepped back and nearly tripped over her tail, which had fallen from her arm during her kiss with Ely. She scooped it up now, embarrassed and just wanting to go home and have a good cry. "I'm actually going to head back to the cottage, I think. Lots of packing to do before tomorrow. Excuse me."

Behind her, Ely said, "Morgan, wait..."

But she was already gone, back into the stuffy house, where too many people in too many costumes were pressed together like sardines. Except now she remembered that Jeremy had driven her over. Damn. As she neared the buffet tables again, she saw him and Sam talking, their heads bowed together, each giving the other heart-eyed looks. Good. She was happy for them. Jeremy deserved his happily-ever-after. At least one of them would get it. She couldn't ask him to leave the party now, but maybe he'd let her drive his car back to the cottage, then she could bring it back tomorrow.

Yes. That sounded good. The rain from earlier had stopped, so it should be an easy drive. She'd walk, but it was night, and the last thing she needed now was to get lost again.

She approached the two men, then waited for a them to notice her so as not to interrupt anything. "So sorry, Jeremy," she said with faux brightness. "But I've just remembered something important I need to do back at the cottage."

Like sob myself to sleep in my pillow.

"Would it be a problem if I drove your car there, then brought it back in the morning?"

Jeremy's gaze narrowed. "Everything okay?"

"Yes, fine," she said too fast, her chest tight. "I just have so much to do before I leave. I've made my rounds here, so now I'd just really like to get back to it."

"I'll take you." Jeremy set his sparkling water aside.

"No, no." Morgan held up a hand in protest, glancing at Sam. "Seriously. I'll be fine. It's not far, and you two are having such a good time, I don't want to break that up."

Jeremy exchanged a look with Sam before sighing and slipping the keys out of his Jedi robes. "Fine. But call me once you get there so I know you made it okay. And please be careful."

"Always," she said, relieved beyond measure. "So nice to finally meet you, Sam."

"Same." They hugged briefly, then she was off to the front entrance, heart racing in time with the steps, hurrying through the crowd like the hounds of hell were after her, because it kind of felt like they were. All the ghosts of her past, all her mistakes, all her missed opportunities, haunting her tonight.

She found Jeremy's car and climbed in behind the wheel, cramming her mermaid tail into the passenger seat, then started the engine. The costume restricted her leg movements, which made working the pedals more difficult, which was why she'd ridden with Jeremy to begin with, but it was too late now. She'd make do. After adjusting her mirrors and fastening her seat belt, she eased out of the parking spot and started down the drive to the main roadway. The sky was dotted with clouds, but the moon peeked through now and again. Between that and her headlights, she could see well enough, though the area looked different at night. Lots of odd shapes and sinister shadows. Very fitting for Halloween.

At the bottom of the hill, she turned out on the roadway,

heading for the cottage. Images from the day replayed in her mind like a movie. Being ill that morning. The positive pregnancy test. Telling Jeremy. Arriving at the party. Kissing Ely goodbye on the patio.

That last one stabbed her hard between the ribs. God, she was going to miss him. Dylan, too. And Jeremy. There was so much she was going to miss about Whidbey Island. But she couldn't stay, not with the way things were now.

Ahead, something streaked across the headlight beams, glaring white. An animal, maybe? Morgan slammed on the brakes, and the car skidded. The road was still damp, and before she knew what was happening, the back end fishtailed off the asphalt and onto the muddy berm. From there it was a slow slide into the ditch on the other side.

Perfect. Right back where she'd started.

Grumbling, Morgan gunned the engine like she'd seen Ely do that first day, but it didn't work. Just sent mud flying everywhere. Next, she got her door open and crawled out, only to end up on her butt on the ground because her tail got caught between the car interior and the door. She fell awkwardly with her ankle beneath her, and pain shot up her leg. Dammit. She wiggled the toes, and luckily, they still seemed to be working. Each tiny movement sent bolts of agony through her nervous system, though. Tried to stand on it, but nope. Wouldn't support any weight. She collapsed back down in the mud as a distant *baa* echoed on the air.

Foiled by sheep. Again.

Cursing, she took a deep breath, then reached into her shell-covered bra top for her cell phone. She turned it on, but of course there was no service out here. Perfect.

Above her, on the roadway, she heard cars pass, but no one could see her down here in the ditch. The engine was still running, though, so maybe she could use the hazard lights to signal for help. Except that would mean moving, and moving was nearly impossible with her sore ankle.

Still, she had to try. For herself. For the baby.

Slowly, excruciatingly, inch by inch, she managed to get to her knees, then hauled her upper body back through the open car door and strained to reach the hazard light button on the dashboard.

Click.

Then, exhausted, she flopped back onto her butt to wait. Wait and pray someone would find her soon before she froze to death out here.

CHAPTER FIFTEEN

ELY STOOD FOR a long moment after Morgan walked away, feeling like his entire world had imploded. Then, oddly numb, he bent to pick up his coat from the ground where it had fallen before looking at Raina. "You were right. I do love Morgan. But I can't ask her to stay here when she wants to go."

His ex-wife crossed her arms, tapping her slipper-covered toe impatiently on the flagstones. "Did you even ask her?"

"No," he said, pulling his coat back on, the stuffed bird sitting crookedly now, but Ely didn't care. "But I did tell her Dr. Greg was going to offer her a permanent position at the clinic. If she'd wanted to stay here, that should've changed her mind. It didn't."

"Men," Raina muttered, walking over to him to adjust his parrot. "She doesn't care about the job. Okay. Scratch that. She does care about the job. Very much. But she also cares about you, Ely." She stepped back and sighed, hands on her hips. "Look. I know you're a control freak. Lord knows I lived with it long enough. And I know you want everything to be certain. But that's not how life works, Ely. Sometimes you have to have to jump first, then look later. Otherwise, you're just going to resign yourself to being miserable the rest of your life.

"Seriously, Ely. You need to give Morgan a reason to stay besides the job. Give her your heart. Let her know how you feel, how important she is to you. There's no guarantee, but I'd bet good money she feels the same. And maybe, if she knew how you felt, that might make all the difference. I know you, Ely Malik. Don't you dare go comparing what happened with us to what's going on between you and Morgan. Don't. Everyone wants different things, and that's great. It's what makes the world such an interesting place. I love my job and it requires me to travel a lot and I'm okay with that. But Morgan doesn't strike me as someone stricken with wanderlust. Just the opposite. So, go find her and proclaim your love. I'll bet good money you sweep her off her feet before the night is through."

Ely wasn't a man who liked to gamble, especially with his heart, but deep down he knew he had to try. He'd let Morgan get away once in his life. Fate was giving him another shot, and he didn't want to lose her again. It had been a long, hard road to get here. But he'd gotten clear, finally.

Because of Morgan.

"Okay. I will." He squared his shoulders, pulled his tricorn hat lower, then headed inside.

The crowd parted before him as he made a beeline toward the buffet table, thinking maybe Morgan had gone back to Jeremy and Sam. But when he got there, she wasn't with them.

"Have you seen Morgan?" Ely glanced around the room. "I was just with her on the patio."

"No," Jeremy said. "She left. Took my car keys to drive herself back to the cottage."

Dammit. He didn't like her being out alone at night. "And you let her go?"

"I offered to drive her myself, but she said she'd make

it fine on her own." Jeremy frowned. "Why? What happened, Ely? Is everything okay?"

"No. Everything definitely is not okay." He stalked off toward the foyer, running into Mrs. MacIntosh, who was dressed like the teapot from *Beauty and the Beast*. He snagged his housekeeper by the handle. "Did you see Dr. Salas leave? How long ago was it?"

"Yes," she said, her nod making her lid hat wobble on her head. "About five minutes ago. Said she was going back to the cottage."

Ely hurried outside. Maybe Morgan was still making her way through the maze of cars out front, but no. Beyond the lighting around the house, it was pitch-dark. Unease bored into his belly. He found his truck and climbed in, heading down the drive.

By the time he reached the main road, he had to turn on his bright beams to see any distance in front of him, and worry sprouted tentacles and wormed through his body. The island might be close to Seattle, but it felt like a world away out here. Occasionally the moon peeked out from behind the clouds, illuminating the land on either side of him. He had the window down and despite the cool night air slapping his face, his skin burned and his pulse raced.

God, why didn't I just tell her I loved her and beg her to stay?

That would've been so easy. But no. He'd had to keep it all inside, just like always. Growing up too soon, it had been a defense mechanism, a way to protect himself. Now, it was just keeping him away from the thing he wanted most in the world. His feet ached in his shiny pirate boots, but that was the least of his concerns. He had to find Morgan. Had to tell her how he felt. Had to beg her forgiveness.

Halfway to the cottage, a brief flash from somewhere below the road to his right made him slow down, then back up, after checking to make sure there were no cars coming behind him. Ely eased onto the berm and put the car in Park, took a couple deep steadying breaths. *Calm down.* He needed to calm down and think. He'd lived here all his life. Used to play on this land as a kid. There'd been a time when he could find his way to the cottage and back blindfolded. Chances were good that Morgan was already home and he was making a big deal out of nothing. Still, he couldn't seem to shake the feeling that something was wrong…

Then, there. Again.

Another flash, from below the edge of the berm, fainter this time. He cut the engine and got out. The moon had completely disappeared behind the clouds now, and from the scent of the air, it would probably rain again soon. If Morgan was still out here, he needed to find her. Ely pulled out his phone and turned on the flashlight app, only to see his battery was nearly dead. Not good. And even if he wanted to call someone to help him search, there was no signal.

Just keep going. Keep moving. Morgan needs you.

In the stillness, waves crashed against the distant shore. Keeping the water to his right, he continued to search, sweeping his phone in front of him from side to side in case Morgan was lying on the ground somewhere, hurt or bleeding. Images of the plane crash that killed his parents flickered in his head—the carnage, the destruction, the death—and they robbed the oxygen from his lungs making him breathe harder. Morgan had been lucky that first day on the island. He'd been there to rescue her then. If he had his way, he'd always be there to rescue her.

Please, God, let her be okay. Must find her. Have to find her.

He hadn't been able to save his parents, but maybe, just maybe, he could save Morgan.

Then a sound. Faint at first, carried on the wind. He stopped and listened.

A voice. Someone calling for help. He headed down the embankment toward the noise, barely making out a huddled figure on the ground at the bottom of the ditch. The closer he got, the more an outline emerged. A woman, with a mermaid tail. Morgan. He'd found Morgan.

Heart slamming against his rib cage, he moved slowly toward her over the craggy rocks. Then she cried out and he threw caution to the wind, leaping and jumping and running, running for her and calling her name, not caring about the mud sucking at his boots or the slippery rocks or the fact he'd probably have to buy this stupid costume now because of the damage. It didn't matter. Nothing mattered except the fact that she was safe. He sank to his knees in front of her and pulled her into his arms, his voice shaky and rough. "Are you all right? I was so worried. What happened?"

"I was heading back to the cottage and then something ran in front of the car. A sheep, I think," she said, wincing. "And I think my a-ankle's b-broken," she stammered, shaking so badly now it was hard make out her words. "S-stupid t-tail. G-got c-caught."

"Shh." He held her closer, kissing her hair, breathing her in. "I've got you. I've got you. I won't let you go. I won't ever let you go."

Morgan went quiet then. Either she'd fainted or fallen asleep. Regardless, he needed to get her inside and warmed up. Ely carefully picked her up and carried her up the embankment to his truck, then drove her to the cottage. He'd send a tow truck to retrieve Jeremy's car in the morning. For now, his top priority was Morgan.

JOIN US ON SOCIAL MEDIA!

Stay up to date with our latest releases, author
news and gossip, special offers and discounts, and
all the behind-the-scenes action
from Mills & Boon...

millsandboon

millsandboonuk

millsandboon

It might just be true love...

MILLS & BOON

THE HEART OF ROMANCE

A ROMANCE FOR EVERY READER

MODERN

Prepare to be swept off your feet by sophisticated, sexy and seductive heroes, in some of the world's most glamourous and romantic locations, where power and passion collide.

HISTORICAL

Escape with historical heroes from time gone by. Whether your passion is for wicked Regency Rakes, muscled Vikings or rugged Highlanders, awaken the romance of the past.

MEDICAL

Set your pulse racing with dedicated, delectable doctors in the high-pressure world of medicine, where emotions run high and passion, comfort and love are the best medicine.

True Love

Celebrate true love with tender stories of heartfelt romance, from the rush of falling in love to the joy a new baby can bring, and a focus on the emotional heart of a relationship.

Desire

Indulge in secrets and scandal, intense drama and plenty of sizzling hot action with powerful and passionate heroes who have it all: wealth, status, good looks…everything but the right woman.

HEROES

Experience all the excitement of a gripping thriller, with an intense romance at its heart. Resourceful, true-to-life women and strong, fearless men face danger and desire - a killer combination!

To see which titles are coming soon, please visit

millsandboon.co.uk/nextmonth

touched him in the past. Linked her hand with his as they'd walked along, talking. Wrapped her arms round him as they'd danced together. Slid her hands through his hair as he'd kissed her. Stroked his bare skin as they'd made love...

She hadn't been prepared for this. She'd thought she was working in a brand-new unit with Ric Fanelli and Henri Lefevre. She'd been so busy over the last three days, packing and sorting out her flight and accommodation and saying goodbye to everyone, that it hadn't even occurred to her to look up the rest of her new department. But clearly Angelo had known she was coming here, because there wasn't the slightest trace of surprise in his expression.

'I didn't realise you worked here,' she said, forcing herself to sound calm and collected—even though seeing him again had sent her into a spin. 'I thought you were in Rome.'

He inclined his head. 'I moved here a year ago.'

And he looked just the same as she remembered. The same unruly hair that he tried to keep neat for work, but it insisted on curling and tended to stick out everywhere by the end of a shift. The same dark, soulful eyes with their incredibly long lashes. The same beautiful mouth that had made her heart feel as if it had done a triple somersault whenever he smiled at her.

Continue reading

SURGEON'S SECOND CHANCE IN FLORENCE
Kate Hardy

Available next month
www.millsandboon.co.uk

MILLS & BOON ®

Coming next month

SURGEON'S SECOND CHANCE IN FLORENCE
Kate Hardy

Sam was still smiling when she walked into the Michelangelo Hospital. At the reception area, she picked up the lanyard with her ID card, and asked for directions to Ricardo Fanelli's office.

When she reached the maternity department and pressed her ID card to the reader, nothing happened; clearly her card hadn't been activated yet. Not wanting to be late on her first day, she pressed the buzzer.

There was an answering buzz, and a few seconds later the door opened.

And her knees buckled for a moment when she saw who'd opened the door to her. She almost dropped the flowers she'd bought to thank Lidia.

It couldn't be Angelo. How could he be working in Florence, when she knew he lived in Rome?

But the name on the lanyard round his neck was very clear: Dottore Angelo Brunelli.

The love of her life. The man who'd told her he didn't love her any more.

'Hello, Sam,' Angelo said. 'Welcome to the Michelangelo Hospital.' He held out his hand, offering her a formal handshake, as if to prove that they'd both got over the past.

The second her palm touched his, her skin felt as if it was fizzing. Memories bubbled over, of how she'd

COMING SOON!

We really hope you enjoyed reading this book.
If you're looking for more romance, be sure to
head to the shops when new books are
available on

Thursday 26th
May

To see which titles are coming soon, please visit

millsandboon.co.uk/nextmonth

They'd gotten so many gifts recently for the baby, but jewelry seemed a bit over-the-top. "Ari won't be old enough to wear that for a while yet."

"Good thing it's not for him then, huh?" Ely creaked the tiny velvet box open to reveal a beautiful antique diamond and sapphire ring. It sparkled in the firelight, or maybe that was the unexpected tears in her eyes. "Morgan Salas, love of my life, mother of my child. Will you please, finally, do me the honor of being my wife?"

She bit her lip, so choked up she could barely speak.

"Oh, God. Yes. Yes, I'll marry you, Ely. Love of my life. Father of my child."

It had taken her nearly a year, and a lifetime of regrets, to reach this point. But now she was here, with Ely, with their family—the one they'd created together, from friends and those they cared for—and she never wanted to leave again. He slipped the ring on her finger, then kissed her.

"I love you, Morgan. Forever," he whispered, his forehead to hers in the firelight.

"I love you, too, Ely," she said. "Forever and ever, amen."

* * * * *

EPILOGUE

Ten months later

MORGAN SAT BY a crackling fire in the nursery she and Ely had painstakingly decorated at Wingate, nursing newborn Ari—short for Arham, after Ely's father. The baby's blue eyes, just like his momma's, slowly drifted closed, and a wave of complete contentment washed over her.

Despite a few bumps in the road, she'd carried the baby to full term. Had been on bed rest for the last six weeks of the pregnancy, which made everyone cranky, but she'd do it all again in a heartbeat.

"Hey," Ely said from the doorway, tiptoeing over quietly to crouch beside her chair, stroking his son's downy head. He'd put Dylan to bed, and finally the never-ending stream of guests and well-wishers over the last few weeks had subsided. She loved the sense of community on the island, but Morgan was exhausted and planned to go to sleep herself just as soon as she got Ari down for the night. Ely looked tired, too, his hair a mess, dark circles under his eyes, a shadow of stubble on his jaw. He was still the most gorgeous man she'd ever seen. He grinned back, shifting slightly to pull something from the pocket of his black sweats. It took her a moment to realize it was a ring box. Frowning, Morgan glanced at him. "What's that?"

with us at Wingate. He said as much earlier, after all. So much wiser than us."

She smiled. "Yep. Smart kid."

"He really is." Ely gave her a squeeze. "So, will you marry me, Morgan?"

It would be so easy to say yes right now. She wanted nothing more than to spend the rest of her life with him. But she didn't want to rush it. If something happened with the baby and he changed his mind about her like Ben had, it would break her heart.

"Give me a little time. Okay? I'm not going anywhere."

He leaned up to meet her gaze. "You're not?"

"Nope." Morgan grinned, not realizing until right then that she meant it. "I'm not. Can't go turning down Dr. Greg's offer, now can I?"

ket falling to her waist. When he finally pulled back, he was grinning from ear to ear.

Her heart stumbled. "Please don't get too excited yet. It's still early and things could go wrong. With my history of ectopic pregnancy, I'll be high-risk either way." Morgan sighed. "I wasn't going to tell you until I was sure the pregnancy was viable."

"Ah, Morgan," he said, kissing her once more before snuggling in beside her. "I know there are still risks, but I don't care. We'll make an appointment at Seattle General for a full workup. And no matter what happens, we're still a family. You, me and Dylan."

"Don't forget Jeremy and Sam, too. Even Raina. Maybe even Dr. Greg and Peggy." Morgan settled in, letting the warmth of the fire and Ely seep into her tired bones. For the first time since the previous morning she was relaxing at last. Maybe they didn't have it all figured out. Maybe they both still had doubts. But one thing she'd never doubt was Ely. He'd more than proven to her during her time here that he was trustworthy. After all the pain Ben had caused her, she could let someone in again.

Let Ely in again.

"You're right," she said finally. "I don't want to waste this second chance we've gotten, either. I love you so much."

"And I love you, Morgan," he murmured against her temple. "I want to grow old with you, side by side. We're meant to be together. We've already wasted enough years." Ely met her gaze, his tawny eyes bright with honesty. "Let's not waste any more time. Please."

"I love Dylan, too, you know," Morgan said. "He's like my own son."

"Dylan loves you back. He'll be thrilled to have you

"Yes, God, yes, I love you! I don't go around calling just anyone my beloved." He shook his head, and his hands dangled limply between his knees now as he flashed a rueful smile. "After I got a stern talking-to from Raina, I went inside to talk to you, to tell you how I felt. But then Jeremy said you'd left and..." He scrubbed a hand over his weary face. He still looked wonderful to her, maybe even more so all scruffy and tousled. "I went after you. I was scared out of my wits. Especially knowing how cold it gets at night and how dark. God, if I hadn't found you, Morgan, you could be dead out there."

His voice broke, and she moved then despite the pain, unable to resist hugging him. "But you did find me."

"I'll always find you, Morgan." He turned and kissed her, soft and sweet and gentle. "I lost you once. I never want to lose you again."

She sighed and rested her forehead against his. There were still things he didn't know. Important things. Maybe the most important thing. Morgan took a deep breath and said, "I'm pregnant."

For a long moment, Ely just blinked at her. "I'm sorry. What?"

Morgan swallowed hard, uncertainty threatening to overwhelm her. But no. This was Ely. She trusted Ely. She always would. "I didn't think it could happen again. The doctors told me it couldn't. But I guess they were wrong. I'd been feeling sick in the mornings for a while, and at first I thought it was the flu, but then my period was late this month and I'm always like clockwork, so I went into town yesterday and bought a pregnancy test, and it was positive, and—"

She didn't get to say anything else then, because Ely was kissing her again, pulling her into his arms, her blan-

horror show this morning. How fitting for the season.

"How'd you find me last night? Did you see my hazard lights?"

"Sort of. I saw some brief flashes from the side of the road, but nothing I could really follow. I'm pretty sure Jeremy needs a new battery in his car now." Ely huffed out a breath and sat forward, burying his hands in his hair. "God, Morgan, what the hell were you thinking? You know what the terrain is like around here. You scared me half to death, wandering off like that at night."

"Sorry." She adjusted her weight, then sighed. "Did you sit there all night with me? What about your party?"

"It's fine. And I don't give a damn about the party. I'm sure it went fine without me." He looked over at her, and just like that, her heart tumbled, the same way it had each time she'd seen him since that very first night all those years ago, the same connection that drew her back to Ely like a moth to a flame and kept her in thrall. She'd always return to him, she realized now. Because he was her person. Ely Malik was the one. And no amount of hiding or running away would change that. Not now. Not ever.

"The only thing I cared about last night was you, Morgan," he continued. "And I'm sorry I didn't say it sooner. I should have, but I was scared." He huffed out a breath, staring at the floor between his knees. "God, I've been such an idiot this past month, trying to control everything, acting like keeping you away would protect me, protect the life I'd built here for Dylan and me. But it was too late. That life changed the minute you set foot on this island. I changed. I'm not the same man I was a month ago, Morgan, and I have you to thank for that. I care for you so much it hurts. I love you, Morgan Salas. Always will."

Her stomach flipped with happiness this time, her pulse trilling like chimes in the wind. "You love me?"

Once inside, he laid her on the sofa and covered her with a blanket, then rekindled the fire. After the flames were crackling again, he returned to her side and knelt on the floor, slipping off her shoes, then taking one of her chilled hands in his. "Just rest, *Janan*. I'll stay here with you."

She peeked one bleary eye open and whispered grog-gily, "Still don't know what that means."

"Beloved." Ely smiled and kissed her fingers. "Because that's what you are. My beloved."

Her smile lit up his night before she drifted off again.

Ely made sure she was warming up, then examined her ankle. Swollen and bruised, but from what he could tell, at that point, at least, not broken. He'd tape it up now, then drive her to the clinic in the morning to get it x-rayed to be sure. Ely went in search of her medical kit for supplies.

Morgan awoke from a deep, dreamless sleep and opened her eyes to find dawn breaking through the windows of the cottage. Ely sat across from her, still wearing his frilly shirt and tight black pants from the night before. She blinked a few times to make sure she wasn't imagining him, then tried to move her sore ankle, but it was taped too tight. Ely must've taken care of it while she'd slept.

"Good morning," he said, watching her over his stee-pled fingers. "How are you feeling?"

Morgan frowned, her head fuzzy as she mumbled, "Sore. Is my ankle broken?"

"I don't think so, but we'll check at the clinic later any-way. Probably still hurts, though."

"It does." She tried to sit up, then winced. He came around to help her, getting her comfortably snuggled into the pillows in the corner before taking a seat at the other end of the sofa. Morgan looked down to find she was still in her costume as well. Great. She must look like a real